CUT AND COVER

CUT

AND

COVER

A THRILLER

BY KEVIN HURLEY

Skyhorse Publishing

Skyhorse Publishing books may be purchased in bulk at special discounts for sales promotion, corporate gifts, fund-raising, or educational purposes. Special editions can also be created to specifications. For details, contact the Special Sales Department, Skyhorse Publishing, 307 West 36th Street, 11th Floor, New York, NY 10018 or info@skyhorsepublishing.com.

Visit our website at www.skyhorsepublishing.com.

10 9 8 7 6 5 4 3 2 1

Library of Congress Cataloging-in-Publication Data is available on file.

Cover design by Rain Saukas
Cover photo: Thinkstock

Print ISBN: 978-1-5107-2649-9
EISBN: 978-1-5107-0150-2

Printed in the United States of America

BROOKLYN

"Do they think we're fools?"

They turned their backs toward the white Ford Econoline parked up the street, rubbed their mouths, and smoothed their beards to frustrate lip readers.

"Apparently," Abdul replied. "I'll take the next bus when it pulls up. You take the one on Lafayette. I'll meet you there."

"There? At the bus?"

"No, you ass, at the *place*." His cousin hadn't paid attention during the English classes they attended at BOCES. Abdul always had to spell it out for the fool. "I'm sure the house is ready?"

"The house is ready."

"*Allah Hafiz*," said Abdul.

"*Allah Hafiz*."

His cousin walked east toward Lafayette Avenue. Abdul stood by the curb and waited for his bus. A Hyundai Sonata with chrome wheels and four muscled teenage boys, dressed as the magazines taught them, menaced and boomed hip-hop and rolled down the street in arrhythmic pulses of brake and accelerator. Abdul glared at them, thought better of it, and turned away.

Abdul looked to the pavement and prayed that Allah would forgive his negativity. Black gum winked up at him from the sidewalk, shiny and smooth from countless footfalls. The tarnished wads were compressed into the concrete, jagged onyx against a gray and glass-sparkled backdrop. Residual antifreeze had pooled along the curb, unnaturally green as it lifted oil and dust from the road.

The persistent *thump-thump*, *thump-thump* beat of the urban jungle gnarled his sensitive ears, clawed at his thoughts, and burned his blood to scabs. Gas fumes slid into his nostrils and muddled his thoughts like cheap perfume. A coupon for Kennedy Fried Chicken stuck to the street next to his sandaled feet, glued in place by sugary soda and road sand.

A drop of sweat slipped off his tanned and wrinkled brow, held for a moment on one long lash, and splashed into his eye with a salty burn. He raked his finger over the socket to soothe the itch, but pushed too hard and scraped his eyeball so even more tears gushed out. He tried to blink away the irritation and temporary blindness.

The closed left eye compromised his peripheral vision. His right eye spasmed and twitched in sympathy. A rumbling came from down the street. The beat coming from the Hyundai dwindled as the rumble grew stronger. Abdul's ears focused on the bass sound to compensate for his temporary sightlessness.

What is it? Just the city bus. Praise Allah. It was the 38 going back over to Lafayette. It wouldn't stop here. He would wait for the 26 bus.

Abdul blinked harder through his tear-filled eyes and made out a blurry flock of pigeons fighting for position on the mosque's dome. A man on a bicycle? A delivery guy? Riding so close to the bus? Some swine at least tried to keep their bodies sound, though their minds remained cesspools.

He tilted his head skyward, extended his neck, closed his eyes again, and said a quick prayer to Allah for his health. More tears rolled off his cheeks. The Brooklyn 38 bus rumbled and hissed as its driver tapped the airbrakes.

The long-bladed dirk cut through Mohammed Abdul Bari's slender trachea, sliced his larynx, and ground his esophagus against his spine. His carotid artery hung helpless in two parts, pouring his life into Brooklyn's catch basin.

"Put it up on the screen again. Play it again."

Kieran Gilchrist raised his voice one decibel beneath a barking St. Bernard's and pointed his finger at the play button on the computer touch screen. He tapped it twice in frustration. The surface sponged in and out, leaving a ghostly fingerprint as the gas in the monitor expanded and contracted. The technician slid the mouse over the play button and clicked it once. A black and white image on the computer screen began to play. Kieran watched the recording made by the FBI stakeout team that had been positioned on Lafayette Avenue in the Ford Econoline.

"What do you see, sir?" Stephen Walker asked the senior official in charge of the FBI's Counterterrorism and Counterintelligence division, who stood at his right shoulder and exhaled warm coffee breath onto the screen. Desktop tappers annoyed Stephen, but in the interest of self-preservation he kept his opinions to himself.

Stagnant air hung in the room of the White Plains satellite office because the HVAC engineers hadn't been able to get the thermostats to work with any accuracy. Kieran stared at the image on the screen, his brows knit together, his ruddy complexion a contorted portrait of primal angst. He loosened his tie another inch and unbuttoned his collar.

Kieran resembled a fading professional wrestler, minus the steroids and greasy hair. He had piled thirty extra pounds on his muscular frame since the divorce, and it made the dry heat that much more unbearable.

"Play it again." His voice was more a yip than a bark this time.

"I can put it on repeat, and we can watch it over and over," said Stephen, in a practiced balance between helpfulness and sarcasm.

"Play the damn thing." Kieran's hoarse, growled response initiated quick clicks from Stephen's adept fingers.

They watched the screen replay four more times, believing nothing would change, but hoping for different results. The eye becomes bored by repetition, but the brain might rearrange the images until something changes and a clue appears.

The blue and white Metropolitan Transportation Authority bus came into view on the screen's right side in a mosaic of fuzzy gray pixels.

"Stop." The command grated a nerve that ran from Stephen's right ear to tense muscles in his neck. He clicked the mouse and froze the digital world that had captivated the last forty minutes of their lives.

"Is this the first time we see the bus?" said Kieran.

"Yes, sir," Stephen replied.

"And on the left, that's the first time we have Abdul Bari on the screen with the bus?"

"Yes, sir." Stephen moved the mouse over Abdul Bari's image to show he knew what was going on, confirming which of the Arab-featured people on the busy Brooklyn street was their man.

"Why is the 38 bus coming down our street? That bus route goes from Lafayette to DeKalb Avenue. Why is it down here on Graham?"

"We checked, sir," Stephen replied. "There was construction on the normal route, so the driver was in the process of cutting down a few blocks and then cutting back up to Lafayette. The driver—"

"In the process? What do you mean, 'process'?"

"Just, just that he is driving, sir," Stephen said. "I mean he is in the proc—"

"Who's the driver?" Kieran wiped his forehead with his sleeve and left a gray stain on his white, heavily starched cuff.

"Jeffrey Hirsch," said Stephen. "He's been with the MTA for eighteen years. Big fat guy, two kids, and no connections to crime. He's a dead end, sir. Another schlub doing his job. He was back at the bus depot before we even got ahold of him. He had no idea what happened. He kept going and made the next right. The agents said he cried, he was so scared. Like a baby."

Kieran scissored his meaty fingers through his thin red hair and rubbed both sides of his tense jaw until the tendons crackled. Pressure bands released in his skull. He dropped his right hand to his navel and scratched through his undershirt.

"Forget him for the moment," he said. "He never stopped anyway. He couldn't have reached out the door and cut our guy, unless his arm was seven feet long. How high are the bus windows?"

"There are different models of this bus . . ." Stephen realized his mistake too late.

"I don't care about any model but this model. Understood?"

"Yes, sir."

"Go on."

"None of the windows open," said Stephen. "The bus—*this* bus—is air-conditioned and the windows are sealed. Only the door opens to let people on and off."

"In and out. People don't get on the bus. They get in it."

"Yes, sir."

"What about the other passengers?"

"There were none, sir," Stephen replied. "His route doesn't officially start until he gets up to Lafayette."

"Put a picture of a Brooklyn MTA bus on the screen."

Stephen performed a Google Image search and pulled up the model of the bus Jeffrey Hirsch drove. Kieran noticed that even if the door was open, a killer would have to lean way out and down to reach someone of normal height who was standing on the sidewalk. It was unlikely.

A driver posed through the large tinted windshield: a multi-ethnic model who satisfied the MTA's politically correct photo op requirements. The MTA would have everyone believe no one was black, white, or Hispanic in Brooklyn anymore. To portray Brooklyn as a multihued rainbow of racial bliss couldn't be further from the truth. Kieran snorted at the hypocrisy.

"And the bus windows were intact, none broken, all the seals in place?"

"We had two agents push all their body weight against every curbside window. They didn't budge; all the seals were in perfect shape. The bus is fairly new."

The closest seat was up front, curbside, and a few inches from the door. If the bus slowed down and the driver opened the door, a well-trained, physically fit, and nearly acrobatic assassin could lean out and slice a throat. A rider could have jumped down into the stairwell where passengers boarded, and dealt the killing slice. But Jeffrey Hirsch would have to have been an accomplice or a hostage for this theory to ring true. Someone had to open the door to the street.

"You sure you found out everything about this driver?"

"Hirsch is a union member waiting to get his pension," Stephen replied. "He loves the job. Everyone on the route knows him. No religious affiliation, but he was born a Catholic. He's forty-two, five foot nine, 240 pounds of Almond Joy, minus the almonds and the chocolate." Stephen checked for a grin, saw a frown, and continued. "His wife's a nurse, and his kids get good grades. Nothing remarkable about him, except the fact that he spent the last eighteen years driving that bus route and didn't kill himself."

"Don't hypothesize unless I ask you, Walker," said Kieran. "This unremarkable bus driver is the only person close enough at any time to assassinate Bari. Unlikely, but he's all we have for now."

Stephen kept his eyes forward on the MTA bus he had Googled.

"No openings anywhere on the curb side of the bus where someone could slide a knife through, say, at neck height?"

"No openings anywhere on that side, sir. Except some baggage storage below." Stephen moved the cursor to the baggage compartments and made a few circles with the cursor. "But it's not used because these buses are short-run. We checked it out. Nothing but cobwebs in them. The latest models don't even have storage. This was the last one made with this design."

Kieran exhaled and attacked his itchy naval again, convinced something from the dry cleaners caused the irritation. He put both hands in his pockets, spun a quick circle in place, and jangled some loose change.

"How fast was the bus going?"

"Look at the screen's lower right-hand side, sir," Stephen said. "There's a mile-per-hour indicator." He pointed to it with a flick of the cursor. "The bus is traveling at about thirty-two miles per hour when it comes into the screen, taps its brakes lightly once, and slows down to about twenty-two as it approaches the subject. It maintains that speed until it gets close to the end of the block and, of course, slows to make the turn."

"Of course. Roll it again. Let it roll from the top, and stop before we lose sight of Bari."

Stephen clicked replay.

"Stop just before we lose sight of him." Kieran stared at the flat screen. "Close-up on the face." Mohammed Abdul Bari's eyes were shut as he faced the sky. Tears slid down his cheeks. Was he emotionally distraught? Did he want to die? Did he see the blade coming and stand there like some pacifistic suicidal recipient? Why didn't he move? Maybe Bari didn't know it was coming, maybe he was unprepared to die. But why was he crying?

"Who kills a man on the street in broad daylight, Walker? And what man stands there and lets his neck be sliced like a holiday turkey?"

"If I may, sir?" said Stephen.

"Go ahead."

"As to who killed him, the weapon's simplicity lends itself to an Al Qaeda or other trained soldier making a statement about a traitor. And this is what happens to bad jihadists when they get out of line."

"Go on." As much as Kieran rode Walker, the young man interpreted the meaning behind the silence inherent to surveillance videos better than most. In fact, Walker improved with no sound, whereas most people were lost with full audio. To mute one's sense of hearing sharpens the viewer's eye, and leaves his mind open to possibilities buried by the brain when it has to simultaneously sift through both audio and video. "And the tears?"

"I don't believe he's crying, sir," said Stephen. "The rest of his facial muscles are flexed slightly upward. This indicates a "presmile," if you will. This man was, if not happy, at least content for the moment."

"Happy he was going to die?"

"You mean these are tears of joy for the afterlife?"

"Perhaps he was waiting for the knife like a fly waits for the spider to crawl down the web. Maybe he'd given up."

"Take a look at his eyebrows, sir. Notice they're pulled forward, toward the center of his brow."

He leaned a little closer to the screen. He didn't know what it meant, but he might never have noticed without Walker.

"When a person is in a presmile, the eyebrows involuntarily come closer together as the cheek muscles lift upward," Stephen explained. "You have to try and lift your eyebrows upward if you're ready to smile. That would be a put-on face, an act. This man isn't acting. Also, the upper eyelids droop slightly in this expression. Please try it, sir. You'll see what I mean."

Kieran pulled the corners of his mouth back a little and felt his eyelids droop the slightest bit.

"Do you see, sir?"

"Maybe. So what?"

"He isn't faking," said Stephen. "If he was ready to die, or lifting his tearful eyes to Allah in acceptance of the knife with his head in the position, chin up," he pointed at the screen, "his eyebrows would have been lifted in a passive expression. Like Jesus is portrayed on the cross."

"So you don't think Bari is ready to die. You think he probably doesn't even know he's going to get his throat slit like a sheep, and he's happy as a clam because the bus is coming?"

Stephen offered a slight laugh at the similes. Kieran remained straight faced.

"It's useless for us to conjecture why he might be smiling," said Stephen. "But we know he's happy or, at the very least, content."

"Then why, Sam Spade, is he crying?"

"Spade? Sir?"

"Don't sweat it, Walker. There's no app for that. You will agree that he's crying?"

Walker closed in on Bari's face a few more percentages and scrunched his eyebrows together.

"I wouldn't say crying. I think his eyes are watering from the sun, or some irritant. He's not unhappy. He's not giving up his spirit. He has no reason to cry, in the emotional sense. He has tears. We shouldn't read anything into it without more evidence. Based on his face, I would let that theory drop, sir."

"Then why did Hirsch tap the brakes?"

"He probably tried to slow down for the curb. You have to let a little pressure out at a time, so the bus doesn't jerk the passengers."

"But there were no passengers, Walker. The bus was empty."

"It's a habit. He's slowing down a little for the curb."

"Maybe he had to slow down to get a good angle on Bari. A signal to someone next to Bari to take action."

"Maybe," said Stephen. "But I think it's the way they all drive, letting off brake pressure to ease into the corner."

Or maybe, Kieran thought, *Hirsch's accomplice has learned to hide between the pixels of this two-dimensional screen.*

They rolled the tape until the sun went down.

LOWER HUDSON VALLEY

John Rexford performed a quick perimeter check with a casual left-to-right head shift as he reached forward, pulled the keys from the ignition, and stepped into the bright, early afternoon summer sunshine. A pale blue cloudless sky faded into space. Humidity glued his shirt to his skin. A few more minutes and his sweat would bleed through the cotton. Air entered his lungs like syrup poured over waffles, thick and warm. He had to think about his breath. Not so in the Afghanistan mountains where he had spent the last seven years and where the air all but parched a man's lungs.

The Blue Mountain Winery was a restored eighteenth-century dairy farm minus the dairy. The cornfields and cows had been replaced by ninety acres of hybrid vinifera root stock that had won the owner several gold medals in US and European competition. The property rolled up from the Hudson River to one hundred feet above sea level and rested on a gentle hill with southwestern exposure. A constant water supply, from rain runoff and deep wells tapped into the aquifer, fed the grapes. The fertile sandy loam drained well. The Hudson River acted as a massive heat pump, regulating the seasons. This temperature moderation allowed Blue Mountain Winery to start work earlier in the spring, and postpone harvest another three to four weeks later into the fall than other locations in New York State. Management had started a small bistro to smooth out the revenue in slower months. The bistro went organic, and business boomed.

The restaurant's website boasted authentic fare and eclectic cuisine. Eclectic meant that even if John was lucky enough to find cheeseburgers on the menu, they would come with avocado, or a lemongrass and chutney puree, or some other equally piquant and unpalatable topping.

John had been dormant for eighteen months before he was called up for his first stateside assignment on the streets of Brooklyn. Follow-up orders instructed him to check a public website called HudsonVhappenings.org on the third Sunday of each month. The last restaurant listed on the page, farthest to the right and bottom, would be their rendezvous point. No matter what the restaurant, John was to meet his contact there at 1330 hours on the last Friday of the month. The manner in which the meetings had been orchestrated ensured that even his contact didn't know where they would rendezvous until he or she read the website on the third Sunday of each month. They both had to read it at precisely 0600 hours to ensure a new web posting didn't send them off in different directions.

He was meeting for the first time with a man who's name he did not know, and whose face he had never seen. But John knew that all the missions he was given through his handler in Afghanistan came directly from the this contact.

Several shoebox compacts were parked in the lot, but most of the spaces were empty. No ostentatious black SUVs or Crown Vics, not even an old LTD. Had his contact walked? Helicoptered in? He glanced to an open field behind the lot, half expecting to see a tethered bird. A Spanish guy weed whacked ornamental shrubs and rye grass along the left side of the building. He wore orange and black plastic earmuffs. Not likely a communication device, more likely safety equipment. Cut grass, fertilizer, and two-cycle engine exhaust plumes commingled into a familiar summer fragrance. The landscaper looked up for a moment, and then refocused on the grass blades as he lopped their tops to an acceptable height.

John picked a spot that gave him the best view of his Subaru from any window seat on this side of the building. He glanced at the bumper and read the scratched-and-peeled I'D RATHER BE BIKING sticker. He wanted to get this over with, get back to the mountains, and get back to riding.

The lunch crowd had already filtered out and the afternoon bar crowd had yet to flood in. It was a good hour for spooks, both spectral and corporal. Meeting his CIA contact on the last Friday of the month for their prearranged appointment would work out fine. At this hour on a Friday, most places were either crowded with despondent or elated salesmen, or they were deserted. Both scenarios could be utilized as good cover. Backslapping salespeople were a loud bunch that made it difficult to eavesdrop on private conversations, and a deserted restaurant left few places to hide prying eyes. This first meeting with a stateside agency contact put John Rexford's radar on high alert.

He hoped the next restaurant review on HudsonVhappenings.org was for Señor Frog's in Cancun, where noneclectic items such as tequila could be ordered.

He checked for out-of-place reflections in the tinted glass windows, and noticed his eyes looked a little darker than usual. Maybe he celebrated too much last night. Maybe it was the tinted glass. Satisfied, he walked up the restaurant's manicured sidewalk. Nothing out of order, no movement behind him or at the parking lot's tree-lined border. Eerie spooks hid so well that you didn't feel you were being watched, but he knew better.

His Italian mother's beautiful olive skin had been diluted by his father's genes, and her dark eyes were tempered by the recessive blue of the fighting Irishman. Eyes are an asset, a weapon in the human arsenal that must be maintained. John's were light brown, with dark capillaries around the eyelids that allowed him to blend in with Middle Eastern, Mediterranean, or South American cultures, so long as he maintained a good tan. Blond-haired, blue-eyed operatives were limited in where they could be stationed in the war on global terror, or as some politicians preferred to call it, "man-caused disasters."

Upscale locals and day-trippers from New York City usually packed the place. The Blue Mountain Winery's product was so popular, they often turned down wholesale buyers so they didn't run out of wine for the restaurant. Selling other people's wines before your own, in your own restaurant, would be gauche.

He followed the maître d' to a private table in the back. It had a window view of the parking lot. A man sitting at the table jumped up and pumped John's hand in a show of zealous salesmanship.

"Johnny." He sang the name like a game show host: *John-aayy.* His hair was coiffed à la *Jeopardy*'s Alex Trebek: salt and pepper, not a lock out of place, sideburns at mid-ear. "I'm glad you could make it," he said.

"Hey," said John. He hadn't been given his contact's name. "Yeah. Good directions."

"Please sit down." The man gestured to the chair opposite him.

"Any problems finding the place?"The man waved his napkin like someone hailing a plane, and smoothed it on his lap.

"No." John checked the parking lot through the window. "The directions were pretty clear. Where do we begin?"

The man's raised palm arrested further conversation.

"Hold on, John. Take a look at this." He handed over a business card, and placed a small computer on the table.

"What's this?"

"This, my friend—and you can call me Pete—is so cool." Porcelain veneer shone brightly at his upper bridge, perfect in every way, except those teeth belonged in a much younger man. The lower teeth were real, slightly misaligned with coffee stains. He tapped at the business card with his index finger.

John looked at the card, then back at the electronic device on the table. It resembled a mini netbook but was half the size. "What's up, Pete?"

"This is the latest and the greatest. Ever see one of these?" Pete pressed the power button and turned the five-inch LCD toward John.

"I've seen one, but not that small."

"That's a fact, Jack," said Pete. "It's made by General Dynamics, but it's not for sale. It's a prototype."

"It's nice." John raised his eyes and twitched the corner of his mouth in a tiny smirk. "Thank you for showing it to me."

"Shhh . . . shhh. Hold on. Ahh . . . yes." Pete slammed the clamshell lid closed without turning it off, and placed the device on the bench next to him. "We're good. So what's up, Johnny?"

He ignored the question. "What was that?"

"Damn things are worthless. Tell me who, other than the little geek engineers, can get their fingers on the keyboard? Totally worthless." Pete grabbed the drink to his left and took a big slurp. Ice chinked and the gold bracelet dangled on his wrist like a fishing lure. "You want a drink?" he said.

"Why did you show it to me?"

"I had to scan you," he said. "How the hell do I know what little bugs you got all over your body from living up in the woods the way you do? Besides, it's not you I'm concerned with. Parasites have a way of attaching themselves to their hosts unnoticed. No one put any bugs on you."

John raised an eyebrow. "You think I brought a surveillance device with me?"

"Noooooo. I said nobody put any bugs on you." Pete winked, finished his seltzer, and chewed the lime. "Just a precaution. You're clean as a whistle."

"So now what?" His contact was either very paranoid or very smart, maybe both.

Pete flattened his palms on the table. "I'm a regular double-o-seven here, Johnny. I don't think you understand, son. I have full and complete trust in you. You've been vetted by the best. I'm the guy who checked you out." He leaned back and smiled. "But I don't know who's been sticking things in your pants. You know, like *Get Smart*, Agent 99, one of those spy gadgets. Can't be too careful." He motioned for service. "Take a look at the card."

Pete's business card was embossed in shiny, navy blue ink and a ritzy font: C. PETER CHOCKER, SENIOR ACCOUNT EXECUTIVE, INTERNATIONAL FIBER RESOURCES. A web address and contact information followed.

"You see, *compadre*, if this little digital device made a funny sound when its microwaves coursed through your body, we would be humming a different tune: paper products."

John looked up from the business card. "That's your cover? C. Peter Chocker?"

"We're a major supplier of specialty face stock to the pressure-sensitive label industry, including florescent, latex-saturated, and thermal transfer. IFR fabricates tamper-proof security metallic coated grades. Our experienced sales and customer service staff yada-yada-yada." He rattled off the rehearsed pitch with smooth eloquence and grinned like a vaudeville monkey.

"You're chock full of answers, aren't you?"

"Chock full. Yeah, I get it, John. And I'm chock full of quality and care for my clients." He waved a waitress closer. "You want a beer?"

"No, thank you. I'll have a Coke."

"Good man," Chocker said. "I don't drink myself. Two Cokes." He held up two fingers in a peace sign, and the waitress walked away.

"Why don't you drink?"

"Because, my friend," Chocker paused for effect, "I'm a Muslim." He looked into John's eyes, straight-faced and serious, and placed his hands on the table, palms down. He chuckled and shook his head. "Seriously, John, you've got to lighten up, dude. Life's too short."

Chocker motioned the waitress back. "Get me a scotch, please, single malt, a double. Glenfiddich if you have it. Sure you don't want anything, John?"

John shook his head. He stared at the waitress as she walked away.

"Those hajjis make you a teetotaler when you were in-country?"

"Nah. It's a little early for me."

The waitress placed the Coke and scotch on the table, and John sipped the soda.

"You sure you don't want something? Beer?" Chocker asked again. "Come on, everyone has a beer. We had Billy Beer, J.R. Beer; even the Pittsburgh Steelers had a beer. Even you can have a beer. We'll call it Johnny Beer. Breakfast of champions. Put you right up there on the Wheaties box with Sugar Ray and Lance."

"Coke's fine."

"No problem. I got something for you, Johnny." He placed a small flip phone on the table. "The smallest satellite phone ever made."

John picked it up and rolled it over a few times in his hand.

"That, my friend, is a phone like no phone you've ever seen." Chocker pointed at it. "It has a built-in get-out-of-jail-free card. My number is in there. You call me anywhere, anytime, anyplace in the world, and I will be at your twenty in a flash. No matter where you are on this planet, I can be there in less than half a day."

John cleared his throat. "Look, Pete," he said, "I ain't saying you're full of shit, but . . ."

"But you're saying it."

"Half a day? The Blackbird can't do that. Even at Mach 3 you still have to refuel."

Chocker gave a self-satisfied chuckle. "Don't you worry about me, son. I can hop an F-15 Strike Eagle quicker than most people can book tickets on Expedia."

"Not a real practical mode of transportation."

"Do I look practical?"

He looked at the scanner on the table, at Chocker's scarred hands, his electric blue eyes, and his dark blue Armani suit, and decided not to comment.

"I fly with the best of the best, son," said Chocker. "I'll pull your ass from the fire, if need be." He made tiny hoof beat sounds on the table with his fingertips. "But you have to compute loading the plane, getting up to speed, finding a decent place to land, connecting flights, meals. It can be a real hassle." Chocker laughed to himself, like he just remembered a funny joke. He looked out the window and said, "All I'm saying is that I'll be there for you."

A waiter placed some bread, chilled butter, and a small knife on the table without a word and left.

Chocker grabbed a piece of bread and spoke while he chewed. "So anyway, about the phone. Don't ever use it."

"What?"

"Keep it charged. Any standard Nokia charger will work. Put it in a safe place."

He rolled the phone over in his hand some more. There was no brand name. "Why can't I use it?" he said.

"Becaaause . . ." Chocker drew the word out. "If you do use it, I'll become nervous and worried."

John powered up the phone.

Pete raised an eyebrow and smiled. "Curious George. Listen, if I pick up my phone and see your number on it, I will have to assume you're in deep trouble or compromised. Either way, it's no good. I will say one word into the phone: 'cock.' That's it."

"Cock?" John repeated. "Christ, you couldn't come up with something better?"

"Don't be a pervert, John. It's slang for rooster. Think of me as Foghorn Leghorn, if it makes you feel better."

John rubbed his face in his hands.

"And if I hear anything other than 'a-doodle-doo' from the person on the other end, or something even close to a-doodle-freaking-do, I hang up my phone and we never see or hear each other's sweet voices again." Chocker hesitated, his eyes locked into John's. "I'll assume you're dead or soon will be. You got it?"

"What is wrong with you, Chocker?" He wanted to retract the statement immediately upon hearing his own words, and then added, "Sir."

Chocker laughed and took another pull on the scotch. He shrugged. "Nothing. It's our secret code. We all need a secret code, right?" He switched to serious mode, his lips pulled tight together, and his eyes bore down on John. "Are we crystal?"

Chocker's eyes were Cowboy blue, like Pat Garrett in *The Chisholm Trail*: intense, sparkling, all-American. "I got it," said John. "Cock-a-doodle-doo." He took a sip of Coke. "Do we have to go through all this?"

"There's so much more we should go through." Chocker let out a sigh and realigned his silverware. "But life is too short, and this is enough for now. We need to keep this simple. Cock-a-doodle-doo will do."

They sat in silence for a moment, surveying the room, and then Chocker spoke.

"You're an all-star, John. Get your game on, like the song says."

"And you're the guy who's gonna pull my ass from the fire when things get hot?"

"Like the whale saved Jonah, Johnny. Like the whale saved Jonah." Chocker raised his glass and clinked it against John's. "You're gonna be like that guy Jonas from *The Unit*, you know, the TV show."

The show had been off the air for a while, but John let the dated reference slide. He figured a guy like Chocker wasn't getting much face time with the idiot box. Besides, Dennis Haysbert was still so popular he had his own DH6 clothing line and his face was all over Allstate Insurance commercials. "Except I'm not a six foot four, 250-pound black guy with muscles in my ears." He hesitated, and then added, "And I'm not the leader."

"I don't need leaders," said Chocker. "You're an army of one. I don't need you, and you don't need me. You do what you have to do, and I do what I have to do. We're independent. We're not followers, Johnny." Chocker shook his head. "You never were."

Chocker smiled, reached across the table, and gave John's shoulder a buddy punch. His long reach and wide shoulders stretched the stitching in his coat when he flexed. Deep cuts on his hands had healed and left shiny scars.

"It's why you ride the bike," Chocker continued. "Maybe it's why you bowed out of pro ball." Chocker turned his palms up. "You were never made to wallow in teamwork. You're not a team player, Johnny."

Who was this asshole to tell him he wasn't a team player? John bit his lip and took a drink, thinking now he should have ordered the scotch.

"And I love it, John." Chocker put a thumb to his chest. "I don't need team players. I'm not one. Who needs a bunch of suck-asses high-fiving each other, not getting squat done? You know what the problem with a team is? You're only as strong as your weakest link. Some leech is always gonna pull you down. Your enemy will keep on hammering the weak link until it breaks and snaps, and the whole chain suffers."

A waiter hovered a few feet away, cautious of their personal space. Chocker waved him off with his hand. The man nodded and returned to the other tables.

"So what happened to you, anyway?" Chocker asked. "I mean, hell, man, All-American at Rutgers. I saw the films. You were awesome."

"How did you see films of me?"

"Johnny." Chocker smirked and shook his head. "I got films of films filming films. You were a tight end. No one could touch you. You ran your skinny ass through those primates like they were statues. You were awesome. Third-round draft choice. Not number one." He raised his index finger, and then waved his hand away. "But hell, it was the NFL, after all."

John was uneasy with this focus on his past. He didn't view that chapter of his life as a success. "I was all right," he said. "I had speed and good hands."

"So why did you turn down the draft and volunteer yourself into this hellish existence?"

"Look, Pete," said John. "I'm one sixty-five, five foot nine. Granted I'm fast, but when you stand in line with the pros, you realize those animals are six foot four, 225 pounds, have good hands, and can run even faster." He looked at his empty plate and back into Chocker's eyes. "I would have sat it out for a few years and never seen the field. The third draft's a joke. I don't even know why they do it."

"Maybe." Chocker smiled and bowed his head at John.

"As soon as my spikes hit the turf, they would have crippled me," John said. "It ain't college ball. The objective is to reduce the number of eligible players on the opposing team. Vegas odds are set by the number of starters on the disabled list, not necessarily by talent. I didn't want to end up in a wheelchair." He took a drink. "Can we change the subject?"

"Yeah." Chocker looked concerned. "But football aside, why did you enlist?"

"My second love was the bike," John replied. "But I knew I wouldn't make the Tour de France because I don't dope and I didn't have the backing. I didn't want a real job, and I already had a degree. My dad did pretty well in the Marines, so I figured what the hell, I'll kill a few years."

"And a few hajjis." Chocker adjusted the gold cufflinks on his sleeve and gave John a sideways glance.

John looked around the room for eavesdroppers. "That came later. Tora Bora changed my perspective."

"And took you away from racing?"

"Story of my life. You can't serve two masters." He looked out the window. His car had been unmolested, so far.

"Don't worry. It's just me." Chocker smiled and cracked his knuckles in rapid-fire succession.

Another waiter appeared tableside.

"My name is Clarence. I'm your host and wine steward. May I suggest the organic Brunello?"

"Clarence, my good man," said Chocker. "Would you tell us more about the Brunello? I like mine on the light side. Not true to the Italian masters, but not so damned oppressive either, if you know what I mean."

"You're familiar with the Brunello?" Clarence flashed a smarmy grin.

"Certainly," said Chocker. "Sampled it myself in Montalcino. How, might I ask, are you allowed to use the name Brunello?" Chocker cocked an eyebrow but kept his convivial smile.

"As you probably know," Clarence responded with even more affectation, "unlike Bordeaux, there's no copyright on the Brunello name." He hesitated for a moment. "We borrowed the name. We promise not to involve you in a lawsuit."

Chocker tut-tutted with a finger wiggle. He leaned back from the table and sat straight in his chair.

"Well, please bring it on, Clarence," Chocker said. "And thank you for the education."

"My pleasure," said Clarence. "I will prepare your wine." He lowered the wine list to his hip like a schoolboy with a new binder.

Chocker leaned in. "That was one ugly ass Ichabod Crane–looking wine steward, wouldn't you say, Johnny?"

John shook his head and tried not to laugh. Chocker didn't need any encouragement. "Does he make you nervous?" said John.

"I have a rule," said Chocker. "If I can smell a man's cologne, he's too close to me."

"Where did you learn about wines?" John asked, trying to break Chocker's rhythm.

"A historian is a vintner, or vice versa. Something like that, anyway," said Chocker. "If you want to remember history, follow the grape. You can follow wines from the Stone Age, Egyptians, Babylonians, and Caesar."

"After listening to you two carry on, I think I'll have a beer." John placed the cloth napkin on his lap and drank some water.

They perused the menu until Clarence delivered the Brunello to their table. He held it the way a nurse displays a newborn through hospital glass. The label bore an impressionistic rendering of Blue Mountain Vineyards' barn, in vibrant red and black brushstrokes. Clarence waited for them to say something. Chocker kept silent to see how long the wine steward would stand there. Finally he said, "Beautiful. Please open it."

Clarence went through a lengthy uncorking ritual and filled one glass with a taste. Chocker grabbed the stem with his thumb and forefinger, swirled it, nosed it, and gulped it like a professional. He closed his eyes, smacked his lips, and set the glass down.

"Excellent, Clarence. How *do* you do it?"

"We never use the same oak casks twice," said Clarence. "Too much tannin. And no harsh fertilizers. I have to tell you . . ." He leaned into Chocker, inches from his ear. "Sheep shit."

"What?" Chocker leaned back in his chair again, obviously uncomfortable that his personal space had been broken.

"We release our own sheep into the Brunello plot each fall," said Clarence. "They're grazers and don't touch the vines. The organic fertilizer gives it a special finish. I'm sure you noticed." Clarence spoke barely above a whisper, as if this was their little secret.

Chocker placed his hand on Clarence's shoulder. A friendly move, implying closeness, but also suggesting that Clarence should not continue any farther.

Chocker looked across the table at John. "Do you have any allergies?"

John almost blurted out, 'What the fuh?' but just shook his head.

"Then, if you don't mind," Chocker said, "I think it would be nice if Clarence chose our meals for us. What do you say, Clarence?"

Clarence puffed up as if a culinary medal had been pinned on his chest. "It would be a splendid idea." He nearly clicked his heels when he spun away.

"I guess a cheeseburger is out?"

"That should keep him busy for a while," said Chocker. "Let's get to it." Chocker smiled for the benefit of any onlookers, but his eyes glowed the angry blue of burning propane. He let the visual reprimand sink in for a few seconds. "Be careful of those broad daylight antics. I'm giving you full authority on how you complete your tasks, but we don't need to see you on YouTube. If the feebs, or even the hajjis, get wind that someone of your talent is behind the project, then time's up, over, *bloah*." He made a quick fist and released it. "Back to the lab again, yo."

The reference to Eminem's "Lose Yourself" wasn't lost on John. It was cool that Chocker knew the lyrics. If Pete whipped out a crack pipe, however, he would have to pinch himself to 'get back to reality,' as Marshall Mathers would say.

"Understand, Major?"

The rank implied an order, not a request.

"Yes, sir."

In a microsecond, Chocker's expression switched from anger to just another salesman pitching a client. He released the flash drive cupped in his hand and placed it beside John's plate with the ease of a three card Monte dealer. John raised his glass to block the move from anyone to their left. The wall was to their right, so there was no danger there. John put the drive in his pocket.

"Don't feel bad," said Chocker. "About the biking, I mean. Not everybody gets to be top seed. But all the people who try to get there? Those are the people you gotta love."

"Yeah," John said. "I'm still biking."

"You sure as hell are."

"Was that you in the Econoline?"

Chocker shook his head. "The FBI. Those feebs stuck out like a Barney float at Thanksgiving." He laughed and swirled the wine in his glass. "Look at it this way. The grunts in the service—and I love them all—report to their direct commanders: a sergeant, a major, right up the line." Chocker arranged the salt and pepper shakers, some sugar packets, and little plastic half-and-half tubs on the table. Then he grabbed the Lea & Perrins bottle and placed it right in the middle of the arrangement. "We serve at the will of the commander in chief," he said. "*El presidente*, the Big Cheese."

"The president knows what we're doing?"

"Whether he does or doesn't is immaterial, because it would be plausible deniability regardless."

But not if you're talking directly to him, John thought.

"Some people think it's okay for our enemies to come here and kill us on our soil," said Chocker. "But somehow it's not okay for us to defend ourselves. I disagree."

"So now I serve you?" said John. He tilted his glass to Chocker and took a sip of wine.

"You serve America, son."

"So I don't get a ribbon from the commander in chief?"

"Not a chance in hell." Chocker shook his head. "I'm a guide and your savior, if need be. We all need someone to protect us. That's why I gave you the satellite phone. You're here because you want to be. You saw what happens when religious fanatics and drug dealers get ahold of a country . . ."

"You mean like ours?"

"Touché," said Chocker. "But there's no comparison, and you know it."

John wondered, but kept his thoughts to himself for now. He hadn't fully tested the limits of his latitude with this new mentor.

"You'll find schematics on the flash drive of an underground superstructure relating to a very large water supply. Let me tell you what isn't there." Chocker gulped a half glass of Blue Mountain Brunello, checked to make sure Clarence hadn't rushed over to fill it in his obsessive need to please, and poured himself another.

"The FBI's Joint Terrorism Task Force works real tight with the NYPD," Chocker explained. "They've been trying to stick their thumbs in all the security holes in the New York City reservoir system since the towers went down. Problem is, there are too many miles for effective counter controls." Chocker pulled a small spiral notebook from his pocket, flipped it open, and showed John a three-by-five-inch condensed aerial photograph of the region.

"This is the entire system from the Catskills to Manhattan. Over one hundred miles of above- and below-ground tunnels, siphon chambers, support buildings, and cut-and-cover aqueducts. Impossible to protect at all times."

"Cut and cover?"

"The Romans invented them. Water channels lined with stone or concrete, and closed on top, so they were less detectible by enemies. The good thing is, there are only five CCPs."

"New acronym for me, Pete."

"You call them choke points, jarhead. In hazard analysis they're referred to as critical control points. Places where severe damage to the entire body is most likely to occur—the heart, arteries, brain—you get the picture."

John nodded. "Understood."

"This is one of the hottest CCPs, and the goddamn feebs haven't done a thing to protect it except put some motion alarms and trout troopers in there." Chocker pointed to a small star superimposed on the map. "It's the Kensico Dam."

John shook his head. "Trout troopers?"

"The trout troopers—my simple backwoods friend—are the DEP police. They're mostly amateurs, one step above conservation officers. They have a fully equipped task force, but upper management keeps them locked down so tight they can only respond post-incident. They have no reconnaissance."

Chocker closed the notebook and slipped it into his jacket pocket.

"One hundred eighty feet below the surface of the dam is where all the aqueduct tunnels converge and flow into New York City, via the Hillview Reservoir. If it is compromised, nine million people will have about a week, and they'll be drinking from the Hudson—a fate no one deserves."

John listened while he reviewed a mental image of the water supply from Chocker's notebook. "Why not blow Hillview?"

"The Hillview Reservoir is tiny by comparison," Chocker said. "A couple billion gallons. You'd have to get into the Hillview gate chambers and attack there. It's completely sewn up: security cameras, motion detectors, heat sensors, and a healthy dose of paranoia are everywhere; and the police substation is on site. Twenty-four-hour armed guards with machine guns, and dogs. Hillview also has a series of backup valves that can divert the water to the Croton Reservoir. It would be an inconvenience to take out Hillview, but not a tragedy. They did their homework here, Johnny."

"Who?"

"I'm getting to that. School's in session, so listen up."

"So Hillview is out. Why Kensico?"

Chocker leaned in. "Kensico has something else."

He looked around the dining room again as if he might be looking for a waiter. Clarence appeared as if on cue, and delivered the cheese platter and more bread. Chocker had eyes in the back of his head. John broke off a piece of crusty Italian bread from the wicker basket on the table, and covered it with a healthy swath of Caprino goat cheese.

Clarence asked if he could get them anything else, and then left the two men to their conversation.

"So water is disrupted for a few days," said John. "Don't they have the same capability at Kensico?"

"Kensico was never upgraded. Plans were made, money budgeted, and then moved elsewhere after 9/11."

"Where'd the money go?"

"Down the rat hole," said Chocker. "To fund better communications between emergency services."

John shook his head at the irony. The geniuses in power moved money away from a hard target to fund walkie-talkies for local responders. Meanwhile, New York City sat ripe for the picking—or drowning.

Chocker lowered his voice even more. "Fifteen tons of rusting chlorine gas tanks are stored in a side chamber next to the main tunnel." He waited for John to absorb what he had said, and then added, "The Canadians want to release the gas and simultaneously stop the water supply. Primitive or what?"

"Canadians?"

Chocker rolled his eyes and mouthed, "Terrorists." He raised his voice and continued: "Wind, water, and fire, John. The wind will drift the chlorine gas several miles, all the way to White Plains, maybe even Scarsdale, killing tens of thousands in the process. The water will flood the Bronx River and take out billions in real estate and roadways. By the time the first responders arrive, the roads will be underwater, inaccessible."

Chocker sipped some wine and let John digest the image of thousands of people choking, their lungs deteriorating from chlorine gas. Emergency crews stuck, unable to access flooded roads, helpless to do anything but watch, as their friends and relatives drowned or suffocated in their own decomposing lung tissue.

"If they manage to take out the chlorine and the tunnel," said Chocker, "New York City will have no potable water, and only a two-day supply to fight fires. After which, these pieces of garbage are going to let loose a wave of arson on the five boroughs like we've never seen. It'll be a firestorm once the gas mains go." Chocker paused, and then said, "It's a good plan, John. You've got to stop it."

"Why me?"

"I handpicked you, son," said Chocker. "You're good with any weapon, and even better with your hands. I need primitive here, John, no traces. I know your work. I was the one responsible for getting you stateside."

"Nice trick. You're quite a magician."

Chocker explained that the spillway would be shut down at the end of the month for repairs downstream, allowing the terrorists to crawl up the tunnel and into the screen chamber.

"Once the water supply is cut off, they'll be able to draw down half of what they need from the Croton Reservoir. That is if, and only if, every single man, woman, and child in the five boroughs drinks, eats, and bathes with bottled water. The nine million self-centered urbanites will horde at least five hundred million gallons on the first day, in sinks, bathtubs and bottles, leaving firefighters with big, shiny, impotent nozzles in their hands."

A new waiter unfolded a tray stand next to their table. Clarence brought plates from the kitchen and placed them on the stand. He set the entrees in front of them, careful to keep his elbows low and not obstruct their view of one another. When Clarence finished, he stood back from the table and smiled, with his hands crossed over his groin.

John looked at the meal and vaguely recognized its components: bread, meat, vegetables, and snails.

"What have we here?" said Chocker.

Clarence described each platter, its preparation, and place of origin. There was *gougère* (a choux pastry made with cheese), *escargots au Chablis* (snails in Chablis), *jambon persillé* (ham jellied with parsley), *gardiane d'agneau* (lamb stew with olives), and *moules aux amandes* (mussels with an almond stuffing).

"Fabulous, Clarence," said Chocker. "Where did your chef receive his training?"

"The Escoffier school in France, and here at the Hudson Valley's own CIA."

John stiffened. Chocker suppressed a laugh.

"A fine school," said Chocker. "Thank you, Clarence."

"Most certainly, sir," Clarence grinned. "Is there anything else I can get you?"

"Not at the moment. Thank you."

Clarence made a hand signal to his assistant. The young man picked up the folding tray and they hurried back to the kitchen.

"The CIA?"

"You should have seen your face," Chocker snorted. "It's the Culinary Institute of America. If only I had my secret spy camera in my lapel. It would have been precious."

He looked at Chocker's lapel and wondered where the camera was, in fact, hidden.

"Do you know the gestation period of a Norway rat, John?"

"Let me think." John's eyes shifted toward the ceiling. "Nope. Got me there."

Chocker laughed. "Twenty-one days. They can have fourteen pups per litter if they have enough food. Once people leave the city, the rats will be humping like . . . well, I was going to say like rabbits, but hell, like rats, I guess. And that means disease, John. Typhus, rat-bite fever, hantavirus, meningitis, and the list goes on."

"Understood. Even after these assholes leave and the fires are out, the aftermath is going to take years to clean up."

Chocker nodded. He slurped a mussel from the shell. "They haven't shut this thing down in a hundred years, and they probably won't for another hundred. This is a once-in-a-lifetime opportunity for these assholes to pull a 9/11 redux."

"How did the bad guys find out about the gas?"

"Big Brother." Chocker shook his head. "All municipalities have to report hazardous material storage annually to the local fire departments, local emergency planning committees, and SERC, the State Emergency Response Commission. It's all public knowledge under community right-to-know laws."

If John wasn't already aware of how much our freedoms endanger us, he would have been disappointed. "How do I proceed?" he said.

"What you need to know is in your pocket. You burn these, capiche?"

John nodded.

Chocker raised a finger and said, "Let's go over what isn't on the drive." He pulled a cell phone from his waist and flipped it open. He stabbed the keys until he found what he wanted. "There will be two demolition experts brought in from outside the country, probably Yemen. We don't know much more about them, except intel says they can get the job done."

He gave Chocker a look that said "bring it on."

Chocker's phone vibrated in his hand. He checked the number, then stood up and walked to an empty area of the dining room without saying a word.

John checked the parking lot for Canadians.

WHITE PLAINS

Kieran Gilchrist sat at Kisco Kosher with a hot corned beef sandwich, coleslaw, and a pickle sliver for company. An almond horn in the dessert case was provoking him when his eye caught the television screen. A local cycling team member was giving an interview on Channel 7 News. Westchester County closes down the Bronx River Parkway for four hours each Sunday in September for cycling traffic only. The woman talked about carbon footprints and exercise with a smile on her face that made her look like she was ankle high in the Fountain of Youth. Kieran asked the guy behind the counter to increase the volume on the TV, but by then there was already a commercial showing a cheerful father taking his family for ice cream in a Lexus SUV. He threw his lunch in a paper bag and ran out the door.

Kieran's right heel throbbed from plantar fasciitis as his shoes slammed into the concrete with each painful, half-jogged step. His breath sputtered in choppy bursts through his nose and mouth. He blew past his office staff, collapsed in his chair, and caught his breath. Corned beef and pickle juice leaked on his blotter through the flimsy paper bag. He threw it in the trash can beneath his desk.

Kieran grabbed the phone. "Get Walker in here now," he said. "I want the Bari surveillance clip on the screen." He put the phone down and remembered the diet iced tea he'd forgotten in the dripping bag. With a grunt, he fished it from the trash.

Stephen Walker turned the wall screen on remotely, and was in Kieran's office before the iced tea was gone.

"Where should I start rolling, sir?"

"I want you to take it right from the beginning."

Walker rolled the surveillance video, and they both watched as the blue and white Metropolitan Transportation Authority bus came into view on the screen's right side. Neither man said a word as the digital film clip played. Walker looked at Kieran for a command.

"Play it backward."

Walker complied without question. The bus rolled comically backward as wispy smoke plumes appeared and sucked back into the exhaust pipe. Small pieces of paper materialized from nowhere and floated upward from the street. Abdul Bari became visible, his face to the heavens, as the MTA bus rolled in reverse.

"This time, take it frame by frame. I want you to concentrate on the wheels."

"Forward or reverse?"

"Forward," said Kieran, annoyed.

Walker gave him a nod and zoomed in on the lower half of the screen.

"Can you focus the damn thing better?" Kieran leaned forward as if the extra inches would improve the picture quality.

"Not if you want a close up. I've already digitally enhanced this version to make the edges less fuzzy."

"So this isn't the original?"

"No sir," said Walker. "I always save the original and use copies to view. That way if anything goes wrong with the equipment—power surge or whatever—I still have the original stored elsewhere."

"Anything? What do you mean?"

Walker already knew he had slipped up with his vague response. "Anything at all. Worst possible scenario. Could be a virus, electronic circuitry malfunction, or the building burning. Anything."

"If the building burns, then it's all lost, isn't it?"

"No sir. This footage is stored on an FBI server in Washington. The servers are all over the country, I mean the actual storage device. Well, it's not actually in DC, you see. Everything we see here is stored on my intranet site; it's our own personal cloud. We'll never lose the original—"

"Enough! Fine. I understand. I trust you, Walker." Kieran clapped his hands together. "Go for it. Let's check this out and see what we can see."

Walker smiled. If he was ever to receive a compliment from Kieran Gilchrist, that was the one.

"Stop!" Kieran stood up quickly and limped a little as he stared at the screen. "What is that?"

"I can't see, sir."

Kieran backed away from the screen and kept his finger on the spot that had drawn his interest. Walker zoomed in and lost total focus, and then zoomed back out until the image was identifiable.

"Right there," said Kieran. "What is that? A puddle?"

"That is the puddle we noticed in a previous viewing. It looks like a reflection from under the bus."

"That is not a reflection from under the bus. Take a closer look. Get up over here and stand right beside me, and tell me what you see."

Walker went to the screen, leaned in and out, and stood at different angles. "I think it's a wheel reflection."

"It is. And it's coming from the street. Look at the edge of the puddle. You can see some tiny squares. Do you see them?"

Walker leaned in, and his face changed from skeptical scientist to enlightened believer. "They look like rectangular reflections from the building on the blind side of the bus."

"And therefore, that wheel reflection cannot be from under the bus because the angle of reflection shows the building windows. So the wheel reflection has to be on the street. Would you agree?"

"It's someone on a bike, sir."

"I know it is, Walker." Kieran sat back down on the sofa. "I know it is."

Both men were quiet for a moment, and let the static image of the bicycle wheel sink in. Kieran broke the silence.

"It's why we didn't see anyone kill Bari. And it's why we couldn't figure out how anyone on the bus could reach out that far. There was no one on the bus except the driver."

"Sir?"

Kieran cocked an eyebrow. "Yeah?"

"That bus was traveling at thirty-two miles per hour when it came on the screen," said Walker. "And about twenty-two as it passed Bari. I ride a bike, and I can tell you that to maintain that speed you would need to be a world-class cyclist."

"I understand. And you don't think the average person could pull off that speed?"

"I don't. At least, not and slice a throat at the same time."

"Excellent," said Kieran. "That means we're not dealing with the average person. It narrows the field down considerably. We're looking for someone with a very specific skill set."

Kieran's intercom made one soft beep, and blinked. He picked up the receiver, irritated at the interruption. "Go ahead, Christine."

"I thought you might like to know that Patrick Corcoran is stateside."

"What? He's supposed to be fighting a war in the Mideast."

"I know, Kieran," said his senior security administrator. "I just got word. Supposedly he has taken some personal time."

"That prick hasn't taken a vacation day in his life."

"Would you like me to have him contact you?"

There was never a moment he could think of where the words *like* and *Patrick Corcoran* belonged together.

"Get him in here," said Kieran. "But be gentle. I don't want him on the defensive. Tell him we need his help."

Kieran sat back down next to Walker, and they directed their attention to the digitally frozen puddle with the bicycle wheel reflection.

"Anyone I know?"

"Indirectly," said Chocker. He closed the cell phone cover. "We have to hurry this up."

John nodded.

"I know you can handle the bad guys. Here's the real problem." Chocker pushed the keypad with one calloused, scarred finger, and turned the cell phone toward him. "Get a little closer."

John took the phone from Chocker's hand after a small tug of war. *Just a big kid*, he thought.

The video showed two men locked in battle. The man on top was getting the worst of it. He had his back arched, and there was an anguished expression on his face. The man underneath straightened his legs and arms, and the guy on top went limp. The entire clip lasted about fifteen seconds. John was grateful there was no sound. He didn't like snuff films.

"Did you get a look at the killer?"

"No." He handed the cell phone back to Chocker.

"No one else has either. I call him Yoda. He's like us, John: trained in several schools of the martial way, expert in all, I'm afraid. But he has a skill unlike anyone out there."

"And that would be?" John poked at the jellied ham and then changed his mind.

"First of all, he's a sociopath. A rare trait, even among us. He does it for the art, supposedly." Chocker's benign stare unnerved John.

"Whose team does he play on?"

"Nobody's. He does it for ego and money. But he's not on our side and never has been."

"You seem disappointed." John gave up on the questionable ham and took a spoonful of the lamb stew.

"Hardly. Yoda is unmanageable. He wouldn't last a day in a structured environment, and he's killed a lot of his handlers on principle."

"Principle?"

"He's got a distorted sense of morality," said Chocker. "A couple times he found out his targets weren't who his handlers said they were. So he went back, collected his money, and retaliated. He takes instant camera photos of people who really piss him off and sends them to their bosses. Very effective advertising."

He eats his own—a real jackal. "Instant camera, so there's no digital trace?"

"Correct," said Chocker. "Don't think of him as a Canadian. You'll have your head in the wrong space. Canadians need to belong. Their psychological motivation is the group dynamic. They don't tolerate dissent. This guy's a loner. His motivation is to prove that he's the best. The only jobs he takes are ones that put him in a position to kill, either as a bodyguard or as a direct assassin. He wants omnipotence."

"Where was the video taken?"

"An underground fight somewhere in Russia. One of our guys won it in a card game. Sick, huh?"

"So he knows some ground maneuvers," said John. "What's the big deal?"

"*He* is the big deal." Chocker sipped some wine and swished it in his mouth. "Never underestimate him. He only kills up close and personal. He won't use a gun or a weapon. He enjoys it, John. He lives for it."

John had known gung ho guys in the Mideast who talked a lot. Some even bragged about their kills. But those guys were rare, and most of them were full of it. Few soldiers liked it up close. The good distance killers, the snipers, didn't talk about it and kept to themselves. If Chocker was correct, Yoda wasn't a talker.

"So what's this skill he has?"

"He was raised in a temple. We believe in Bhutan."

"Bhutan, China?"

"Close," Chocker said. "Near Tibet. The monks taught him yoga. The guy's a yogi of the highest order. I'm talking drop-your-eyeballs-on-your-chin-and-roll-them-around, pass-a-pin-through-your-intestinal-tract skill level. He's a complete contortionist. The move you saw on the video is his own invention. Once he gets his arms and legs around you, he applies pressure to your main arteries and you pass out. But he kills you first. A real dickhead." Chocker poked at the jellied ham and then retreated to the lamb as well.

They ate in silence for a minute, and then Chocker asked, "Did you get a good look at the move?"

"It looked like a variation of a vertical four quarter lock. It hurts like hell, but there is a defense, even when you're in it."

"If you're facing the guy, you can bite him or rake his eyes before he gets the hold on your arms. If you're limber enough, you can slide a free arm below his. But let's face it, once you're in, it's over."

"True of any hold," said John. "But you don't find it used very often in two fighters of the same skill. It's too hard to get around a guy's back."

"I don't think you got a good look, John. First of all, those two fighters were of the same skill. The man on top, who ended up with a broken spine, was one of mine." Chocker looked out the window at the parking lot as if he expected someone or something to appear. "He split my guy right down the middle, as if the Jaws of Life had opened his ribcage."

"Sorry." John looked down at his plate. Chocker appeared to blame himself.

"Anyway," Chocker said, "the thing I wanted you to get—which you didn't, by the way—was that Yoda attacks from behind. It's not a vertical four quarter lock. A four quarter lock is done face to face."

Chocker was right. If you put the double grapevine on your opponent's legs from behind, he only needs to move his legs outward and you lose all your leverage. How did he do it, then?

"I'll show it to you again, another time. Needless to say, we can't do it even if we try. Yoda wraps his feet one and a half times around his victim's lower calves to initiate the lock. This freak can stretch his ligaments so far apart that his bones can wrap around his prey." Chocker checked his watch.

"Handy."

"No one has ever beaten him, John. If you encounter him, you use a weapon, or you run."

"I don't think I'll run. But he can't wrap around a slug."

"Two reasons you can't do that." Chocker warned him with two fingers in the air in a peace sign. "One, a slug will penetrate the chlorine tanks down there, and neither one of you will make it out." He dropped one finger and added, "Two, no one can know you're there. That means nothing left behind. No guns, slugs, or prints." Chocker paused for effect. "No debris, no collateral damage of any kind. Everything goes in the drink."

"By drink, I assume you mean the tunnel."

Chocker smiled. "At the end of the aqueduct there's a screen to filter out anything larger than, say, a toaster. A couple times a year, the watershed maintainers pull up the screen and take out the debris. Soft things go through."

"Like fish?"

"Yeah, like fish." Chocker grinned. "Imagine a human-sized cheese grater. Clean as a whistle." He pressed his palms on the table and leaned in a little. "But never, ever, do you engage one-on-one with this guy. Got it?"

John remembered the Play-Doh machine he had as a kid. He and his sister would shape the blue clay into tiny people and then run them through a plastic press, where they squished out on the other end.

He took a drink and finished off the lamb. It was tasty, but it had nothing over a thick cheeseburger and fries. A few seconds passed, and Chocker's face started to redden.

"I'm serious, son," Chocker said. "You stay away from this guy unless you can take him from a distance. I want him, but I want you more."

"How can I take him from a distance without a weapon?"

"You're the professional," said Chocker. "Improvise. Throw a spear."

He ignored the ridiculous suggestion. "Why is he here?"

"To cover these assholes as they prepare to eliminate hundreds of thousands of our fellow citizens. He's the bodyguard—close personal protection."

"And you want him alive, don't you?"

"If possible." Chocker looked surprised. "Why do you ask?"

"I'm seldom told not to engage. I don't mean to sound disrespectful, or to pry, but . . ."

"But you will."

"Yeah, I guess. You don't want the FBI to know anything, not even after the fact. Correct?"

Chocker grabbed some bread and tore it apart. He dipped it in olive oil and waved it at John. "Go on."

"What?"

"Go on," said Chocker. "You're going to tell me your thoughts. I can feel it. Enlighten me."

"Considering you asked, you probably got the video from one of your guys. But the other information—accessibility to tunnel, the schematics, the construction work—that came from the FBI, who got it from the DEP. If I leave a trace there, then those guys are going to wonder how you, or whoever sent me, got ahold of the intel. If I end up dead on the floor of the tunnel and they can trace my DNA or teeth, which are all on file with the military, then you're going to have a lot of 'esplaining to do, Lucy.'"

Chocker's blue eyes sparkled. Crow's feet tap-danced around their edges.

"You win the door prize, Johnny boy. I'm proud of you. But you're only partially correct. The FBI doesn't know about this CCP, or at least they haven't placed it on a priority list. I don't want you dying down there and screwing up the works."

"How considerate," John said, and then had an afterthought. "You've got a man inside."

"I can neither confirm nor deny, but the feebs aren't as stealthy as they think."

Son of a bitch! These guys don't trust anyone. Now John was covering for the CIA while they spied on the FBI. Homeland security at its finest.

"Is there a problem?" Chocker asked.

"It's nice to know my welfare isn't your top priority. Keeps it all in perspective."

"Bullshit." Chocker locked eyes with John. "If I wasn't concerned about you, I'd send you in blind and armed to the teeth. The point is, you're the only one who has the skills to pull this off without anything other than hand-to-hand combat or primitive weapons."

He understood why Chocker wanted everything primitive and low-tech. He wanted John's mind in Cro-Magnon mode. Look what Thag can do. Bam! Hit the guy with a rock.

Chocker made small talk about the food and changed the subject to the weather as he scanned the room for a moment. They both picked at their meals.

"Why do you call him Yoda?"

"Because he's a master yogi and he is DA-angerous. Plus the little prick can't talk right. They say he had some speech impediment as a kid. Says everything backward."

"Yeah?"

"Nah. I'm playing you. I had you, though, didn't I?"

The child returned. It was a relief to see Chocker smile again. "What do you think of this place?" he said.

"West Coast wannabees trying to serve the funky quaint attitude," John said, and took a drink. "It doesn't blend with

East Coast snobbery. But the cheese is good." He paused. "People should stay in one place."

"You want to elaborate?"

"It was easy over there. It felt like I was in one place and I knew the rules. Now I've got to keep changing my skin. I'll take any mission you have, but after this we should consider getting me in another post."

Chocker pushed his plate to the side and sipped his wine. "What if I told you I don't have another post for you?"

"Then we'll cross that bridge when we come to it. At some point I'm going to have to make an honest woman out of this girl, and you know what that means."

"She'll be a liability. Whether or not she knows what you do for a living. You can't live in two worlds, John."

"I am right now."

"I know. And with your legs straddling both worlds, you're pissing all over yourself."

"Don't think I'm not grateful, not dedicated. But I'm looking at things a little differently, Pete. In Afghanistan, there were no distractions. Here, well, I guess things seem more real."

"And people like you make it real, John. But remember, you can't be a little pregnant, and once you're out, you're out."

"I understand, sir."

"I don't think you do. No more flying by the seat of your pants. No more toys, no more tracking, hunting, no more using the skills you were born with. Will you be happy blasting clay pigeons on weekends with a bunch of overweight gun club types?"

"I don't know if I will be happy with my decision. I definitely won't join a gun club. That's just silly."

"Just an example."

"Yeah, pick a better one next time."

"How about the complete and utter boredom associated with doing the same thing for thirty years and then moving to The Villages in Florida to learn ballroom dancing and drive around in a golf cart?" Chocker took a breath and settled back. "Better?"

"I don't live that far in the future."

"Wise."

Clarence placed their check on the table and tried to engage Chocker in more small talk. Chocker cut him off and the maître d' took it as his cue to exit.

"I know you've thought of this, but—"

Chocker interrupted and smiled. "Curious George."

"Why don't we take all three of them out on our own?"

"In the words of our greatest president, Abraham Lincoln, 'You can't kill all the people all the time.'" Chocker grinned. "We don't know exactly where they are, and we can't wait until they're together, because then we might have to let the Feds in on the party."

"But why not have the FBI protect Kensico during the repairs?"

"Critical thinking. I like it. If these rats get a whiff of the feebs, they'll crawl back into their burrow, and we will have missed a golden opportunity."

"And you'll never catch Yoda."

"I sense a tone of insubordination, Major."

"No, sir. Not at all." John wanted to rephrase his previous statement, but the bird had already flown from his mouth. Chocker made it easy to let your guard down. But forgetting your place was a dangerous career move. "I believe he's a high priority and we will gain useful intel."

"Good save." Chocker clinked his wine glass against John's.

"If we can get one of these Three Stooges, we'll interrogate them, and backtrack the who, what, where, and when of their organization. I want the overseas people."

"Permission to speak freely?"

"At all times."

"If you let the FBI in, they'll want to know how you got the intel, and might find out about your inside man . . ."

"Neither confirmed nor denied, John."

"Nonetheless, they'll suspect."

"They will. And we're all supposed to share info and play nice-nice."

"Except for Yoda."

Chocker leaned in, his fingertips pressed against the white linen tablecloth, his expression deadly. John looked for a weapon of opportunity, then realized running away might be his best defense against C. Peter Chocker. His mind flashed on the fox that took the gingerbread man across the creek and then ate him. He was the gingerbread man, and he wanted to run, run, run, as fast as he could.

"Let me educate you. No one has ever killed an agent and survived. Ever." Chocker's second "ever" was exaggerated. "We've tracked every scumbag down, interrogated him, got intel, and then eliminated him. For every one of our people who goes down, we take ten of theirs. It's what keeps us sane and the United States a world power. It's why the president asks us, and tells other agencies."

"Sorry." John wanted to say something else, but Chocker was on a roll.

"Here's a newsflash for the CNN bobblehead inside your brain, Johnny. OBL's top generals are all dead." He took a big gulp of the Brunello and let that sink in for a moment. "There were a lot of agents killed in those two towers. We tracked the bastards down, cooled their core temperature to where they could barely think, and interrogated each of them all the way down the Celsius scale. Then we warmed them up a degree at a time and asked the same questions. Do you know how painful it is to thaw out from frostbite?"

He could only imagine.

"It makes waterboarding feel like an amusement park ride," said Chocker. "As they thawed, we removed parts of them. A lot of our friends were massacred by those bastards, John. There was a lot of hate to go around. One tiny piece at a time, no matter what they said—and they said a lot. Every major organ was intact when they finally went to Allah, but they were nothing but skeletons with a brain, veins, and a heart."

"Jesus." *So this is what it takes to run the world's largest covert intelligence operation.*

"It's the old saying, John," said Chocker. "The only people who think torture doesn't work have never been tortured."

John wanted to change the subject, but he couldn't think of anything to say. Chocker flattened his palms against the tablecloth, and the color returned to his scarred skin.

"Of course," he said, "it's worthless now. All new players in the game. But trust me, OBL's team talked plenty. Every one of them gave us another piece of the puzzle."

"So why the war on terror? We got them, didn't we? Don't tell me this is about oil?"

Chocker took a drink and smirked. "Oil is the biggest scam ever perpetrated on the earthlings." He shook his head, disgusted. "Earthlings" were what they called civilians in Marine Special Forces Operations School (MARSOC) at Camp Lejeune, North Carolina. John's instructor said their job would be to walk among and protect the earthlings anonymously. Nod your head and smile, but don't interact outside mission parameters.

"Even when Jimmy Carter pulled that crap in the seventies," Chocker continued, "we had more oil than the world could use. There's enough oil in Saudi Arabia alone to last four hundred years, and that doesn't take into account improvements in technology. The US can sustain current usage with natural gas and our own untapped coastal reserves."

"It doesn't make sense. I'm sorry, Pete. Maybe I'll keep my mouth shut."

"I wouldn't want you sitting in front of me if you didn't know how to sift the hay from the chaff, John. I expect it from my people."

They toasted, but John had the feeling he didn't want to enter into this conversation.

"Four hundred years is a lot of regime changes, princes, and presidents," said Chocker. "As long as the status quo is maintained, we can continue on for the betterment of the world. This is the first time in history a superpower has had a stronghold across the entire Mideast. We've got armies and forward posts in almost every major country. Iran's surrounded, and the Russians won't even consider sending their boys in after the Mujahideen kicked their ass."

"I get it," said John. "Not about oil, just military influence."

"Military influence to protect our country and to spread democracy. This country runs on its military, always has. The more of us there are around the world, the safer the planet. Anyone, anywhere, tries a major attack on our allies, we will be at their doorstep in minutes, not days. And I don't mean some delegate from the State Department or the UN. I'm talking about marine battalions, offshore naval bombardment, tomahawks in their windows, and UAVs dropping ordnance from nowhere and everywhere."

"So it isn't about AQ?"

"It's all about them. The only time we've ever been able to successfully express our way of life throughout the world is through our military. Heard anything from the Peace Corps lately?"

John wasn't sure the Peace Corps even existed anymore, and shook his head.

"The more tentacles we have, the more people get to know us. Guns and butter, Johnny. These drug addicts with their summits in Copenhagen and the UN are milking us."

"I don't follow."

"You ever see a wind generator built by the UN?"

John shook his head.

"We helped build two of the largest wind farms in the world: the Philippines and South Africa. Did the UN give our engineers credit?" Chocker shook his head, disgusted. "Without boots on the ground, we would never have known about Kensico. So there are a lot of layers here, John. And you're a part of it."

John looked at the empty wine bottle and wondered if he had followed Chocker down the rabbit hole.

"Your days as a Pollyanna are over, son. Welcome aboard." Chocker raised his glass and mouthed a silent "Hoorah." "Let's get back on point. Are you with me?"

"One hundred percent of my heart and soul, sir. When I'm in, I'm all in. This will get done right. We have no choice."

"A lot of people are going to bite the dust if you drop the ball."

"Relax. Have I ever not delivered?"

"No, John. You're the best of the best."

He nearly cringed when Chocker checked his watch like the White Rabbit.

"Why don't we just advertise what we do?" said John. "You know, let the country know how truly bad the bad guys are, and how to handle them."

"Everything?" asked Chocker.

"Well, not everything." John realized that some details should never be disclosed. "But enough so the world knows we're not the bad guys."

"If you take man out of the picture," said Chocker. "The most dangerous animal on the planet is the killer whale."

"Yeah?"

"And the only time he gets harpooned is when he sticks his head up and spouts off."

They made small talk about benchmarking, product positioning, and e-commerce as they waited for the bill. John exited to the right and got in his Subaru. He started it up and watched Chocker get into a Buick LaCrosse. Not bad. No government plates, and much more discreet than a black SUV or a Crown Vic. It took some pull to get a vehicle without government plates. Chocker's pockets and influence ran deep, but John had already suspected as much.

He pulled the satellite phone from his pocket and found one preprogrammed number in the directory. He pushed SEND and waited.

"Cock," said a voice on the other end of the line.

"A doodle-freaking-doo," said John.

C. Peter Chocker's husky laugh filled the Subaru's interior. "You all right?"

"Just checking."

"Curious George."

CATSKILL MOUNTAINS

She was light and feathery between his legs. She held him steady with a firm and pleasing constitution, and a latticework of components only God could put together in one instrument of pleasure and pain. Every component integrated to perfection. When he pushed down, she bent with his weight and climbed upward with no resistance. When he pulled up, she absorbed his sweat and muscle into her body and transferred it to the earth. If he tucked in, his hips low and pressed tight against her willing frame, she relaxed and let gravity swallow them both, downward, at the edge of control.

He smiled as he climbed—sweat, push, pull, and sweat, up, up, up.

"Thank you, God," John giggled.

He thanked God for the ability to bike. He felt bad for people who couldn't walk; people in wheelchairs dependent on their surroundings, limited to where they could go; diabetics who'd lost their limbs; Wii addicts. Cycling put the world in perspective and increased the gratitude in his attitude.

The killing, the suffering, the constant dredging through sand and brush as a soldier in his country's name so that he and others could be free—it all vanished on rides. The intensity of physical action put him in the moment, in the present, like a Buddha.

She was carbon black with flecks of fire-engine red. Her color would change when his mission went live. Her given name was the Specialized Tarmac S-Works SL3 Super Light—haughty, like her design. He called her Baby.

Her ultralight chain had alternating red metal links cast from a unique alloy to give it both strength and flexibility. The red links accented her soul's cool blackness with a glint of fire. She dressed nicely in Zipp 404 wheels, all carbon and Kevlar body armor beneath him, protecting him from slips, rocks, and nasty falls at fifty-plus miles per hour.

With the custom carbon saddle, Baby was unique.

The bike he rode at the Olympic trials for the summer games in Athens didn't hold a candle to Baby. Not that he would have won with her, but with Baby's frame at just under three pounds, there would have been a definite edge.

He had tried to make the Olympic road cycling team in his senior year at Rutgers, right after passing on the NFL offer. They told him to come back next time, and to shed ten pounds. He had gained too much weight from football and couldn't make the top ten for the time trials. His decision to enlist in the Marine Corps came several months later. He hadn't thought about it too much. He had settled for the next open door after life had closed two more behind him.

He pushed the disappointment from his mind and stretched out farther over Baby's downward-curved handlebars. The pretty red highlights would have to go when the rubber met the road, or the Kevlar tires, in this case. Baby must be indistinct to prying eyes before she was mission-ready.

He whipped around the Ashokan Reservoir's winding roads, climbed Ohayo Mountain in a flash, and coasted into Woodstock. He stopped for a triple espresso at the Bread Alone Bakery, then headed back onto the bubbling asphalt.

Today's test took him to the hills outside of Phoenicia, with fast, ten-degree grades for the warm-up before he reached Platte Clove Road, one of the most difficult climbs in the northeast: in total, about forty-five miles that would take one and a half hours if he could hold his average speed to thirty.

Baby sported a Dura-Ace crank set with ceramic bearings for increased strength and less weight. He preferred clipless pedals—step-ins—to put more power to the ground. The cyclometer displayed an average speed of twenty-nine miles per hour, with a cadence of one hundred. John's heart rate ramped up to the race level of one hundred sixty. His breath flowed with little effort at that pace, a smooth inhale through his slightly opened mouth, air sliding over his teeth, and then an exhale through the nose and mouth. Repeat as necessary to power the machine.

The solitude of man melded with machine kept him physically grounded to the road. But spiritually he flew with the hawks and eagles that came down from the clouds and pulled a duck or trout from the reservoir. Wind whistled in his ears, and the tires hummed as they lifted microscopic tar and placed it back on the road.

Head down.

He reviewed the motions he knew so well. Head down to cut resistance and relieve neck strain. Keep the spine as aerodynamic as possible. Head down kept the target small, the bullets out of his skull. Head down so the whistling threat passed by him and into the rocks, or some unlucky bastard bringing up the rear.

He made a conscious effort to stay in the moment. To stay right here, riding, and keep his thoughts away from the perilous hills of Tora Bora, Nangarhar province—a place of poppy fields, children sold to human traffickers, and Pashtun clans ready to take any side for a dollar and switch between tribal loyalty and profit at the drop of a hat. John glimpsed those phantoms behind every rock outcropping along the road, in the trees, under bridges and sluices that guided the Esopus Creek into the Ashokan Reservoir. They showed themselves in flashes of tribal garb among the swiftly passing forest, black turbans and filthy beards hiding gaunt faces in Catskill ditches.

Sweat dripped off his brow and into his eyes, making the enemy more lifelike, harder to see, fuzzy fleeting forms teasing him to come closer. They jerked their rifle butts in his direction, feigning live ammo like little boys playing army.

Get off the bike and let us see what you're made of, Major Rexford.

He pumped harder, rode faster, and came back to the Catskills, in the actual moment, alive with sweat and aching muscles and in love with the escape Baby gave him.

The LCD display on his wrist told him he had left the working heart range of one forty and entered the low end of his max heart rate of one eighty-three. He would keep his heart rate here for a few more miles, and kick it up a notch at the start of Platte Clove Road.

He reached down for his water bottle and took a drink. He pedaled harder, away from the past but not its responsibilities, and into the present.

Out of the moment, he lost focus and went back there, adjusting the canteen on his belt. Grass and scrub trees dotted the earth, low on the mountain ranges outside Tora Bora. Higher up, thin tire tracks veined the mountainside; and even higher, rock-strewn capillaries spidered the landscape where only natives and goats walked with proficiency. Vehicles were worthless in the mountain of caves. A Daisy Cutter's last smoke plumes crawled along a distant horizon and evaporated into gray skies.

He dug his heels into the dirt and climbed higher.

The air smelled fresh, devoid of hajji sweat, but sounds of small rocks rolling into gullies unnerved him. Was it the enemy, or wind and gravity? Nature ultimately reduces all mountains to beaches.

He pressed harder. The taut cables in his legs strained against the incline. His soles slipped and his knees bled into the foreign dust and dirt.

On the last hilltop before the next valley, he chambered the 7.62 NATO round into the Dakota Scimitar tactical rifle. He preferred the M40A3, but they wanted him to try out the Scimitar. It was one of life's coincidences that a scimitar is a curved-blade saber, a weapon of ancient Persia. Aesthetically, this would be a good kill.

Major Rexford's martial arts and hand-to-hand weapons training had prepared him physically for this desiccated high mountain terrain. His ability to cluster five rounds of the NATO projectile into a six-inch target at a thousand yards made him the obvious volunteer for this mission: keep Osama and any other Al Qaeda leaders in Afghanistan until reinforcements arrived, specifically in this kill zone, and then await further instructions.

Sheikh Ahmed Salim Swedan drew on a hand-rolled cigarette near the fire, inhaled to the bottom of his lungs, and held the smoke. Probably laced with opium. No one held their hits that long unless they wanted to get high. He downloaded Swedan's photo and profile into the handheld he kept in his pack, and confirmed with 100 percent accuracy that he had located one of the top dogs in Osama's kennel of mongrels. He opened a signal and waited for a response.

"Zero-One-Niner, Lucy. Please respond."

"Hazmat-One-Bravo, Lucy. Over."

"Go ahead."

"The cabbage is in the garden, ready to pick. Over."

"Hold your position, Hazmat. Repeat. Hold your position."

"Requesting permission to proceed. Over."

A series of squawks and clicks followed.

"Negative. Do not engage. Repeat. Do not engage. Over."

"Hazmat out." And very pissed. This went on for three more days while the CIA waited for reinforcements to close the back-door from Afghanistan into Pakistan. The administration decided to leave it up to the Afghan warlords, some of whom were Osama's known allies, to halt the retreat. Major Rexford hung his head as he watched the ragtag Al Qaeda terrorist army march away from the valley and into western Pakistan, where they were untouchable by US forces. Had he been a mercenary, Major Rexford would have earned two million dollars for this kill. As a marine, he received a twenty-one-mile hike back to base camp. Defeated, he pushed his boots into the arid soil, one in front of the other.

Push harder. Come back to the now. He forced himself against Baby's pedals, and the pain brought him back to the Catskills.

Push, pull, push, pull. The cadence rolled through his brain as he climbed Platte Cove Road. *One, two, one, two, push, pull, push, pull.* He pedaled rounds, keeping his power even throughout the chain ring's 360-degree revolution.

Ain't no use in callin' home, Jodie's got your telephone . . .
Ain't no use in lookin' back, Jodie's got your Cadillac . . .
Push, pull. Sound off. One, two. Sound off . . .

Heart rate: one ninety.

He envisioned a tiny door in his throat that let the air in, swung the other way, and let the air out. *Breathe in the moment. Breathe out the moment. Breathe in the moment. Breathe out the moment. Over and over, up and up. In and out.*

Higher and higher, baby . . . it's a living thing . . . what a terrible thing to lose . . .

He stood on the pedals as the incline steepened an eighth of a mile from the summit. He trained to push harder at the top. His Olympic coach had taught him to use his momentum to carry him over the top. *Never slow down near the crest. Push harder at the top.* The memory of this encouragement moved him forward.

He bellowed "Hoorah" as his momentum took him over the crest. Baby carried him the rest of the way. He coasted to the dirt roadside, turned his head, and looked back at where he had been. The soldiers, the Buddha, the enemy, the air, aching muscles, bleeding knees, and his breath were separate elements rolled into one. He had spun them with his crank into shiny nuggets where they dissolved like tigers into butter in a children's book, round and round the tree, chasing their tails until they melted. He took a drink from his water bottle, huffed the sky, swallowed the green leaves, and exhaled clouds of victory. He rested his head on the handlebars and watched sweat pearls roll off Baby's ebony frame.

Still in oxygen debt, he laughed and snorted between gasps, because he had done what few people could. It was elation borne of exclusivity. It erased any failures or mistakes from the past for this impermanent moment, and brushed the residue from his life's chalkboard. With new breath came new life, and he would descend with a clean slate.

He clipped back in and let Baby and gravity do the rest. Time for a personal record. With his eyes closed, the wind evaporated any doubts. Bike and rider picked up speed.

"Fucking faggot!"

The horn blast rocked his reverie. He grabbed the handlebars tightly, eyes wide in adrenaline shock, fingertips on the brake levers, ready to launch into the rock and thistle–choked ditch.

The black pickup truck's modified mufflers stuck up over the cab. A cartoon boy pasted on the rear window pissed on the world. The truck pulled up beside him, with two men in the cab. A scraggly bearded, red-eyed redneck with bad teeth and a beer can in his hand sat nearest him on the passenger side.

"Get off the road, queer-boy," Bad Teeth spit through his moustache.

Stringy snot clung to John's helmet. His digital heart meter broke two hundred and flashed a warning. He pulled tight on the pistol grip brakes and skidded to a stop at the edge of the road. The truck kept going. He raised his left hand high, put his right hand on his crotch, and flipped them the bird. The driver slammed on his brakes, yelled something incoherent, and threw an empty beer can out the window.

John popped up on his pedals and attacked. When he got within twenty feet, the truck peeled away and shot gravel into his face. Both men in the cab extended their arms and flipped him off.

With his serenity shattered, revenge episodes played over and over in John's head. He had already killed them three different ways before he got back up to speed. He tucked and coasted down the four-and-a-half-mile descent.

His body began to tense from a buildup of aggression caused by conflict with no resolution. He unclipped his right pedal, raised his leg behind him, and rested it on the saddle for a quadricep stretch, holding the position as he gained speed. Twenty miles per hour.

Heart rate: one hundred six.

He switched to the left leg and repeated the stretch. Thirty miles per hour.

Heart rate: one hundred eight.

With both feet back in the stirrups, he grabbed the straight part of the handlebars, lowered his crotch onto Baby's top tube, tucked his helmet behind her head tube, and pulled his knees tight against her frame.

Speed: thirty-five miles per hour.

Heart rate: one hundred nine.

He pulled his elbows inward for a more aerodynamic approach, but surrendered a large degree of control in doing so. To steer in this position, he leaned slightly left or right and nudged the handlebars by micrometers to guide Baby into the turn's groove. Forty-five miles per hour, and she didn't shake—not a shiver, not a squeak. Baby held the road like the thoroughbred she was.

Stand up, buckle up, shuffle to the door.
Jump right out and count to four.

Sweat burned his eyes, but he couldn't take his hands off the bars at this speed.

If my reserve don't blossom round
I'll be the first one on the ground.

Heart rate: one hundred thirty.

Speed: fifty-two miles per hour.

He heard his platoon sergeant yell. *Sound off. One. Two.*

His heart grew lighter as he got closer to the kill, closer to the action.

Not a shimmy at fifty-eight miles per hour. He raised his head to catch a little wind and slow Baby down for the curve ahead, the last turn on the road. The rest of the road would be a straight, steep decline. He had to get past, this, one, last, curve.

His thighs ached from the static position. His forearms cramped up as he pulled out of the curve and headed for the straight away at sixty-two miles per hour—a personal best for the 1,200-foot vertical climb of Platte Clove Road.

The black pickup rolled slowly one hundred yards ahead in front of a deli at the intersection. He slowed down to ten miles per hour as he passed, and squirted the driver's face with his water bottle. The truck lurched and skidded to a stop. Noisy grunts and curses came from inside the cab as John pulled over and rested his bike on the post office mailbox in the small parking lot. He left his helmet and glasses on, and finished off the water bottle.

Heart rate: one forty-five—optimum combat level.

Speed: zero.

The rednecks jostled and shouted at each other inside the truck cab, unable to formulate a plan. They wondered why the crazy little bastard on the bike didn't pedal away to safety. This confused them. They bickered back and forth in the cab's safety, and somehow convinced each other that together they could kick the little faggot's ass. They jumped out and swaggered toward him, chests puffed, guts sucked in. If inside the truck they had waffled between fight and flight, fight had won.

"You got a problem, boy?" the short redneck asked. He had made the faggot comment.

John looked into their eyes. They didn't see his through the iridium-coated Oakleys. He smelled fear. *Breathe in. Door swings open. Breathe out. Door swings the other way.*

"Yeah," the taller redneck chimed in. "What's your problem, faggot? You sprayed me with your water bottle. You think a bottle's gonna save your ass?"

John saw no weapons, but he made no premature plan based on this information. A weapon usually accompanied fear and empty bravado.

"That was piss, fat boy." He stepped away from Baby.

The short redneck came in fast, hands up like a boxer. The steel-plate bottom of John's cycling shoes connected with the man's kneecap, and the cartilage popped like bubble wrap. He went down with both hands grasping his useless limb.

The tall redneck snapped his hand into the air and waved an expandable police baton. He took a roundhouse swing, and John let the baton pass inches from his chin. John gripped his attacker's wrist in an instant, twisted upward, and struck a tight-fisted blow to the man's triceps that ripped away collateral ligaments and separated the radius from the ulna. He eased the injured man down with a kick to the back of the calf, and let him collapse on the short redneck.

John and Baby took the back roads home to avoid any police or ambulance on their way to help the the men he had left on the ground. It added twenty miles to the trip, but was better than sitting in a police station justifying the assault.

A little of the serenity he had earned from the climb returned as he spun sprocket and chain back to his house. He remembered a John Lennon lyric: *There are no problems, only solutions.*

So far, this had been one excellent day.

Henry Clay Hall pushed off the floor for momentum, setting the oak rocking chair in motion as John road up the gravel driveway.

"You're a little early, Major," said John. "Or the senility's kicking in. The rent isn't due for another week." He coasted to the porch and slammed on the brakes, fishtailing Baby's rear end.

Henry leaned forward on his cane. "If I needed rent money, I wouldn't have leased this fine property to a jarhead low-life who spends his days pedaling the countryside."

John dismounted and carried Baby onto the porch. He kicked the cane's rubber tip and sat down on a plastic lawn chair next to Henry.

"Gonna be a nice sunset," said Henry.

"Yep. You want a beer?" John rotated his wrist, holding an invisible can.

"Beer? I thought we were friends."

"There's Jack Daniels inside. Why don't you come in and watch me undress?"

"You ain't my type," Henry replied, peering over his bifocals. "But if you get me drunk enough, we'll see." Uneven and cracked teeth peeked through the salt-and-pepper beard that rested on his chest. A gold cap glinted in the back of his mouth. He gave the rocker two hard pushes, leaned on the cane, groaned, and stood erect. "How's the missus?" he said.

"She's all right. She's coming over later. Something about surprising me with dinner."

He placed a half-full rocks glass in front of his landlord, and went into the bathroom off the kitchen to shower.

"You better hold on to that one," said Henry.

"What?" John yelled back through the sound of running water.

"I said you better hold on to that one. It ain't likely you'll get another schoolmarm to come calling in this backward town."

"I got something for you to hold on to," John shouted back over the patter of water drops that hit the antique claw-foot bathtub's enamel finish.

"All I'm saying is she's a good looker. Got a good job, and you ain't exactly a prize." Henry waited for a smart-ass reply, then added, "Look in the mirror lately?" He took a swallow of Jack Daniels and set the glass back down one-quarter full.

John turned off the shower. "When will you learn to speak American? You spend so much time in those civil war books, you're starting to sound like a Johnny Reb." A moment of silence passed. "Hey. You still out there?"

More silence.

"Henry? You still out there?"

"Yeah," Henry mumbled. "What do you want?"

"Why aren't you talking?" John walked into the kitchen, pulling a T-shirt over his head.

Henry grinned. "You insulted me."

"Then have another drink, you old bastard."

Henry mumbled that he didn't mind if he did, and swallowed the rest of his whiskey.

"How's the book coming?"

"Maybe you should read it. I'm worried it won't make the Ivy League bestseller list," said Henry, and poured himself more whiskey.

John scratched his wet hair. He took a drink of the Jack Daniels that Henry had poured him in a tumbler glass, no rocks. His pumped and dehydrated body absorbed the warm alcohol burn like a thirsty sponge.

"Maybe I should have gone to Rutgers and majored in English," said Henry. "You know, to learn myself better."

They toasted. "Here's to your West Point career and the class of 1901," said John.

Henry let that one slide. "All I'm saying is you ain't getting any younger, and she's a looker." He put the glass back down.

"Is that what you were yelling about when I was in the shower?" said John. "Did you actually say 'schoolmarm'?"

Henry rubbed his stiff fingers over the top of his cane. "I did," he said. "And it's a real word, jarhead. Look it up." Henry took another sip, smacked his lips, and used his tongue to collect whiskey droplets. "Your problem is you got no class. You moved in here six months ago, and I moved into my trailer across the road so you could have a life."

John shook his head. "You moved into the trailer, as I recall, because I needed the barn to work my iron, and you like to cash the checks."

"Speaking of wrought iron," Henry said, "I saw what you did over at Torcia's store with the chairs out front. You got some talent, son." He looked at the wall behind John. "You see that?" He pointed at photographs of John winning the Tour de Champlain and other cycling races. Next to them hung team portraits of the Rutgers's championship Scarlet Knights, with John in full uniform. "The problem is, there ain't no ladies in any of those pictures, no children, no family. You want to end up a crippled old barracks rat like me?"

"Other than the heartbreak of ugliness, you don't seem all that pitiful, even for an army grunt."

Henry snorted and shook his head. "You don't have any service photos hanging. What's the story?"

"I don't need photos of the place. All I have to do is turn on the TV and get live recon 24-7."

"I suppose." Henry took another sip and rubbed his hands together. "John, I'm not here to pry. Just looking out for a fellow soldier. You know, passing on the knowledge and all that crap. What did Shaw say?"

"Shaw?"

"George Bernard Shaw, you ignorant Yankee."

"Oh, that Shaw. He said Vietnam vets should stay in hospitals and decrease the surplus population."

"He said, 'Youth is wasted on the young.'"

John turned toward the window. Two lush oak trees pushed a shrinking sun into the horizon. A gentle wind turned their leaves. It looked like rain. "Hey, not to change the subject—"

"But you are."

"Would you like to join us for dinner?"

Henry stroked his long beard and sipped more Jack Daniels. "Thank you. I got something cooking with Abe's assassination and want to see if I can put the puzzle together."

"You sure?" said John. "That Abe thing is pretty much wrapped up. I hear they got the guy." He raised his index finger. "Wasn't it some asshole rebel, slave-hating, KKK guy?"

Henry poked at John with his cane. He used the table for balance, lifted himself from the chair, and beckoned John into the living room. Everything was as Henry had left it when he relocated across the road to his single-wide trailer. The furniture looked like it came from a Cracker Barrel catalogue, but about a century older. In one corner sat an old cane English rocker covered in a blanket and dust. An oak serving buffet had its own wall, with two Scottish terrier bookends on either side of it. Unmatched Victorian armchairs in need of reupholstering filled each corner. Photographs of twentieth-century wars hung on the drab green plastered walls. Time and temperature changes had cracked sections of the plaster into irregular spider web patterns.

"I'll get these out of here soon," Henry said. "I haven't had the time."

"Don't sweat it," said John. "I'm in no rush."

"I know this ain't much for entertaining the ladies." Henry gave him a nudge. "That is, having this stuff on the walls. But it comforted me when I was bored with no one around."

It's the old bastard's way, John thought, *of telling me he likes having me around.*

"Take a look at this one." Henry tapped a photo with his cane. "This was taken in '68. I was twenty-one years old, fresh out of the Point, and full of piss and vinegar. Handsome cuss, wasn't I?"

John had noticed the photograph before. Henry Clay Hall stood in full military dress with his platoon outside their barracks in Saigon. It was apparent that he was in charge, even if you didn't know he was the West Point graduate.

"You look pretty dapper," said John.

"Yeah." Henry cocked an eye. "Now come down here."

They walked around the lion-footed sideboard to the spot on the wall where Henry's cane tip rested.

"Take a look at this one," said Henry, "taken right after we mopped up Saddam's elite chickenshit Republican guards. I headed up the USCENTCOM Army Materiel Command in Kuwait City."

"Impressive, Major."

"We were in charge of technology, acquisition support, and logistics to ensure dominant land force capability. Take a good look at me." Henry tapped the glass protecting the photograph.

"To be honest, Henry, you look a little worse for wear." Everyone in the picture was smiling except Major Henry Clay Hall. He was staring at the camera with a hardened look.

"Would you like to guess why?" Henry looked over his glasses at John, a full head shorter.

"Never was good at guessing."

"It was just over twenty years since I left Saigon. We didn't have anything called post-traumatic stress disorder back then. Those of us who stayed in the military were lucky. The rest of those boys came home to a world of emotional hurt, and those who were physically wrecked had to deal with that, and the emotional stuff."

"But you stayed in."

"I didn't have a choice, John." Henry rubbed his hands together again. His dry skin made the sound of broom bristles on a sidewalk. "I had no one to write to except my parents—no women, no real friends, being a West Pointer. The regular army didn't associate with us. No one I could hang with. Long story short, I mulled my life away from station to station." Henry winced. They went back into the kitchen and sat down.

"You see, John, I went in all pumped up, got a little screwed up in Asia, and then spent the rest of my career stuffing it. When I started hearing bombs go off again, in the desert, I lost it. I started drinking. They had to send me back to the States. One night I was sniffing around for this lady I knew in Fort Drum during one of their typical snowstorms and landed flat on my back outside a bar. Everyone thinks I'm out from a war injury. I got booted, son."

He tried to pour Henry another drink, but Henry covered his glass.

"You put in your time," said John. "They got more than they bargained for from you. Vietnam. Desert Storm. What the hell? You're all good in my book."

"Son, I ain't looking for pity," Henry said. "I'm trying to tell you that if I had someone to write to, it might have been different. Who knows?" Henry tapped John's foot with his cane. "You got a head on your shoulders, a good education, and a girl who thinks the world of you." He groaned and pushed himself up from the table. "I'm getting the hell out of here before the schoolmarm shows up."

He followed Henry to the door with a hand on his shoulder. "You sure you don't want to stay?" said John. "Maggie says she's making something special. Could be SOS, or hash browns and ketchup."

"Shit on a shingle? Tempting, but thank you, no," Henry replied. "I'll go get with my boy Abe and see where he takes me." Henry walked to the edge of the steps leading to the broken cement walkway. "Which reminds me . . ."

"Yeah?"

"The local yokels didn't get their boy today."

John didn't take the bait but sipped his whiskey instead. A warm rush tingled through his brain. Muscle fibers relaxed beneath his skin, and the world had an alcohol-induced gentleness.

"Turns out some numbnuts in a pickup got their asses kicked in by a biker up near Roxbury," said Henry.

"Motorcycle gang?" John attempted sincerity.

"No, John, it wasn't. A guy on a road bike kicked their asses good, so the witnesses say. They didn't get a good look at him, though, what with the helmet and sunglasses on."

"Ain't life a bitch? Where do you get all this gossip anyway?"

"I wouldn't consider myself true Catskill Mountain trailer trash without a scanner to put me to sleep at night."

"Have a good night, Henry."

The screen door banged against the jamb. Henry turned and walked down the stairs.

"If the guy has a brain, he'll take Roxbury off his route for a while," Henry muttered.

"What?" John spoke through the screen, as if he hadn't understood.

Henry waved his cane and kept walking.

John had chosen carefully before renting Henry Hall's Catskill farmhouse. His handlers had told him to find a country setting within two hours of Manhattan to set up shop. They approved of the location's proximity, tucked away in pastoral farmland and the forested mountains of the Catskill Park. Uncluttered cycling was another positive feature. When you lived in the mountains, long drives and roof racks were unnecessary to get away from it all. John could get his gear on, open the front door, point Baby's wheels in any direction, and challenge some of the biggest hills and fastest descents in the northeast.

Snow seldom accumulated before January in the Catskills, and hardcore riders only lost the first couple of months each year to icy roads. Martial arts, cross-country skiing, and snowshoeing augmented John's winter training regimen. By March he was back on the pavement, devouring miles of empty back roads.

Inside the weathered, two-story pine-board building, an ancient cast iron combination coal/wood-burning furnace rested on a solid concrete slab, cured rock-hard by one hundred years of moist hot summers and cold dry winters. Henry had upgraded the unit to natural gas in the seventies so he could convert the barn into a rental home. The plan never materialized, but the furnace remained.

Cancer took John's father and left his mother with a college-bound son and younger sister to care for. The meager death benefit awarded military widows, and an even smaller monthly check from social security, left a hefty gap between a tuition scholarship at Rutgers and the cost of books and spending money. His football coach found him a job at a thoroughbred horse ranch in Heathcote, New Jersey, about fifteen miles from the Rutgers campus in New Brunswick, where John mucked stalls and built and maintained fences on weekends.

The ranch employed an old hippie named Thai, who shoed the horses. Under Thai's guidance, John learned the basics of forging, drawing or lengthening the metal, and bending and welding different iron grades. His blacksmithing skills were further honed after he enlisted in the marines, where he found himself among primitive blacksmiths, courtesy of Uncle Sam, who specialized in twentieth-century small arms.

Thirty miles past the last outpost in Afghanistan, where neither the Afghani nor any other single military power had control, was a tribal territory known as Darra, the world's largest open-air gun market. Access by invitation only. There was a five-thousand-dollar cover charge to enter city limits, and if you weren't introduced by someone already known to the locals, you might not leave. People who tried were tattooed with a third eye. Few outsiders had the balls or a good reason to visit Darra unless they were buying guns, or hunting people who bought guns.

John's unit spent three months with Darra's Afridi tribesmen, studying the gunsmith's painstaking craft. John also learned how their product wormed its way into world arms markets.

The Afridi were a fierce, independent faction that answered to Allah and money—preferably US dollars—but would trade in any currency for a fee. Their equipment wasn't much different from that of the early Iron Age, where socioeconomics favored the use of iron implements and weapons over bronze. The Afridi were able to price their dollars, euros, and afghani to within pennies of the major currency exchange rates each day, and adjust their prices accordingly, with little access to modern computers and the Internet.

John watched twelve-year-old boys make replicas of rifles, from a 1914 US Enfield and accompanying .308 ammunition to a modern bolt-action Remington 700 BDL—an excellent low-budget sniper rifle for third-world scumbags. The "stable boy craftsmen," as they were known, could pump out two to three complete rifles a month using nothing more than hand tools and a wood-fired furnace. The most astonishing detail about these guns was that they fired modern factory-made ammunition flawlessly. What Thai didn't show John about hand-forging metal, he picked up by watching Afridi youths contribute to the modern arms race with primitive tools.

The stable boy craftsmen were also experts in knife and sword fabrication. Pulwars (a broadsword of Afghanistan), dirks, and tactical knives hung from every storefront. They sold for as little as two dollars US. John observed as fourteen-year-old boys fashioned knives in about two hours from scrap metal salvaged off burnt-out Jeeps and Land Rovers. The knives' hardened rubber handles were made by melting worn-out tire strips, shaping them, letting them cool, and then laminating another layer of melted rubber over the previous one. After three layers, the results were beautiful, black-handled, perfectly balanced throwing knives and daggers.

Knife-making had become indispensible to John's profession. He never used the same weapon twice. When he completed a mission, he melted the evidence into a steel ball.

So when the realtor showed him Henry Hall's barn, complete with an old crucible furnace for metalworking, he didn't need to see the house. He had his bike routes laid out before he moved in, and he negotiated full access to the furnace before he signed the lease with Henry. He invested in a used sixty-inch sandblasting cabinet though eBay and, with a few odds and ends such as acetylene torches, helmets, and asbestos gloves, John was in the wrought-iron railing and metal repair business.

John used the sandblaster to remove rust from scrap metal he bought at a local junkyard. The business started as a good cover, but he soon found out there wasn't a blacksmith around for a hundred miles, and demand for his skills was high. He turned down bigger jobs to keep people away from the place. He didn't need the artsy crowd dropping in on weekends to check out his studio and his cover.

Blacksmithing brought him Maggie. She needed an antique wrought-iron birdfeeder fixed, and had heard that the new guy in town was handy with an anvil. After she ran out of metal on her property that needed bending, and excuses to visit John, she decided to invite the reclusive artisan to dinner. He declined, so she told him that she would bring it to him. He liked her perseverance, and conceded.

Whenever he cleaned his equipment, he recited the Marine Corps Rifleman's Creed to stay focused and remember why he had chosen this life.

This is my rifle. There are many like it, but this one is mine.

Baby lay on a canvas tarp, stripped of all her parts.

My rifle is human, even as I, because it is my life.

He placed her brakes, chain, cables, crankset, handlebars, wheels, seat post, and derailleur on the floor in the order he removed them from her frame.

I will learn its weakness, its strength, its parts, its accessories, its sights, and its barrel.

He ran his fingers over her stripped-naked 2.6-pound base weight. His plans to paint her jet black had changed after the incident on Platte Clove Road.

He remembered Henry's warning: "If that guy had a brain, he'd take Roxbury off his route."

The old bastard was right. The police couldn't identify him with the glasses and helmet on, but he didn't want some redneck cousin bent on revenge to run him off the road because his bike looked like the bike the guy rode who messed up Billy-Bob and Beauford.

Chocker had sent Baby via UPS a few months ago, courtesy of International Fiber Resources. John didn't think the CIA would mind a color change. He didn't want a bike that could be recognized as being at the location where two rednecks had recently been assaulted. He also knew Chocker would be happy for one more degree of separation tying him to any illegal activity. With the NSA checking every American citizen's emails and phone calls, less contact was always better.

John picked up her slender frame and placed it inside the sandblaster cabinet. He turned the air compressor on and filled the hopper with five pounds of finely ground silica. Once the pressure had reached the proper level, he reached his arms inside the glove holes in the cabinet and grabbed the bike frame. He used his foot to regulate the silica flow as he looked through the glass view window and maneuvered Baby at different angles inside the cabinet, making sure the abrasive blast made contact with all exposed painted surfaces.

After a half hour of delicate sanding, he had removed every speck of black and red pigment from Baby's surface. Her brushed aluminum and titanium frame lay naked before him.

I will keep my rifle clean and ready, even as I am clean and ready. We will become part of each other.

He pulled her from the cabinet and let the metal cool to room temperature, then cleaned all traces of dirt, abrasive, and oils from her skin. He wiped her down with an alcohol-soaked cloth and then a dry chamois. Once her surface had dried, he locked Baby into a floor-mounted bike stand and went to the paint cabinet to choose a color.

He turned the aerosol paint cans so the labels faced him. Black spoke to authority and power—too antagonistic. He wanted something people on the street would notice, but then look away. Nothing to say, "Hey, look at me."

White was pure and innocent, but it stood out in almost any backdrop and attracted attention. It also showed dirt, and John loathed a dirty weapon.

Yellow and orange were attention getters. They were used in safety signs, because they were too bright for the average person not to notice.

He pulled a can of dark purple from the metal shelf. It was the color of royalty. Baby deserved something regal. The label read DEEP PURPLE. It was the name of a classic rock band, and he hummed the riff to the song "Smoke on the Water" as he shook the can vigorously and walked back to Baby. The glass pea inside the can rolled smoothly from top to bottom with a click-clack sound. He pulled off the cap and set it on the worn wooden workbench.

The barn leaked air, and a thirty-foot open-beam ceiling eliminated the need for active ventilation. John made some perfunctory passes along Baby's frame without pushing the aerosol can's nozzle. When he had the right distance and hand speed, he depressed the nozzle and watched the shiny brushed aluminum turn to deep purple. Baby's frame took on a completely different personality as pigment covered the alloy canvas.

He applied one coat, waited a few moments, and then another. He stood back a few feet and watched Baby dry, impressed with the smoothness of her new finish.

So be it, until victory is America's and there is no enemy, but peace.

He had a slight buzz from the inhalants inside the aerosol can, so he wasn't sure whether he had heard something or felt it, but the hairs on his neck bristled. He wasn't alone. He kept his position in front of Baby's frame, not wanting to alarm an intruder by making quick movements.

How close was the bench? There were knives on the bench, and some throwing stars in a box near the sandblasting cabinet. He kept no guns in the barn. A weapon of convenience? The aerosol can in his hand. No flame source, so it remained a projectile.

Dry straw crunched beneath the weight of footsteps behind him, inside the barn now, and a little to the right. One forward roll would place him at the bench with a knife in his hand. Expert at the range, he fashioned his knives for the explicit purpose of killing at distances of twenty feet or less. As long as the intruder didn't get in a shot—or if he did, and missed—there would be at least one chance for an offensive throw. John took the weight off his left leg and dropped his right shoulder as he readied himself for a standing Aikido forward roll.

"Boy, are you focused."

Maggie's voice relaxed the tenseness in his body. He turned and saw her beautiful, slim silhouette against the open barn door. *Note to self: close door when working.*

She stepped closer and into the filtered light of the windows. Straw chaff and dust flecks glittered in the air between them.

"What are you up to, John?"

He saw her warm smile, the dark brown eyes, and straight black hair pulled back and tied in a scrunchie. She wore a baseball cap labeled ONTEORA, the school where she taught third grade; a tight-fitting black T-shirt with a V-neck; blue jeans; and running shoes. He couldn't take his eyes off her. Her sheer bra might as well have not existed.

Maggie could have had a weekly spot on Fox News, where they showed famous women who wore too little. Maggie had too much class for that, and he was attracted to her the minute he laid eyes upon her.

"Take a picture; it'll last longer." She closed the distance between them with a bouncing gait and slight hip gyration, and then kissed him on the cheek. "Eww, what a manly smell."

"I'm putting the finishing touches on this bike," he said. "Are you early?"

"Nope." Maggie pursed her lips. "I brought you Chinese. Remember? Tuesday night Chinese? Every Tuesday night we have a date at seven o'clock for Chinese food, and if I was ever late you'd have to spank me."

"I remember that part. Are you late?"

"Nope. Right on time."

"My loss."

Maggie tried to wrap her arms around him for a kiss, but he backed away. "What's the problem?" She feigned sadness with a pouty lower lip.

"Nothing, Maggie," he said. "I stink. I haven't taken a shower since I rode, and I've been working on this bike for hours."

She pushed his hands away, stepped inside his guard, and planted a wet kiss on his lips.

"I like the smell of a working man," she said. She gave him a come-hither smile and looked over his shoulder at Baby.

"Is that your bike?" she asked, and then added, "Why did you change the color?"

He hadn't thought of a rational explanation yet, but he was quick on his feet.

"I dropped it on the ride and scratched it up pretty good."

"Dropped it" in bike parlance didn't mean you dropped the bike while holding it. It meant you took a spill and hit the asphalt.

"Purple was the only color I had close to anything I liked," said John, "so I went with it."

"Oh, John, are you hurt?" She gave him a once over.

"I caught my shoe on a dismount."

He couldn't tell her he screamed down mountains in excess of sixty miles per hour with nothing separating his skin from the asphalt but a micro-fine synthetic bike jersey and a thin layer of crushable foam to protect his skull. Most people wouldn't attempt this for money. He did it for kicks.

"You ride too fast, John."

He gave Maggie the universal I'm-a-stupid-little-puppy guy look, and she changed the subject. "I like purple," she said. "Purple is supposed to have positive power in the universe. All the Wavy Gravys in Woodstock wear it. Ever notice?"

"Nope." He walked over to the bench and wiped his hands with a rag.

"They even have a purple year and purple days. We should go over and check it out sometime." She changed her voice to mimic a sixties hippie and rolled her eyes. "It's like, wow, purple, man."

"I don't think it would be safe for me to spend too much time with the anti-everything crowd," John said. "I'd end up in jail on manslaughter charges."

"We should go over and see the town sometime anyway," said Maggie. "It's got lots of nice shops and restaurants. We could spend the day checking out galleries. I know, I know." She put her palms up. "You're a tough guy. But hey, a little culture never hurt anyone. And I could eat tabbouleh and you could get a hamburger."

"Not a veggie burger?" He threw the rag on the workbench.

"If you spend an afternoon looking at art with me, I'll buy you the biggest, reddest, bloodiest, cheddar cheese bacon burger and fries you can wolf down." She opened her mouth like a wild animal and growled.

"It's a deal," he said. "Can I go inside and get cleaned up?"

"I'll set the table."

"How about we eat in front of the television?"

Maggie nodded. "That's what I meant. I'll set the couch, and you clean off your grimy self. I brought over *One Fine Day* with Michelle Pfeiffer and George Clooney. Have you seen it?"

He shook his head as his chick-flick radar spiked.

"You'll love it then."

She took his arm in hers and walked him to the house.

Michelle Pfeiffer played a hardheaded single mom in *One Fine Day,* with a controlling personality and a no-nonsense approach to her busy executive life. She was offset by Clooney's likable self. Clooney played a divorced dad who had trouble juggling his busy executive life and children from a failed marriage.

John fell asleep before the movie ended, with his head in her lap, and she allowed herself to cry as she watched Pfeiffer and Clooney nod off together on their couch in the final scene.

Few things irritated Patrick Corcoran more than meetings, and he avoided formal meetings with suits at all costs. Even more irksome was when the thing inside the suit was an FBI agent. They were chain yankers, he liked to call them "chainkers." The big Irishman, Kieran Gilchrist, topped the list of FBI chainkers. Gilchrist was no more of a prick, pencil-pushing attorney than the rest, except he had an impractical moral compass that forced him to play by the rules. Kieran was good, and he had a nose for the hunt. Patrick would play his cards close to the vest, appearing agreeable to full disclosure among the Homeland Security agencies.

Today's meeting was nothing more than a disguised interrogation. Interrogations involved people trying to act like they wanted to help you, when they only wanted to burn your ass. Patrick avoided going to his small office at the CIA's counter terrorist center in Washington, DC, for this reason. Office politics were subtle interrogations employing the techniques of deception, suggestibility, and body language. To Patrick, meetings and interrogations were the same: torture.

Former CIA Chief Tenet had tapped Corcoran to head the CTC's strategic assessment branch in the fall of 2001 to "digest vast quantities of information and develop targeting strategies." After a few months poring over NSA surveillance and chatter from around the globe, Patrick realized he could no longer waste his time and talent. He complained, or rather suggested, to the brass that his skills would be better utilized in the field, managing assets. Someone had their thinking cap on that day, and Corcoran soon found himself in the Middle East, heading the new special operations branch of the CTC. They had one mission: to find Al Qaeda, engage it, and destroy it. It was a much clearer goal than "digesting information" or "developing targeting strategies." Hunt and kill. Simple, clear, concise.

Almost immediately, Patrick handed the administrative tasks of running the branch to his second-in-command and embedded himself with his men in the field. The presence of high-level management willing to get blood on his hands kept his team's morale high. Since 9/11 he had managed the finest hunter/killer stable the United States government and the world had ever known, and he loved his work. Unfettered by budgets, pointless team meetings, and endless red tape, he traveled the globe and picked flies off the terrorism manure pile.

Some meetings bore fruit. When he was in his Gulfstream V, communicating via scrambled satellite phone with an operative, explaining that a target had the green light—now *that* was a meeting.

Patrick Corcoran struggled to unzip the identity of C. Peter Chocker and leave that custom-tailored suit in the closet. The senior sales representative for International Fiber Resources existed on another plane that chainkers like Gilchrist would never appreciate.

The security guard perked up when Chocker walked into the lobby. Chocker looked out of place in his black French beret, goatee, black slacks, black suit coat, black sneakers, and black square-framed glasses. It was the standard costume of the artsy-fartsy types who inhabited the Tribeca section of Manhattan, a neighborhood recently ranked by Forbes as one of the most expensive zip codes in the country. Chocker employed the Patrick Corcoran or Mr. Tribeca OK disguise as his antithesis, which made it easier to peel off when he had real work to do.

"How can I help you, sir?"

"I'm here to see Kieran Gilchrist."

"Your name?"

"Patrick Corcoran," said Chocker.

"Is he expecting you?"

"I hope so."

The guard asked Chocker for some ID and made a call upstairs. Chocker showed him the Patrick Corcoran ID, passed through the metal detector, and headed up to Gilchrist's eighth-floor office. He introduced himself to the receptionist, signed the roster, and was buzzed into Gilchrist's inner sanctum. He pulled the black beret down to the top of his thick-framed glasses, averse to having his photo taken, even by his own side.

"Hello, Pat." Gilchrist reached out with his meaty paw to shake. Chocker gave him a limp response.

"Kieran. How are you?"

"Fine. Have a seat." Gilchrist motioned to the heavily padded brown leather chair across the desk. Chocker sat down and crossed his legs.

"How's life in the CTC?"

"In the words of Mae West, so many terrorists, so little time."

Gilchrist chuckled. "Wasn't that quote attributed to Cecil Rhodes?"

"No." Chocker shook his head. "I'm pretty sure it was Mae West."

The sparring had begun.

"I understand you took some time off."

"Yeah. I missed the amber waves of grain."

Gilchrist grinned, moved some papers around on his desk, and opened a manila folder. He searched for something to handle, to control. "We've got a problem," he said.

"I don't think so. I think you've got a problem." Chocker removed his black beret and picked a lint speck from the fabric.

"Why do you say that?"

Chocker set the beret on his lap, ran his fingers over the inside flap, and pulled out a six-inch white plastic strip, serrated on one side and smooth on the other. He held it by the handle and pointed it at Gilchrist. Gilchrist's hand instinctively reached for the buzzer under his desk. Then, thinking better of it, he tapped his fingers on the manila folder.

"And what's that, Patrick?"

"It's the weapon I would have used to gut you, if I was a bad guy. Your sharp-eyed agent and his state-of-the-art metal detector were oblivious. Christ, Kieran, don't you guys make people take off their hats when they come in here?"

Gilchrist reddened and cleared his throat. "We were under the assumption that you were a friendly."

"Bad assumption." Chocker held the blade up and twisted it in a slow pirouette. "It's EVA, ethylene-vinyl acetate, undetectable by metal detectors. The Brits were using them to teach field surgery to military doctors at Cambridge. Our boys at Stanford took the base plastic, fiddled around with it so it would bend easily." He bent the blade until both ends touched, then let it spring back. "Now we have a flexible, durable weapon that—dare I say—even the FBI can't detect."

"And why did you bring it here?"

"As a gift," he said, and threw the plastic blade on Kieran's desk with a smile. "Give this to your boys in the city. It fits nicely in a beret."

"Thanks." Gilchrist picked up the blade.

"Spirit of cooperation, Kieran. Spirit of cooperation."

"In that light, do you know why you're here?"

"Because you love me and because the head of Homeland Security asked my boss to ask me here." He paused, and then added, "Don't take this wrong, Kieran, but I've got a lot of balls in the air, and I need to keep juggling so Mr. and Mrs. Q. Public can pay the mortgage. Can we get down to business?"

"More specifically," said Gilchrist, "you're here because I asked the head of Homeland Security to ask the president to *tell* you to be here, because I knew you would find a way to delay as long as you could."

"Perceptive. Now what?"

"I've got people dropping like flies in the New York metro area, and I would like you to shed some light on the situation, if you can."

"Consider me a beacon, but you'll have to give me more information." Chocker raised his chin and smiled.

"A few days ago a Muslim man, a naturalized citizen, was assassinated in front of a Brooklyn mosque."

"Assassinated? The papers said it was murder."

"Murders tend to happen in private, or in a fit of passion. This guy was tracked and had his throat cut at a bus stop in broad daylight."

"Who was the passionate one?"

"That's just it." Gilchrist set the blade on his desk. "There was no confrontation."

"Any leads?"

"I hoped you could help me out there." Gilchrist looked into Chocker's eyes for a reaction. When he didn't get one, he added, "What do you know?'

"I'm not sure what you mean." Chocker shrugged and added, "I probably know what you know. Unless there's something, and I'm sure there is—you wily bastard—you're not telling me."

"What might that be?"

"Do you want me to guess?"

"Go ahead. Indulge me."

"You first.

"No, please. Go ahead."

"No. You first." Chocker grinned, and waited a few seconds for the frustration to build in Gilchrist's bloodstream. "Just kidding. I'll go first." He looked toward the ceiling as if his memory were stored there. "Mohammed Abdul Bari, an Afghan national, immigrated here on an asylum visa three years ago, got his throat slit while waiting for a bus. He was on a watch list, mostly because he fit the terrorist profile for age, socioeconomic background, and place of origin. He's a Sunni Islamist, though not tied to the Taliban. He despises western culture—don't they all? He and his brother-in-law and a cousin had some civil disobedience planned."

"Civil disobedience?"

"Well, in jihad terms of relativity, yes. They want to kill Americans," said Chocker.

"Any idea how?"

"They had some weapons in a van: guns and explosives. You have them now." Chocker paused for a moment, and then said, "Are you going to ask me a lot of questions you already have the answers to? It could get tedious, Kieran."

"I'm trying to see if you can give me insight."

The compliment did not fool Chocker.

"Do you feel enlightened?" said Chocker. He gave an irritated look toward the black television screen on the wall, and then back to Gilchrist. "Let's cut the crap, Kieran. What do you want to know?"

"I want to know what you had to do with Bari's death. I want to know why, when we get close to someone in the Muslim community who might, and I mean might, be linked to terrorist activities on US soil, they end up dead."

"Bad karma?"

"Hardly."

"And you think I have something to do with it? Look, sometimes things are exactly as they seem. I'm not trying to tell you how to do your job, but let's look at the facts."

"Okay, let's."

"You've got a Muslim nut job who ends up on the street with his throat cut. Did you check the wound?"

"It was ragged and deep. Something long and thin, a serrated dagger maybe." Gilchrist's eyes shifted to the plastic blade on his desk.

Chocker leaned forward. "That's pretty consistent with an inside hit from his own community. These guys like to do it old-school: cut the throat, lots of blood, embarrass the family, and put fear into his friends." He sat back in his chair. "Look no further."

"But we never found the weapon."

"So?" Chocker was nonplussed. How often did anyone find a homicide weapon?

"We checked every storm drain, garbage can, and Dumpster in the vicinity and we interviewed hundreds of mosque members. No one knows anyone with a weapon like that."

"Let's not comment on your naïveté, Patrick." Chocker rolled his eyes like a bored teenager. "All right. Let's. You expected cooperation?"

"I expected something. This was too clean for an amateur." The only noise in the room came from the tiny fan inside Gilchrist's laptop. "I need to know why you took out Abdul Bari."

"And I told you," said Chocker, "Bari wasn't us. We don't use primitive tools in broad daylight, Kieran. I don't need the exposure."

Gilchrist balled his fist and leaned over the desk. "He was a US citizen, Patrick."

"Even more reason to take him out quietly—which we would never do, by the way. I don't need the publicity. It only serves to create speculation from people like you who don't understand what's going on out there."

"Out there?"

"Don't take it personally, Kieran. But this isn't a criminal investigation. It's war, and you're not geared up to fight it . . . at least not the dirtiest parts."

"And you're a goddamn super spy?" Gilchrist waved him off and smirked. "Give me a break."

"I'm not going to get into a pissing contest with you, Kieran. But realistically, if you follow all these rules you've set up, you can't win."

"Do go on," Gilchrist said.

"Remember Operation Amber? Ahmend Hashim Abed told investigators that he was punched by his captors—three decorated Navy SEALS—who all had to face a court-martial. He had a bloody lip, for God's sake. And that bastard mutilated four security guards in Fallujah."

"Are you saying you don't have anyone working this operation?"

"What operation? We're supposed to work together, Kieran. As much as I have a reputation for going off the reservation when I need to, I don't disobey direct orders from my president."

"Come on, Corcoran, give me a break."

"You're barking up the wrong tree. You have a dead Muslim on your hands, and you're getting a political hailstorm blown your way because you don't have a handle on it. About right?"

"A big hailstorm." Gilchrist didn't think it weakened his position to repeat what his colleague in the CIA already knew.

"But you're so hungry for a bad guy, you're missing the obvious."

"Which is?"

"It was an inside job done with a knife, by another Muslim, no doubt. It's not the American way to slice a throat in the street. Ever heard it done before?" He waited for a response. Gilchrist shook his head. "Didn't think so. It was likely someone who was pissed at Abdul Bari for a laundry list of reasons." He let that sink in for a moment.

"It's a possibility. But let's explore another."

Chocker nodded and sat back in the leather chair.

"You have people you don't like living here," said Gilchrist, "sending money overseas to the bad guys, and you can't arrest them because you're CIA. And you won't give them to us, because you know we won't kill them. And the bottom line is, you want them dead."

"And this is the FBI's theory?" He laughed, took a breath and exhaled with his eyes closed. "Can you hear yourself, Kieran? You sound like some dope-smoking conspiracy theorist. By the way, did you find the other shooter?"

"Shooter?"

"Yeah, the guy on the grassy knoll. I hear he's still on the loose."

"Bite me, Corcoran."

Kieran removed a list from the folder on his desk. "Peruse this and see if anyone's familiar."

Chocker recognized every name on the list. They had all been considered at one time or another for CIA recruitment, and some of them were special ops before their battle injuries.

"Where did this list come from?"

Gilchrist ignored the question. "Recognize anyone?"

"Nope." He shook his head and continued reading. "Not yet."

"They're disabled veterans who do bike rides a couple times a year. They raise money for widowed military wives and their children. It's a good cause. Gets a lot of publicity."

He put the list back on Gilchrist's desk. "What about it?"

"We reviewed the tape of the Bari killing in Brooklyn about a couple million times, and finally found a reflection, like a shadow image, coming from the bus's blind side. We didn't see it at first because the reflection rolled at the same pace as the bus tires, and we thought that's what it was: just a reflection from the bus tire. But after a closer look, we know that the guy who killed Bari was on a bicycle."

"I thought you were supposed to cooperate, Kieran. How come I didn't know? Where's the love?"

"What? I just told you."

"Nothing like the eleventh hour. As to your next question: no, I don't have any operatives running around killing people on bicycles."

"John Rexford." Gilchrist gave no buildup, no question in his voice.

Chocker kept his game face, but his breath stopped for a second and his gut muscles tightened. "Yeah?"

"Know him?"

"Is he on the list?"

"Here's the thing: he's not. But he should have been."

"What do you mean?"

"He signed up for the ride and sent in his money. But then, strangely enough, he didn't show for the event."

"Why is that strange?"

"You tell me."

"Come on, Kieran, I don't have time for this nonsense. Why didn't he show for the ride? And what difference does it make?"

"We don't know why he didn't show. I thought maybe you'd help me with that."

"Sorry."

"Sorry you won't help, or sorry you don't know?"

"I don't know the guy. Why is he a suspect?"

"Because the day he didn't show for the ride was the same day Abdul Bari was cut like a goat at the altar." Gilchrist pushed another folder toward Chocker. "Take a look at his file."

Chocker flipped through the file for a couple minutes, nodded, shook his head, and pursed his lips. "Marine Corps Expeditionary Medal, Purple Heart, Silver Star, wounded in action, disabled. The guys a hero, Kieran." He looked back at the file. "Wish I had got to him before they tore his knee up. Is he the guy who didn't make the race?"

"He's the guy. Lives in the Catskills, upstate."

Chocker closed the folder and placed it back on the desk. He looked at his watch to get the point across to Gilchrist.

Gilchrist sighed. "I'm trying to get a handle on this. I'm sorry I was a prick before, but I've got to figure this out, and you're not always the most forthcoming son of a bitch." He smiled, stood up, and put his hand out.

"And you're a real cocksucker yourself, Kieran. I'll sniff around and see what I can find out about this Rexford."

Kieran let go of Chocker's hand and sat back down, a cue the meeting had ended. Chocker walked to the door, put his hand on the knob, and turned to Gilchrist. "One more thing."

"Yeah?"

"Would you validate my parking?"

Gilchrist waved him off and put his attention toward the pile of paperwork on his desk. After a few minutes alone, he picked up the plastic blade and ran the sharp edge over his fingertips. He pushed the intercom button and his assistant answered.

"I want to see the medical records for all the veteran bikers on the list. And I want to review the tape of this meeting."

KENSICO

In judo and jiujitsu, the *gi* are very similar, though some Brazilian jiujitsu schools prefer a tighter fit around the cuffs and pant legs, providing less material for the opponent to manipulate. Yoda had studied the ground fighting techniques, chokeholds, and arm locks of both schools of martial arts, but he'd abandoned the classic garb. He held no belts.

A student could not be promoted in most schools without the traditional wearing of a *gi*. Yoda wore it so his instructors would accept him. When he had mastered what he needed, he left the formal classrooms and traveled the world to hone his own skills, his way. He mastered his deadly techniques in less ceremonial clubs, places where an arm lock meant you broke the arm. Tap outs were unacceptable in the damp caves, dusty basements, cold warehouses, and back rooms where Yoda perfected his trade. Yoda knew as well as any surgeon the locations of pressure points, arteries, and where the thin-walled veins ran closest to the skin's surface.

He struck his victim's pressure points swiftly, paralyzing or outright killing him.

He spent thousands of hours devoted to kung fu muscle-strengthening techniques while stretching his body into deeper and more powerful yoga poses. This combination of strength and flexibility, and a will that didn't accept defeat, made him unwelcomed, albeit respected, wherever he showed up to fight.

Yoda occasionally haunted an old dojo and flaunted his skills with the best student who dared to spar with him. His constriction technique neutralized all comers without a blow. Some still had enough juice in their limbs to try and tap out; others watched the faces around them shrink into small dots and disappear before they lost consciousness. He considered staying with these students, perhaps teaching them his "way," or even becoming the new master. But the dress codes were too strict, and Yoda didn't stand on ceremony.

When he was five years old, he'd had no food other than what the villagers brought to the monastery, and only the brown robe given to him by one of the monks to cover his thin frame. Yoda's mother, father, and little sister had been killed by communist bandits when they crossed the border into Bhutan from China. To cope, his headmaster in Bhutan taught Yoda the serenity of deprivation. At the age of sixteen Yoda was a thin, lanky, and introverted youth who wouldn't sit still. Had he been born in a western culture he would have been given Ritalin. In Bhutan, he was taken into the monastery, where the monks forced him to sit for long hours to control his breath and clear the weeds in his mind. Though they had taught Yoda—whose real name was Jigme Dorji Wangchuk—the art of breathing for serenity, he had none.

His mother had hoped that, by naming him after one of Bhutan's great leaders, her son would develop leadership skills. But young Jigme didn't make friends, so he had no one to lead. The monks made him practice the yoga asanas, or poses: up dog, down dog, bridge pose, bow pose, scorpion pose—all which the headmaster believed would humble him further, and through an awareness of self, body, and spirit, reach a true peace with his surroundings and the weeds that cluttered his mind. Instead, Jigme used his exemplary skills in yoga's spiritual practice to twist and turn himself on the other boys in the monastery and make them howl in pain.

After he cruelly constricted a stronger but dimwitted older boy, the monks stripped Jigme of his royal name and gave him the name *Zopa*—patience. They hoped if he heard this name pronounced often enough, he would become humble and patient with other life forms around him. Jigme hid at the sound of his new name.

Patience evaded him. Jigme, once again, maimed a fellow orphan with his self-designed yoga bastardization. Unwilling to tolerate his behavior any further, the headmaster asked him to leave the monastery for the community's good. He was the first and last person turned away from the benevolent Mahayana Buddhist temple in Bhutan's lofty mountains.

Yoda traveled west, out of Asia, through Europe and eventually throughout the world. He taught yoga and stole to survive. He developed his own martial way and absorbed the skills of others like a sponge. His skills as an assassin, and his obsession with staying off the grid, eventually earned him a reputation as the most elite and sought-after killer in the underworld.

The ability to kill without weapons and slink away through the tiniest openings paid Yoda very well. So well, in fact, he need never have worked again, and only took new projects as he saw fit—projects that challenged his skills and increased his esteem in the dark world he inhabited, far from the clean air and monks in the high mountains of Bhutan.

The latest challenge designed to further his self-aggrandizement had brought him to America. It was how he came to find himself in New York State, dressed in black, tight-fitting spandex and black ballet slippers with neoprene supports in the heels and toes. His thin black gloves were custom-made from eel skin and formfitted to every contour of his hands. Yoda chose eel skin because it was more durable than other animal hides, and yet became softer and suppler with use. It was the uniform in which Yoda was most comfortable in the work he performed.

Slippery spandex contoured his body so no one could grab him; and better still, zippers and seams could not inhibit him from encircling his prey like a constrictor. Black was stealth for melting in the shadows. The silken spandex allowed him to slide up and down his victims' bodies and lock them into an arterial-crushing death hold. The ballet slippers left no shoe prints, were light and silent, and allowed him to slither around his prey's legs.

The only addition to his regular uniform tonight was a slim-profile, tight-fitting backpack designed to hold a laptop computer.

Yoda carried no weapons for defense. His arsenal was self-contained. He practiced the closest, most sexually arousing kill at the most personal range. There was no gun, no blade, and no garrote to separate him from the intimacy of his actions.

He watched from the shadows as the guard walked his German shepherd around the perimeter of the Kensico Dam gatehouse.

"And I'll be home first thing in the morning," the guard said into his cell phone. "Yeah, I know you worry, honey. There ain't a damn thing to worry about."

Terry Bailey sighed as he listened to his wife's lonely sobs.

"Doosey's right here with me," Terry assured her. "He isn't gonna let anything happen to my fat ass."

Doosey looked up with big, devoted brown eyes, and cocked his head when he heard his name.

"All right, sweetheart," Terry said. "You call me in a little while if you want. If I don't answer, it's because I'm in the tunnel doing my rounds. Keep trying. I'll call you back as soon as I can."

Yoda scaled the fence beneath a maple tree and slid down the other side. He made no sound as he gripped the chain-links with his fingers and toes. He was like a sheet of black paper blown against steel gray fence by a soft wind. The fence didn't rattle like the bodies he'd strangled.

Yoda had to get into the tunnel from this side of the gatehouse in order to open the escape door for the two Yemenites. They would set the explosives in the tunnel below. A car was ready for them at a Dunkin' Donuts across the street, where they would resurface from the empty spillway tunnel. The two explosive experts would enter the spillway about six hundred yards downstream, where the water had been turned off for tunnel repairs. Once inside, they would climb the sluice gate cable and plant the explosives in the chlorine chamber of the aqueduct, and then exit through the storm drain with Yoda. He would drive them to a hotel, make sure they both bathed, and then kill them. Afterward he would leave them naked in a compromising position in the cheap room where the maids would find them. What would the authorities make of it? Who cared? Yoda would be in Yonkers, where his own escape was already in place.

"What do you think, Doosey?" Terry asked his canine partner. "Should I have divorced her when I had the chance?" He scuffed the shepherd's thick hair and bony skull. Doosey made a talking noise and looked up at him, eyes pleading for more affection.

Glass-covered mercury lights illuminated the gatehouse exterior. Another assassin might see this as an impediment, but Yoda saw opportunity. He moved slowly, unseen within the shadows, like one blade of grass in a field of many.

A large portico, added fifty years after the building was first constructed in 1905, protected the steel entrance door from the elements. The new city architects decided it would lend an historic, albeit remarkably incorrect, feel to the place. The portico served no function and added $300,000 to the budget. The addition allowed Yoda to slink along the building's right wall, unseen by security cameras, and wait for Terry to slide his plastic security card into the electronic lock.

"You want a treat?" Terry teased Doosey with the dry meat in his hand. Doosey sat on his haunches and licked his jowls; his long tail brushed the sidewalk. He made a quick circle in place and sat again. Terry eased a piece of beef jerky between Doosey's long, arced canines, and the powerful German shepherd gently nibbled it from his hand.

"Good boy." Terry stroked Doosey's furry ears as they walked inside the gate chamber. "In three months we'll both be retired and we can keep her company."

Yoda bunched the long sleeve of his spandex suit over his fist and slid it between the strike plate and the latch before the metal door clicked shut. He adjusted the child-sized mini backpack and closed the door behind him without a sound.

The gatehouse interior was one large room with steel I-beams supporting the ceiling and overhead cranes. The oil-stained concrete floor was smooth. Puddles formed along the walls where the stonework dripped with condensation. Soft incandescent lights lit the interior walls, but not enough for night work. It was barely enough to allow a person to walk around and not bump into the old diesel engines and pumps that controlled water flow through the aqueduct. The machines raised and lowered the gates and were controlled by a remote office over fifty miles away in Grahamsville, near the Rondout Reservoir in the western Catskills. Other than infrequent maintenance and repairs, and the sounds of Terry and Doosey's nightly rounds, the gatehouse building was uninhabited.

Terry went to the chamber's south end and opened the office door. The small room was designed as a workplace for the men who had controlled the valves and diesel engines before remote controls were installed in the seventies. It was empty now, except an old steel desk, a trash can, and two metal folding chairs.

Terry flicked on the light, pulled up a chair, and plunked his tired bones down in front of the steel desk. He kept a plastic baggie of beef jerky in his utility belt to stave off hunger when he got the midnight munchies, and to share with Doosey. He slid his hand over his large paunch and pulled out a piece, tore off an inch for his partner, and chewed loudly on the dried, peppered beef. Doosey gently nibbled another piece of jerky from his hand, spun around three times, and plopped on the floor. He licked and nibbled the jerky between his padded paws. Most big dogs gobble treats. Doosey was a connoisseur of hard tack, and he savored every strand.

Yoda walked softly over the water puddles near the walls. He skipped his ballet slippers along the surface, rather than risk making tiny splashes the dog might hear. The smell of old oil and mold penetrated his nostrils. He saw the security guard through a small window in the office. The fat man leaned back in his chair and chewed something.

Yoda crept deliberately forward. He had no fear of the German shepherd, but he didn't want to alert the animal until he was closer. He had killed much more dangerous dogs: pit bulls, a Belgian Malinois, and even a wolf in Georgia. The largest and most deadly canine he'd faced was a two-hundred-pound Caucasian shepherd, a dog whose sole purpose was to kill wolves that attack sheep. Yoda had originally tried to help the dog kill a wolf. When the wolf was dead, the Caucasian shepherd still thought Yoda was coming for the sheep. After much teeth-gnashing and bone-cracking, the big dog went under and never awoke.

"Checking in." Terry clicked the button on his handheld radio and set it down.

A minute later the radio squawked. He picked it up and responded with an all-clear.

"Roger that," said the voice. "Check back in two. Over."

"Out."

It was one o'clock in the morning. Yoda and his team had two hours to set the charges that would blow the aqueduct and rupture the chlorine gas tanks, and then get back to the motel.

Yoda leaned against the doorjamb. He breathed deeply and deliberately from his diaphragm. Doosey jumped to all fours and barked once, his back legs crouched in typical shepherd defense posture, ready to pounce. Not the angry growling bark yet, more like the "Hey, are you a friend?" bark that could quickly turn into the "I want to bite your genitals" bark. Terry had his feet up on the metal desk and his eyes closed. He turned first to his partner and then the door. The man's presence in the doorway startled him. Terry kicked his feet up and off the desk in an attempt to stand, but instead fell over on his side. His hip hit the concrete floor with a dull crack, and all the air left his lungs.

"Who the hell are you?" Terry croaked, and then rolled onto his belly, his face contorted from the intense pain in his broken hip.

Doosey growled with instinctive hate, and saliva strings drooled from his teeth and lips.

Terry forgot the months of training he had gone through with Doosey. His heart rate and blood pressure soared, and he saw white stars around the edges of his eyes. The pain in his hip kept him from getting up and facing the perpetrator. The man's camouflaged face and onyx eyes sent a shiver through his body. At that moment it occurred to Terry his wife might spend the rest of her life alone.

The command. What was the command? What was the command?

Terry's mind stumbled over the words, but nothing came from his lips.

Doosey looked at his partner, his eyes begging for the command to strike. His head turned toward the man in the door, and back to his partner—the one with words, the one who could fix this problem with one word, but where was the word?

Doosey glared at Yoda, the hairs on his back raised high. Where was the command? He almost broke position, but eleven years of police training kept the obedient German shepherd in place.

"What? What?" Terry wanted to say, "What do you want?," but he couldn't complete the sentence. The air had not returned to his lungs. His words escaped in tiny burps. His hand instinctively went for his gun but only found his corpulent waist.

Yoda stepped into the light of the room and raised his palm to Doosey, and then his finger to his lips. He remained calm and did not make eye contact with the dog. He hissed, "Shhhhhh."

Doosey's ears pressed flat against his skull, and a low growl vibrated from his throat.

Yoda walked over to Terry, unholstered the pistol from his utility belt, and set it on the metal table.

In slow-motion, Yoda reached his hand into an open compartment at the bottom of the backpack. He pulled a damp slab of four-inch-wide London broil out and let it dangle at his thigh. Doosey caught a whiff and barked. Yoda had used the strategy with success a few times in the past. London broil is a tough cut with a strip of connecting fiber that is difficult to break. Once the dog grabbed on, he would not likely let go. If it didn't work, Yoda would have to kill him. Killing animals for free did not interest the assassin. He had killed a monkey once that would not stop harassing him in a tree. But that monkey's death had been mission-critical. This loyal dog was not.

Yoda stood still, calm, not making eye contact, as he held the meat closer to the German shepherd. Doosey looked to his master for a command, but none came. Terry drifted in and out of consciousness as his brain helped him to cope with the pain of a broken hip.

Doosey took a couple fake snips at the meat and then grabbed on and twisted his head from side to side, his long white canines locked into the thick, bloody slab. Yoda made a semicircle and slid the dog over the worn concrete floor. Doosey let go, and then grabbed on again. It became a game as Yoda pulled, Doosey growled and twisted, and Yoda pulled him another few feet across the floor. Yoda eventually worked the dog so that he was angled in front of the open bathroom door. He pulled extra hard one more time. Doosey pulled back hard, his haunches low, nails scratching the concrete. Yoda released the meat and the dog slid backward, half his body inside the bathroom. He slammed the steel door shut and turned back to Terry.

Terry lay unconscious on the floor, his white and mole-marked belly stuck out from his shirttails. Yoda placed his right knee in the center of Terry's spine, and cradled the fat man's chin with interlaced fingers. He used his left leg to push off the floor, and pulled Terry's head upward until he heard the cervical spine vertebrae crack as hard cortical bone fractured. Yoda released the flabby chin and stood over his kill.

He unlatched the plastic security key from Terry's chain and checked the bathroom door one more time to make sure it was secure. The dog had satisfied his initial anxiety with the raw meat, but was whining behind the door.

Yoda walked outside the office into the gatehouse's main room and searched for a casket. He would need something considerable. A fifty-five-gallon oil drum rested on the floor against the far wall. The lid pulled back easily, and it was empty except for a few inches of spent lubricant in the bottom.

He put the pistol back in Terry's holster and carried the corpse over his shoulders to avoid leaving any drag marks. Terry's body made a tiny splash as his head hit the bottom of the filthy drum. A dull clang vibrated off the stone walls. Yoda paused and listened to the last echo as it trailed into nothingness. Terry's legs stuck up above the rim, so Yoda crossed them and stuffed them down into the container of old oil.

Where many an assassin had a weapon in the small of his back, Yoda kept a small three-by-four-inch Fuji Instax instant camera. He turned on the flash, leaned over the barrel, and took an up-close and personal photo of the dead security guard. He waited a few moments for the film to dry before sliding it into the camera case, and then placed the steel lid back on the drum and returned to the office.

A few beef jerky slices were in a plastic bag on the table. Yoda wasn't hungry, and besides, he was a vegetarian. He slid the jerky under the small space between the bathroom door and the floor, then balled up the plastic bag and threw it in the metal waste can next to the desk.

The dog locked in the bathroom would confuse anyone looking for the guard. They would immediately start a search upon finding Doosey, so Yoda had to be out of there before anyone became suspicious that Terry had not checked in. No one would bother to look in the fifty-five-gallon oil drum that had probably rested against the same wall for decades. Terry's fellow officers would assume the guard had left his post for some reason or another when he didn't check in or answer his phone. Yoda guessed they would search the tunnels and find nothing. It was only a matter of time before the stench from the corpse drifted from the oil drum. Yoda and his team would be long gone before this occurred. Even with the threat of the guard and his dog contained, Yoda still walked noiselessly between the light and in the shadows, across the damp gatehouse floor.

With the tunnel schematics committed to memory, Yoda descended the stairs into the dark hallway that led to the chamber door where the chlorine gas cylinders were stored. He smiled to himself in the darkness as he ran his fingers along the wet tunnel walls—prideful, like a snake was pleased when the mouse was inside him.

The Kensico Dam rose over three hundred feet from its base and contained nearly one million cubic feet of masonry and concrete, cured with time by frigid Catskill streams. Thirty billion gallons of water pressed, pushed, and bore down upon the century-old framework. The New York City Department of Environmental Protection purchased the property in 1963. A thirty-million-dollar project to rehabilitate the dam's stressed infrastructure and crumbling façade was approved and slated for completion in 2007, but regulatory and safety concerns halted the flow of work.

The dam impounded the Bronx River, a trickling stream that would never, by itself, fill the thirteen square miles of earth buried beneath its surface. This gigantic pool pulled water from the Catskill and Delaware aqueducts, which in turn drew down from six Catskill Mountains and four downstate reservoirs. Over one hundred and sixty miles of underground tunnels, cut-and-cover aqueducts, steel siphons, and pressure tunnels flowed from the Catskill Mountains and squeezed the water into a siphon chamber 1,100 feet below the Hudson River, where it resurfaced on the east side in Putnam County. From there, the aqueduct dumped its precious cargo into the Kensico Reservoir to feed New York City's unquenchable thirst.

The 9/11 attacks forced government agencies to take a new look at the world, this time through the eyes of a terrorist. City engineers determined that a large explosive charge, brought in by a truck or van, could blast a hole big enough to flood Valhalla and parts of White Plains, only a few miles further south. Vehicular and foot traffic were banned on top of the dam—another restriction courtesy of the Al Qaeda network.

As with any large government project, many resources were wasted or left behind during construction. People, animals, and heavy equipment were lost in the mud, tunnels, and deep water as engineers pressed onward to complete the project on schedule.

Mayors come and mayors go. Watershed commissioners served at the mayor's will and floated in and out with election tides. Fortunately, for New York citizens, gravity powered the water's flow, and the overengineering typical of a century ago compensated for the lack of care the reservoir received in the present day.

In the 1950s chlorine was introduced into the system to eliminate bacteria from the potable water supply. In subsequent years, lab analysis determined Catskill aqueduct water was so pure, no treatment was required. The chlorine tanks were taken off-line. Once off-line, they became off-budget. When the chlorine gas flow stopped, so did its funding. With the money diverted elsewhere, bureaucrats lost interest, and only a few low-level watershed maintainers even knew the tanks existed.

It was precisely this lack of legacy detail that brought John to the dirt road where he stood. He'd left his car back at the Graham Hills Park in Mt. Pleasant, five miles due west, parked at an angle in the open lot so that a passing patrol officer wouldn't remember the plate number a few days from now. It was perhaps an overly cautious step, but John remembered something Confucius said:

The cautious seldom err.

Baby was safe at home, too delicate for this mission. The trails in Graham Hills Park were geared toward experienced mountain bikers. Sharp rocks and steep gravel inclines would destroy Baby's wheels, designed for smoothly paved roads. When John could ride no further because of thick brush, he placed his mountain bike about ten feet into the woods, beneath an undergrowth of ferns and dead branches that had fallen beneath the pine trees during a recent windstorm. He hiked the steep ravine that led to an old service entrance for the aqueduct. Thorn bushes and sticks poked his feet and shins as he made his way through the brush in light black running sneakers. He would have preferred stiff hiking boots, but stealth—as was often the case—was a more important factor than comfort.

He gripped a twenty-inch steel crowbar in his hand to pry open the diamond-plate steel door to the shaft if need be.

He wacked brush with the crowbar in the darkness, alert for stray coyotes, which were almost as prevalent in Westchester County as house pets. So far he had only heard their yelps in the distance. They hunted in packs at night and ran for miles, trying to scare up a rabbit or swoop down on a cat or dog whose owner had left them outside too long to do their business.

Shrubs and thorn bushes covered the overgrown path to the entrance. It took him a half hour to pull them up from the ground and cast them aside. He stopped every few moments and listened, to see if the hunter had become the hunted. *Never assume you're alone in your pursuits, especially when you're an army of one, with no point man or anyone to bring up the rear.*

A plaque commemorating Frank E. Windsor, the engineer in charge of construction of the Kensico Dam, was bolted to the diamond-plate door. The local townspeople whose lives were uprooted and whose homes, barns, and businesses were buried under billions of gallons of water would be less than amused at New York City's tribute to the man responsible for the interment.

Out of options, most locals left the area to go further upstate and farm in the early 1900s. Others got jobs building the dam with mostly Italian, African American, and Russian immigrants who flocked to the area for work. Over 1,500 men had worked on the Kensico Dam at the height of construction. The mayor appointed a water supply board, which in turn mounted a police force to quell any uprisings among the locals. With trains of liquor shipped in to keep the workers happy, and tons of dynamite for blasting, the police force was a necessity.

Chocker had given John the schematics of the tunnel system from Manhattan Island to the Catskills. He wondered if his enemy had the same. Did they know the three ways into the chlorine chamber?

The path of least resistance was through the gatehouse, an unlikely route considering it was locked and patrolled by armed guards and police dogs.

The second option was to enter through the street by climbing down a catch basin and travelling through a series of low tunnels that eventually connected to a waste weir leading to the spillway. The spillway is used by the Bureau of Water Supply to release excess water from the dam during periods of high rainfall. All major dams had spillways to release water and protect the dam's structural integrity.

Excess water flowed through the waste weir, down the spillway, and into the Bronx River, where it blended with New York City's East River. A perpetrator could travel several miles inside the waste weir tunnel and be directly underneath the gatehouse, where the aqueducts converged before they sent water to New York City. The waste weir was a concrete tunnel with ten feet of headroom. There would be no water running through the weir for the next three days due to construction downstream, as Chocker had indicated. At the weir's end the terrorists could climb up a forty-foot cable that held the sluice gate in place, then pop up inside the gatehouse next to the large diesel engines used to raise and lower the five-ton gates.

Only once in a hundred years had the sluice gate been closed and water diverted for maintenance. With hundreds of millions of gallons raging through the gates, they weren't normally a security risk. No man could fight such a powerful current, access the sluice gate cables, and climb into the gatehouse chamber above. With the water arrested, a person could gain access. This was the most likely route the enemy would take.

Chocker could have simply notified the FBI about the security breach. The FBI would assign guards to monitor the sluice cables during the repairs, and this would all be an unnecessary risk. But Chocker had a hard-on for Yoda. John had seen it in his eyes. Another instance where CIA and FBI priorities aren't aligned and, as a result, American lives were put in enemy crosshairs.

Option number three was right here, at the bottom of a ravine near the Gate of Heaven cemetery, but still on New York City land. This tunnel section had been built first and left to atrophy when it was replaced by new construction. Most bad guys wouldn't have access to the diagrams showing this entrance. Of course, Chocker did. But did the Canadians?

He stood before a shaft used in the old days to cart coal into a room forty feet below the gatehouse floor. Diesel engines replaced the coal-fired steam engines that raised and lowered the gigantic valves that controlled the water flow. This section of the tunnel had been mothballed, and the chamber that previously held diesel engines now stored chlorine gas for disinfectant. The horizontal tube of steel and concrete hadn't been accessed in over fifty years.

John put his ear to the cold metal and listened. He smelled rusted steel and wet dirt. The hum of far-off traffic from the Taconic Parkway vibrated through the metal plate against his cheek. He thought of Indians in old westerns with their ears pressed against railroad tracks, listening for the iron horse.

Rust had made brittle the steel plate's edges, but the center was solid. John gave a halfhearted pull on one side, and it gave an inch. It was bolted to the tunnel, but the bolts had slackened over the years. He jimmied the crowbar into the gap and pressed against it with his chest. If someone else had decided door number three was the best entrance for a terrorist act, John wouldn't have time to recover once the plate was off. It was like riding a three-pound titanium bicycle down an asphalt road at sixty miles an hour: sometimes you had to trust in the universe.

John broke off six of the twelve rusty bolts holding the door in place, and pulled it away from the stone wall enough to get his body inside. He slid through the opening and carefully replaced the door behind him. It would look normal to the casual observer.

The humid air inside the shaft smelled like rotten potatoes. John's feet bumped against steel rails used by the coal carts decades before. He sat for a few minutes and listened. His heartbeat reminded him he was alive, a machine powered by muscle, full of determination and the will to persevere. He accepted that tonight he would end the same heartbeat of at least one other human, or risk losing his life. There were no obstacles, only solutions.

Heart rate: one hundred ten.

He was calm and ready.

His palms are sweaty, knees weak, arms are heavy . . .

It had been so out of place for Chocker to quote Eminem. Was there anything he didn't know? *Does he know if I will die tonight?*

Water droplets plinked into small puddles farther down the tracks. He couldn't see them, but he imagined expanding ripples in a tiny pool. He reached down and touched fine powder and smooth flakes of coal dust along the rails and ties. Heavy crushed stone ballast supported the tracks. He reached up and touched the ceiling three feet above his head. He would have to duck-walk or crawl two hundred yards to access the chlorine chamber.

He threw small pieces of coal and gravel in front of his path to scare off any rats or other small, biting mammals. Cobwebs stuck to his face and made him itch so much he had to stop every few feet and wipe them away with his shirt. He tried not to think about the poisonous brown recluse and wolf spiders that love the dark.

He crawled and duck-walked until he saw a glimmer of light at the tube's end. He listened for sounds of life, other humans, or machinery. Water thundered through the aqueduct beneath him.

A bat flew inches from his eyes as it escaped the tube. His heart smashed against his chest. He took some deep breaths, flexed his entire body, and relaxed his muscles. The technique allowed oxygen to rush into his bloodstream and give him back psychological, and eventually physical, control of his body.

He sensed the water's power as millions of gallons rolled through the aqueduct and the rails beneath him hummed. He sat down, listened to the water, and waited for his heart to find a rhythm with the confined river. In a few feet, he would no longer be protected by the tunnel.

Heart rate: ninety-five.

Not bad, considering the bat.

Either the guests had already left, or he was the first to arrive at the party. He committed to the room.

Chamber walls rose to a concrete ceiling, with thick rebar bracing twenty feet overhead. Yellow and white minerals had leached from the concrete over years and left crusted stains. Four standard household incandescent bulbs lit the room. His eyes traced the wires strung like vines along the walls, up the stairs where they dead-ended at a door near the top of the chamber. No switch. It must be on the other side. The schematics showed this door led to more stairs, down several hallways, and eventually up into the Kensico Dam gatehouse.

Three antiquated coal carts sat rusting in one corner. John checked them out and found that workers had used them as trash bins over the years. Assorted remnants of America's throwaway mentality littered the carts: plastic bags, paper bags, beer bottles, soda cans, cookie boxes, and lots of plastic water bottles.

Two large metal fans hung motionless from the ceiling. Snot-like, dust-covered cobweb strings hung from their six-foot blades. A louvered opening in the ceiling above trickled light a few feet from the fans. The louvers allowed airflow when the room was occupied. There was no other way in or out except for the door at the top of the stairs and the coal tunnel. If a chlorine tank sprung a leak, any workers inside would have died from asphyxiation within minutes. Chlorine gas corroded lung tissue into jelly. OSHA became law in 1970, too late for the midcentury working stiff.

He looked to his right and saw the terrorist's targets: fifteen one-ton chlorine gas cylinders painted yellow with red DANGER signs. Twelve were stacked, one atop the other, all the way to the ceiling, separated and secured in heavy metal frames. Three cylinders had been placed on large scales where the precise amount of gas could be metered into the water system. An overhead crane mounted to rails on the ceiling had lifted and lowered them into place. An octopus of pipes dead-ended at the release valves of the two tanks resting on the scales. Once connected and the valves opened, these pipes metered gas directly into the aqueduct for disinfection. The pipe's path led to a six-square-foot hole in the floor. John lay on his stomach and looked into the hole. The sound of rushing water this close was deafening. No chance he would hear an attack from behind.

He climbed down the steel ladder and stood over a hatch on top of the aqueduct. His sight, smell, and touch were the only senses left to detect unfriendlies in the area. He continuously scanned the room and the opening above. He pulled open the aqueduct cover and a freezing blast sprayed into his face. He stuck his head inside the hatch.

Fresh potable Catskill water raced beneath him like one unbroken black plastic sheet. A little light from the incandescent bulbs above broke the plane of the hatch. The tunnel was a dark, confined space from which there was no escape.

The black plastic sheet rushed forward at millions of gallons per minute through the aqueduct, then downstream into Yonkers, where it spilled into the Hillview Reservoir and was routed to New York City. Before it dumped into Hillview, it passed through large steel screens, where the fish and debris were filtered out and eventually brought up in a basket and disposed of by NYCDEP watershed maintainers.

Chocker's cheese grater.

He closed the hatch and crawled back up the ladder to the chlorine chamber. He heard the clang of metal against metal. The steel door at the top of the stairs moved. He sprinted to the nearest coal cart, rolled over the open top, and buried himself beneath the trash. Something sharp poked through his shirt. Broken glass cut his hands. He stuck his fingers in his mouth, sucked hard, and swallowed. The less DNA he left behind, the better.

Chocker's orders had been clear: no debris, no collateral damage of any kind. Everything goes in the drink.

John hadn't had a chance to strike and was already wounded. He erased the defeatist thought from his mind and focused all his concentration on separating the rushing water's background noise beneath the floor from sounds within the chamber.

A door hinge creaked. They were inside. How many were there? How long would it take them to walk down the twenty-five steps to the floor? Thirty seconds, maybe? If they weren't running. It wasn't wise to rush with high explosives. What if the plan had changed? What if these guys were suicide bombers and had decided to blow themselves up along with the chlorine, the aqueduct, and this marine? Would he get to see the virgins? He doubted it. He heard Maggie click her tongue at him. He didn't like to bring the workplace home with him, and now he had brought home to work.

They spoke in conversational tones, not muted or whispered. Just a couple of Yemenite explosive experts chatting it up. These guys had no fear of anyone else being in the chamber. After all, what idiot would be down here at three in the morning on a Wednesday night?

He nearly screamed in primal panic when the coal cart shook.

One of them said something in an Arabic dialect and then laughed: not Afghani, probably something like Algerian or Moroccan. John picked up the hint of a French accent. Hadn't Chocker indicated they were from Yemen? Perhaps Yemen wasn't their home base. Did it matter who shook the goddamn coal cart at this point? When he killed them, he would say a multilingual prayer.

The man kicked the coal cart and John nearly broke point and attacked. More laughs, and he sensed the man walk away. When you spend your adult life working alone in this profession, you tend to rely on a sense of things more than what you can hear, see, smell, or touch. John didn't have a visual, but in his mind's eye he saw the man turn and walk away from the cart. It was a talent, a gift, not something spooky or paranormal. It was a learned trait where you trusted your gut and followed the mind's eye. John was still alive because he trusted his instincts. He had survived all opponents. It was all he needed to believe in the process.

With one hand on a throwing knife attached to his belt, he slid his other hand up the cart and turned his head to the side so his left eye peeked over the rim and showed less of his skull.

A man's head disappeared into the opening in the floor. The other guy hunched over the hole on his knees.

Heart rate: one hundred twenty-nine.

He breathed in slowly, held it, and exhaled deliberately. *Keep the adrenaline low to the last minute. A killer's body changes when he is about to strike. Blood expands in the vessel walls and his vision narrows.* John needed complete control. He needed to see everything.

He rolled over the cart's edge and pulled the nine-inch dagger from its sheath. He had serrated the knife's edges on a grinder back at Henry's barn. It would cut going in, and with a slight twist, shred meat and arteries when it was pulled out. He had two more thin, nonserrated, and perfectly balanced throwing knives on his belt, good for up to ten yards. Air friction made them unreliable beyond that distance.

Where was Yoda? Where was the third member of this confederacy of bastards?

He checked the door at the top of the stairs. Still closed. Maybe they didn't need Yoda? A third person increased the chance of exposure by 33 percent. A hidden, third killer was an added distraction. He compartmentalized Yoda, leaving the program running but minimizing the file.

He slinked toward his mark with a tai chi gait, imitating the synchronized padding of a cat as it stalked prey. The Arab was too focused. He didn't hear the soft steps only three feet behind him. Long, greasy hair hung over the thug's camouflaged jacket collar. He was five ten, five eleven, maybe 150 pounds. John would use a chokehold, and then drag him away from the hole. If a struggle ensued, John would have two assailants to battle simultaneously, a less-than-optimal scenario. A pistol grip protruded from a leg holster under the man's coat.

"Yeah, yeah, yeah." The man spoke in Arabic, mumbled something under his breath, raised himself from his knees and stood up.

John grabbed his hair and collar together and plunged the serrated blade into the thug's back at kidney height. The enemy was instantly paralyzed, his mouth agape.

He opens his mouth, but the words won't come out.

John slid one step closer and reached around the bearded neck with his left arm in a chokehold. He twisted the knife and raked it back and forth like a fishtail as he pulled it out. One more spear to the kidney, and he eased the man to the floor several feet from the hole.

A quick room check for other assassins. No one. The team had shut the door when they came into the room. John put the dying man on his back a few feet from the floor opening. His glazed, open eyes didn't register much. John watched his eyelids droop as the muscle tension decreased. Blood oozed from his mouth and pooled beneath his coat.

He crushed the man's windpipe against the concrete floor with his heel until the gurgling stopped.

Heart rate: one hundred forty-five.

A sprinkle of stars encircled John's vision. He had to calm down. He took some deep breaths and went back to the rabbit in the hole.

"Bassam?" The rabbit shouted up the hole. "Bassam!"

John took a prone position one foot from the hole and saw part of the room below at an oblique angle. The rabbit had opened the hatch to the aqueduct and exposed quarter-inch cables that led into the hole. He only saw the top of the rabbit's head as he adjusted the cables. In a neat row on top of the aqueduct rested a dozen Composition 4 detonators. The rabbit had yet to insert them into the plastic explosive. A dozen detonators meant there was enough C-4 in the hole to take out this chamber, all the chlorine tanks, and maybe even the gatehouse above.

"Bassam?"

The rabbit sounded nervous, his voice soft and unsure. He cursed something that translated roughly to "ignorant ass."

The rabbit placed a portable electric drill next to the detonators. He had put something else next to them, but John couldn't get a good visual. A weapon, maybe. He deliberated between an all-out assault in the hole, or waiting for the rabbit to pop his head up. The rabbit had to come up the side of the hole with the steel ladder. It was too risky to jump down, and he sure as hell wasn't going to stroll down the ladder and ask for ID.

He crawled on his fingertips and toes to the opposite side of the hole, and waited. The rabbit's right hand came up first, then his left, as he grabbed the rungs and pulled. He muttered the same dialect of "ignorant ass" but not so loudly this time. The tone of his profanity exposed his jumpiness. *Any animal, even a rabbit, is most dangerous when he is nervous, ready to strike.*

Rabbit's head reached the ladder's top rung, his eyes at floor level. Something made the rabbit grab for his gun—a sixth sense, a gift perhaps. He unsnapped the holster and turned his head.

John sprung off both haunches and into the air like a tiger, with the serrated blade in his right hand. Clear, vitreous fluid spurted from the rabbit's skull as the blade entered his right eye socket and cut through panicked gray matter. He pulled the rabbit's paw off his gun holster with his free hand. They fell through the hatch opening and onto unforgiving cement ten feet below. John landed on the rabbit, his hand still on the knife handle, the blade wedged firmly in the man's skull. The man's neck twisted on impact, and his tongue rolled over jagged teeth. No need to check for vitals. This guy was real dead.

He would have to clean the blood from the rungs before he left. He wiped his hands on his pants, and peeked above the hatch for number three. The door was still closed. He peered across the floor and looked under the coal carts for feet, someone that might be hiding on the other side. Nothing.

Back at the hole, he dropped his head inside the aqueduct's opening and counted six C-4 bricks tied to thin steel cables and suspended above the water. Six more lay on a towel next to a backpack on the floor beside the dead man. The tunnel would sustain maximum impact only if the C-4 were placed inside. Had the rabbit placed them on top of the tunnel, most of the blast wave would be forced upward, damaging the infrastructure but not the aqueduct's ten inches of hardened steel and concrete. John pulled the explosives from the hole, careful of booby traps and detonators. The rabbit must have been checking the cable lengths when he was rudely interrupted. The bricks did not have attached detonators.

He separated each C-4 brick from its cable to make sure he hadn't missed anything, like a blasting cap, and dropped them into the water where they would roll along the bottom and eventually break into a thousand tiny pieces. C-4 needed a specific shockwave to detonate. It couldn't be set off by slamming it on the floor or even shooting it with a gun. It was so stable, in fact, that Vietnam soldiers would break off small pieces and use it for cook fires. When you held a lighter to it, C-4 burned slowly and emitted a steady heat—perfect for grilling K-rations before the invention of MREs—Meals Ready to Eat.

He dragged the would-be assailant's cooling body to the opening, and dropped him headfirst into the fast-moving water. There was a faint splash as the raging current swept the corpse away. A few miles downstream it would be grated into bite-sized chunks and slurped up by sucking carp lips.

Something in the air changed. John's ears pulled up on his head, and the hairs on his neck bristled. His right hand instinctively moved to the knife on his belt as he felt the snake-like body of Yoda slide over his back.

In less than a second, Yoda had him wrapped with both legs and locked them around his ankles. He slid both his arms under John's armpits and tried for a full nelson and a quick neck break, but only got one arm in as John grabbed for his knife. Yoda left the half nelson with his left arm, and wrapped his right around John's elbow and forearm to block him from using the dagger.

The master yogi straightened his legs out, arched his back, and fell backward onto the floor, employing a radical half-nelson suplex. He turned his head away at the last moment, and John's skull and neck took the full impact of their fall.

John's breath stopped. He tried to pull his knife from its sheath, but Yoda's right arm kept his locked tightly against his ribs. Yoda straightened his body, extended his legs, and lengthened his spine vertebrae by vertebrae, like a human torture rack. John's knees crackled as they were forced backward against the joints. He flexed with all his strength to break the hold, but they only rocked together on the cement floor. After expending an enormous amount of strength, he went limp and tried to breathe. Yoda constricted his hold even tighter.

Whichever side he rolled to, Yoda rolled with him, their hips seemingly glued together. Yoda's pubic bone jammed under John's buttocks as if they were attempting an intimate coupling.

He snapped his head backward, but Yoda had positioned his cheek against John's, leaving him no space to maneuver. Yoda's warm breath and thin wet lips pressed against John's skin.

John had the dagger out but couldn't raise it above his waist. Yoda's spandex-covered thigh pressed beneath his own, so he couldn't stab downward and cut the bastard's leg without impaling himself. His head pounded and claustrophobia drew the walls in around him. Yoda extended John's spine a little more, and John felt a small electric shock in his knees.

The filthy snake has put pressure on both femoral arteries, and he's going to put me to sleep.

John's left arm started to tingle. A sharp pain pulsed in his elbow. He heard a tiny pop as his knees reached their breaking point. Another fraction of an inch and they would buckle backward against the joint. His vision began to fade. He blinked to refocus but the edges faded away to black.

His hand was numb, but still sensed the dagger. There was no place to stick this bastard without cutting himself first, and no time left to worry about a few stitches. He was dying.

John plunged the throwing knife's nine-inch blade through the meaty inside of his own thigh, careful to avoid any main arteries, and poked it out the other side and into Yoda's thigh. Yoda twitched a little, but didn't release his patented death hold.

Is this how I'm going to die? Cutting myself until I bleed to death in this animal's grip?

"No fucking way," John said out loud.

He drove the knife all the way to the hilt, through his hamstring, and cut Yoda deeply. Their blood spurted into the air like droplets from a spray can, as their hearts pumped harder. Even as they tried to kill one another, they exchanged life-giving fluid. Yoda loosened his grip a fraction and began to retract his legs, but he kept a tight lock on the arm that held the dagger.

Air sucked through the wound as Yoda pulled away and the blade slipped from the hole gouged in his thigh. Yoda rolled and stood up, a sad look on his face. Not angry, but disappointed that John hadn't surrendered to his deadly maneuver. He had been slighted for the first time in his professional life. He picked up a towel from the floor and applied a light tourniquet to his bloody thigh, inches above the deep cut.

John rolled onto his stomach with the blood-dipped knife still in his hand. He tried to get to his knees, but his legs were still asleep. He wanted to throw the knife. The distance was perfect, but he had no leverage lying down.

Yoda stared blankly at him—exotic eyes that registered nothing human—and then climbed the ladder. John got up and hobbled toward the opening, knife in hand. Yoda was out of the hole before he could throw the weapon.

John turned a quick three-sixty at the top of the ladder, expecting an ambush, but Yoda was already walking toward the stairs. John scrambled on all fours to Bassam's corpse, pulled the pistol from the dead man's holster, and clicked off the safety. Yoda heard the noise, and performed a series of backward rolls toward the chlorine tanks, then stood up in front of a one-ton gas cylinder. John crouched in a firing position, one knee down.

Yoda grinned and raised his hand with his index finger up. He shook it back and forth like a schoolteacher scolding a student.

The trigger pressed against his index finger. John's hands shook as he willed himself to fire, but his body wouldn't comply. It knew what his brain didn't want to admit. A miss or ricochet here would bring two deaths. At the very least, his own death. He wasn't sure if this animal breathed chlorine gas, or if he might hold his breath long enough to get out. He kept the front sight trained on Yoda's smile.

Yoda reached his slender arm around his back and pulled the Fuji Instax from its case; his eyes never left John's. He pointed the lens toward John and took a picture. The chamber was silent except for the slight whir from the camera as a sheet of self-developing film the size of a credit card spit out like a black tongue. Yoda held the photo in his hand for a few seconds, looked at John, then back at the film, and nodded in approval. He kept one eye on John and simultaneously slipped the photograph and the camera back into his waistband.

Yoda turned his back and scaled the steel frame that held the chlorine cylinders. He climbed like a floating monkey up the framework to the ceiling.

When Yoda reached the top, John had him. He would climb up and engage. The only way out was through louvered vents in the ceiling that lead to the gatehouse floor above. There was eight, maybe ten, inches of space between each metal louver.

Yoda stood atop the steel scaffolding and shook his arms and legs like an Olympic swimmer taking the block. The towel around his thigh was dark red. He jumped up and grabbed two louvers, turned his head sideways, and pushed it through the small opening. With both hands through the metal louvers he wiggled his body from side to side and pulled his upper body into the gatehouse above. His hips were too wide to make it through the opening. As he pushed down on the grates from above, Yoda's legs grew longer.

John heard a slight *pop, pop,* as Yoda separated his ball joints from his hip. Both legs dangled lifelessly beneath the louvered opening. Yoda pulled his floppy hips through, and his rope-like legs followed behind.

John hobbled toward the stairs to get a shot off before Yoda recovered, but his legs wouldn't cooperate. His left side was still numb as he dragged himself forward like a stroke victim.

At the top of the stairs John pushed on the door, but it wouldn't budge. He pushed again, and something heavy behind it rattled against the knob. Yoda had blocked him in. John slumped to the floor and let the gun drop to his side.

Chocker was right. *You have to fight these guys with primitive tools—no gun—or you're at a disadvantage.*

John tore Bassam's shirt off, sat down, and used part of it to bandage his thigh. He put the remaining swatch in his pocket. The bleeding slowed. He had missed the femoral artery. There was no permanent damage, but it throbbed with every heartbeat.

Heart rate: one hundred twenty.

He had a lot of killing left inside him, but no one to play with. He smashed his closed fist against the floor several times, and laid back. The small louvered opening looked big enough for a train to go through. He closed his eyes and started to drift, but caught himself, and sat up with a grunt.

He dropped Bassam into the pit, and then through the aqueduct's open hatch, along with the drill and the backpack.

The place had to look like no one had been there: Chocker's rule. John took an old broom from the corner and swept coal dust and dirt from the floor over the pool of Bassam's blood. He spread it over the floor and then kicked more dust over the stain to make it look a little more natural. In a couple days it would all settle out and look like no one had been there, at least to a casual observer. Close inspection would prove otherwise. But with no explosion, and no bodies, there would be nothing to investigate.

He sanitized the pit with Bassam's shirt and wiped down places he had touched: the aqueduct, the ladder, the rim of the coal carts, the door handle at the top of the stairs, the broom handle, and the railings. It wasn't perfect, but he doubted anyone could pull a print from this dusty floor, and the bodies had taken their evidence with them.

After a throbbing crawl through the coal tunnel, he pushed the diamond plate back and escaped into fresh autumn air like a convict who had finally made it to freedom. The moon stepped in front of the clouds, and he could see better than when he had entered. After a cursory attempt at replacing the vines and bushes in front of the tunnel, he gave up the remedial landscaping and fought his way up the ravine and to his bike.

He ignored the pain in his leg on the ride back to Graham Hills Park. He wiped the crow bar clean and hurled it into the woods. Ordinarily he didn't like to leave anything behind, but the crowbar would rust. Even if someone did search the area, and on the remote chance they found it, it was meaningless. Maybe some kids had used it to get into the coal tunnel to party.

He tossed the bike in back of the Subaru and grabbed a blanket from the back seat to sit on and protect the upholstery from bloodstains. This mission had been sloppy enough.

Twenty miles from the scene of the crime, three New York State trooper cars passed John in the opposite lane going south. They were lit up, sirens wailing, and had to be going over one hundred miles per hour. They looked like giant tracer bullets fired down the thruway from a cannon somewhere ahead. A few more miles and the road lit up again, this time with fire trucks, ambulances, and more police cars—not just troopers but every cop that was on duty was pouring southbound and not taking any prisoners. It had to be one hell of a pile-up.

He grabbed a few aspirin from the bottle in his car, chewed, and swallowed them dry. He kept to the speed limit all the way home and parked the car close to the porch. He had to take care of the wound before bacteria dug in. He checked for the knife in his waistband, though there was not no time to check for perpetrators, and no reason there should be any.

Special forces soldiers were provided with a small pharmacy of amphetamine and antibiotics, along with basic surgical supplies.

The Joint Chiefs of Staff don't advertise this in their recruiting posters for fear they'd have to weed out junkies and young punk thrill-seekers looking for a rush. John had used some of his stash in the mountains of Tora Bora and brought the rest home with him. As a scout, he worked alone and sometimes stayed awake for three to four days tracking the enemy. Amphetamines gave him an edge. The hajjis didn't believe anyone would stay on their trail for that long without sleep. Special forces soldiers were monitored on a regular basis to check for a buildup of drugs in their systems. Uncle Sam wanted the kills, but he didn't need an army of tweaked-out assassins with unlimited firepower running wild among the earthlings.

John kept a pharmaceutical go-bag in a dresser in the spare room. In the bag were OxyContin blister packs, the time-release version of oxycodone. The little pills were known on the street as "killers" (which he thought appropriate given his line of work), OC, and "hillbilly heroin," for their popularity among rural drug addicts.

John grabbed the bag and went to the bathroom. He chewed on a five-milligram OC tablet, took two azithromycin, and downed an eight-ounce glass of Jack Daniels. It would hurt regardless, but he had to sew himself up or the wound would close and get infected. He sat on the toilet seat and gave the whiskey ten minutes to get into his system. OC was time-released, but by chewing it you could get around the sustained release coating to get a euphoric rush similar to heroin. He wasn't interested in the high, only pain suppression.

He pulled back the flap of skin around his self-inflicted wound and dispensed isopropyl alcohol into the hole. Most of it poured down his leg. This wasn't going to work.

He grabbed his toothbrush from the sink, poured alcohol over it, and used it to pry open the wound. This time the isopropyl alcohol burned exposed nerve endings and dripped out the hole on the other side of his inner thigh. He took another drink of whiskey and used a povidone-iodine solution as an antiseptic. The iodine didn't sting at all, but it left a brown streak down his leg and pooled on the floor.

He threaded a length of absorbable catgut and performed an approximation suture, which secured the sides of the deep wound. Then he made a continuous, uninterrupted suture along the wound's edge. He pulled back on his thigh muscle and performed the same surgery to the hole on the other side. The bloody gauze, instruments, and catgut went into a small garbage bag under the sink. He would clean up when he woke up.

The procedure had been sloppy but quick. John needed sleep. He placed his head on the pillow and let another OxyContin take him to hillbilly heaven.

The vulture's voice was smooth—not unlike his own—but nasty, with an edge:

"This is the end for you. You haven't accomplished anything. Lie there and rot."

John had heard the voice before. It came when he no longer had a goal on which to focus. The voice itemized his faults, his failures. The scavenger on the headboard hunched over, glared, spit at him, and tore the air with its sharp beak. It ruffled its feathers, hissed, and dropped a white and gray soupy present on his forehead. It felt wet and sticky.

He stretched his heels away from his calves, and wiggled his toes. Everything worked that far away from his heart. He extended his arms over the sides of the mattress. The pain in his ribs and his muscles urged him to stop. His skin tingled, and his tongue was swollen as it rolled inside his dry mouth. The sensation of being halfway between slumber and wakefulness made him edgy. He tried to will himself awake.

"You're pitiful," said the vulture. "Spend the rest of the day staring at the ceiling. You're ugly and nobody likes you. They pity you. She's lying. She wants a man. You're convenient, that's all. A means to an end."

He rolled to his side and curled into a fetal position and listened to the music.

It was an old Bachman-Turner Overdrive hit, "Taking Care of Business."

"Taking Care of Business"? He remembered it playing in his father's cassette player in the battered family pickup truck. His dad had been a Bachman-Turner Overdrive fanatic.

John squinted one eye toward the alarm clock. He never set it, and it didn't have a radio. He straightened his legs and felt where he had been stretched like Gumby and slammed against the concrete floor.

"And when this is over, the CIA will kill you. You failed. You let the Yoda live."

Had they followed him here? Was he home? Maybe and yes. Was there someone in the house? It wasn't Maggie, because she had a day job. She went to work, regular hours.

The music faded like a ghost slipping into a gray fog. He sat up too quickly and gagged dry air. He was too tired to put in the effort for a good puke. The skin on his head ached and his temples pulsed from the OC hangover. He went to the bathroom, took a piss, and downed three aspirin. He lay back down on the bed. The vulture's words drifted now, from somewhere outside the room. He heard the words, but he couldn't get a handle on their exact meaning.

He couldn't keep this up forever. Assassins had a lifespan. Even the best, deadliest kung fu *sifu* in the world gets old.

Regardless of expertise, a young and unbreakable Mike Tyson would cripple a ninety-year-old kung fu master.

This has got to end. But how? How would he tell them? How would he tell Chocker it was for real? How could he resign from a job that didn't exist?

If it were easy as fishin', you could be a musician . . .

If you get in with the right bunch of fellows . . .

He snapped into a sitting position, reached behind the head board, and pulled out the long throwing knife he kept there, hidden in a sheath, duct-taped to the wall.

This was real. This wasn't a dream. He didn't have any Bachman-Turner Overdrive music in the house. It wasn't Maggie surprising him either. BTO wasn't her era. Some sick bastard was teasing him before the kill. He wasn't ready to die. There was too much self-loathing ahead.

He belly crawled down the stairs headfirst to keep a low profile, fingertips supporting his weight on each step like a spider, gently, like water rolling over rocks. He had a complete view of the living room. It was empty aside from dusty furniture. He looked at the living room windows and Henry's framed photographs on the walls for a reflection of any movement from the kitchen. He hesitated at the stair bottom, pulled into a crouch, and then duck-walked to the kitchen archway. The stitches in his thigh pulled against the swollen flesh.

Most of the night came back to him: the tunnel, Yoda, the rabbit—but he still didn't remember the ride home. How did he get home?

The music had stopped. He peeked in quickly and snapped his head back, expecting the *pfffftt* of a silenced weapon followed by the metallic clang of the slide action. Nothing. He looked again. Someone was playing a game and wanted him to keep coming.

He crouched low and walked into the kitchen, raising his head every few feet to look out a window. No cars in the driveway. Henry's cat sat at the edge of the road and looked in his direction. Sunlight filled the room and left no place for an assassin to hide in the small country kitchen. John stood up with his back in the corner, knife in hand, and scanned the room. He saw the toaster, refrigerator, stove, table, and chairs. Some dirt was on the floor, but he had probably brought it in last night. The sink dripped a steady beat every ten seconds or so. Nothing seemed out of the ordinary. But what didn't he see?

Look around. What don't you see? What was missed or added?

The LCD screen on the sat phone Chocker had given him blinked a silent warning. He had placed it in the charger after last night's mission. He walked over to the charger and picked up the phone. Chocker had never called him here—never called him at all. He had made it clear at the Blue Mountain Winery that communication via satellite phone was one-way—John to Chocker.

"I'll assume you're dead or soon will be. You got it?" Chocker had said.

His muscles tensed, and he felt like puking again. He slid to the floor with his back against the wall to take the pressure off his legs.

The phone vibrated in his hand. He almost dropped it for fear it would detonate. Maybe someone had planted a charge inside. A number came up he didn't recognize, so he let it ring again. When the BTO song came on, he pushed the talk icon.

He didn't say a word. He waited, unsure of the protocol going in this direction. There was no code if Chocker called him.

"Is that you?" It was Chocker's voice.

"Cock?"

"A-doodle-doo. Enough already. We need you, John."

"I'll call you right back."

It sounded like Chocker, but the paranoid spook would never break protocol unless something serious had occurred. Had someone exposed Chocker? Or kidnapped him, and was trying to get to John through him? Was Chocker in trouble?

He was torn between redialing and getting in his car and running the hell away from this town, this life. Then he remembered what his father had told him about the American flag: *These colors don't run*.

He pushed redial.

"Cock."

John replied with the "a-doodle-doo."

"Satisfied?"

"We'll see. What is it?" He kept his voice steady, emotionless. He smelled a setup.

"You all right?"

"Been better."

Chocker took a deep breath and exhaled into the phone. "What happened, John?"

"All three of them were there. Just like you said. I got two, dumped them in the grater, but Yoda got away."

There was an uncomfortable silence. John wasn't sure if Chocker was pleased at his success or disappointed in the failure of Yoda's escape.

"Sorry," John said.

"Tell me again," said Chocker. "What in the hell happened, soldier?"

"Sir?"

Something was wrong. John recognized the tone. Chocker was pissed and didn't believe his story.

"Did you turn on the news today?" Chocker's voice was monotone, without emotion.

John was about to say, "Yeah, right after I saved the inhabitants of New York City and sewed up my own wounds, you cocksucker," but he just said, "No."

"Six thousand Westchester County residents evacuated to Connecticut, New York City, and New Jersey. Eight hundred confirmed dead so far, and the hospitals are treating people in their parking lots!"

John's sense of reality shifted. He felt weak and dizzy. He leaned forward to puke, but his stomach was empty.

"Now are you going to tell me what really happened?" Chocker's voice raised an octave.

John remembered police cars racing by him, emergency vehicles, and fire trucks. But wasn't that all a dream? Wasn't it just an accident on the highway?

"When I left the location, all ordnance was neutralized and disposed of. Two enemy in the drink. All ordnance disposed of . . ." He couldn't think of anything else to add. His memory was nearly blank from the point when Yoda slipped through the ceiling. He remembered the bat, but wasn't that before the engagement? Then the troopers, and after that, he was home sewing his wound.

"John!"

Chocker's voice brought him back to the kitchen. John imagined he was sliding down the wall, and then felt his ass hit the floor. There were trees outside his window. No sand, no scrub brush. He was in the Catskills, wounded and alone.

"What happened to Yoda?" Chocker's voice was steady, firm. It wasn't a reprimand, just a commander looking for an answer, a report on the mission.

"We engaged, sir. I cut him bad. He escaped through a vent in the ceiling."

"When you left, was he already gone?"

"He ran, sir. He ran . . ."

"Well, directly thereafter, the situation went Charlie Foxtrot."

Cluster fuck, thought John. But he had done everything right. Yoda had run. He cleaned up. The bad guys were in the drink . . . except Yoda. Yoda had run. All ordnance was—

"John?"

"Sir?"

"Are you all right?" said Chocker. "Are you wounded?"

"I have a puncture wound on my leg. I cut him bad, sir. I cut him bad. But I had to cut me to get to him. It was the hold . . ."

"Do you need a doctor, John? Should I send someone?"

"No. I took care of it for now."

"Someone put some ordnance in there, soldier," said Chocker. "Either that freak came back, or there was a second team."

"He couldn't have come back," John replied. "He was cut and bleeding real bad. He needed a doctor. I'm telling you, sir. He did not return to that location. I'm sure of it."

"The feebs are calling it an accident so the whole goddamn country doesn't go on full alert," said Chocker. "Maybe they know what happened, maybe they don't. In the meantime, we've got work to do."

"Work, sir?"

"You're not done, Major. I want you to boot up, go to the site, and rendezvous tomorrow. Understood?"

"You want me to hunt him down?" John heard the words come out of his mouth, but didn't feel the conviction in his own voice.

"Yoda's so far gone, we'll never find him now," said Chocker. "I've got something else for you. Are you fit?"

"I'm fit, sir." John slid all the way to the floor now, his back flat against the linoleum, half-opened eyes staring at the ceiling. "I'm sorry, sir. I saw no other ordnance."

"Go to the website, find the location, and meet at the regular hour. You are still my man here, son."

"But I failed you, sir."

"FIDO," said Chocker and hung up the phone.

Fuck it, drive on.

The number of surveillance cameras on the FBI satellite office in White Plains had been doubled since the deaths of 812 citizens after the Kensico chlorine release. Fourteen of the dead were NYCDEP police and first responders.

Kieran Gilchrist didn't look up and didn't smile as he entered the building. He wasn't concerned about anyone blowing up his office. It wouldn't have the political and horrifying impact of a gas release. He didn't think anyone in this drab building would be on any bad guy's list. As for himself, aside from a few people he worked with, he didn't think he'd be missed. The only time he heard from his ex was on the back of his checks.

What the enemy wanted was to drive fear into the hearts of the citizens he was paid to protect. Killing a few was a bonus, but the fear that John Q. Public could die at any moment from a cloud of deadly gas had a far greater impact than blowing a building with FBI agents inside.

Gilchrist had been one of the first people on the scene on a cool day in January 2005 when two Northern Suffolk rail trains collided near the Avondale Mills plant in Graniteville, South Carolina. A railroad switch had misaligned, funneling the railed behemoths together into a sculpture of twisted steel. Sixty tons of chlorine gas had been released into the atmosphere.

Eight people died almost immediately from the accident, one later from chlorine inhalation. Due to the corrosive nature of chlorine gas, 5,400 residents had to be evacuated for two weeks while the cleanup took place. The strong oxidizing effect of chlorine produced corrosive tissue damage. The gas penetrated cells, reacted with cytoplasmic proteins, and destroyed the cell structure. Any living thing it encountered would break down at the cellular level and die. This modern marvel could be attributed to a German chemist, Fritz Haber, who created the gas for the specific purpose of destroying the enemy in WWI.

There was no antidote for chlorine poisoning, and the results of exposure occurred within minutes. In humans, internal and external tissue blistered until it popped and released life-giving fluids. The estimated cost to Norfolk Southern Railroad at the time was in excess of fifty million dollars, irrespective of future litigation. The immediate area surrounding the release was not nearly as populated as Westchester County. The city of New York had already set up an escrow account with several law firms, in the neighborhood of a half billion dollars. Most legal experts agreed that would only begin to cover the cost of future litigation and medical claims.

The true devastation of Graniteville occurred months and then years later, when people began to complain of lung disorders, aggravated asthma, reoccurring skin rashes, ocular damage, and sleep apnea. Some victims lost a large percentage of their lung capacity and had to be put on steroids that, along with forced inactivity, made them gain weight and become lethargic. More than half of the five thousand evacuees were later treated for psychiatric disorders that ranged from low-level anxiety and depression to nightmares, post-traumatic stress disorder, and flashbacks. The flashbacks could be triggered by the sound of a train, large crowds, chlorinated swimming pools, or even something as simple as the smell of burning diesel fuel.

For Kieran Gilchrist, the Kensico catastrophe—as it was now being reported in the press—was an all-too-personal flashback to what had happened at Graniteville. Though the EPA and OSHA required risk management plans at the Graniteville plant, local volunteer fire department first responders entered the release area without first donning their self-contained breathing apparatus. And who could blame them? A thorough records review proved that some of the mandatory, on-going training had been skipped and, when performed, was lackluster at best. Moreover, the panic and sense of urgency that occurred when your friends and loved ones were in danger tended to make people forget about their own safety. Security footage of the Kensico release showed a similar response.

To Gilchrist, it was like watching a trained firefighter enter a burning building without proper turnout gear.

Gilchrist took the elevator to his eighth-floor office and prepared to review the devastation one more time. The secretary of Homeland Security had tasked him with personally reviewing the situation and preparing a response for the mayor of New York. It was his job to craft an accurate response so that the mayor didn't offend anyone or reveal any further weaknesses in the current RMP that terrorist organizations could exploit.

Gilchrist's normally polite and professional security administrator said good morning and gathered papers on her desk, along with a list of messages, to review with her boss. Small talk had left the office the morning the first deaths were reported. Everyone's previous sense of infallibility disappeared along with the vapors, and the White Plains satellite office had morphed into a somber place. The security administrator brought him coffee, something Gilchrist never asked of her, and waited for him to speak.

"Let's fix the worst first," said Gilchrist. "Shall we, Christine?"

"Priority one would be to call the DHS secretary and tell her where you are with the mayor's next response." Christine put that message on the left side of his desk. "Next, the mayor of New York City wants to know how far you've gotten with the mayor's response." She placed that note on the right side of his desk.

"How far have I gotten?" He gave Christine a weak smile and tried the coffee. He raised the mug to her and nodded thanks.

"You are finished with the response," she said. "That is, unless some breaking news comes in before 11:00 a.m. today." Christine gathered the press release she had spent most of yesterday and last night writing and put it in the middle of his desk. "You need only review it. I think even the mayor can get this one right. I've pared it down to several sound bites, an emotional outreach or two, heavy condolences and, of course, a promise of complete transparency."

"Thank you," said Gilchrist. "You know I can't do that stuff. You've saved my ass again."

"You can do it, Kieran. The problem is, you don't know the proper way to tell the truth."

"And that would be?"

"You tend to let the facts get in the way."

Senior Security Administrator Christine Sparks had spent the last seven years of her career working personally with Kieran Gilchrist and had followed him up the bureaucratic hierarchy of promotions. Security administrators assigned resources, scheduled services, requisitioned equipment and people, and performed every other bureaucratic function required to prepare operations teams for their tasks. Kieran Gilchrist was effective, and he found the shortest solution to any problem he encountered. Together, they made a crack team. The problem was that he didn't know what parts of the story to leave out. It had cost him political capital and a few promotions along the way.

"You're a little frank this morning, considering."

Christine smiled and said, "This isn't the end, Kieran. You're the best at what you do. You've just got a lot on your plate, and your personal life isn't helping. So don't be hard on yourself, and let's get through this."

"On the bright side, I haven't given up drinking."

"You see," Christine made a fist and shook it. "There's always hope."

She had a way of helping him to realize that the entire world wasn't an icebox of mortality. Kieran slapped his hands together to indicate he was ready to dig into the mess with more gusto.

"Did the fatality numbers change?" he said.

"No. But there are a lot of people showing up at the hospital with pulmonary problems, headaches, and other ailments." Christine rifled through the papers and pulled up a black-and-white photo of a man, with accompanying personal statistics. "This is Terry Bailey, a security guard at Kensico. He's disappeared."

Gilchrist picked up the paper and took a hard look at the man's photograph. "Is he the connection? Is this our Benedict Arnold?"

"I don't think so, Kieran," Christine said as she shook her head. "He's pretty much true-blue from what we can find. The DEP performs thorough background checks once a year on their law enforcement staff—DWIs, police records, drug problems. He was clean as a whistle and about to retire. He does have one stressor that could set him off. It turns out his wife is a little unstable, but not enough so that their medical plan covers her particular problems. She burns up all allowable psychiatric services in the first few months of every year, and then self-medicates with the bottle."

"What's her problem?"

"She's got a rare form of anxiety disorder. But we don't think this guy—at least so far—had anything to do with it. His DEP canine partner was found in the chamber, dead from the chlorine gas. So somehow these two got separated."

Gilchrist put the photograph aside and asked, "What else have you got for me?"

"As you are quite aware, I'm sure," Christine said, "the DEP controlled the flow of information regarding the gas release from the point it was detected in their sensors, up until the status changed from an incidental release to a catastrophic release."

Gilchrist jotted quick passages on a pad as she spoke, and then asked, "At what point did it switch over? I don't mean the information flow. I mean the status."

Christine referred to a report in her hands. "The DEP indicates the ambient air above the chamber exceeded one part per million at around 5:00 a.m. Not to beat you with details, but one ppm is still considered an incidental release."

Gilchrist shook his head almost apologetically. "No, no. Please don't leave anything out you think I might know. God knows I'm not running on all cylinders with the sleep I'm getting."

"You really should take something, Kieran. A sleeping pill won't hurt."

"Imagine what would happen if I was half-looped on Ambien and I got the call at three in the morning from the secretary that some other crisis has popped up?" He made believe he was turning a steering wheel and had a dopey grin on his face. "I'll be right there, madam secretary. I just need to drive off the Tappan Zee Bridge first, and what did you say your name was?" He took his hands off the wheel. "No thanks."

"Have it your way. I took them when I got divorced and saved myself a lot of grief. Sometimes a little memory loss is healthy."

"Not when you're sitting on this side of the desk, Christine."

"Good point." She pulled the pen away from the side of her mouth. "Back to the status. This is a report from the computer that monitors the sensors inside and outside the chambers." She slid the report closer to him and then sat back.

"Let's not waste time," he said. "I know you highlighted these sections for a reason, Chrissie. Please explain."

"The ambient air outside the structure was zero ppm at about 4:00 a.m." She gave him a moment to find the line indicating this reading, and continued. "Now take a look at sensors twenty-one through twenty-six at 4:00 a.m., and follow them to 5:00 a.m."

He scanned the chart and looked up. "Nothing. Zero ppm. What's the significance?"

"The significance is that sensors twenty-one through twenty-six are in the chamber that held the chlorine gas cylinders. There were six sensors in that area, all reading zero ppm up until 0501 hours, when the exterior ambient sensors picked up the incidental release."

Kieran leaned back and covered his face with his massive hands. He rubbed his eyes until he began to see stars. The report revealed why the first responders entered the release area without donning SCBA. They probably figured it was a sensor malfunction because the inside readings showed no chlorine in the atmosphere. When they opened the chamber doors they were engulfed in levels exceeding the catastrophic ten-ppm exposure level.

"Please get Walker in here," said Gilchrist. "I want to review the security footage. Tell him I want it on the wall screen."

In fifteen minutes the high definition screen on the office wall was queued up and ready to go. The images were in black and white, with the date and running time on the bottom right of the screen. Gilchrist and Stephen Walker sat on a comfortable leather couch that faced the television screen.

"Let it roll," said Gilchrist.

"Yes, sir."

Walker used the keyboard of his laptop as a remote control and could stop, start, zoom, and play back any frame via wireless Internet that ran from the server in his office. No sound had been recorded. The screen was split into three sections showing the vantage point of three separate security cameras. The first view was at the main door to the chamber, the second came from a steel light pole that covered the area where vehicles would drive up, and the third was a bird's-eye shot from the roof of the building.

"Nothing's happening," said Gilchrist.

"The time is 0503 hours," said Walker. "They would not have had time to respond to the sensor yet."

Gilchrist checked the printout Christine had given him: 0501 hours was indicated as the time of the first sensor alarm. The DEP police had armed guards at Kensico, and the Eastview precinct was only six miles away. He wondered how long it would take them to show up. He was not optimistic.

When he saw the first patrol car pull onto the screen, he ordered Walker to stop the tape.

"At 0526 hours?" Gilchrist was exasperated. "It took those trout troopers twenty-five minutes to respond to a potential gas leak from six miles away? Wasn't anyone on patrol? What about the officers assigned to patrol West Lake Drive around the reservoir?"

"They were the first on the scene," said Walker. "But as you can see, the Valhalla fire department showed up at the same time."

Beautiful, Gilchrist thought. *The local volunteer fire department showed up as quickly as the paid police force.* "How far away were they?" he said.

"Actually, the DEP station in Eastview is a little closer, depending how you drive."

Gilchrist indicated with a twirl of his finger that Walker should play on.

The police officers pulled up to the doors with their emergency lights off. Four officers exited their cars and turned toward the oncoming fire trucks that were lit up like Christmas trees. They waved their hands in the air and motioned for the trucks to pull over to the right so that the police cars wouldn't be blocked. It appeared a couple of the firefighters were prepared to don full turnout gear and SCBA, but hesitated as their chief walked over to the police, who were only dressed in uniform. They talked for about a minute. The lead police officer talked with his hands on his utility belt. The other three stood off to the right, near the cruiser parked closest to the chamber doors. The officer and fire chief grabbed the receivers of their two-way radios several times and nodded their heads as they spoke.

It was precisely at this point the decision was made that would kill all fourteen men.

A firefighter exited the cab of the second fire truck with a small electronic device in his hand. Gilchrist recognized it as a toxic gas leak detector, similar to the one used at Graniteville. It could detect chlorine gas in parts per million. The lead police officer held up his hand and spoke into his shoulder-mounted two-way radio. All fourteen men stood still.

"What's happening right now, Walker?"

Stephen Walker stopped the tape. "Take a look at the print out Christine gave you. Match the reading with the time on the screen."

Gilchrist checked the time on the screen—0531 hours—and then found the corresponding line on the paper in his hand.

"The reading shows zero ppm," said Gilchrist. "But a minute before it showed one ppm. What happened?"

"We interviewed the DEP employees in the control room shortly after they were evacuated. They thought it was a good idea to reset the monitors outside and see if it was just a glitch in the system."

Gilchrist bent over and rubbed his face even harder as he listened to Walker. The pressure on his eyes somehow relieved the tension building up in his brain. He listened, though reluctantly, as Walker finished the explanation. "I'll roll it back a bit," said Walker.

The NYCDEP police security tape picked up again at the precise moment the lead officer was speaking into his two-way. Gilchrist raised his head, and his empty stomach growled from the coffee he'd ingested.

"You can see the officer raise his hand and listen for a response from the control room. The control room supervisor told our investigators that this officer—the one on the screen with his hand in the air—asked them what the reading was at that moment. They responded 'zero ppm.' The officer responded, 'Roger that,' and waved his hand at the firefighters here." Walker stopped the tape for a second, then hit PLAY again. "The firefighters understood this to mean that they did not need their SCBA."

Gilchrist's stomach growled so loud that Walker turned toward him and gave a weak smile.

"Skipped breakfast," said Gilchrist. "Proceed."

"What the officer did not understand, and what the control room failed to tell him, was that it takes a few minutes for the sensors to clear and refresh the readings. It was during this time that the officer—and this is only conjecture because we do not have sound—told them the meter read zero ppm and the building was clear."

"So the control room didn't bother to say that he needed to wait for the sensors to ramp up?"

"The control room supervisor told us he had no indication that the officer in charge would attempt an entry at that moment. They said they were waiting for him to ask for the next reading."

"What's the protocol?" asked Gilchrist.

"It appears there is no protocol for this exact situation, sir."

"They didn't see him open the doors?"

"The control room monitors water flow and various types of sensors. The security cameras are monitored by the DEP police."

Gilchrist gave a solemn nod, as if listening to a eulogy. He put his hands together between his knees and looked up at the screen. He could already hear the cable news bobble heads: "Neither law enforcement personnel nor first responders were trained, drilled, or prepared for this scenario." It was going to be a shit hailstorm in the papers. The mayor would need to up the escrow account a few billion. Gilchrist twirled his finger in the air again.

Gilchrist and Walker watched as the first officer closest the door punched in a code to release the electronic lock. Two of the other officers stood behind him. The lead officer and the firefighters turned toward the doors and followed about twenty feet behind.

The first three officers instantaneously brought their hands to their mouths and fell to their knees. One of them grabbed for the pistol on his belt before he began to shake and roll on the ground as his larynx, trachea, and bronchi immediately inflamed. At this point, a mist rolled out the chamber doors.

The firefighters stepped forward to help the fallen men, but were quickly engulfed in the gaseous vapors. They hit the ground in a similar fashion. Most of them vomited and tried to cover their eyes, noses, and mouths as they choked to death. Though Gilchrist couldn't see it, he knew their lungs were blistering from the high levels of chlorine gas that had accumulated behind the metal chamber doors.

Gilchrist noticed the time on the screen: 0533 hours. It had taken all of two minutes from the time of the last transmission to the control room for all fourteen men to die a gruesome death. He was sure it seemed much longer to them.

"Do you want to see more, sir?" Walker asked.

"Not at this time," he responded. "I want to know why those sensors malfunctioned."

"The sensors outside were new and worked perfectly," said Walker. "The sensors in the chamber containing the chlorine gas were older and had metal parts."

"And chlorine corrodes metal."

"Yes sir. Over the years incidental leaks of one part per million or less had occurred in the chamber. I mean, when the chamber was actually in use. No one realized at the time that these incidental leaks had slowly corroded some of the internal components and wiring. The way the old system in the chamber worked was that if one sensor malfunctioned, the electric feed to the others automatically went down, and the area was considered contaminated until air samples were taken."

"But that protocol was ignored," said Gilchrist. "Because the ambient exterior air was where the reading was showing gas, and they assumed there was no problem below."

"Yes sir. And the massive amount of chlorine interrupted the chamber circuitry, so no reading was sent to the control room."

"Anything else?"

"I have nothing specific at this time," said Walker.

"I do."

Both men turned to see Christine Sparks's tall, full-figured body standing at the threshold of Gilchrist's office.

"Christine?" Gilchrist cocked an eyebrow.

"Mr. Walker will need to leave the room," she said.

Gilchrist nodded at Walker and he was gone in a few seconds.

"What is it, Christine?"

"Our HAZMAT team found traces of mercury fulminate powder and potassium chlorate powder in the chamber."

"Any sulfur?" Gilchrist asked, his tone flat. He hoped the third ingredient needed to make a detonator was missing.

"No, Kieran," said Christine. When he almost looked hopeful, she added, "Our lab tells us that chlorine in those concentrations could have affected the sulfur and made it unrecognizable."

Gilchrist's heart sunk in his chest. "Will we have to change the mayor's response?"

"Not at this time," said Christine. "But madame secretary will need the unabridged version."

"How long will it take?"

Christine Sparks put her fingertips on the senior official in charge of counterterrorism and counterintelligence's shoulder and handed him a single typed page on FBI letterhead.

PHILADELPHIA

Forty-eight hours had passed since his battle with the highly skilled American soldier in the aqueduct tunnel—the first adversary he had not succeeded in killing in hand-to-hand combat in his career as an assassin. Yoda had managed to get to Yonkers, awaken a contact that was supportive of the Muslim battle against western tyranny, and secure a doctor who could sew up his wound. Yoda was not personally concerned about western tyranny or any battles religious zealots fought with one another. He just needed to survive. His contact and the doctor were very helpful. It took thirty-seven stitches to close the wound, and he was instructed to change the dressing daily.

Yoda refused painkillers, but he did take the antibiotic samples the doctor gave him. He thanked them and then killed them both. There were only two people on this planet left who could identify him and what he did for a living. One was the American soldier, the other his death broker—a middleman in Yemen who set up his jobs and arranged payment. He was in need of that man now.

Before Yoda left the doctor's office, he took surgical supplies and a vial of prescription drugs. He had already anticipated their need.

Yoda hated killing people for free, especially when there was no challenge to the act. The soldier in the tunnel had made it a necessity, and for that he would pay dearly. But first, Yoda needed to identify the man.

Philadelphia had an Asian population of around five percent, depending on who was taking the census. The University of Pennsylvania, just over the Delaware River from New Jersey, had an undergraduate Asian population of nearly 25 percent and sat in the center of the city. Yoda chose Philadelphia as his secondary staging point for these two reasons. It was just under a three-hour drive from Westchester County, and he had left within minutes of eliminating the two men in Yonkers. He was unaware of the history of religious and political freedom the town represented, and might have considered his situation there ironic had he known.

Yoda had used the ill-fated Yemenis' car parked at the Dunkin' Donuts to get there. He left it in a twenty-four-hour public parking facility near the campus. With so many Asians in the neighborhood, he would go unnoticed walking the streets or driving in the rusted Honda Civic.

Yoda wasn't sure exactly how old he was. He never really believed anything the monks had told him before he left them more than a decade ago, and his real parents had been killed when he was so young, he didn't remember birthday parties or bedtime stories. He was sure, however, that he was young enough to fit into the college crowd without a problem.

Yoda handed a small photo to the young girl in the Staples copy department near campus.

"I need this scanned and put on a disk."

He spoke humbly, in slightly broken English, the way he imagined an insecure international student in such a large and modern city might converse. He wore a crisp, new University of Pennsylvania T-shirt with a smiling red-and-blue Quaker mascot printed on the front, and a twill baseball cap with the school logo. His blue jeans were new but torn, and purposely stained with coffee. He completed his ensemble with a pair of cheap sandals he had purchased for five dollars from a street vendor.

"You want a disk?"

The young girl screwed up her face like something was wrong with Yoda, or his question. He was irritated, but he put on a humble act anyway. "Is that okay?" he said.

"Dontcha want a flash drive?"

She looked at him, looked away, and looked at him again. She kept doing this as she shifted her weight from foot to foot, avoiding eye contact the whole time. Yoda found everything about her to be rude and irritating. He hated that she questioned him, that she was fat, and that he needed her help, if only temporarily.

"Which is better?" he said. Yoda only used computers to send a rare email to his death broker. He did not own one, and found he had no use for them. His was a cash business where money was transferred to numbered accounts in various friendly banks in Europe and the Caribbean. He always called them to make sure the deposits were made. He went to them when he needed money.

The girl smiled like she was trying to be nice—a pleasant employee—but her tone came off like she thought he was from another planet, or somehow mentally handicapped.

"The flash drive is smaller," she said, like an adult would talk to a child, and showed him one on her key chain. "You can carry it anywhere, and just plug it into a USB port. You don't need a CD drive."

"Okay. Flash drive then." Yoda smiled and tilted his head in a slight forward nod the way he thought this American idiot might appreciate, considering she probably thought he was Chinese.

The girl scanned the photo into a large digital copier, pushed some buttons on the keypad, and inserted a new flash drive to the USB port. She also printed an enlarged color copy of the photo and brought it back to the counter with the original and the flash drive. He could tell she questioned why anyone would have a photograph of a soldier in a dark room pointing his gun at the photographer. You can take just about any photo to a copy shop in America without raising an eyebrow, as long as it didn't contain naked children or animal abuse images. Still, crouched soldiers with semiautomatic pistols were out of the ordinary.

"Film major," said Yoda, and pointed to the smiling Quaker on his chest. "Make movies."

The girl's eyes lit up in comprehension. She smiled and said that was cool.

He paid her in cash and waited as she bagged his purchase.

"You show me one thing on machine? Okay?"

"For a film major?" She smiled. "Sure. But you've got to put me in your next movie."

Yoda nodded with a smile and walked behind the counter to the copier the girl had used to scan his photo.

"You can make another picture for me?"

"Sure." She scrolled the keypad and pulled up the last entry. She was about to hit COPY when he interrupted her.

"May I?"

"Oh, yeah."

He studied the keyboard for a moment and found a delete button indicated by an "X." He moved his fingers toward the copy button and let his thumb push the delete button first.

Words came up on the screen, asking him if he was sure he wanted to perform this action. Yoda mumbled "make copy" and clicked YES before she could stop him.

"No," she said. "Now we have to scan it in again."

The girl had an expression of disappointment that would have been appropriate if Yoda had deleted the final version of a nine-thousand-word treatise on the history of film. He thought about snapping her neck and stuffing her in the copier's cabinet, but it was just a thought, something to amuse him and temporarily redirect his frustration away from the American. And there were always the cameras in this country, ever watchful, ever present.

"That's okay," said Yoda. "I will come back another time. You are most helpful. Thank you."

There is a market for every service and a middleman to make smooth the transaction between buyer and supplier. Yoda never met his clients. He was more comfortable using a middleman and the layer of separation it afforded him. He had only met the man he thought of as the death broker once, and could contact him by email or cell phone. The broker had no way to contact Yoda. The yogi took orders for his service on his own time.

Farther down the street he found an Internet café and paid cash for time on a machine. He accessed a generic email account and sent the photo to his death broker. In the text box he wrote the city and state where the man was last seen, that he needed a positive identification, an address, and any further contact or personal information available. He expected his response within twenty-four hours.

After Yoda's work in New York, Homeland Security had raised the terrorist alert level from elevated to high. All the news stations were still reporting the deaths in Valhalla and White Plains as most likely caused by old chlorine tanks stored in the tunnel chambers of the aqueduct system. For now they were blaming it on human error. Yoda understood that the US government may not have had time to figure out exactly what had happened, or they were just keeping a lid on it to stop public panic and a mass exodus from one of the largest cities in the world. He would need to keep away from bridges, shipping ports, and government buildings.

Even cheap hotels had security cameras now when you checked in, so hotels were out of the question. Yoda took a cab to Fairmont Park in western Philadelphia, used a newspaper as a prop, and sat on a bench while he decided what to do. He had given his contact one day to get the information he needed, so he would have to stay in the Asian section of town during the day and sleep in the park at night. He liked parks. They were green and generally quiet at night.

He waited until dusk, and then climbed a fifty-foot elm with an equally large canopy. The branches were thick, and he was able to find one that was more or less horizontal. Yoda assumed a full lotus position with his straight back against the main trunk. He listened to the far-off traffic as he aligned his spine and focused his energy toward the wound in his leg. He meditated until pin needles of morning sun rifled through the old elm's myrtle-green leaves.

John had considered staking out the restaurant before Chocker arrived. Did he trust his contact? It was always the question overseas, but he had to remember that he was home now. If he didn't trust his contact here, then he was in the wrong job. On the other hand, a lot of American citizens were dead and dying, and John knew he was the only living link—aside from

Yoda—that could give testimony as to why. Sure, he hadn't killed them. Hell, he'd tried to save them. But that didn't mean the operation he had performed on behalf of C. Peter Chocker, senior account executive, International Fiber Resources, was exactly legal—far from it. Would Chocker want to tie up any loose ends? Yoda was in the wind, and with John gone, Chocker would be free to move on to his next project. And if John didn't show? The answer to that was obvious. He would be hunted down and killed. Decision by indecision was not an option.

If Chocker did nail him for the surveillance, it would put a serious damper on their relationship. Pissing off a deep-cover, wet-work CIA operative with unlimited funding was a sure way to have your cerebral wiring rerouted, or worse, a complete power outage. Despite his melancholy perspective, John preferred his current state of consciousness to the alternative—one unaltered by the chemical cocktails of C. Peter Chocker.

John was ten minutes early. It was safe to go inside without appearing the anxious date.

He tried not to limp as he pushed the door open with the side of his wrist. He didn't like to leave finger and palm prints anywhere. The bartender stopped racking glasses for a moment, smiled, and gave John a nod.

He committed himself to the room, realizing he was already made if Chocker was there. Sometimes these pricks show up two hours in advance so they can watch who you bring with you, or if you're hiding anything outside the place, like a weapon. Some get a kick out of watching you watching for them. He wondered which category Chocker fit into.

None of the dozen or so preoccupied Amsterdam Flavour clientele looked up when he came through the door. Every person in the room represented a threat, a potential enemy, or someone hired for the explicit purpose of killing him.

He scanned their shoes, clothes, faces, and body language—*threat, no threat, threat, no threat*—and saw no immediate danger. Most were wrapped up in private worlds of adultery, money, and drink. Alcohol and the clandestine don't mix. Loose lips sink ships, and all that. Chalk this up to a business meeting.

He purposely hadn't taken any painkillers that morning so his head would be clear for whatever curves Chocker threw his way. He wanted to be able to read the subtle clues in his mentor's body language to see if they contradicted the words that left his mouth. Still, the hillbilly heroin had a lingering effect.

The restaurant décor was brass rails and dark, shiny wood, complemented by the smoking hostess walking toward him. She wore black and white with a card dealer's armband around her left bicep and a menu pressed flat against her chest. He had no idea about the significance of the armband, but it looked cool and nicely accented her toned physique. Fashion faux pas are easily ignored when stretched over an athletic teenage blonde.

"*Goede middag*. I'm Cindy." She bobbed her head from side to side and fidgeted with the stitched edge of a leather-bound menu—a girlish figure bottled in a black vest, long-sleeved white shirt, and tight black polyester slacks.

"*Ola*."

She laughed and displayed bleached enamel orthodontic sculpture framed by plush, purple lips. "Are you waiting for someone?"

"Yes, another gentleman." He paused for a moment, then said, "A business meeting."

"Of course." She gave him a knowing look he thought was apropos of nothing. *Did she know? Was she the one?*

The men's room door swung inward, and a tall, fit man in a dark blue suit extended his hand. John checked if it held a gun, or worse, was wet, and then reached out his own hand. They shook like old friends, lots of pumping.

"Johnny." It was the game show host smile again. "I'm glad you could make it."

"Yeah. Good directions." John pulled his hand away from the firm grip.

"Let's take a seat. My table is over there by the window." The man gestured to the wall closest to the parking lot.

So he saw me pull in. "Sure. You lead."

The tables were varnished, rough-cut pine with clustered initials carved on the top. The Amsterdam Flavour wasn't the place to which people brought knives. The owners had the initials put there for ambiance, to give the place a sense of an older time and to offset the chic modernity.

John waited as Chocker let the small computer perform its scan. Chocker closed the lid and set it on the chair beside him.

"I'm compromised, sir."

"Explain." Chocker's eyebrows came together and his jaw jutted out a little. The bags under his eyes had a purple tint, and his skin was shiny, like he hadn't showered this morning.

A waiter interrupted, placed their food on the table, and left.

"I ordered for you, buddy." Chocker put his face over the warm plate and inhaled. "We don't have a lot of time today."

John nodded.

"Can I get you anything else?" Cindy hovered a few feet away.

"Just a dessert menu, please." Chocker mouthed almost half the burger in one bite, and the waitress hurried away.

"He took my picture." John leaned in closer to Chocker. "He used that instant camera and took my picture."

"How far away were you?"

"I don't know, thirty, maybe forty feet."

Chocker swallowed hard and gulped some water. "Don't worry. Eat your fish."

He glanced down at his flounder piccata. The lemons looked suspicious. "Easy for you to say."

"It's good fish, John. This place is first-rate."

"Not the fish, the picture."

"Oh. Don't give it a thought. The camera is crap. From that distance there won't be any definition, especially under poor lighting. The place was poorly lit, wasn't it?"

John nodded and poked at his fish.

"You look like hell, son. Are you sure you're all right?"

"I'm just tired, Pete." He pushed away the capers and forced some of the tender filet into his mouth. "I'll be okay in a few days."

"And your leg?"

"I stitched it up right away. Had some antibiotics in the go bag. I'll be okay."

"Maggie?"

"She's in Albany at a teacher's conference until Sunday. I'll think of something by then."

Chocker pushed his plate to the side and swirled a french fry in a pool of ketchup. A busboy asked if Chocker was finished, and just got a stare. It was apparent to John that Chocker was in no mood for small talk.

"Give it to me again." Chocker pointed the red end of a french fry spear at him. "From the top."

"I took out both targets: one in the upper chamber, one in the tunnel chamber. Both went downstream. I found twelve bricks of ordnance and appropriate detonators and several feet of thin wire. All flowed downstream directly after the targets. Yoda engaged me at this point." John waited for a question, an interruption. Chocker just stared without blinking. "We struggled. I cut through my thigh to get to his, so he would break that constriction hold, and he exited up the stairs to the main chamber."

"You saw him at this point? His face, I mean."

"Perfectly," said John. "I pursued and took a gun from the body upstairs—"

"What body?"

John looked at him quizzically and said, "What do you mean?"

"You said both men went into the stream. What body?"

"It wasn't in that exact chronology. Sorry. I—"

"Then put it in that exact chronology, John. I asked you for a report, not a fairy tale."

This was not how John wanted the conversation to flow. He wasn't giving a report. He was being interrogated.

"Target one was eliminated. I left him, went downstairs, and eliminated target two. As I finished disposing of target two and the bricks into the tunnel, I was engaged by Yoda. We struggled; he escaped. I followed him to the main chamber and acquired a pistol from the corpse of target one. I took aim at Yoda, but he was already climbing the tanks, so I couldn't get off a round."

Chocker balled his fists until his knuckles whitened. John heard the crack of cartilage. "I told you it had to be primitive with these guys," said Chocker.

"It was not my intent to use a weapon, sir. I couldn't match him on the climb up the scaffolding. He was too fast, and I was unable to respond with my leg—"

Chocker raised his palm to stop John from explaining this detail further. "Now tell me how he got out of there. I checked the schematics. I don't see how. You tell me exactly how he got out of there."

"You think I'm embellishing, Pete. You want me to drop trou right here?" He grabbed his belt-buckle with both hands and glared at his mentor, letting him know he wasn't afraid of him, Yoda, or any other prick that wanted his shot at the title. The conversation was steering away from the professional arena and feeling more and more personal, and John didn't like it. "I'll show you the wound," he said.

Chocker took a deep breath and exhaled. "I just want to know how he left that chamber, John."

John saw something flash behind Chocker's eyes that he didn't like. As if someone had injected Chocker's soul with Novocain, devoid of all emotion. John realized his decision to work with Chocker required a separation from humanity, and his own emotions.

He had already surmised that no one in any government hierarchy knew who he was or the nature of his work except Chocker. He knew he was as far off the reservation as anyone gets: no traceable phones, nothing in writing, a one-man operation. He was no less a solo operative than Yoda. It was just a matter of perspective as to which side of right or wrong the unreliable scales of justice tilted.

The generic flash drives were probably downloaded from a computer far away from C. Peter Chocker's office—wherever that might be. John didn't even know if Chocker *had* an office, though he must. A deep-cover operative named Canaan had recruited John in Afghanistan, ostensibly for undercover assignments with the CIA. Everything had checked out so far: the checks came in the mail, Chocker had appeared at the winery, the missions were real and the intel accurate—well, almost. It was now possible that another team, a backup squad, was in the tunnel the whole time. On the other hand, who the hell was Canaan? He didn't report to any base. He was running around with hajjis, delivering contraband, raising goats, and fathering Afghan children.

John drank some water and stared back at the man who controlled a large part of his future. On the other hand, if Chocker didn't make it out of this restaurant alive, John's future was in his own hands. The clandestine nature of the operation worked both ways. Just as he was the only one alive—except maybe for Yoda—linking Chocker to the tunnel mission, Chocker was the only one alive linking John to the killings. The blade cut both ways, and blades were John Rexford's specialty.

"He climbed up the scaffolding in black spandex and ballet slippers," John continued, "and went out the louvers that vented to the upper chamber."

"You want to run that buy me one more time?"

"Imagine a tall black Asian weed with ballet slippers." John tasted the rice. It was heavy on butter and salt, just the way he liked it, but when he tried to swallow, his throat tightened up, so he abandoned it and drank some water. "One minute I'm alone with the dead guys, and the next I've got Captain Stretch Pants sucking my air and squeezing the life from my limbs." John remembered the sweet banana smell of Yoda's warm breath as the yogi had brushed his thin, moist lips against John's neck. The hairs on his nape prickled in recollection.

"There's no implication, John." Chocker gulped some scotch in the glass next to his empty plate. He licked his lips and added, "No implication whatsoever. I just want information. I need to know how this freak left the gridiron before the game was over and still managed to score a touchdown." Chocker smiled the slightest bit. "Clear?"

"Crystal." He stretched his legs and winced when the stitches pulled against his raw wound.

"You need something, soldier?"

"No, sir. I'm good."

"Just let me know if you do. We do have a medical plan, you know."

John tried to smile, but his heart wasn't in it. "He turned and took my picture by the tanks. Then he climbed the scaffold, jumped up, grabbed the vent louvers—the ones you must have seen in the schematics—and pulled himself right through, slippers and all. I watched his legs dangle for a moment, heard the pop, and he just pulled himself right up through. I'm sorry, Pete. I couldn't take the shot."

"Pop?"

"I think he separated his ball joints from his hip."

"Yogi freak." Chocker rubbed his palm against his mouth and chin. He cracked his knuckles in rapid-fire succession. "You sure you don't want a drink?"

"A beer would be cool."

"Now you're talking." He waved Cindy back to the table. "Get my friend here a Harp on tap. Would you do that, Cindy?"

"Certainly. Be right back. *Dank u.*"

"*U bent welkom,*" said Chocker.

"You speak Dutch?"

"Nine languages, buddy. Even some freaky Farsi dialects no one knows except people on the India/Pakistani border. But English will still get you around most of the world, thank God." Chocker grabbed another french fry and chewed on the burnt end.

John wondered how many more layers there were to C. Peter Chocker that he wasn't aware of and that he might never know. His stomach turned sour and he felt like he was going to lose the flounder for a moment. The fish swam up his throat, and he forced it back down with a swallow. He'd been in far tougher spots in his life and kept a cool head, but suddenly the whole room didn't seem right and a wave of paranoia rushed through his body, threatening his very existence. How many languages was Chocker not fluent in, but spoke well enough that he could get by? How many places could Chocker hide with his seemingly unlimited financial resources? What could a man like John Rexford do against a force like this?

"You okay, John?" Chocker pushed the water glass closer to him. "Take a drink. You look white. You need a doctor?"

John knew he wasn't okay, mentally or physically. He shook his head, drank some water, and surveyed the room. How many people here belonged to International Fiber Resources? It wasn't healthy to be this paranoid. He felt exhausted, but a marine learns to function through exhaustion. He was trained to continue and will the body forward, though it thought it couldn't go on. The brain knew it could always go a little farther—just put one foot in front of the other. *Your left, your le-eft, your left, right oh left . . .*

"Let's turn him in."

"What do you mean?" Chocker cocked his head.

"Send his info—description, injuries, who he works with, everything. Send it to the FBI."

"That is so far out of the realm of possibility, it doesn't warrant discussion."

"Then let me go after him, Pete." John unconsciously picked up the steak knife beside his plate. He pointed it in Chocker's direction as he spoke. "You give me everything you have on this bastard, and I mean everything, his complete file. I'll find him. I'll track him down and kill the bastard."

Chocker raised his hand cautiously, using his fingertip to guide the knife away. John looked at it, as if he didn't know it was there, and set it back down on the table.

"Listen to this once, soldier. We do not work with the feebs. They are not aware of our transactions, and if they were, you and I would go away for a long time."

"So you've turned me into a criminal. Thanks, Pete. Thanks one whole hell of a lot."

"What do you want, John? Did you think we were going to get a ticker tape parade down Broadway?"

"I don't need glory. I just need to hold my head up high, and I can't do that if you let Yoda go free."

Chocker lowered his head and clasped his hands together, then looked back up at John. "If he surfaces, I'll make sure you have the first crack at him. But don't hold your breath."

"That's not enough. I want his file. I'll know how to hunt him down, but I need more background. You give me what you got on him, and you will not regret it."

Chocker glanced at the parking lot. John looked out after him, as if they were both waiting for the same person.

"It's only me, John, really. You can relax, son." Chocker's voice was paternal, concerned. But was it his real voice? Who the hell was this guy?

"How do I know he's not coming after you, Pete? Maybe just being with you is compromising my position."

"Because no one knows me, John. It's the nature of the beast."

"So why don't you just contact me through the Internet?" Then you won't have to scan me and mess with my sperm count.

"Nice to know I'm working with a real eco-weenie. You mean like a URL posting?"

John nodded.

"They work to a point, but are only as secure as the people using them. I like face-to-face." Chocker chewed on the last fry and pointed it at John. "We had an agent working deep cover who communicated with a solo via URL. She was a real top gun . . ."

"An outsider?"

"A freelancer," said Chocker. "The best in the Asian theatre. She was a real looker, too. She was under our surveillance. We watched her go into an Internet café, checked out her terminal, made a call to the NSA, and traced every URL the computer pinged during her time online. From that point on we were able to intercept some of her messages, and even back-hacked the URLs she used."

"Damn, is nothing sacred?"

"Like I said, only as secure as the people using them," said Chocker. "I like face-to-face."

"You know about the man in Tora Bora, right?" John didn't wait for acknowledgement. "Canaan. The guy who eventually recruited me after I pulled him out of a tight spot. The guy who was supposed to save me if the desert burned." John looked at the parking lot again. Dark clouds bumped shoulders over the trees, and it looked like rain. "He smelled like burro shit, tobacco, and BO. I knew he was American, but I have to tell you, the man even fooled the Taliban. He looked Afghani, smelled Afghani, and spoke like a true believer. When I looked in his eyes. . . . You know how you can always tell by the eyes?"

Chocker winked through the ice at the bottom of his glass.

"There was no perceptible difference between him and the natives," John said. "He even took a wife. Married a local, raised goats and chickens. Rode a little Honda scooter. The tribal leaders didn't hassle him because he took a job running mail for the mayor and some other backwater smugglers who ran the town."

"I can't say that I know him, John. You know that. But it resembles a myth called Hell on Wheels.

"Who?"

"Hell on Wheels," said Chocker. "The story is that he is no longer there. The myth is that he's the best there is. Maybe even better than that slippery scum Yoda."

"Where is he now?"

Chocker gave a self-satisfied chuckle. "You're one funny bastard, soldier," said Chocker. "I told you it's just a story."

The sense of being the last man out annoyed him even more. "I need to see him," said John. "I want to talk to him."

"Maybe you're not getting this." Chocker leaned closer with a blank stare and said, "He's no longer available to you, John. I'm your fearless leader. Understood?"

"Then I'll ask you. When is this over?" John's tone was serious, interrogative.

"It's over when you say it's over, John." Chocker gave a closed-mouth smile. "You volunteered. No one drafted you. What's up?"

"I know. And I don't want out. I'm just wondering if there's an end in sight. In your plans, I mean?"

"Hey, Johnny, is it the girlfriend?"

"Yeah, Pete, it is the girlfriend. I'm starting to feel maybe I'd like to get a piece of this American dream I'm fighting for, and stop living like a ghost. You know?" John drank some beer to loosen his throat. The hillbilly heroin had a dehydrating effect. When Chocker didn't respond, he continued, "What's the meaning of life, and all that ephemeral bull. Maybe sell paper products."

Chocker chuckled, checked the platinum Rolex on his wrist, and leaned back in his chair. "We don't hold you, man. This isn't servitude, only service. Right now we have several more opportunities for you, after which you can make a decision if you want. It's always on you, my friend. You say the word and we pull the plug on this." Chocker hesitated, and then added, "If that's what you really want."

Chocker scanned the room and looked back at John, waited a few seconds, and said, "You already paid your dues, son. This country is safer because of you. You're doing it for every asshole out there who throws a fit because his wife only brought home vanilla ice cream and forgot the pistachio like he told her." He gave another almost imperceptible glance at his timepiece.

"Somewhere to go?"

Chocker ignored the question. "You're the guy who makes it so the fat dweeb's wife can safely go get ice cream instead of being burned alive in a suicide bomber's fantasy. But you stop when you lose the gut feeling that makes you tick." The flame in Chocker's eyes burned hot. At that moment, John realized he didn't want to face this bastard down in a firefight, or even at a closing for paper products. Chocker was unflappable in his resolve. On the other hand, if he was thrown in the river, someone would have to pay the ferryman, and Chocker was the only shark swimming in these waters.

"No problem. I'm just wondering how many more earthlings we have to save, is all?"

"I'd like to tell you it ends when all the bad guys are dead, but it won't happen in our lifetime. So it doesn't end." Chocker sighed and pulled his fingers from the joints with several small pops. "You're hell on wheels here, Johnny, what we need. We can't win without boots on the ground right here."

"So what's gonna happen when I'm done? I mean when I can't do this anymore?"

"Uncle Sam and IFR have got your back for the rest of your life, Johnny."

"IFR?"

"International Fiber Resources," Chocker said. "That government check is programmed for delivery to the little painted mailbox in front of your Catskill home for the rest of your natural life, and your wife's life, should you marry.

You don't have to worry about a damn thing. Your health benefits are covered no matter what happens with Obamacare."

Cindy appeared beside them with a cheery grin, her hands behind her back and her breasts comfortably corralled in the vest, but nudging at the buttoned gate.

"How about dessert, gentlemen?"

"Coffee and apple pie for me. What do you say?" Chocker looked at his fellow diner.

"Sure," John said. "I'll try some pie. No coffee. Thank you." He wasn't really hungry, but he remembered he had a part to play.

"Would you like another beer?" Cindy asked. John shook his head. "*Zeer goed*." She gyrated back to the kitchen.

"I thought about that, Pete."

"She's a little young, but not illegal," Chocker encouraged. "Go for it."

"No." John rolled his eyes. "Not her. The doctors."

"What about the doctors?" Chocker's expression turned quizzical.

"What if I ever have to prove I'm disabled? Won't that blow my cover?"

"Not going to happen," said Chocker. "You're on full disability. No one would have a reason to go back and check on you. You're in like Flynn, kid. Never gonna happen."

John swallowed the last of his Harp. "Not under this administration, or maybe even this president. But I'm only twenty-eight. It won't be so easy when the records say I have shrapnel in my knee and they take an x-ray and find healthy cartilage. I mean, it's nice having an excuse to set off metal detectors, but if I went through one, nothing would happen unless I was strapped."

"Not gonna happen, son."

"Here's another scenario," John said. "What if they come up with some new technology the government wants to try out on me and fix me? How the hell will I explain the metal in my knee melted away? No shrapnel. Not even a bullet in there."

John knew Chocker could sense the anxiety in his voice, though the soldier within him tried to maintain calm.

"Didn't our boys slice you up good and leave a few long scars to scare away any doctors?"

"That works for regular doctors. Some butcher from the military may want to try out a new program on me." John paused, and then whispered, "What do I do when they don't find any shrapnel in my knee?"

A waiter asked if they wanted anything else, and placed the pie gently on the tablecloth.

"Who's waiting on us here?" Chocker asked, bemused. "Is it you or Cindy? Because being hot, she gets the bigger tip, you know?"

"At Amsterdam Flavour we work as a team, sir. We pool our tips."

"Lucky for you." Chocker chuckled and patted the waiter's shoulder. "Just kidding, son, you're doing a great job. Could we have the bill when you get a moment? We have another engagement."

"Of course." The waiter walked away.

Chocker took a swallow of apple pie and slurped his coffee. He wiped his mouth with the linen napkin. "I know the bureaucrats running this country can't be trusted. But I can, Johnny. You don't worry about doctors or the FBI or anyone else." He pointed his fork at John. "Hell, if we have to, we'll put some goddamn shrapnel in your leg. Screw the doctors."

Another pseudo operation would be absurd, but John liked Chocker's flexibility. "I'm good with that, Pete."

"Good," Chocker replied. "Because I need you on point, 100 percent. Let's eat some pie."

When they had finished, Chocker slid a flash drive over the table. "Everything you need to know is in there. Burn it when you're done."

John palmed the flash drive. "I only want to know what I need to know, Pete."

"But?"

"But I usually have a little broader perspective on mission goals."

"Let me help you out." Chocker wiped his hands with his napkin and set it on his plate. "Brooklyn wasn't a prelude. It was a separate mission, but still relevant to the current op. Bari had supplied the Yemenis with the plans and ordnance. What you have on the flash drive is an after-the-fact order that needs to be fulfilled."

"After-the-fact?"

"We found where Brooklyn got his support," said Chocker. "How his training was financed overseas, and who paid off the people that gave those goons—who are now fish food, thanks to you—the tunnel schematics and dates of vulnerability. The current project is like going in and shutting the door after the horse is out; however, it will stop the rancher from buying more horses for a long time."

Brooklyn was a soldier. Now it was time to cut off financing. John felt better that the links in the chain were beginning to coalesce.

"You will be apprised as needed," said Chocker. "I don't want you thinking too far ahead. Stay on point, keep limber in mind and body."

"So we have a chance to break the bank here?"

"One of many banks, unfortunately," said Chocker. "This guy collects the money, sends it over there, where they train assholes like Brooklyn to come back here and do the damage. It's a wide circle of scumbags using American generosity against us. But what goes around comes around."

"I understand, Pete. I'll complete the circle."

"I know you will," said Chocker. "Now let's review the present before we get too far ahead of ourselves. Yoda is in the wind. We've lost all contact with him. You stopped them from cutting off the water supply and burning the five boroughs to the ground. Give yourself an attaboy and don't dwell on what you can't control."

John gave a nod and said thank you.

"It's not up to us to do damage control on those casualties in Valhalla. Leave that to the FBI and the mayor of New York. They're used to making excuses for themselves anyway. You've got to take this next guy out, or he'll just hire more people like Yoda—and believe me, our plate is already full."

A waiter placed the check on their table; Chocker gave it a cursory look and slid some bills into the server book.

"The whole country is on high alert right now, but the feebs are playing it down. My guess is they already know it was sabotage, but they don't want to start a panic. Or maybe they don't know yet, but they will. In the meantime, keep your head low, because everyone is a suspect and the tri-state area is going to be crawling with law enforcement. However you act, keep your head below radar at all times."

"SOP."

"I know, but you don't want to get caught in some chance roadblock and not have a reason for being there," said Chocker. "Look, John, I know you know your job. I'm just saying that everyone's so tweaked up right now, you have to do everything in classic form. Parse out your sectors methodically, have a good cover wherever you go . . ."

John's smirked a little, like a kid whose father told him he did a good job.

"Just crank it up a notch, if that's possible."

"I'm always cranked up a notch, Pete. It's my nature."

WOODSTOCK

The broker had given Yoda the requested information on Major John Rexford, retired military. He also informed Yoda that only half the money that was owed him for providing close personal protection to the two jihadists would be paid into his account: half for releasing the chlorine gas, nothing for failing to blow the aqueduct. Along with the constant pain in his thigh, this gave Yoda two hundred thousand good reasons to kill John Rexford.

The death broker found John Rexford's identity through a private, nonprofit organization that managed the nation's organ transplant system under contract with the federal government. He had used a highly paid contact in the organization's IT department in the past to track people down, knowing through experience that many military and patriotic people donated their organs so that others could live. Some people filled out a donor card and carried it with them, but many states had a donor registry and people simply signed off on the back of their driver's licenses. The contact ran John's approximate age, height, and weight through the national donor database, cross-referenced it against New York and New Jersey driver's licenses with facial recognition software, and got a match. All of the information on John Rexford's drivers license became available: full name, address, height, eye and hair color, and corrective vision restrictions, of which John had none. It was more than Yoda needed to help John die so that others may live.

Yoda had spent the last twenty-four hours performing surveillance by driving by the road that passed between John's home and the old man that lived in the trailer next door. After midnight, Yoda found a dirt road a few hundred yards from the house and drove his rusted Honda Civic into a thicket of pussy willows and small poplars. He spent the rest of the night taking catnaps and waiting for something to happen. He hated waiting. It reminded him of the monks in Bhutan and how they tried to teach him patience, how they humiliated him with that name: Zopa—patience. Planning was one thing and a necessity, but sitting for the sake of sitting was for fools.

The old man had left only once in his truck and returned with a brown paper bag of groceries. Rexford had returned last night, and his car remained in the driveway. Another car, a late model Chevrolet Cobalt sedan, had been in the driveway since yesterday and had not moved.

The next morning, that changed. A young woman in her late twenties left the house at 7:00 a.m. Yoda scrambled to his car and headed in the direction he had last seen her drive. She drove slowly, below the speed limit, and he was on her in less than a mile. He hung back and waited until she pulled into the entrance to Onteora High School. *So our assassin has himself a schoolteacher,* Yoda mused.

After giving her time to get to her class, Yoda parked in the visitor's parking area, entered the building through the main entrance, and followed the signs to the administrative offices.

"Can I help you?" A middle-aged woman with hair dyed black looked up at him. She used one hand to pull down on the frame of her glasses as she gawked over the rims. The nameplate on her desk read SALLY FROST.

"Yes. Hi."

"Hello," she said, and gave Yoda a smile that he knew was insincere, as if he didn't belong there.

"I'll be moving here shortly, you know. I have a small child, and she will be in school." Yoda smiled and spoke to her like a new immigrant who was proud that someone in his family might get an education from so stately an institution as the Onteora school district.

"You can't speak to anyone now." The woman continued typing at the keyboard. "School's in session, but you can make an appointment, if you like, with a counselor. How old did you say your daughter was?"

"I did not say." Yoda smiled and gave a slight bow. He knew that Americans liked it when Orientals bowed to them. They felt like they had the upper hand. "But she is six, you know."

"That would be Mr. Watkins, then. He counsels all the lower grades."

"I do not need to see him now. I'm just curious about the school hours," said Yoda. "I must make arrangements for after-school activities for little Sally."

"Your daughter's name is Sally?"

"Oh yes. Not her original name. Her original name is Salimu Chang, but Sally is easier, you know."

"I see," she said, but clearly, Yoda thought, she did not. "Well, Mr. Chang, the school closes for classes each day at two thirty."

"Two thirty? Good time to see a dentist." He smiled and bobbed his head as if she would get the joke.

"Pardon me?"

"It's old Chinese joke, you know. Not too funny."

The woman started typing again and kept her eyes on Yoda. "Is there anything else, Mr. Chang?"

"Oh no, I'm not Mr. Chang," said Yoda. He knew he couldn't kill her, not for free anyway, so he thought he would just play with her head for a while. "I'm Mr. Lee. Sally is adopted. Her parents died when Tibet massacred our people in the mountains, you know. You saw on CNN?'

"I'm very sorry," she said. "That is so terrible. I heard something about that. The Dalai Lama was involved, wasn't he?" The woman's lips formed a pout, and her eyebrows rolled up like a bespectacled beagle looking for a treat.

"Oh yes, his soldiers killed many of my countrymen. Very bad man. I must go now."

Yoda turned and left the room, leaving the woman with the most convoluted misrepresentation of the Tibetan independence movement he could come up with on short notice.

He drove back to the dirt road, hid his car again, and kept an eye on John's house with Leica Ultravid binoculars that fit in his palm as he perched from a vantage point thirty feet off the ground in a hemlock tree.

John left the house on his bicycle at noon. Yoda thought about going inside, but the old man's truck was still in the driveway, and he didn't need a potentially nosey neighbor calling the police. He snaked around the woods, up one tree and down the next, capturing all the angles of John's property he could without being seen. Yoda found the solitude pleasant and would have liked to stay longer, but two thirty quickly approached.

He drove to the school and parked across the street at an IGA grocery store. He had a few minutes to kill, so he bought himself a banana and a pint of plain yogurt and drank from the cup as he waited for the woman. He wasn't sure if this was John's girlfriend or wife at this point, and it didn't really matter. He was told that if you kill a man, he only dies once, but if you kill his loved one, he dies each day upon awakening.

The hot sun began to heat up his small car, so he rolled one window down. He didn't want to, but the heat was becoming unbearable. It was always best to keep your windows up during surveillance. Small bits of dirt and reflections distorted the view for anyone looking at the driver.

A convoy of school buses was parked in front of the school. Once the buses were all loaded with children, they began to pull out one by one. State troopers were parked at each end of the lot with their lights on, warning traffic to slow down. About fifteen minutes later, the teachers and other school administrators began to file out of the lot in their cars. John's girlfriend was one of the last to leave.

Yoda pulled into traffic with a two-car buffer between him and his target. He followed her ten miles into a small town called Woodstock. Over Main Street hung a banner that said World Awareness Day. *WAD*, he thought. In native Bhutanese there is no such thing as an acronym. Yoda found them fascinating.

Yoda watched her pull into a municipal parking lot in the center of town. He entered the same lot but through a different street, and parked at the far end. The woman left her car carrying a small backpack in her hand. Yoda followed as she window-shopped, never closer than one hundred feet away. There was no chance she knew him or was aware of his presence. Still, he followed the rules of engagement and crossed the street several times, used storefront window reflections to watch her every move, and ducked into a store here and there if her head turned his way.

The town was packed with people who seemed to be out of place. *Certainly they could not all be from here*, thought Yoda. They were all so different—not just a mix of races, but a mix of dress and attitude within the races. Most of them were white, some black, and a small percentage were Asian. They all wore the same pasted-on smile, like something wonderful was about to happen, or had already happened, and Yoda missed it.

Blue jeans or khaki shorts were the standard outfit for the crowd. Married couples, mostly in their late fifties or sixties, made up a large percentage of the people. They tried to look poor, or at least humble in their khakis and jeans, but Yoda knew better. Closer scrutiny revealed manicured fingernails and toenails, and hairstyles meant to be slightly edgy and cool but which cost fifty dollars every couple of weeks to maintain. The women always gave it away: expensive, handmade jewelry hung from their throats, wrists, and fingers. Even their tiny white toes were ringed in gold. For all their attempts at being laid-back and part of the scene, this group of whites dripped pretentiousness.

The teenagers were different. They appeared to actually be poor and lacked a high degree of personal hygiene. Yoda smelled bhang on their clothes. The sweet smell was familiar to him and reminded him of India, the first place he'd fled after leaving the monastery.

The woman went into a store that sold chimes. Yoda took the opportunity to get closer to a curious group of women on the street corner who were dressed in black and holding cutouts of large black hands stuck to broom handles. The women were protesting something, and Yoda wanted to know what it was.

He stepped closer and picked up a brochure that identified this group as Women in Black. A quick glance at the brochure told him that Women in Black was a worldwide network of women committed to peace with justice, and was actively opposed to injustice, war, militarism, and other forms of violence. They claimed to use nonviolent and nonaggressive forms of action to protest what they thought were bad behavior in others.

He laughed to himself when he read the part about how they took action by sitting down and wearing black clothes to mourn the dead. They were all middle-aged and well-fed. It was obvious they had never experienced war or any of the violence Yoda knew firsthand. American television, he had learned from watching, showed very little of the real killing and how it was done. *This country likes pictures of bombs blowing up. Close-up hatchet work doesn't sell cars.*

He nodded to one of the Women in Black who took notice of him. She nodded back but did not say anything. All the better. She wore expensive black jeans, had tinted hair, and sported shoes that cost more than a man in Bhutan made in a year. Yoda was about to ask the woman how many people her group had saved, because he had traveled to over thirty countries and had never heard of them.

Rexford's woman stepped from the doorway of the chime store and crossed the street. Yoda broke away from the WIB group and stepped into a store full of colorful T-shirts. He bought a shirt that was two sizes too big and put it on, then picked up the trail again.

A tall old man walked past him pulling a wagon. The man smelled very bad—not sweet like bhang, but more like piss and sweat. In the wagon was a small television set connected to a VCR that ran off a battery. A black-and-white home video played on the small television screen. The images were of people laughing around a table, and then the tape just kept looping over and over. This man hadn't come to visit WAD. Yoda realized that the man somehow belonged there, that he fit in perfectly, but that he was too far gone mentally to engage in conversation. He stepped away from the man. A simple rule of surveillance was to not engage anyone who stood out. On the other hand, the man seemed to be the less obvious standout of them all, because he looked like he belonged. He carried himself like he was there, in the moment. Yoda respected him, but did not interact.

Main Street rolled to the center of town, to a square with a little park with benches and well-maintained landscaping. Yoda had heard the drums beating the moment he left his car in the municipal parking lot, and now he saw the origin of the sound. Different sizes of drums were arranged in a circle, and it appeared anyone could sit down and beat them as they wished. Yoda recognized the conga, and a few tam-tams, and a Japanese taiko drum. He had been to Japan; he had killed there. WIB had not been there to protest his actions or offer any help to the dying.

Yoda listened and liked what he heard. At first, it seemed everyone was just beating away in his or her own rhythm. After a minute or two he began to hear an undertone, a simple beat that emanated throughout the circle. It was strange to him how these different people who had never practiced together could create a oneness of beat. The longer he stood there, the stronger and more hypnotic the beat became. He felt it bump against his heart. He began to rock in a slow side-to-side motion with the people standing around him.

John Rexford's woman took an open seat in front of a conga, set her small backpack on the ground beside her, and picked up a wooden drumstick with a soft cloth ball on the end. She was timid at first, not striking too hard. The sound her drumstick made was all but drowned out by the other players, but

Yoda could hear it. It came to his ears in small circles and pushed against his brain as he watched her delicate hands wave the stick down against the tight skin of the drum, and then up into the air near her tanned face. Down against the tight skin, and up toward her straight black hair. Down against the tight skin and up to her soft brown eyes and the corners of her mouth, and the lips, the soft lips.

She gained courage and banged the drum harder until her tempo and volume matched the other players in the circle and she became one with them. Yoda heard two sounds now: the steady rhythm of the group thumping a slow bass beat in unison, and the woman's individual beat as she waved the drumstick and brought it down against the tight skin of the conga.

The woman did not belong to this crowd. She wore blue jeans, true, but the rest of her outfit was a white T-shirt and cheap sneakers. She wore no jewelry and did not tint her hair. Her face was free of makeup, and her body was lean and fit like a runner's. The woman shown above the others in the drum circle like a young seedling in a garden of overripe fruit. She didn't wear the pasted-on smile, and appeared to be naturally happy with her own presence. John Rexford had chosen well.

A seat opened beside her as a chubby man in khaki shorts hoisted his bulky frame with great difficulty and hobbled away. Yoda took the seat in front of the vacant conga beside her and picked up the orphaned drumstick. He breathed in slowly, cracked some small bones in his neck to relieve tension, and hit the drum with a metered beat. He listened for the deep bass sound he had heard before, the sound that the group made. He focused on it and clicked with the cadence immediately. A smile spread across his face, and the woman turned toward him and smiled.

Yoda gave her a sideways glance and smirked as if to say he was a badass drummer, and didn't she think so.

Just when Yoda had begun to feel the strength of the beat, a man stood up in the center of the drum circle and raised his hands. One by one, each person stopped drumming.

"A moment of silence for the sick and suffering around the world." The man raised both hands and bowed his head ceremoniously.

"I am Jigme," said Yoda. He smiled his own relaxed and genuine smile, not the phony one he used for copy shop employees and high school secretaries. He put out his hand slowly, to show that he was no threat.

"Maggie," she whispered. "I'm Maggie. Nice to drum with you, Jimmy." She put her small hand in his, and he shook it gently. His hand did not linger in hers but politely pulled away after the customary American two to three shakes. There were no rings on her fingers. It proved nothing in these times; still, a man like Rexford would want to mark his territory with a diamond.

"Let us clear the air for a moment," said the man in the center of the drum circle. "And when you feel like it, please drum again. But remember where your sounds are going and whom they are for. If we don't remember those who suffer around the world, no one will. Keep them aware."

Yoda leaned a little closer to Maggie to indicate what he said was semiprivate. "He is a little self-centered, maybe? Do you think?"

She laughed softly and put her drumstick to her mouth for a second. "I suppose there are more people out there than us who can remember the suffering."

"Dreams and anguish bring us together."

"What a strange thing to say." She said this politely, with questioning eyes.

"I don't mean to insult anyone," said Yoda. "It's just that none of us here are actually suffering too badly. Maybe a blister on our thumb." He smiled and raised his drumstick. "We can go home and have our spouses lick our wounds today."

He waited to see if she would respond with anything that indicated she had someone to lick her wounds. Maybe something like "my man doesn't lick wounds," or, "wouldn't that be nice."

"Dreams and anguish," said Maggie. "Are you saying if we, I mean other people, didn't suffer, then they would not get together?"

"I have seen that most people come together at times of suffering more than other times. Look at all these strangers—even me and you. We would not be here to beat the drum if this town had not come together to worship suffering. Everyone would be at home, or shopping."

"Where are you from, Jimmy?"

"Jig-me."

"Oh, sorry."

"It's okay. My name is a strange one, even among by friends in Tibet."

"Tibet," said Maggie. "Then maybe some of these drumbeats will make it all the way there."

Yoda lowered his head for a moment. "These people are nice, Maggie, but this sound does not help the poor of the world. If you're in need, would you go to a poor man or a rich man?"

"I guess a rich man."

"Perhaps," said Yoda. "But I have found it is always the poor man who will give you a hand."

"You have a good point, Jigme." She said his name slowly to get it right and Yoda smiled, pleased at her consideration. "But I think these people here today are just trying to make a spiritual connection. They are not asking for anything."

"In my travels, among poor people, I haven't found any asking for the help of drum noise. I'm sure they care very little about the drums."

A young girl began to beat her drum, and in a few seconds the circle started up again, tenuously at first, and then with a cohesive pulse. Maggie picked up her drumstick and softly struck the conga skin. When she didn't say anything, he added, "Perhaps they ask for nothing, but I don't think they have been asked either. These people will be the same when the drums stop beating."

Maggie kept her rhythm and stared straight ahead.

"Would you like to get some tea or a drink?" Yoda asked.

"No thank you. I'm just going to sit for a moment and then go home. But thank you."

Yoda placed his drumstick on the conga and stood. "Have a nice day then."

He walked behind her, leaned close to her ear, and said, "The living need charity more than the dead."

Maggie beat the drum for another minute and then risked a slight turn of the head to see if he was still there. She exhaled in relief to see a little boy and his mother waiting behind her to take her seat at the drum circle.

At home, in her kitchen, Maggie dumped the contents of her SpongeBob backpack, looking for the grocery list she had prepared during a break between classes. She wanted to add mozzarella for the chicken cutlet parmesan she would make John this weekend. She had to have buffalo mozzarella, and the only place to get it was a family-run Italian deli in Kingston. Her mother never served her father anything but buffalo mozzarella because it wasn't dry like the factory processed cheese, and the few times she had, Antonio Castalia had made a fuss.

Key chain, gum, small notebook, calculator, tissues, hand lotion—*where was it?*—pens, rubber bands, sunglasses, sunglass case without sunglasses in it, cell phone, hair scrunchie, sunblock SPF 80, aspirin—*damn!* The bottle was empty—small brush, Wite-Out, crumbled yellow sticky note with illegible writing, tiny flashlight with dead battery, ChapStick, handheld mirror, hand sanitizer. By the time she had hit bottom, all that was left was the partially sucked and rewrapped menthol cough drop she hadn't wanted to waste. She checked the side pocket: nothing there but a brochure from the Women in Black. She didn't remember picking up a brochure and putting it in there. *Strange how the mind works*, she thought, and went about starting a new list with buffalo mozzarella as the first entry, and aspirin second.

THE WESTCHESTER

Dark blue nipples protruded from the ceiling every one hundred feet, and directional cameras monitored the dead spots. John couldn't avoid security camera detection in the mall, so he stuck to the walls and kept his head tilted downward. He wore his baseball cap low on his forehead and kept his folded windbreaker around his neck. Law enforcement wouldn't be looking for him if everything went right, but it was prudent to keep his face covered just the same. He had to focus not to limp.

The Westchester was a high-end shopping mall whose name took advantage of the county's blueblood reputation. It was a place where upscale mommies could leave little Tiffany and Parker with the Nebraskan nanny while they badgered their private shopper over acres of marble and carpeted floors, and sucked on bottled spring water or latte under fluorescent lights that accented their Lancôme tints. Neiman Marcus and Nordstrom were The Westchester's anchor stores.

It had been ten days since the chlorine release, and the FBI stuck to their story that it was an accident. The more paranoid and less trustful citizens still hung at the fringes of Westchester County and stayed with relatives and friends, but most were back at their jobs. The mall had suffered for a few days, but consumers had already returned in full force, whether in blissful denial or because they needed their fluorescent-washed spending fix. The teenagers, with youth's innate sense of indestructibility, came because they needed a place to hang out.

John wolfed a quick order of orange peel shrimp at P.F. Chang's China Bistro to settle his growling stomach. Next stop: Neiman Marcus, where he paid cash for two hypoallergenic, synthetic, yet somehow "green" pillows and a black windbreaker.

He went into the men's room, walked to the last stall, and stuffed the memory foam pillows into his shirt. When he had positioned them correctly, they hung over his belly and gave the illusion of pudgy back fat. He buckled his belt and covered up with the black windbreaker. Next came the yarmulke, beard, and thick glasses he'd purchased earlier at Beyond Halloween Costumes in Yonkers. They had everything a good spook needed.

He put his shoulders back, splayed his feet a little, and looked down his nose through nonprescription, Coke-bottle glasses. A good semiorthodox Hasidic Jew waddling through the mall. The image staring back from the mirror told him he had nailed it. He favored his right side a little with the waddle. It was a nice touch, and easy to perform with a healing gash in his thigh.

Amateurs get hung up trying to make a disguise perfect. First impressions are all the average person sees—a vague outline with a few focal points. The observer's mind fills in the rest of the picture based on previous knowledge and prejudices, like an airbrushed centerfold. Porn lovers only see pigment on two-dimensional shiny paper but imagine three-dimensional perfection, minus moles and scars. The eye picks up every detail, but the brain glosses over warts, and we see what pleases us. Only through intense hypnotherapy can a subject be made to recall unsettling details the brain has airbrushed. A bearded, fat white guy, with a white shirt, black windbreaker, yarmulke, and a pronounced pigeon-toed waddle was all anyone at the Westchester would need to develop an image. Their blueblood upbringing would fill in all the blank spots and brush over the unsightly details. Bigotry completed the finishing touches.

He stuffed the Neiman Marcus bag in the trash and went out among the masses, the earthlings.

Few of the earthlings carried shopping bags. Mid-September was traditionally slow, and the Dow Jones Industrials weren't helping matters. Back-to-school sales were winding down, and few shoppers were pumped for Christmas. A herd of teenagers and unemployed adults pressed cell phones into their craniums, soaking up the microwaves. If he had known ten years earlier about the coming boom in cell phones, he would have gone to medical school. Brain surgeons were going to hit a Klondike when the tumors started to metastasize.

He didn't see well through his glasses, so he kept them near the tip of his nose. He stopped at a kiosk that sold handmade, all-natural soaps, and feigned interest. In the next kiosk a man sold remote-control helicopters. Two wide-eyed young boys looked on as the man paced the helicopter through several takeoffs, aerial maneuvers, and landings. He talked the entire time he piloted the miniature flying machine. *Chocker would love this guy.* Best of all, he sounded like a Russian. *Sometimes life throws you a softball.*

"Not like Brookstone," said the salesman. "They have one channel. Helicopter goes round and round, like this." The Russian's eyes narrowed and he smiled as he picked up the Hasidic Jew in his peripheral vision. The miniature helicopter flew around and around in a drunken pattern. Then, either by accident or design, the pilot crashed it into the kiosk.

"You see? Round and round. But it is strong. It can take a crash." He held the chopper in his left hand, and manipulated the remote control in his right until it took flight again. "You need two channels to do this."

He maneuvered the bird back and forth in a straight line and around in a circle to show what a one-channel did, and then back and forth in a straight line again to show the advanced movement achieved with two channels.

The kids walked away, their fingers rapidly texting details of the presentation to their friends. John filled the void with a two-step waddle.

"Does it hover?" He pronounced the "h" with a throaty Hasidic roll.

John waited for a hint of prejudice, an annoyed expression. Russians, in general, didn't treat the Jews any better than Hitler; and in their current monochromatic society, old prejudices remained. But he felt no animosity or disdain from the salesman.

"Hover?" He pronounced it "hoover," like the vacuum cleaner. "No. Two channels does not hover. Look."

The Russian tried to make the helicopter hover, but only managed tiny circles by manipulating the toggles. He scanned John from yarmulke to floor, as if sizing him up. Some Hasidic Jews lived like paupers, having given their money to the rabbi, who then doled it out in a monthly stipend. The others—the prosperous ones—owned their own businesses, tithed a small amount to the rabbi to shut him up, and kept the rest. The Russian wasn't sure which he was dealing with, so he gave an inviting smile and held out the controls.

"Go on. Give a try."

John suppressed an ear-to-ear grin. He had loved remote-control toys since childhood, but the Rexfords had little disposable income, so he had settled for playing with other kids' remote-control dune buggies and Batmobiles.

His first attempt at a takeoff crashed onto the gray marble tiles. He had used too much rudder and throttled up too fast. The little electric engine had torque.

The Russian took the controls, gave the toggle sticks a gentle *tap-tap-tap*, and said, "Like this, easy." He patted John's shoulder and gave him an encouraging nod to try again.

The little bird spiraled in ever larger circles and maintained a holding pattern at an elevation of about fifteen feet.

"What's the range?"

"Range?" the Russian repeated.

Do these Russians always have to repeat the question?

"How far can it fly?" John said.

"One hundred feet, give or take." The Russian tilted his open palm from side to side.

John smiled as if to say *not bad*, and took the helicopter up to the ceiling, where it circled beneath the Westchester's skylights fifty feet overhead. The Russian's expression lost its equanimity as he watched his inventory disappear on a path that would likely lead to a crash-landing. John brought the hissing bird earthward at full speed. He pulled up from the dive just as the landing skids buzzed the salesman's matted black hair.

"Jesus in Christ. What the hell, man?" The Russian's expression changed from fear, to anger, to laughter in a split second. "You are damn good flyer. You want to buy one?"

Always ask for the sale.

"How long does the battery last?"

"Battery?"

Yes, the battery, Boris.

"Twenty minutes for normal person," he said. "For you, probably ten. You drive like a crazy man." He patted the sleeve of John's windbreaker.

"How much?"

"Twenty-five dollars."

"You will take a credit card?" He already knew the answer.

The Russian gave an apologetic look. "I'm sorry. The machine does not work today." Russians were black market masters. In a society where the best means of survival was to stick it to the Kremlin, cash was king. They brought this inherent distrust of banks and government to the United States with them.

"I don't think I have enough cash," said John. "Let me see." He reached into his left pants pocket and pulled out a crumbled twenty and three singles.

"Twenty is good. No problem." The Russian was quick to close the deal. He put two boxed helicopters on the counter. "Green or black?"

The black was a close replica of the Apache Longbow. John had spent a few hours aboard them in Afghanistan. Against all regulations, the pilot had let him fire the cannons. It was like reaching out with a long arm and pulverizing the earth. He pointed at the Longbow.

"I need a bigger one, too. One that hovers." John laid the accent on heavier than ever. He wanted Boris to remember the Jew. He motioned to the boxes under the counter. "What do you have back there?"

"Those are the best," said the Russian. "I have not put them up yet. Just came in. You want hover? This baby can hover. And she is RTF. You don't find that in a big bird like this." The Russian placed the helicopter on the counter.

"RTF?"

"Ready To Fly. Charge the battery for eight hours, turn it on, and you are in business."

The helicopter they had flown was five inches high with a ten-inch rotor diameter. This chopper's box boasted a twenty-eight-inch main rotor diameter, seven-inch tail rotor diameter, and thirty-four inches from canopy to tail. Red, white, and blue, it resembled a corporate jet copter chassis more than a fighting machine. It had a pleasant karma about it, not like the little killer wasp John had purchased.

"This hovers?" said John.

"Like a seagull. Nine channels, twenty-two-volt lithium battery with extended life. She can fly for over one hour, even with you for pilot." He gave a real Russian *ha-ha-ha*. "Comes with AC adapter and charger."

"How fast can it go?"

"How fast?"

They really do repeat everything. Maybe the Russian needed time to formulate a lie.

"You know, miles per hour."

"I don't know." The Russian responded with a tone that said no one had ever asked, and then said, "Let's look at box."

And moose and squirrel.

Sweat ran down John's armpits from the pillows insulating his waist. It wouldn't be long before his perspiration bled through the windbreaker. He had to move this along before all his pores opened.

He had kept his glasses up by his eyes so the Russian didn't get a good look at them, but now he rested them toward the tip of his nose and read the helicopter's technical specifications from the box. The manufacturer claimed it traveled at four hundred miles per hour, scale speed. Actual airspeed was closer to eighty miles per hour. Still, no slouch.

"How much?"

"Two-fifty."

"Maybe I should get a gas-powered one?"

"No, no, no. You want to mess with gas?" Boris shook his head. "First of all, it's going to cost you at least six or seven hundred dollars to get one like this in gas version. Then you cannot fly anyway because of noise. Every town has restrictions on gas planes. You have to go to special club. Pain in the ass."

John had no intention of joining a hobby club. But he didn't want the machine gun sound a gas-powered piston engine made on his mission either. He had played with friends' Cox gas-powered model airplanes as a kid, and they were anything but discreet.

"Plus, they're not so easy to fly." Boris wasn't giving up. "You are good, but you need two people to fly them. They do not take off so good, and sometimes go out of range. You need a range finder so you don't crash. Big headache."

The Russian had a point. John needed something fairly quiet, though complete silence wasn't required, and he couldn't employ a copilot for this mission.

"Remove it from the box," said John. "We'll have a look."

The box advertised in bold yellow and black that inside was the ultimate flying machine: a radio-controlled Super Rat RTF helicopter.

Boris opened the box and placed the Super Rat on the counter. Together the men gave the helicopter a once-over worthy of two Underwriters Laboratories technicians. The Super Rat had a carbon fiber body and frame, which made it light and strong, but not necessarily good for smashing into things. The carbon-fiber canopy wouldn't withstand much impact. Would it disintegrate from a top-speed crash with a stationary object?

John lifted the cockpit doors and looked inside. He found what he had hoped for: two separate injection molds, anchored by rivets to an aluminum bar, supported the canopy. The bar riveted to both sides of the cockpit maintained structural integrity and connected to another bar in a "T" shape to support the nose. It would have to do. If not, he would have to go gas-powered.

He had checked the Internet before this trip to the Westchester. The gas-powered helicopters had more metal parts, more powerful motors, and lifted a heavier payload. He didn't want to make structural modifications unless absolutely necessary. This mission required that the machine look like it had just come out of the box.

"Two-twenty," said the Russian. He patted his shirt pocket and put his hand back on the counter. A smoker, or someone trying to quit.

An uncomfortable moment passed, and then Boris broke the salesman's cardinal rule and spoke first. "What do you think?"

John wanted to Hasid him down a few more dollars to stay in character, but his crotch and armpits were saturated.

"I'll go to a cash machine," said John. He pointed at the Super Rat. "You wrap it up. Throw in an extra battery, okay?"

"No can do, boss. Battery cost me thirty dollars. I will give to you for my cost."

Well, you got your two-fifty, Boris.

"Wrap it up. I'll be right back."

"You got it, boss. The remote control takes two C-cell batteries. Rechargeable. No charge for you."

There was a pun in there, but he wasn't sure Boris got it.

John took the food court escalator to the floor below, and dawdled in front of Tiffany & Co. He didn't go in, because he'd been there before, and their engagement rings started at about ten grand and climbed quickly.

The combined aroma of Taco Bell and Cinnabon didn't sit well with the orange peel shrimp in his stomach. A seltzer might help, but he changed his mind when he realized he needed to get out of there before his clothes dripped to the floor.

John had a little more than two thousand dollars in his pocket, but hadn't wanted to show it to the Russian. He had planned on spending around three hundred on the chopper, and guessed he would need the rest for his proposition to Boris.

He kept his back to the other shoppers, counted out two hundred and fifty dollars, folded it, and placed it in his right pocket. He counted another eight hundred in one-hundred-dollar bills, placed them in his left pocket, and put the rest in his back pocket. He lingered around for about the amount of time it would take to find an ATM and went back to Boris. He took the stairs and came at the Russian's kiosk from a different direction. Boris fished for opportunity with a small copter.

John pulled the money from his right pocket and handed it over.

"What's your name?" said John.

The Russian raised an eyebrow and counted the bills.

"Uri."

"I'm Yoseph Mandelbrot. Call me Yossi."

"Good to meet you, Yossi." He shook John's hand softly. "You need receipt?"

"No, no, no." Uri would appreciate the small-scale tax evasion. "I have a proposition for you, Uri."

Uri gave him a "what bullshit is this" look.

"My group is having a picnic in a couple weeks," John said.

"A small, family-style get-together. We will be at FDR Park. There will be many kids, and I would like to hire you to come and fly your helicopter. No selling. Just fly the birds so the children can enjoy."

"Yeah?" Uri stuffed the cash in his pocket. "I don't think so."

"You should bring a few planes—"

"Helicopters," Uri corrected him.

"Of course." John slapped his own forehead with the palm of his hand in a symbolic "Oy vey, what a schlemiel I am," and then said, "One for you to fly and maybe a couple for the kids. The parents would love it. It will keep the children entertained. I wouldn't ask you to sell anything, understand. But bring a few extra and keep them in the car in case someone wants one." He winked. "It couldn't hurt."

"I can't leave the business." Uri waved at his kiosk like it was the Taj Mahal. "Who will run it?"

"I have a personal question. How much will you do in sales in a day?" John made a point of looking around. He suspected he had purchased the only helicopters so far today.

"It changes day to day."

"Our picnic is on a Saturday . . ."

"Oh, no." Uri raised his hands in supplication. "That's my biggest sales day. I could sell maybe two thousand that day. Sorry."

"But two thousand isn't all in your pocket." He patted his pant leg. "I'm saying I will give you five hundred dollars to work at our picnic for two hours, maybe three. You can enjoy the park, nosh a little, and hire someone to run the store. Surely, you know someone who could handle the store for a few hours?"

Uri rubbed his chin stubble.

John took the roll of bills from his left pocket, counted off five hundreds; careful not to touch them with his fingertips, folded them, and palmed them so only Uri could see. Uri looked around, and then back at the hand with the money.

"Where is this place?" Uri asked.

John motioned Uri back to the counter. He pulled a pen from his shirt pocket and flipped over a flyer to write on. He wrote the address, date, time, and lot number for the picnic in block letters with left-handed doctor's scrawl, careful not to touch his fingertips on the paper or countertop.

Uri looked on with interest. "I will lose some sales. Not to mention having to hire someone I can trust. Eight hundred."

John pulled the remaining three one-hundred-dollar bills from his pocket, put them with the others, and smoothly moved his hand toward Uri. Uri took the money and nonchalantly put it in his pocket.

"It's all right here, Uri." John pointed at the paper. "Franklin Delano Roosevelt, Saturday in two weeks, two o'clock to maybe four or five. Stay at least until four. Remember, please don't try to sell helicopters to the children. You are entertainment." He winked again, and then said, "But if you have a few in the car, it couldn't hurt."

"And what if I don't show?"

This was a good spot for a Bruce Willis snappy comeback like, "I'll turn these helicopter rotors on high and use your balls for a piñata," but it would spoil the mood.

"Then you give the money back," said John. There was an uncomfortable silence. The chance Uri might not show lingered in the air. "I'll be there a little after three. You set up and don't worry about a thing." He patted Uri's shoulder. "Tell them you're with Yossi if anyone asks, and play with the helicopters. The children will be so happy."

He shook Uri's hand to seal the deal and walked toward the food court. He glanced back at Uri, who was talking with a customer, and then took the stairs to the street. He rode a shuttle bus to the Mamaroneck Avenue lot where he had parked the Subaru. It was several blocks away, but it was an outdoor, daytime-only lot with no security cameras.

He removed his Yossi Mandelbrot disguise and the pillows as he drove, and stuffed them into a garbage bag on the seat. He pulled into a gas station two towns over in Elmsford, filled up the tank, and stuffed the garbage bag into a trash can by the pumps, doubtful the police would check every garbage can in concentric circles from Uri's kiosk. Even the feebs, as Chocker liked to call them, wouldn't have the tenacity to go this far from ground zero. Besides, the picnic wasn't for another two weeks, and the pillows, beard, glasses, and yarmulke would be in a New Jersey landfill by then.

How bizarre was this life? He had just purchased a Chinese-made miniature replica of a US helicopter, in the United States, from a Russian, to kill a Muslim. *It truly is a global economy.*

And if Uri didn't show? A Russian decoy iced the cake, but John would still have to bake it.

Yoda had noticed the water in the Ashokan Reservoir was very low. Could it have been from his work in Kensico? Not likely. The chlorine explosion had only temporarily diverted water from Kensico to Hillview. Thanks to John Rexford, the aqueduct was back on line at full capacity. It was late in the year, and the summer had been dry. Large riprap walls led from the road to the water below. Farther out, small islands, previously submerged, poked up to greet the air and gasp breath from the world they had previously occupied, only to be drowned again when the fall rains came. There had been no need to follow Maggie closely to find where she lived, because traffic had been slow and there was little danger of her turning too suddenly for him to react.

Route 28 is a long, mostly straight road with few turnoffs in the section between Woodstock and Mt. Tremper. If you did want to turn off, you had to signal way in advance, otherwise jacked-up New Yorkers in a hurry to get to their second homes for the weekend would pile drive their SUVs into your rear bumper. The long, level straightaways had a calming effect and lulled motorists into autopilot mode that made this section of Route 28 the deadliest in Ulster County.

Traffic tonight was nearly nonexistent. It was 3:00 a.m and almost everyone was tucked in their sleeping bags, except a few hardcore drinkers mesmerized by their campfires.

Campfires dotted the Esopus Creek, guiding Yoda on his way to Mt. Tremper, where he turned off Route 28 to Maggie's side road. He pulled the Civic into a clearing where loggers had stacked felled trees, and hid the car behind a tall pile of thirty-foot timbers.

Coyotes yipped in the distant fields, on the hunt for small game or the stray domestic pet. Tree frogs chorused like a million tiny whistles as they verified one another's positions for a possible mate. Yoda padded silently through the forest in his ballet slippers and black spandex, sliding through underbrush and over soft pine needles that bowed beneath his feet. The smells of forest mushrooms and a nearby wetland filtered into his brain. The dark woods took away the normal distractions of daylight, and his sense of smell and sound were tuned exponentially. Diurnal deer mice and small chipmunks scurried as he approached, caught off guard by Yoda's muted gait. He slid between forest shadows like black ink poured over velvet.

He lay down on the freshly cut grass at the edge of lawn that bordered the small cape where Maggie slept. The windows in both dormers were open, so he could not be sure which room contained his sleeping target. His eyes peered over irregular blades of mowed grass, and he breathed in and exhaled until there was no air left in his lungs. He relaxed his diaphragm and let the air expand his chest a molecule at a time as it tickled the hairs in his nostrils. No mouth breathing, only nose breathing, in this exercise. He needed to smell for pets: dog scat, cat urine, anything that would expose the presence of a domestic animal. As deep a sleep as Maggie's dreams may take her, pet owners were quite attuned to the sounds of their animals. Even the low growl of a dog or the quick scurry of a cat over a wooden porch could wake them. All Yoda smelled was fresh grass and water from a puddle formed under a coiled, leaky hose on the ground next to the foundation—a green python that could trip an amateur.

Yoda stood up and worked his way along the edge of the property, along the ecotone between the mowed grass and the wild shrubs at the lawn's edge. Open Bilco doors led to the basement. He walked down the bluestone and concrete steps, and brushed his fingers against a railroad tie retaining wall to feel for vibrations in the earth. He pushed lightly on the wooden-framed, bent screen door, and stood inside a mudroom. He smelled death immediately. The putrid rot of a small animal lingered near his head. He lightly ran his fingertips over the sill plate until they encountered the swollen body of a decomposing mouse in a trap. Maggie wouldn't set these traps if she had a house cat.

No dog shit on the lawn; dead mouse in the mudroom. It was safe to assume, for the moment, that the only two live mammals in the building were human.

Yoda applied pressure to the basement door. At first it didn't move, and he was concerned that there might be a deadbolt. But a little more careful, consistent pressure, and the door budged an inch inward. He stepped inside the basement and pushed the door almost closed behind him without letting it rub against the jamb. He smelled fuel oil and dust.

He found the darkest spot in the room and stared at it for a full two minutes. This allowed his eyes to adjust and make everything else seem brighter. The basement was cluttered with storage boxes and plastic buckets, the kind gardeners use to start plants in the early spring.

A small electric spark spat a few feet away, and he crouched. It was the boiler kicking on to heat the hot water. He used the background noise to climb the wooden steps that led to the first floor, then waited by the door until the boiler shut off. A slight breeze floated through the basement window screens, cool against his face.

Country people still felt invulnerable in the Catskill Mountains and weren't concerned about break-ins and theft. Only the second homes and camps, abandoned on weekends, were hit by petty thieves. The local residents were left untouched, for the most part. The basement windows could have been used as a primary entrance if the doors were not so carelessly left open, and they were always a possible exit in a pinch. Yoda doubted he would need them for what he was about to do.

He ran his fingers over the wooden door with both hands in two large "S" motions. The bottom of the door was rough and splintered, with deep gouges he recognized as claw marks. A previous tenant must have locked the dog in the basement, where it had clawed for hours, maybe days, whining and scraping in fruitless pleas for freedom. Yoda felt the animal's loneliness linger like a ghost in the damp room.

He paid careful attention to the edges of the door frame for alarm wiring and magnetic strips. Only when he was confident the door was not alarmed did he place his hand on the round knob and turn it slowly, a quarter inch at a time. The latch was sticky and needed lubricant, but it pulled from the door frame, out past the strike plate, and back into the lock. He knelt at the top of the stairs, opened the door slowly, listened for hinge creaks, and waited for any motion or sound in the room.

The air was warmer on the first floor. He breathed in the smell of old carpeting to his right, and turned his head to the smell of spices in the kitchen on his left. He stood and listened to the tree frogs for a break in the cacophony—nothing. As long as their shrill opera continued to play, he could be sure nothing was moving around outside. He stepped to the side and pushed the door back against its frame, but did not close it.

The center steps that led upstairs were carpeted. He ascended like a vapor and turned to his left. The door was open, so he walked in and looked for a body on the bed. There were two beds, and both were empty. The outline of picture frames hung from the walls, though it was too dark to see the images they contained. There were a few stuffed animals on one bed, maybe a lion and a dragon, and some throw pillows on the other. A broken wicker hamper rested off-center on the floor in the corner, empty. A huge glass fishbowl was outlined against the window, but it held no fish, just what looked like a few pennies on the bottom. A digital clock with a soft green glow showed the time.

There was an open door to his right. He walked through it and into the bathroom. The smell of perfumed soap and hand lotion indicated that a woman was close by. Yoda's black silhouette accompanied him in the mirror as he passed by the sink.

Another door in the bathroom was half open, and he could see the lumpy outline of a body covered in a thin sheet in the adjoining bedroom. Maggie was curled with her back toward him. Her hips formed a rolling landscape to her waist, and rose again at her shoulders.

He walked across the carpet and sat in a chair in the corner of the room nearest her bed. Another small digital alarm clock on a nightstand illuminated Maggie's face in an orange glow as she slept.

A closet with no doors was to his right. Clothes were hung and packed tightly in the space. Shoeboxes and another wicker hamper were at the bottom. Laundry that had not made the hamper was scattered on the floor in irregular patterns. They were delicate clothes: woman's underwear and blouses.

Yoda could see the soft curve of Maggie's fleshy breast beneath her arm. He reached out and held his hands with fingers extended over her jet-black hair, the way a pianist hesitates just before tapping the keyboard. He kept his fingertips slightly above her hair, almost touching the dark strands. Static electricity between their bodies pulled delicate locks away from her head until they almost connected with Yoda's skin, before they lost the electric charge and floated down again to rest on her sleeping head. He stroked her hair like this for a while, almost but not quite touching. He leaned a little closer to breathe in her scent, her breath. It was salty, with a tinge of garlic. She stirred.

"Hmmm . . ." The sound came from her throat like a cat purrs. She said a word, then another. It sounded like "on."

A small heart locket on a chain was draped over a wristwatch next to the alarm clock. It was close to 4:00 a.m.. Time to finish the job and get out before early morning traffic began. Yoda stood up and waited until he was sure she had returned to the depths of sleep.

John had no pretense of being Buddha, Muhammad, or a Lama. He didn't consider himself a Christian either, or part of anything labeled religion. After all, some very religious people had spent the last decade trying to kill him.

An assassin's life allowed for plenty of time to read between missions. You could only clean your weapon so much. After a while the brain needed stimulus outside regimented military discipline.

John read books in a search for rationalization of the life he lived, and of the lives he took. Love of country, saving innocents, and killing an enemy intent on destroying your way of life were all good motivators, but he needed something more to keep his wandering mind under control—something that said it was okay to take a life, that it was okay to break mankind's laws. What were laws anyway? Every state, country, and civilization had its own, so there was no sense in trying to figure out who was right. He decided he would live his life based on his own accumulative knowledge, rationalizations, and whatever it took to sleep at night. No one else had cornered the market on morality. So why try?

Blacksmithing and cycling were Zen. Both required that he be 100 percent focused on the moment. Lost focus while meditating left you with poor posture or uncomfortable thoughts, what the Buddhists called "mind weeds." In his Zen, a momentary loss of focus meant a third-degree burn, a busted hand, or a fall where road gravel shredded your flesh at fifty miles per hour.

It was the hunt that put John in the moment. Destruction of America's enemies brought him peace, not the kill. If a man spends his career killing other humans and seeks no moral justification, he is a sociopath, not a soldier.

Shunryu Suzuki wrote, "In the beginner's mind there are many possibilities, but in the expert's there are few." John kept a copy of Suzuki's book next to his bed, and when his mind got twisted, he opened it up to a random chapter and read. When he got too cocky in his missions, cycling, or his metalworking, he tried to remember that the expert was limited, and that the beginner walked a wider path.

Like Baby, John's character was forged in steel, polished best where worn. Because of his nature, he needed to remain in the present at all times to avoid mind weeds of his own.

He liked to warm up before he fired up the furnace and pounded away at the steel. It released the tension. A fifty-mile ride or decent workout delivered the results. He had managed to get in several rides in the last week, all over fifty miles. Though it strengthened the hamstrings and calves, cycling tightened the upper body and back muscles without any gain in strength. Not good when the task required using your body as a weapon. Today he opted for the workout, albeit one which favored his swollen thigh. It still looked puffy, but the sutures were holding.

The Marine Corps provided unlimited opportunities to improve his martial arts skills. While overseas he had attended weekend exhibitions, competitions, and off-hour classes by some of the best fighters in the world. During active duty, when he wasn't in the field, he spent time in the dojo honing his boxing, kung fu, and aikido skills.

But there was no instructor here, no sparing partners—just him and Baby.

He pulled the heavy barn doors closed and ignited the propane furnace. Henry's barn heated up to over one hundred degrees Fahrenheit in a few minutes. He stripped down to his running shorts—no shoes or socks, nothing to protect his hands—and began a yoga routine to loosen up: down dog, up dog, proud warrior, and a runner's stretch on each hamstring.

Once he was limber, he knocked off the first set of one hundred sit-ups, one hundred push-ups, and thirty pull-ups. He completed three sets of each in three-minute increments. Once his upper body felt loose, he pummeled the heavy bag that hung suspended from a thick, hand-hued ceiling beam. It was secured to the floor with a chain and cinder block so it absorbed hooks, jabs, and kicks more like a body. In a gym workout, your partner held the heavy bag in place for you. No such luxury for those who work alone.

He spent a half-hour on sidekicks, mule kicks, jabs, and upper cuts on the leather bag, connecting with whip-like smacks that echoed off the barn walls. He stood seven feet from the bag, stepped forward with either leg, and shot in low on the bag, dragging his other leg behind him. This allowed him to get under his attacker and pop up close. He repeated the motion until his hamstrings ached.

If a quick opponent dropped down to meet the attack, John employed a ground game of joint locks and chokes. But most people didn't know how to defend against a straight shot to the legs, and the fastest way to take out a human was a groin rip (one instructor called it "a monkey stealing peaches from the tree"), and then up the torso for a Ranger choke hold. The choke hold left the aggressor vulnerable for too many seconds while the enemy squirmed and fought back. John deviated from the classic choke hold with an open claw strike: a split-second, brutal squeeze on the soft neck tissue, and a tearing rip as he retrieved the jab.

Two large maple logs rested on the floor, cut into four-foot lengths, with their bark removed. The lighter log weighed forty pounds, the heavier seventy. He started with the small one, cradled it in the crooks of his arms, and stood in a horse stance for five minutes, until his legs and arms began to tremble. After a minute to recover, he repeated the exercise with the heavier log, pushing himself to the point where his limbs trembled again, and then lowered the log to the floor. He repeated this exercise with both logs until he could maintain the position without pain or mind weeds.

He used a ten-pound, ball-bearing-filled canvas sack to increase his grip strength. He assumed a cat stance, with 90 percent of his weight on his back leg. The toes of his front leg rested lightly on the floor. The cat stance was versatile because the forward leg was used to strike, or more often as a decoy to get the opponent to strike you. Your opponent would waste a strike if he went for the leg because it supported almost none of your body weight.

John clawed the fingers of one hand into the ball bearings, then released the canvas bag, and snatched it catlike with the other hand as it fell. It was a tiger-claw, kung-fu-grip strengthening exercise. He repeated the exercise until his fingers ached and he could no longer hold up his arms. As most fighting was done close in, having a good kick or jab was helpful, but not crucial. The fight was over if you could take out a man's trachea in one motion. Five minutes without oxygen, and the brain was dead. Long before that, your opponent choked for air, and every cell screamed out as shock reduced his ability to retaliate.

John found creative ways to practice these techniques while deployed in the Afghanistan mountains, unwilling to chance exposing his location to the enemy's ever-vigilant binoculars. He carried a two-foot-long, one-quarter-inch rope in his rucksack. He spent days watching and waiting for targets while he ceaselessly tied and untied the rope into knots. Each time he untied the tight knots, his fingers grew stronger and his tactile coordination increased. If he found himself in a prone position, with his belly in the dirt, he continued to scour the landscape for targets and dug his fingers clawlike into the rocks and sand beneath him to strengthen his grip and harden his skin into calluses.

He preferred a blade, but they were not always handy. Rapid removal of an opponent's throat viscera was the quickest way to end a fight when no guns were involved. If he noticed his enemy had sharpened fingernails, he would defend in kind, but a knife was always better. Coming to a knife fight with sharp fingernails was imprudent.

Some aikido and jiujitsu proponents asserted that all fights eventually ended up on the ground and, for that reason, the ground game was the most important. They were restricted by codes of honor and rules. Assassins were not.

The ground game was best with only one opponent. The problem was, while you had hajji A on the ground in a neck-breaking choke hold, hajji B was kicking in your temples. In the time it took for someone to get him to the ground, they were breathing through a fist-sized hole in their throat, or their eyes were gone, along with any will to fight. John had done it with bigger, faster, stronger, and more developed martial arts experts who had all practiced various grappling and kicking styles. He respected but didn't fear them. He always checked his opponent's fingers. If the joints were gnarled and calloused from years of hardening techniques, he kept his distance. The best method to control an enemy like this would be a bullet.

One instructor had told him, the best fight is one that happens when you're not there. If he encountered an aggressor that had nothing to do with the mission, someone in a bar perhaps, John did his best to walk away. It was an ego-bruiser, but in any fight there is always the chance you could be the one who ended up as worm food.

His internal chain was relaxed from the workout, so he proceeded to his anvil.

A blacksmith's tools included hammers, chisels, cleavers, punches, hand drills, bellows, soldering iron, files, and tongs—tools that were also excellent weaponry. They also improved his grip and wrist strength especially in a good martial arts workout.

John picked up the hammer, pleased by the heaviness in his hand and the lightness it gave his heart. Metalwork allowed him time to create instead of tear down.

With a pair of twenty-four-inch tongs he grabbed the dirk he had made for the Brooklyn mission. He held it in the three-thousand-degree furnace for a few minutes, until it turned a dull orange. He pulled it from the fire, rested it on the anvil, and forged it into a small rectangle by turning it over and over and striking it with the hammer. The ideal color for most forging was bright yellow-orange, but he only needed to change the dirk's shape enough to make it unrecognizable. He would use the metal for something else later—another blade, or to patch someone's deck furniture. Where the dirk ended up wasn't important, as long as it was unidentifiable as the weapon used on Abdul Bari.

The orange rectangle made tiny pops as it cooled, and gave off metallic vapors that bit his tongue. He positioned it on a steel rectangle of sheet metal on the workbench, next to his grinder, and placed the hammer and tongs on the anvil. He noticed something shiny draped over the workbench vice that was bolted into the wood.

He took off his gloves and picked it up. It was the fine gold necklace and heart locket Maggie wore. She called it her mother's locket. She kept a small black-and-white photo of her mother and father's wedding photo inside. It wasn't something she wore every day, and not something she would carelessly leave lying around. Had she been in the barn without him? What would Maggie be doing in the barn? The last time she was here he had been sandblasting Baby. He thought back. Did she have the locket on that day? He remembered her Onteora baseball cap, the way her black T-shirt draped over her torso, the smile on her face, and how she had kissed him though he was drenched in sweat. He tried to focus on her neck. Was the locket under the T-shirt? He couldn't see it in his mind's eye.

He imagined the locket around her neck, but the memory didn't ring true. Then how did it get there? Was she just snooping around? He let it go for now.

With Brooklyn's evidence destroyed, he felt a sense of relief settle in his body.

Next came a practice course for the Super Rat. He lined up five six-foot rebar rods and uncoiled five more eight-foot, quarter-inch steel cables. He unchained the MIG welder and brought it to the center of the room away from the combustibles. He kept the floor of the barn broom clean.

The MIG welder puts out a lot of heat—in the range of six to eight thousand degrees Fahrenheit—and its harmful light could blind a person in seconds. John slid on asbestos-lined leather welding gloves that went up to his elbows, and grabbed his auto-darkening welder's mask. He left the visor flipped and tied up the laces on his steel-toed leather shoes. Hot metal slag often fell straight down from the working table and onto a craftsman's feet. It burned through plastic and cotton fibers, and could weld one's toes together in a flaming goo. The stable boy craftsman he had studied in Darra had no personal protective equipment, and most displayed the medals of their profession in the form of fused toes, missing fingers, and facial scars.

John placed the rebar rods on a steel table in a small assembly line. He bowed a steel cable until its ends met to form a circle with a thirty-eight-inch diameter. This would give him five inches on each side when the Super Rat flew through the middle. If he couldn't get it to fly through the middle, he would be out one expensive toy, and have to scrap the mission.

With the cable bowed, he overlapped the ends and held them in place with a C-clamp. He flipped down the auto-darkening visor and melted the cable ends together. He let the hoop cool for a few moments, then welded one of the rebar rods to the same spot where he had connected the cable ends. He leaned the piece against the outside of the furnace and stood back to admire his work. It looked like the frame for a giant lollipop mold. After completing the task four more times, he turned off the MIG welder.

He shut down the furnace, put his tools and PPE away, put on his shirt and sneakers, and opened the barn door. The air felt like ice water against his sweat-drenched T-shirt compared to the heat of the barn. He shivered.

Maggie's car pulled into the driveway as he walked up the porch steps. At least she hadn't snuck up behind him unnoticed again. She waved from behind the windshield and shut the car off.

"I hope you were alone in there," Maggie said with a smile.

"Just me and my thoughts."

"Then I'm not jealous, only scared. How's the leg?"

"Getting better."

Maggie had bought the story that it was a careless accident he had while working with an old wrought iron fence. John kept it wrapped in multiple layers of gauze and, despite her pleas to see the injury, he made sure to never remove the dressing while she was around. He had explained that it wasn't a deep cut, but that it was long and took more stitches than it was worth. He told her that the emergency room doctor thought John might want a career as a thigh model, and did his best to reduce scarring. John joked that the tetanus shot had been worse than the cut. Lies masking lies.

Maggie gave him a peck on the cheek and exaggerated keeping her body away from him. "Why don't you take a shower, Smithy, and I'll make us something to eat?"

"Deal," he said. He slid the heart locket from his wrist and dangled it in front of her. "Looking for this?"

Her face brightened as if it were the first time she'd seen it. "My God. I've been looking all over for that. Where'd you find it?"

"It was in the barn." He turned his head toward the open doors. "It was on the workbench."

"The workbench?" She took the necklace from his hand and put it around her neck, first checking that the tiny photograph was still inside. "I was so worried. I hadn't seen it in days. Thank you, John." Maggie's eyes moistened.

"That's weird," he said. "I wonder how it got there." He searched her face for a clue.

"I could have had a senior moment, but I don't know." She tucked the locket under her shirt and placed her palm over it. "Now let me get you fed, my big man."

After he showered the sweat and grime from his body and changed into fresh clothes, hunger pangs set in. He bounded down the stairs, careful of his stitches and sat at the table.

"Well?" he said.

Maggie faced the old gas stove with her back to him. "What?"

"You said something about food?"

She turned toward him and flipped a Frisbee-sized omelet in the air. She placed the sauté pan on a warmer. The sweet smell of caramelized onions and cheddar cheese filled the room. The toaster bell chimed. Maggie spread butter on some blackened bread the way a mason screeded wet concrete.

"Ketchup?"

"I was in the military, remember?"

"Oh yeah," she said. "Ketchup on everything."

"It's a sauce, you know," he said. "Think of it as a sauce. No different than hollandaise, béarnaise, or any other sauce. If it had a French name, you'd have no problem ordering it at a restaurant."

Maggie rolled her eyes. "McDonald's, maybe."

John grabbed the plastic bottle and covered his omelet with ketchup. He gulped a tall glass of orange juice Maggie set before him, and swallowed a piece of buttered toast in two bites.

"Wow," she said.

He grinned and said, "I was hungry."

"Did you start any new projects?"

He anticipated her next question. "No. But I finished a small one."

"Was it Andrea's chair?"

It was the question he had expected. Maggie had made friends with Andrea at work. She had asked Maggie if John wouldn't mind repairing a broken deck chair for her. "Wouldn't mind" meant "please do this for free."

A white lie would keep the peace. "I didn't finish it," he said. "But I got it mostly repaired. It's a weak metal, so I have to go slow. She shouldn't buy her furniture at Walmart."

"She's a teacher, John. We don't have a lot of fiscal choices."

He wanted to change the subject. The deck chair was still leaning against the wall where he had placed it a month ago. "How was your first full day back?" he said.

"Hectic, but I love it already. I went over to Woodstock afterward to do a little window-shopping. It was World Awareness Day."

He snorted.

"I know, I know," she said. "It wasn't my intention. I actually didn't realize it was today. I did have fun banging the drums, though."

"Drums?"

"There was a drum circle, like the kind I guess American Indians use when they have spiritual dances and stuff. It was fun, but I met the strangest guy."

He used the last bit of buttered toast to wipe the plate. "What do you mean?"

"He was in the drum circle. He sat next to me and we talked a little."

"Yeah, Maggie, that is strange."

Maggie rolled her eyes. "He was from Tibet, and we started talking about charity—"

"Tibet?" He gave her a quizzical look.

"Yeah. There's a monastery in Woodstock. Maybe he was visiting."

"Maybe. What did he say that was so strange?"

"We were just talking about the drums, and people in general, and he said something like poor people don't need charity . . ." She hesitated and put her fingers to her lips. "No, no that wasn't it. That wasn't the weird thing. He actually said, 'The living need charity more than the dead.'"

John felt his back muscles tighten and his internal radar switch on. He tried to appear indifferent, but something didn't feel right. "What did he look like?" he said.

"Kind of tall, for an Asian guy," she said. "I don't want to generalize a whole race, but he was taller than most, maybe as tall as or a little taller than you, I guess. He was thin. I got the feeling he was some kind of Buddhist, or someone who had studied that religion."

It couldn't be Yoda. John thought he might be overreacting, but he also knew to trust his gut. The bastard had taken his picture, but Chocker said it would be grainy at that distance. And even if Yoda had a photograph, what good would it do him? There were over three hundred million people in the country, and the majority of them were still Caucasian. John couldn't imagine any way for this guy to track him down, unless he had followed him from the tunnel. Had Yoda waited in the upper chamber, and then snuck back down and followed him through the old coal tunnel? Not possible. Yoda was cut badly, and would have needed a mountain bike to trail John all the way to his car. He tried to relax.

"You shouldn't talk to strangers, Maggie."

"It wasn't like I sought him out. He was in the drum circle."

"Anything else about him you thought was strange?"

She thought for a moment and gave John a quizzical look. "Do you think you know him?"

"No. I just think you're right. It was a weird thing to say to someone you just met." It was time to change the subject. "Are your classes crowded?"

"You mean since they mothballed the old school? No. But you should get anything you want before they demolish it."

"They're going to demolish the old school?"

"It's obsolete. They figured out it cost more to upgrade it than to just tear it down. There's going to be a public auction of all the contents. I'm sure there are old tools or metal scrap you could use."

"I'll check it out again," he said. "How's the new group of children?"

Maggie put a piece of her omelet in his mouth. "They've all got their new clothes, new ideas, and are so eager to make friends. God, John, they're so beautiful at this age."

"Fourth grade is nice. Wait until the little brats go through puberty."

"I know you don't mean that." Maggie fed him another bite of omelet. She had a faraway look in her eyes.

He sensed the "M" word wasn't too far away, followed soon by, "When are we going to have a baby?" or, "Have you thought about kids?" He wanted to marry her, and have kids and all the pain and joy that goes along with them, but she was a liability. If someone wanted to get to him, they would target Maggie. He refused to put anyone in that situation. He felt guilty enough for letting their relationship go this far, but he couldn't back out now.

He knew that Maggie wasn't aware that their life together was on hold until he found a way out of his current duality. She probably thought she had to be nicer to him, show him more trust, love him more, and he would come around. He felt like Batman: half his life with the earthlings, the other half in a cave.

The topic of marriage had been successfully avoided up to this point in their relationship. It would be impossible to manage the "take your daughter to work day" should they ever conceive. So far, he had been able to temper her not-so-subtle hints at marriage. But Maggie had patience and persistence, and was not about to let this opportunity slip through her fingers. The sex was tender and at the same time erotic, and a year had gone by, so why not take their relationship to the next step?

They ate in silence, until the omelet vanished and only ketchup swirls and burnt crumbs remained on the white plate.

"They like to play," Maggie said.

"The kids?"

"Yeah. There's this one boy who has to get everyone together all the time and start a new game. He makes up games, and everyone understands."

"He should get a job with Mattel."

"I guess leaders are born, not made," she replied. "What do you think?"

"It's the man, not the land," he said. "A lot of guys can lead, if they're given direction, but there are very few who can design a plan and encourage others to follow. Sounds like you have executive material in the making."

"Or another Major Rexford." Maggie smiled and gave him a sideways glance.

"Hey, you want to play?" He wiped his grin with a napkin.

"What?"

"You want to play? I've got a new toy."

"Can we save it for tonight? I'd like to get outside for a while. It's so sunny."

"Not that kind of toy, Maggie." He shook his head. "I bought a little helicopter at the mall. Come on."

He grabbed her hand and took her to the counter near the sink, where the small helicopter rested in its charger. The Super Rat was on a charger upstairs, hidden under a bed in the spare room. He would practice with the smaller version first.

"You bought this at the mall?" said Maggie.

"I never had one when I was a kid, and always told myself I'd get one. There it was, so . . . no time like the present." He unplugged the charger and handed Maggie the controls.

"Oh, John." She gave him a quick kiss on the cheek. "I'm so glad you never grew up. Let's go."

They ran to the yard behind the house, where he retrieved the rebar rods with attached hoops. He pushed the rods into the lawn at twenty-foot intervals. He arranged the cable hoops at different heights of four to five feet, while Maggie read the instructions.

He told her that she didn't need to read them. She mumbled back, "Typical man," and kept reading anyway.

Maggie read the basics of powering up the machine and what each control on the remote did, while John stood with his arms crossed and rolled his eyes. When he couldn't take it anymore, he grabbed the remote from her.

"Hey," she said.

"Can we just fly it?"

"I want to go first," she begged.

"And when you break it, what do I get to do? Fix it?"

"Come on, John. I won't break it."

He handed her the remote, and Maggie jumped up and down and laughed. She pushed the power control, and the rotors turned slowly with a soft whirr. The bird went straight up a few feet, and then straight down.

"You have to keep the juice on," he said.

"I know, I know." She pushed him away with her elbow. "Get away. I can do it."

On her second try, Maggie got the bird up and made small, jerky, circular passes over their heads. Then she took it up to treetop level and squealed. "My God. Look at it!"

"Cool, huh?" He watched the bird drift away. "Hey, bring it back, honey. Come on. You're getting out of range."

"I'm trying. It won't respond." Maggie wiggled the control toggles vigorously.

The helicopter made a beeline for the barn; it hovered over the roof for a moment, and then dropped with a thud on the wooden shingles.

"Shit. Shit. Shit." Maggie frowned.

"Don't forget 'damn it.'"

"Damn it."

"Nice job, Ace," he said. "Are you going to go up there and get it?"

"That's support work. I'm the pilot. We don't retrieve."

"Major Gopher, at your service." He snapped off an exaggerated salute and said, "I'll be right back."

He grabbed a ladder from the barn, leaned it against the roof, and climbed up. He held the helicopter and motioned for Maggie to start it up with a twirl of his index finger. The rotors turned in his hand, and the bird drifted off the roof and over the yard. Maggie brought it down to the grass with a gentle landing. She smiled up at him.

"I think I got it now."

He came down from the roof. "I'll leave the ladder there, just in case."

"I thought of something else."

"What?"

"About the guy," she said. "Something that was a little out of place."

He took the controls from her hand and got the bird into the air.

"He wore dance shoes."

John tried not to turn his head and crash the helicopter. "Ballet slippers?"

"No, like Capezios."

Relieved, he said, "Sorry, you lost me."

"Like jazz shoes. Low-cut jazz shoes. The soft kind, black."

He shrugged and mumbled something about Woodstock being an anything-goes town. He ran the bird through the obstacle course until the battery got low and it failed to respond. They went back inside, and he plugged the helicopter into the charger.

"It will take about a half hour to recharge," John said.

"How about you?"

"My batteries are fine."

"It's always best to perform a premission check." She wrapped her arms around his waist. "Don't you think?"

The summer breeze warmed their skin. Sun filtered through the old farmhouse's wavy glass window panes. He lost himself in her earthling-brown eyes. He leaned into her for a long kiss, and Maggie responded on her tiptoes, pelvis pressing hard against him. They went upstairs and fell in love all over again.

While she slept, he looked out the window at the maples and oaks, the weathered barn roof, and telephone wires that cluttered the air. For this kill, he would have to overcome and adjust to every obstacle. Someone's father, brother, friend, even lover, was about to go down, and he had to separate himself from that eventuality, from their loss. Maggie sniffled and pulled the pillow closer to her chest.

Obstacles are what you see when you take your eyes off the goal. He had no strategy to overcome the sniffling, warm hindrance that clutched the pillow on the bed they shared, in this old house, in this small town, in this life of killing.

The swollen wound was worse than yesterday. It should have gone down by now, unless it was infected. He favored his thigh as he blew through a quick forty-five-minute workout on the heavy bag, without gloves, at three-quarter speed. Next came fingertip push-ups, and jump-rope. The leather rope was a quick trainer because it left stinging welts when his technique was poor.

Practice like you play.

John's football coach at Rutgers had repeated this mantra before every practice. His Marine Corps aikido instructor called it *mushin*: fully embodied in the present, when your thoughts and actions are concurrent and spontaneous. It allows a seasoned practitioner to respond automatically to random and unpredictable attacks. If you always trained as if you're fighting, you learned little and never got into the deeper realms of unconscious competence. In other words, repetition of the art would manifest itself in automatic responses during an actual fight. But without careful and deliberate practice, your skills would remain shallow.

He placed a stopwatch on the workbench and set it to beep every three minutes. He alternated between the heavy bag, rope, and calisthenics, with a one-minute rest between reps. This brought his heart rate to where it would be after the twenty-five-mile ride to FDR Park. The remote-control Super Rat was extremely sensitive, and his reflexes, blood pressure, and tactile sensitivity must replicate the actual mission. If he practiced with a slow metabolism and played with a revved-up one, it would increase the possibility of errors in the field.

Preparation for his next assignment meant he must put away the tiny chopper he and Maggie had played with, and with which he had practiced another several hours without her. It was time to practice with live ammo.

He retrieved the fully charged Super Rat from beneath the bed in the guest room and carried it to the metal-hoop obstacle course. He adjusted the five rebar rods with attached hoops to the height of an average man's head, with three sitting and two standing.

He turned on the remote control and then the Super Rat's electric motor. Its remote had two separate, small joysticks and two dials for fine maneuvers. The smaller chopper had only two joysticks, one for elevation and one to circle right and left. With nine channels and a 2.4 GHz transmitter, the Super Rat promised to react quickly to commands, and John needed to work the controls simultaneously to master the bird's full speed and agility.

The Super Rat came with a CD-ROM that showed expert pilots running it though 3-D maneuvers, which were a series of controlled stalls inside an imaginary box in the air. He had already thrown the CD-ROM and the box into the furnace, along with Chocker's flash drive. He didn't need anything left in the house that would connect him to the Super Rat. It gave a whole new meaning to "burning a CD."

There was much more to competition flying than he'd imagined. The chopper's nose was downward in the tic-toc maneuver, and the pilot made the tail rock back and forth like a metronome. The inverted position, which was flying upside down, was a lot harder than the twelve-year-olds in the training video make it look. The funnel, which was flying inverted, backward, in a tornado configuration, was also complicated. And the Holy Grail of 3-D maneuvers, the pirouette flip, wherein the chopper rode an imaginary axis up and down like an elevator while its rotors spun on another imaginary axis, was even harder to execute. When done correctly, the rotors looked like a large dinner plate flopping end-over-end through the air. The manual said that mastery of this move would bring riches, glory, and hot women. Then it went on to say that none of those statements were true, and that women will still be as disinterested in helicopters as they were when you just hovered.

Time was short, but John had two things in his favor. He only needed to fly up and down and in circles, and the unit came with a computer simulator that allowed him to practice on his laptop. The video was very close to what the military had for the UAVs in Afghanistan, without the look down–shoot down capabilities, cameras, and things that go boom.

Maggie was at work, and Henry had left in his old pickup. John didn't want to explain to either of them why a grown man without a real job played with a souped-up toy helicopter when he should be earning a living.

The rotors whined and the Super Rat jumped off the earth as if it would go straight into orbit. He panicked a little and brought it down hard. It pitched to the side and dug up fist-sized grass chunks. John picked up the downed bird and checked for damage. No harm done. On his next try, he eased the joystick more slowly, and the Super Rat climbed skyward. After a few minutes riding an up-and-down axis, he gained some courage and sent the chopper into a large circular flight pattern above the trees at maximum speed. The motor delivered more power than the Super Rat needed. She climbed to one hundred feet in less than three seconds, hovered, and dove to the earth, where she rested gently on the thick green grass.

Giddy from the rush, John giggled like a little kid as he put the helicopter through its basic maneuvers. He took her straight up two hundred feet at full throttle, nosedived toward earth, and stopped three feet from the ground.

My God, this is so cool.

He guided the Super Rat through the cable hoops without a mishap. Practicing with the smaller bird had been a good idea. He could keep the helicopter in the circle's center at half throttle, about forty miles per hour, with no problem. When the time came, and without the hoops as obstacles, he would be able to open up the throttle and sail through a circle one foot in diameter.

He was quickly able to control the helicopter with fewer jerky movements. There was an invisible string attached from his mind to the chopper. He swayed back and forth as the chopper swayed back and forth in the sky. When it went down, his shoulders dropped. When it climbed, his sternum lifted. His breath's rhythm followed the electric motor's changing pitch.

Fragments of his military training came back to him in a scattered slide show: boot camp, special forces school, hand-to-hand combat, and small weapons training. He had been trained for this, to defeat the opposing force.

He slipped back to Afghanistan, where he remembered watching a small handheld monitor in Major Canaan's rough hands while they sat in a shallow ditch in the mountains overlooking the fast-flowing Kokcha River, near the Tajik town of Faizabad, a few days' hike from Tajikistan.

Apache helicopters chopped the air with a war drumbeat in the background. Canaan's voice came to him between the *bat-bat-bat* of rotor blades.

"The world changed after 9/11, John," Canaan said. "We're the good guys again. But we're not an army; we're bodyguards. We're here to protect and serve. It's true what they say. We're the world's police, and like police, we need to know the people in order to win. We have to walk the beat."

Hawks flew overhead, black silhouettes against a white sky. Children played in the village below; their voices floated up to him like the shrill chirping of tree frogs.

"It's against human nature to intentionally put ourselves in the direct line of fire for the sake of another person . . . and yet that's what we do here every day, every day here . . ."

John peeked over the lip of the ditch. He saw a picnic table at a tent's edge and three tethered horses nearby. Children played with sticks, rocks, and old wheels. A camera flashed. A bottle? Maybe sunglasses? A scope?

"The problem is, they don't know yet why we're here. They see someone imposing another restriction on their already limited freedoms. But we'll win them over, John. We'll give them something they never knew was possible . . ."

The camera flashed again. John looked at Canaan, who was rambling on about something, and back toward the village.

"They're sheep that hate the sheep dog until the wolf comes . . . then come running . . . and the wolf wonders when you'll finally catch him . . . when he'll have to test himself . . . fang to fang . . ."

John grabbed Canaan's head with both hands and pulled it down into the dirt as the rocks behind him fractured into small chips from an invisible jackhammer. Canaan fought him at first, out of reflex, and managed to raise his head. The jackhammer blew more sand and stone fragments into the air and into Canaan's eyes before he dropped his head back down. Tiny needles in his eyes blinded him.

John had no target at which to return fire. The rounds came from nowhere. A sniper? Silencer?

He put Canaan's hand on his ankle and told him to stay down and follow. They belly crawled down the ditch, one hundred yards out of the town's view, and tucked behind a rock away from the line of fire.

"Call it in, John. Call it in. Burn the bastards."

Immediate sightlessness put Canaan into a state of irrational panic. Calling in an airstrike on helpless villagers was bad mojo in the best of situations. With no idea who had fired upon them, that plan was off the table. John described the terrain around them in detail to calm Canaan down. They waited in the ditch until sunset. No one pursued.

To sit and wait, blinded, while fired upon, tortured Canaan. Every drop of adrenaline told him to fight back, but he had to hold his position and suck it up until they moved again under the cover of darkness. Hand in hand, with Canaan partially blinded and any backup miles away, they made it back to camp, where a medic flushed the debris from his partner's eyes. A surgeon had to remove the larger shale chips.

Reflections off the Super Rat's shiny rotors brought John back to mushin. How could he drift into a separate part of his brain and still function in the present? He was pleased that the intuitive machine worked so well, but it made him uncomfortable on another level that he had lost conscious awareness of the present, lost his mushin. Someday he might pull into the driveway and find a corpse on his grill.

"I always wondered what unemployed perverts do when no one's around to watch them." Henry had walked up behind him, unheard over the electric motor's whine.

John did his best to act calm. Twice he had let his guard down: once with Maggie, and now with this old bastard. *Get real, soldier, or you'll end up worm food.*

"Jealous?"

"Right," Henry snickered. "Of what?"

"You probably want to get in touch with your inner child, and haven't been able to," said John. "It's a classic predicament for retired old military farts."

Henry let it slide. Curiosity had compelled him to cross the road. "What you got there?" he said.

"This, my friend, is an express ticket back to adolescence. Want to give it a try?"

"No thanks." Henry shook his head. "I don't like my inner child much. I'd probably smash it on you. I'll watch."

John ran through a few more maneuvers and brought the helicopter in for a landing. He had reached a competence level that would ensure a positive outcome. The Super Rat and pilot were mission-ready.

"The battery's getting low. Let's take it inside." John gathered his weapon and they went inside and sat at the kitchen table.

"Where's the schoolmarm?" said Henry.

"Schoolmarming."

"Miss her?" asked Henry.

"It's good to have my privacy back, at least during the day."

"I'll leave if you want." Henry feigned getting up.

"Sit the hell down. You want a beer?"

Henry held out his arm, indicating it needed twisting. John ignored him and went to the fridge.

"Did you ever fly one of those?" Henry asked.

"Nah. Rode a few in 'Stan. You?"

"Never flew one, but the war didn't run in 'Nam without the Air Cav. I got dropped off to a lot of luxurious places on 'em. We had Hueys back then."

"We had Apaches and Chinooks."

"Do you miss it?"

"Nope."

"Not even a little?" Henry pressed.

"Nope."

"I thought a guy like you might miss it," Henry said. "Thought maybe you'd hook up with some police force, or executive security firm, or something."

"Is this going anywhere?" John set the beer can on the table.

"You don't seem like the kind of guy who'd be real happy making lawn furniture, is all."

"So you want my resume?"

"All I'm saying is, there are a lot of enemy here." Henry took a big chug of his beer.

"Enemy?"

"Well, this country ain't what it used to be, John." Henry put the can down and belched. "I figured a guy like you might be comfortable cleaning up the streets of crime, is all."

"That's all, huh? Like a superhero?"

"I don't mean nothing by it. Just making conversation. You looked pretty happy flying that machine."

"I was happy." He scratched his head with both hands and yawned. "Look, Henry, don't take this the wrong way, but what the hell are you trying to say?"

"You're a smart guy, John. And Maggie's a nice woman. I know you'll make the right choice." Henry chugged the rest of his beer, burped one more time, and stood up.

"Which would be . . .?"

"The one that doesn't make your skin crawl when you go to bed at night. The one where you wake up with a warm body next to you." Henry pointed his thumb to his chest. "Instead of four trailer walls, like this old retired military fart."

"I get it. You're still playing matchmaker."

"I'm just saying." Henry grabbed the screen door, pulled it open, and stepped onto the porch. "I'll let you go back to your war games."

"Later, Henry."

The old bastard sure could chug a beer in a hurry. What was that all about? Henry was lonely and didn't want to see him lose Maggie. Sure, he liked to mooch a beer. And sure, curiosity may have gotten the best of him. Sure, sure, sure. *What did he mean by "my war games"?*

John sat at the computer simulator and practiced some advanced maneuvers for the Super Rat he wouldn't be using in the mission, just in case this became a hobby. But it was a lie. He'd never have a hobby like the earthlings, never relax with a toy helicopter, or golf, or fish. The chain links were too taut. As long as he stayed on Chocker's payroll, he would remain wired, awaiting his next fix.

After deleting the simulation software from the hard drive, he ran a scrubbing program to remove any remaining digital traces. He looked at the clock, counted the hours until Maggie would be off work, and decided to take a nap. He slept better in the daylight. All the shadows were accounted for.

When he woke up alone, his skin did crawl. Something in the room seemed out of place. He looked around, saw his reflection in the dresser mirror, and realized what it was.

FDR

The Subaru was parked in the visitor's lot at Chelsea Ridge Apartments, twenty-five miles due north of FDR park. Chelsea Ridge had no security cameras in their parking lot, and was such a large complex that the occasional biker or new face ostensibly visiting a resident wouldn't draw attention. There were lots closer to FDR that offered better cover, but they all had security cameras. A bright detective might check them if he knew the perpetrator was an expert cyclist.

The ability to ride one hundred miles in four hours liberated him, set him apart from the earthlings and gave him time alone to excel in both body and spirit. This practiced discipline allowed him distance from any escape vehicle he needed at mission's end. He couldn't afford witnesses describing a green Subaru in the area of a homicide. His missions were militarily necessary, but the average citizen would side with the judge who put John Rexford behind bars in the event of his apprehension. After all, killing on American soil? *Tut, tut, soldier.*

Maple trees lined Franklin Delano Roosevelt's parking lots and walkways. FDR was one of Westchester County's many bucolic public attractions. It was forty miles from New York City and catered to day-trippers who wanted to fish, sun, or picnic. Buses brought urbanites from the city on hot summer days to cool down in the massive pool, or rent rowboats, canoes, and kayaks to paddle around the lake. The picnic areas had volleyball nets and softball fields.

He pedaled past families grilling hot dogs and hamburgers, kids playing Frisbee, pickup softball games, and some college students jamming acoustic guitars and pounding down beers—a thumbnail sketch of what he protected. Not the skyscrapers and Wall Street bankers, but the average earthling who paid his taxes and only wanted a little explosion-free weekend relief in return for his hard work.

John hopped Baby over a beveled concrete curb and onto a narrow paved path used by bikers, walkers, and skateboarders. He pedaled slowly, like a guy out tooling around, not in a hurry to get somewhere. The moist September air saturated his lungs. White swan tails dotted the pond. Orange feet splashed against the water's surface like tiny flags directing aquatic traffic as their submerged heads nibbled the weeds below. Willow trees offered cover to young lovers on blankets, embraced in the moment, carefree, hugging. Maggie would calm him down tomorrow. Maggie would embrace him and make him feel normal, away from this other life—a life of which she remained clueless. The life that kept him from beneath the willow trees. The riding and killing life.

He found lot 23A and did a few drive-bys. The Muslims had already set up their picnic. Uri was nowhere in sight. The Russian better show. *No time for negative thoughts. He'll be here.*

The tree he had scoped out during reconnaissance was about seventy-five yards from lot 23A: a mature maple, five feet in diameter at the base, maybe three hundred years old, plenty of cover. He rested Baby against another maple fifty feet away. He placed her on the backside of the tree facing into the woods, out of sight of cars and pedestrians.

He scanned the park for anything out of place. Then he closed his eyes, opened them, and did it again. *It's what you don't see that is important, and you never see everything the first time.* Small children played tag, charcoal smoke drifted straight up from hot grills, and a few dogs ran free in violation of the leash law.

Another pleasant valley Sunday, charcoal burning everywhere, here in status-symbol land. The sarcastic lyrics were so cool. His sister used to listen to the Monkees, though they were already considered dated by the time she had heard them. American kids remembered their family picnics. If Muslims placed the same value on the pastime, today's barbeque would be one for the family photo album.

He walked back to the big maple, grabbed the first low branch, and pulled himself up in a graceful arc. Halfway up the massive trunk he found a sturdy limb with a good view of lot 23A and straddled a branch. Its thick green foliage crowned at the top and swallowed him completely.

The distance from the maple tree to the Muslims' picnic was within range of the remote control but too far for the unaided human eye. He would have loved to put a remote camera on the Super Rat, but he remembered Chocker's orders. When you added technology, you increased the evidence trail and the opportunity for something to break. NASA's engineer geeks might argue the point, but all you needed to shut them up was to remind them of the simplicity of the "O" ring, and how it had killed the first teacher in space.

He hung the backpack on the stub of a pruned limb and pulled out a pair of Eschenbach MaxEvent binocular glasses.

They didn't have the range of a good pair of Leupolds or Steiners, but they were fine for up to three hundred yards, and best of all, they were hands-free. They looked like any other pair of lightweight, wraparound cycling eyewear on the outside chance anyone saw him in this tree.

The Super Rat didn't fit into the backpack fully assembled. He had to remove the rotors first. Even so, the tail boom stuck out a little. He removed the components from the backpack and assembled the chopper using a small hex wrench on his key chain. He attached the skids to another branch with two fourteen-inch plastic cable ties, and pulled them tight.

Carpenter ants marched over the tree bark in search of prey and moisture. A few crawled over his legs and arms. He would have flicked them off, but they had a mission of their own, and he gave them a pass.

He powered up the helicopter's electric motor and turned on the remote. The main rotor and tail rotor checked out fine. He squeezed the brightly painted canopy and tried to shake anything loose that may have been disturbed on the trip. The bird was solid. A quick look inside the cockpit told him all parts were mission-ready. He increased the current to the electric motor by manipulating the joysticks on the remote, and the Super Rat bucked forward and backward in an attempt to lift off. A little more juice, and she strained against the plastic cable ties, whining for release like a feral cat.

Preflight checklist: battery power—full; landing gear—secure; fuselage right and left condition—good; main and tail rotor—good; tail boom condition—good; drive shaft and cooling fan—functioning; motor cowling—secure; antennae—good condition and secure; backup battery—power full. He pulled a kite string spool from the backpack and tied a quick-release draw hitch knot to the main rotor shaft. He kept the tag end long so he could give it a quick upward pull and retrieve the kite string without leaving any of it on the helicopter to get caught in the blades.

He had spent hours away from Maggie and Henry's prying eyes running the Super Rat through the obstacle course next to the barn. He had mastered the controls and could open the throttle full-bore and scream through the cable hoops without touching the edges of the circle. Accomplishing his mission would be child's play in comparison.

Two hundred Muslims enjoyed the festivities at lot 23A. They divided their leisure time between singing, backgammon, and food preparation. The women set up the tables and watched the children. The men sat at separate picnic tables and played backgammon, conversed, and smoked. The children played Frisbee and lawn games such as tag, and a Middle Eastern version of red rover. A couple of older boys failed to launch a kite in the flimsy wind. Thankfully, John wouldn't have to compete with nearly invisible kite strings for airspace.

An older model rusted Toyota Celica pulled into the parking lot of 23B adjacent to the picnickers. John put on the Eschenbachs to get a better view of the car and driver. Uri wore casual street wear: blue jeans, green polo shirt, and black sneakers. He looked presentable and clean as he opened the hatch and pulled a small folding table from the car. Uri followed his—or rather, Yossi Mandelbrot's—instructions, and set up his display table at the far end of lot 23B. Close enough so the kids would see the helicopters flying around, but not so close as to inject himself into their private party.

John adjusted the diopter focus on his right lens for better visual acuity. The Eschenbachs allowed him to make out rough details of Uri's face from this distance, but not enough to see his eyes or facial expressions. It would have to do. He would have liked a better pair of handheld binoculars so he could ascertain what Uri said, or even thought, during conversations with the Muslims, but he had to have his hands free to work the remote-control unit.

Uri draped a black cloth over the folding table and placed two shiny blue-and-red helicopters on top. He brought more boxes from the car and put them out of sight under the table. A bird was in the air within minutes, flying acrobatic spins, loops, and dives. John couldn't hear the small electric motor from his perch in the maple tree, but he noticed something had caught the children's eyes, and a few began to wander in Uri's direction. A couple of adults looked over, saw the situation wasn't threatening, and went back to their picnic.

After ten minutes, Uri had a small crowd of kids around the table. He gestured to them to take the controls, but they were all too shy. A tall man got up from the backgammon table and strode toward Uri's display table.

Here it comes. Let's see if Uri can turn on the sales charm and mollify Papa Muslim. Papa Muslim exhibited defensive body language. His palms were up and his chin jutted forward. Uri raised his hands and swung the remote in the air to show how the helicopter flew. Had he dropped Yossi's name? Impossible to tell. Uri put the remote in Papa's hand and urged him to give it a try.

Papa crashed the bird immediately. Uri ran to the fallen chopper, shook his head, and smiled as if to say, "That's okay, it always happens on the first try." He put the remote control back in Papa's hands and held the helicopter five feet off the ground. The rotors turned, and the helicopter began to rise with up-and-down jerks, until it took off skyward and made big circles over their heads.

The children jumped and screamed, thrilled to have an adult in their game. They squealed and urged Papa Muslim on with frantic hand gestures. Uri stood back and let the toy work its magic. A few men from the backgammon tables yelled over and waved. Papa turned his head and the bird crashed to the ground. He reluctantly turned the controls over to Uri and shook his hand. It appeared the blessing had been given. Papa Muslim went back to the adults and sat down.

Uri handed the controls over to the largest boy and took another helicopter from a box beneath the table. He had four birds in the air in less than fifteen minutes. The children clambered for their place in line to get eager hands on the remote controls.

So far, so good.

The women set the picnic tables, and the smell of curried lamb and onions lured a few men over prematurely. The ladies shooed them away and put the finishing touches on the meal. Dinner would be served shortly. John's window of opportunity fast approached, and with it the anxiety of expectation.

He scanned the crowd for the face he had studied from photographs on the flash drive. Amjad Ali Khan was five eleven, a little chubby, and grew his hair long, but kept his curly beard shorter than most true believers. He needed to blend into the western culture more than the others, so that he could fleece Americans of their generous contributions.

Amjad had emigrated from Qandahar, a city of 250,000 in the southeastern section of Afghanistan. His family controlled the wool trade there, and most of his brothers and male cousins were employed at the airport. Some handled baggage; others were in security. Access to money, exports, and flights with lax security checks made it easy to fly into Qandahar with dollars and other contraband. Flying smuggled goods out was much harder, and was almost never attempted. Though they could get anything as small as a kilo of heroin and anything as large as a rocket launcher on board, flights from Qandahar were closely scrutinized when they landed in the West.

Qandahar was the command post for the Soviet military occupation in the '80s. As a teenager, Amjad Ali Khan had been trained by the CIA in the ways of war, and how to defeat a larger, better-equipped and technologically superior adversary. The CIA had taught him that you can't fight a holy war without lots of money. Even homicide bombers had their families taken care of after their tickets were punched for heaven, and their reservations confirmed for the special martyr package which included unlimited sex with seventy-two virgins, all of which would be beautiful like rubies, and have complexions like diamonds and pearls. This passage, of course, was not in the Koran, but most terrorists had never read the Koran.

Amjad Ali Khan wasn't of the mindset to kill himself, but he did spend every day obtaining finances for those who would make the ultimate sacrifice against the Great Satan. He believed this work would get him a lesser package than the full seventy-two virgins, but still a good deal—and he got to live.

Amjad had earned a degree in financial accounting from the State University of New York in Albany, partially paid for courtesy of the US taxpayer, and then returned to his homeland. He dropped off the radar after the Soviets were ousted and the CIA had no use for him. Al Qaeda later recruited him for his business acumen and familiarity with American language and customs. Amjad set up a series of franchises under the cover of the Afghan Children's Relief Fund, and soon had hundreds of thousands of dollars a year coming into the coffers. This money filtered through banks in Dubai, Switzerland, Germany, and Australia. Eventually the money made its way to Qandahar, where his uncle controlled the three largest government-run banks in the city. From there, the cash filtered back into the right hands by way of bogus loans with hypothetical collateral, where it funded terrorism at its point of origin: the United States.

Removing Amjad Ali Khan from the financial equation would, in effect, remove one head from the medusa that supported training camps and illegal arms deals abroad. Of course, in time, someone would take his place, but the CIA relished any gap in leadership at this level.

It wasn't hard to connect the dots from the ACRF to Taliban training camps, and from there to Saudi Arabia and the 9/11 massacre. The money trail had cooled, with no direct link to Amjad, but John didn't need a direct link to justify his actions.

Most of the men wore black slacks or light-colored robes. A few of them wore a long, knee-length dress with baggy trousers known as a perahan tunban. Despite his short beard, Amjad dressed more traditionally than the other men. He wore a black robe and beaded skullcap, or kola. The orange, white, and red beads of the kola made it easy to keep an eye on him, but John still needed the binocular glasses to ensure he didn't miss. Collateral damage would not be a publicity problem, because there would be no link to the CIA, but he only had only one chance at this mission. A mistake would drive Amjad underground, but not so far that the money wouldn't continue to flow back east. John would be the bank regulator who closed Amjad's account permanently.

John checked for pedestrians and saw none. He lowered the helicopter inch by inch to the ground below the maple tree. With a quick tug on the draw hitch knot, the Super Rat was ready to explore the wild blue yonder. He increased the juice with his joystick, and the electrical motor whined. The chopper rocked and begged for more. He gave the joystick another push, and the bird hovered a foot from the ground. The electric motor's high-pitched whine was out of place at ground level. He eased her out and away from the lower branches, and gave her half throttle until she was away. One hundred fifty feet in the air in three seconds.

When the Super Rat neared the limits of its range, a red light on the remote console blinked. John took her out about six hundred yards. At this range, he couldn't see the helicopter without the binocular glasses. The warning light came on and he brought her back, but he made sure she stayed away from his nest in the maple tree. The bird covered six hundred yards in less than twenty seconds. She handled better out here in the open than he had imagined during the test flights back at Henry's barn.

The women herded the men and children toward the tables. Children sat at one table, men at another, and the women hurried about serving the crowd. An elderly man with a long, white beard sat at the head of the men's table. Amjad Ali Khan sat three men down from the leader's position. From their head movements and gestures, they were a talkative bunch. They conversed with plenty of finger-pointing, head-shaking, and hand-waving.

When the wind shifted, he smelled the pleasant odors of saffron, curry, coriander, and black pepper—favorite spices for lamb and beef among Afghanis. Large platters were displayed at the head of the table. The old guy with the white beard would get the choicest picks before he passed them.

Afghans traditionally ate from the same platter with their hands, careful to stay on their side of the dish. In this picnic setting, food from large platters would be grabbed by hand, and placed on the paper plates in front of the diners. One of the ladies brought a plastic jug and metal saucer and placed it next to the elder. He poured some water into the saucer and washed his hands. The same woman gave him a white cloth, and he dried his hands. She took the jug and saucer away with a slight bow, and the old man stood up.

The bearded elder raised his hands, palms upward, and the Muslims bowed their heads. The prayer lasted about a minute, and he sat back down. Seconds later, the picnickers used their right hands to take food from the main platters, and passed them along. When the men and children had all served themselves, the women went to their table and ate as a group.

John brought the helicopter to an elevation of one hundred feet directly above the picnic tables. The whining engine caused a few children to look up and point skyward. The men craned their necks to see what had caused the commotion. A few pointed at the bird and shook their heads.

Were they mad, annoyed, or unconcerned? The binocular glasses weren't strong enough for that level of detail. It would have been ideal to see their expressions and adapt to their mood as needed.

John kept the helicopter at half throttle and flew it in toward Uri, who flew a smaller chopper of his own. Uri looked up at the sound and the picnickers turned their heads toward him. He waved at them.

John took the Super Rat higher over the crowd, out of sight and sound range, and brought it around to the proper attack angle.

Amjad Ali Kahn had his back to the maple tree, his head down more often than not, as he shoveled food into his mouth with his hand. He raised his head to talk and gulp his tea. He had the habit of tipping his head up and back each time he drank. This would be the best time to strike, and would provide the largest target for the helicopter.

There would be no second chance. He had to get it right the first time, or he would kill an innocent—or worse—blow the mission entirely. Either outcome was unacceptable.

He initiated the attack with large circles, two hundred feet in diameter above the crowd. He followed a mental line from the helicopter down to the ground. In order to get this right, he had to imagine a straight line from the nose canopy to the target, and use the line as an imaginary laser that would cut through Amjad's skull along a dorsal contour. He kept the Super Rat at three-quarters throttle, and would increase speed on the final approach.

At one hundred feet high, no one paid attention to the electric motor's hum. Amjad sat at the center of the bird's circular flight pattern. He gobbled food from his hand and gulped more tea. A young boy noticed the chopper and pointed. Every mission had a point where it could still be abandoned. It was now or never.

John took the Super Rat around for the final approach and back up to two hundred feet. The helicopter broke from the circular pattern behind Amjad and cut a sharp radius to the epicenter where his beaded kola bobbed. John cranked the throttle to full, and the engine whined so loud he heard it from up in the tree. Amjad tipped his head up as if he'd heard something. He imagined Amjad's eyes darting to the side as he drank his tea and thought, "What *is* that noise?"

The Super Rat's nose canopy slammed into Amjad's cervical spine, where it connected to his skull, and the rainbow-beaded kola flew straight up, hung in the air for a moment, and then dropped on the couscous platter. The carbon canopy shattered on impact. Plastic shards and metal slivers soared upward and across the table in a 180-degree spray pattern. No one, especially Amjad, had time to duck.

His head slammed down on the paper plate, and fragments of brown sauce, food, skull, and brain matter splattered like a rotted pumpkin onto the picnickers. Amjad's head rebounded off the wooden table and snapped back, pulling his upper body vertical. His ruptured skull ejected pulverized brain. His bloody head dangled from his spine and rolled to one shoulder, all but severed from his body.

The guy next to him freaked out and screamed so loud that Uri looked up from his table and then ran to the scene. The screamer pushed Amjad's lifeless body away from the table, and it slid onto the grass. A couple of the picnickers wiped food and blood from their eyes as they stumbled away from the table. Everyone backed away from the body and circled around the mess, hands covering their eyes and mouths. They backpedaled over one another to get away from whatever had caused Amjad's head to burst. The smaller children who were unable to see over the larger adults laughed, believing the commotion was part of the entertainment. The bearded elder leader crawled under the table.

Heart rate: one hundred ten.

John had to get down as fast as possible and yet unseen. He placed the remote control and the Eschenbachs in the backpack, and swung down from a branch on the maple tree's far side, away from the picnickers' view. He put the backpack over his shoulders and casually strolled to the tree where Baby rested. He clipped in and road the bike path away from the Muslims, fighting the urge to look back.

A mixture of Pashto and English screams rolled down the hill from picnic lot 23A. As much as he wanted to stand on the pedals and race away, John had to tool away from the park as if he was on a casual day trip. With tinted sunglasses and helmet on, he kept his head low and shoulders hunched as he went through the entrance gate.

Uri's rusted Celica raced past him at an intersection and almost clipped another bicyclist driving on the wrong side of the road. *Perfect. If the dumbass had stayed, he may have been able to explain that he wasn't operating the Super Rat.* They would have taken him in anyway, but with time, he could prove his innocence. Now he was a fugitive who had fled the scene. The authorities would assume his guilt and be able to hold him longer for questioning, maybe even get him to say something incriminating on tape, before his lawyer showed up.

John was lightheaded as he turned onto the main road. Adrenaline coursed through his bloodstream with such force that his hands and legs trembled. He had to calm down. Too much adrenaline affected his peripheral vision, and he didn't need an accident right now. He concentrated on his breathing and had it under control after a few miles.

He made the twenty-five-mile ride to Wappinger Falls in just over an hour. He disassembled the remote control into several pieces and dropped them in various garbage cans along the route. He threw the string used to lower the helicopter into a pond at Chelsea Ridge Apartments and watched some minnows fight over it. They got bored in a few seconds and disappeared into the brown water. The waterlogged string floated down with them.

The aftereffects of adrenaline left him hung over and spent by the time he got home. He put Baby in the barn, wiped her down with a chamois, and greased her chain with Teflon lubricant. He threw his riding clothes in the washing machine, turned the dial to HOT, and then took a shower and tried to rest. The sun was too bright for sleep, even with the blinds closed. He drifted in and out of consciousness.

He saw pumpkins, Afghanis, and death on his eyelids. He fought off the temporary guilt that followed a kill. It was real, but it wouldn't last. Someone's friend, brother, lover, lay dead. The mission was mushin, and all obstacles faded.

"Hello, Pat." Gilchrist stayed seated and didn't bother to reach out his hand.

"Kieran." Chocker nodded. "Getting to be a bad habit, don't you think?"

"Us meeting?" said Gilchrist. "Just add it to the list of many."

Chocker didn't try to be funny. The situation was too serious: dead civilians, Yoda in the wind, and the possible exposure of his team. "Any updates I missed on Valhalla?"

Pieces of surveillance video rolled through Gilchrist's mind. What he had learned later, and what wasn't captured on the security cameras, was how the civilians had died.

The first to go were people taking early morning walks. Next were those who lived in homes at the edges of the park. They were mostly on their own when it came to the initial evacuation because the local fire departments and police were too busy trying to figure out what happened and how to contain the gas leak. They had no idea that it was a catastrophic release caused by an explosion. A few early risers heard the sirens and walked into their yards or opened their windows to see what was going on. The chlorine gas was heavier than air, and it rolled downhill from the Kensico Dam, seeking a place to settle. People who weren't immediately overcome by the gas tried to flee, but they had difficulty starting their vehicles as the chlorine worked with humidity and shorted their ignitions. Later, many complained that their cell phones didn't work.

This phenomenon was also attributed to the humidity and high concentrations of gas.

The community had an emergency telephone ring-down system to alert all police, fire departments, and key government personnel, but it hadn't been activated until just after six thirty, nearly a full hour after the fourteen first responders had died. To make matters worse, the initial message told people to shelter-in-place when it should have told many to evacuate. The NYCDEP failed to make the call to the National Response Center, as required, until almost 6:45 a.m.

"You were briefed, I'm sure," said Gilchrist. "You know it was a detonation."

Chocker gazed at his lap and back up at Gilchrist. "Where are you in the investigation?"

"We're not about to go public with the information yet, if that's what you mean."

"I figured as much," said Chocker. "The horse is out of the barn, and whoever blew those tanks is long gone. We've got chatter across the board, mostly emanating from Yemen. Nothing concrete, just celebration of the death of Americans."

"They're not taking any credit?"

"Nothing yet. This was really on the down-low."

"I want you to watch a video with me." Gilchrist pointed a remote control at the large LCD television on the wall.

A surveillance video in black and white rolled across the screen.

"What am I looking at?" said Chocker.

"The Westchester in White Plains. Keep your eyes on the fat guy with the beard and glasses."

They watched a heavyset man, apparently a Hasidic Jew from his clothes and beard, walk along the storefronts, window-shopping. As one camera lost him, another picked him up farther down the mall. He walked through the food court and into a Brookstone. He stopped at a kiosk and watched some kids and a salesman play with remote-control helicopters. The man flew a helicopter for a few minutes and then walked away.

"Riveting," said Chocker.

"Give it a moment." Gilchrist fast-forwarded the tape ten minutes. The Jew returned and handed some money to the salesman, then took one small and one large helicopter with him in a plastic bag.

"Any idea who this is?"

"Nope."

The Jew walked the mall for a few more minutes, keeping his face away from the cameras, and looked in several storefronts before entering a jewelry store. He spent about a half hour in the jewelry store, and came out with the same bag he had before.

"This is where we lose him. He took the escalator to the ground floor and walked outside the building."

"Do you have cameras outside?"

"Yes, and in the parking garage. We followed him to a bus stop, but didn't see him get on."

"Where do the buses go from that stop?"

"They're mostly shuttles that hit the main stores around White Plains and some parking lots. When mall parking is full, shoppers can park off-site and still get to the mall in a few minutes."

"Any cameras at the lots?"

"Apparently not the one he went to. He disappeared after the bus stop."

Gilchrist shut off the screen and placed the remote in his top drawer. He folded his hands on the desk and scrunched his brows together like he had a headache.

"Ever see the guy before?"

Chocker shrugged. "Never."

"Never?"

"Let's not start with the inquisition, Kieran."

"Goddamnit, Patrick." Gilchrist pushed his chair back from the desk but didn't stand up. "I've got over eight hundred dead civilians in the morgue, two Muslims murdered in two months, no good leads, and it sure as hell looks like they're related. The whole goddamn thing stinks of your kind of operation. Are you going to sit there and bullshit me all day that you're here on vacation?"

"I'd love to, but I'm late for a root canal." Chocker smiled, but Gilchrist's face was a stone. "What do you mean two murders?"

"Another man was killed at FDR Park last week . . . another Muslim. A naturalized citizen."

"It was in the papers," said Chocker. "Bloody way to bite the dust." Chocker rested his palms on his crossed legs, head tilted. "And before you ask, Amjad Ali Kahn was mujahideen before someone turned him against the US. So, yes, I do know of him."

"There's a connection. It turns out Abdul Bari had worked at the same airport where Amjad Ali Kahn's family works."

"Works?"

"Kahn's family is on security detail there, as well as other tasks related to running the airport: baggage checks, food service, maintenance—you get the picture."

Chocker shook his head. "That's one hell of a connection for a man who runs a children's charity."

"Are you going to sit there and tell me you didn't know?"

"I wasn't telling you anything," said Chocker. "Of course we knew about Kahn. He used to work with us in Afghanistan against the Russians—before my time. And yes, we knew he had connections at the airport. But Abdul Bari had never popped his head above the wire before. He was off the radar until his life dead-ended in Brooklyn."

"I can let the dagger thing go. I mean, it could have been some tribal dispute among the clan. But now I've got another Muslim with his head smashed into a couscous platter in the middle of a picnic."

"No, Kieran," said Chocker. "What you've got is another dead bad guy who likes to kill Americans, with his head in a permanent prayer position. But, from what I hear, he was killed by a helicopter, a model helicopter, right?"

"Yeah. Like the one you just watched in the video."

"And you have an illegal Russian in custody, who happened to be flying helicopters in the same park a few feet away. Is this right so far?"

Gilchrist nodded.

"So why am I here again?"

"Because the Russian didn't do it."

"Sure. I believe him. Who wouldn't?"

"The Russian says the guy in the video bought two planes from him and paid him to set up at the picnic," said Gilchrist. "He said the Jew was part of the group that hired him to entertain the children. But nobody at the mosque ever heard of this guy."

"Heard of him? You've got a name?"

"The Russian says the Jew called himself Yossi Mandelbrot."

"Ah, a fine Muslim name." He shook his head and laughed.

"I know, I know. But he said he was with the mosque, so the Russian assumed he was Muslim."

"Of course. Russians never lie."

They sat in silence for a few moments. He wouldn't offer Gilchrist the next bit of information, whatever it might be. The first person to speak loses.

"Look, Patrick." Gilchrist leaned his thick forearms on the desk, hands folded. "I need to know if you have a NOC working this thing."

"A NOC?" He smirked. "We don't use nonoperational covers for wet work. NOCs are deep cover to get information, and then get the hell out. They're not assassins. Where the hell did you go to spy school?"

Gilchrist ignored the insult. "I know you have a man masquerading as a civilian. I need to know who it is."

"If I had such a man—which I don't—you know I couldn't divulge mission details, Kieran." Chocker folded his hands behind his head and stretched his legs. "Come on."

"You went over the line, goddamn it. Way over."

"And since when do you draw the line? The attorney general has your manacles so tight, all you can do is beat yourself to death with them. You're hurting your own cause, Kieran."

"We're on American soil, and I don't care what you do overseas . . . not really," Gilchrist said, his face red. "But you're in my backyard, and I need to know what you're doing."

"Your backyard?" Chocker snorted. "I didn't see your name on the deed."

Gilchrist lowered his voice to a raspy whisper. "Don't be a smart-ass. You are not authorized to operate on US soil."

"Read the motivational posters, Kieran." Chocker's face turned to stone. "Strategic counterintelligence is our mission."

"I read them," said Gilchrist. "Your missions are ad hoc and don't include armed conflict with the enemy on US soil."

"That's debatable."

"Hardly." Gilchrist glowered at him. "And even if it was, it wouldn't include covert assassinations of Al Qaeda or any other group."

Chocker snorted with a disgusted grin. "You couldn't find Al Qaeda if they drew a map and exposed their location with one of those damn pushpins you're always sticking in the wall."

Gilchrist cracked his knuckles and took a breath. "You come in here all high and mighty, Mr. Wet Works." He motioned to Chocker's hands. "You wear those scars like they're medals, and you've never even served. I know about the farm—and I don't mean Langley, where you guys go to learn your hand-to-hand combat." He shook a finger. "But that's not for here, not against Americans. You're not special, and you're not above the law. One day you'll slip up, and who's going to cover your ass then?"

Chocker hid his surprise at the reference to his secret martial arts training unit in Connecticut. No one outside a handful of people knew, and he guessed Gilchrist had just heard a rumor or was shaking a tree to see if any fruit fell. Still, he would check for leaks within his team later.

"The law?" said Chocker. "You've been following the law since 9/11, and you geniuses, with all your data, let a scumbag Nigerian Fruit of the Loom bomber into the country on Northwest Airlines with an explosive jock strapped to his nuts." He grabbed his crotch and shook it. "And this guy was already on your watch list. Was that your Christmas present to the American people?" He leaned back in the leather chair. "I can't run my operation like you do, Kieran, or the whole goddamn country will go up in smoke."

Gilchrist's face turned bright red and he bit his lip.

Chocker sat up straight. "Isn't it possible the Russian did it?"

"Not a chance."

"Why not?"

"We checked the remote control he used. It's on a different frequency than the one that killed Amjad Ali Khan. We also checked the Russian's inventory against the video. Yossi Mandelbrot bought the same model from the Russian that was used to kill Amjad."

"Could there be other helicopters that look like it?"

"The serial number on the helicopter in the park matches the Russian's inventory."

"Which puts the Russian at the top of the list."

"Except his remote wouldn't work the helicopter that killed Amjad Khan."

Chocker had another way to solve the problem, but he was reluctant to give Gilchrist a clue. The chainker would feel better if he reached the conclusion on his own. "Maybe another Russian did it."

"What?"

"What if the Russian had an accomplice in the park?"

"Already thought of that. It's possible, but we have nothing to take us in that direction."

"It was obviously a disguise. I mean, the guy wasn't likely a real Jew. My guess is he wasn't fat or pigeon-toed either."

Gilchrist mulled this over a bit. "You think they were working together, and the whole time they knew they could use Yossi as the fall guy and clear the Russian?"

"It would explain why we have no Yossi Mandelbrot, but still have an alibi for the Russian. Pretty smart. Smells like beets and wodka to me."

"I think you may know more about the Kensico catastrophe than you let on."

"You mean the KFC, don't you?"

Gilchrist didn't need to be told what the "F" stood for. He threw a plastic baggie across the desk. "That was priority mailed to our New York office this morning. Don't open it. We still have some tests to run."

Chocker picked up the clear baggie as if it contained a disease. Inside was a small credit card–sized photograph. The image was of a man on a bicycle wearing a helmet, sunglasses, and a backpack. He turned it over and read the handwritten name: JOHN REXFORD, printed with indelible ink.

"Rexford?" said Chocker. "That's one of the guys from your list."

"He's not one of my guys," said Gilchrist. "Yours, maybe?"

Chocker needed time to come up with a response. "Who uses a Polaroid camera anymore? Japanese pieces of crap."

"Polaroids were invented in America." Gilchrist cocked an eyebrow. "It's not a Polaroid. It's a Fuji Instax. Which means we know the image wasn't computer-generated."

Chocker gave Gilchrist a look like he'd just pointed out that water was wet. "It's not real clear who it is or where it was taken. What makes you think it was Rexford?"

"Because whoever sent it wrote 'John Rexford' on the back." Gilchrist smirked.

"They could have written Humpty-Dumpty, Kieran."

"We ran the image through our software, and it gave us the person's height and weight. It matches Rexford."

"And how many other people are on your list?"

"Four," said Gilchrist. "But none of their names were written on the back of the photograph."

"There was hardly room," said Chocker. "This picture could have been taken anywhere."

"It could have been, but it wasn't. We checked out the grounds at FDR. Take the rider out of the picture, and you've got a western-facing view from FDR Park, about three lots down from where Amjad Ali Khan lost his head."

"Any idea who sent it?"

Gilchrist shook his head. "Someone who doesn't like John Rexford. Maybe someone on his team who wants to rat him out."

"Or maybe someone who wants to send you down the wrong fork in the road."

"I thought of that, but I can't come up with any real reason someone would want to do such a thing."

"I've got one," said Chocker. "Have you looked inside your organization?"

"What?" Gilchrist turned his head a little and leered through puffy eyelids.

"You guys leak information like a sieve. Maybe they've got someone inside the FBI—hell, probably—who wants an American to go down for this."

"I'm not going to entertain your insults, Patrick. What I am going to do is request a joint meeting with the DHS secretary, and you and your boss, and we're going to find out what you're not telling me."

Chocker stood up. "You're going to find out what there is to know: nothing. And worse, you'll be wasting valuable time that neither of us can afford. Call me if you have something that can help nail the real bad guys. I'll check on Rexford, too. Maybe someone knows something on my side, but I doubt it."

"Yeah, I'm sure someone knows something." Gilchrist watched the back of the CIA officer as he walked out the door. He buzzed Christine Sparks on the intercom.

"You have the names of the four riders who fit the physical description?"

"Yes, sir."

"Get them in here ASAP."

"Some of them live on the West Coast."

"Then fly them here. Tell them it's a matter of national security, and we'll cover their expenses. And get Rexford in here today, if possible."

If Rexford was Chocker's man, the less time Chocker had to contact him, the better.

The cautious seldom err.

Equipment checks were standard operating procedure. Whether it was a weapon or something as uncomplicated and seemingly innocuous as a bicycle, SOP was to check for defective or worn parts, the least of which were the brakes. He checked his car brakes on wet or snow-covered roads by getting up to speed and pumping the brake pedal to confirm how well the vehicle would track, and how fast it stopped. He did the same with Baby when there was any chance of wet roads or sand bringing him down.

John took Baby up to twenty miles per hour at the first small decline, pumped both brake levers on the drop-down handlebars, and successfully fishtailed the rubber and Kevlar tires from side to side. He performed this maneuver on dry or wet pavement. Daily adjustments were made, depending on heat and humidity.

He smiled, overcome by the sensation of perfect balance. Baby held him up with no more than a few square inches of their combined mass in contact with the earth. He thanked God and didn't care if there was no God, or if God was too big-picture to get involved with something as basic as riding a bicycle. There was more to the universe than John Rexford, and he wanted to thank whatever it was out there for allowing him his own piece of the action.

It had rained all night long, and fog clung to the evergreens like watered-down milk. From a distance it was thick and palpable, but when he reached that point up ahead, the fog was already gone. It appeared again farther down the road, but when he rode closer, it was gone again. He pedaled faster. Just a little faster, and he might catch the ghostly steam before it disappeared.

Baby's Kevlar tires held the road nicely. He sensed how far he could push the thin rubber bands before he would drop. He wouldn't be caught off guard if someone pulled out in front of him, or a chubby woodchuck decided to make a frenzied dash from the ditch.

On a group ride in New Jersey, a flock of wild turkeys had nearly decapitated him when they chose to fly across the road at the same time he had decided to break fifty miles per hour on a downhill run. He careened into forty or more ten-pound flapping and gobbling birds, and the next moment he was on the other side. It was as if someone had picked him up and placed him on the other side of the flock, or time had stopped for him, but not the turkeys. After the turkeys had crossed, his time began again, and he had cleared the collision.

When you do something, you should burn yourself completely, like a good bonfire, leaving no trace. It was a favorite quote from Suzuki's book on Zen meditation. John applied this practice to rides and workouts. Funny thing about Buddhist sayings: after reading them once, and even if he didn't study them for months, they came back when he needed them. He sometimes thought he should go for it and try to focus on the Way, as the Buddhists called it, but he never did. He just dabbled, and hoped the good stuff stuck.

Suzuki's quote, however, stayed with him and popped into his head on almost every ride and workout. *Burn yourself completely, like a good bonfire, leaving no trace.* The brain found it difficult to just be. Suzuki taught that humans usually think before they act, and this thinking left traces or shadows on our activity. It meant that we're not completely in the activity's moment but are distracted by what we have attached to the activity, thereby tainting the pureness of what we do with the stain of our own ego.

He burned all traces when he rode. A good bonfire.

His ideal pedal cadence hovered around one hundred revolutions per minute. He kept his eyes focused ahead. He felt his breath's vibrations going in through his mouth and out through his throat, where a small door opened and closed, mixing his soul with the atmosphere around him. If his ego was in check, and he truly burned the fire, there was no difference between him, the air, the bike, his breath, or the earth. It was all one as it passed through his breath's swinging door.

Any time was a good time to ride. But September was one of the best months in the Catskills. Second homeowners went back to New York City and New Jersey, high school kids were hopefully in school and not driving around high during free periods, and the family vacations were over. The days were still long, with lots of sunshine and the oppressive heat and thick Hudson Valley summer humidity already in retreat, chastened by cooler Canadian arctic air.

Bikers had to look out for leaf-peepers coming up to see the colors change. September was a little early for them, but he never ruled out an elderly couple driving at ten miles per hour around a blind curve because they saw crimson-tinted sugar maple leafs.

Maggie, the next mission, the next twenty years, weighed on his thoughts. Not enough mushin. He had to burn the fire, leave no trace, or his spirit would be shackled to the road.

He dropped down a gear and pedaled harder.

Past stone walls that lined the country roads where they had been placed by hand over one hundred years ago. Stacked shale and bluestone delineated property boundaries and kept the cattle on the appropriate side of the rock fence. Some of the stone walls had been laid down by surveyors to mark property lines. Others were piled high by farmers' cracked and calloused hands before planting spring crops and winter wheat, thrown on a stone boat, and placed in rows between fields to mark irregular plots of grazing land. Now they were overshadowed by new growth forest, relics in a land where few farmers remained.

Past dilapidated barns whose broken backs bent with the weight of time as it twisted their wooden spines and forced them back to the ground. Lilacs, arrowwood viburnum, firebush, and thorny blackberries crawled over the weathered beams and dragged them to the dirt. Woodchucks, snakes, squirrels, and beetles burrowed through the stone walls, opening air pockets and letting in sun, rain, and wind to erode the foundation. With time, they too left no trace.

Past summer cabins, built in the forties and fifties for weekenders, now converted into year-round homes where low-income families and retirees lived. The Catskills' senior citizens were dying and had no one to leave their homes to because their children left the state years ago to warmer climes for employment. Half of their life's labor was auctioned off and given to the government to cover a usury inheritance tax.

Past old lumber yards and mills converted into empty warehouse space, where the Catskill region's lucrative tanning business had thrived in the early 1800s. Hemlocks were sacrificed to support the leather and fur industries. Their high tannin content made hemlocks perfect for curing hides. Trees were stripped of bark and the dead wood left to rot. When the hemlocks were gone, the tanning industry went with them. All that remained were signs memorializing the once bustling town of Tannersville, and third-growth hardwoods intermingled with a few straggling hemlocks that had survived man and the wooly adelgid.

Past the killing. Could he get past it? *Pedal harder. Burn completely.*

Over there he killed with completeness, in the moment. Everything outside himself was gone. He didn't deliberate whether it was good or bad. In his heart it was right for him, to protect his country, to eliminate the enemies who would tear society apart. It was a Zen moment for him, wherein he burned everything and left only ashes.

Why the afterthoughts here? If he had done something so completely perfect and without attachment, why did it leave shadows? Maybe the truth was that some things always left a shadow, and some actions couldn't be burned in a lifetime.

Too many thoughts. No good.

He breathed in, and the universe came through his throat's swinging door. He breathed out, and his self left with each breath through the door to the universe. His breath came in, and he went out. *Pedal, pedal, pedal, and breathe.*

He picked up speed on the downhill run to the Ashokan Reservoir. At 190 feet, the Ashokan was the deepest body of water in the Catskill reservoir system that fed New York City's unquenchable thirst. Over one thousand residents had been relocated in the three years it took to fill the reservoir. Farmers, loggers, and quarrymen were forced to uproot and find another way of life, to start from scratch and leave their livelihood for the betterment of a people one hundred miles south—people they had never known, people who needed their water. Roads, homes, shops, churches, and mills were relocated or abandoned. Buildings that once held the heat of wood stoves, the smell of food, and the laughter of children were torn down or burned. The city unearthed crumbled and worm-eaten coffins of ancestors and recently departed loved ones, and relocated them to less hallowed ground, to dirt with no memories.

The local unwashed weren't allowed to swim in the clean reservoir once it was filled, for fear their filth would trickle downstream to the taps of the city dwellers. Their children weren't allowed to fish or boat without a special permit from a bureaucracy that existed, it seemed, for the sole purpose of taking their property and making them pay for its use.

Fog clung to the trees and rested on the asphalt causeway that covered the reservoir dam linking the Ashokan's east and west basins. John removed his riding glasses and hung them from his jersey collar. Dewdrops of fog had beaded over them, so he couldn't see anyway. Better to squint than look through blurred lenses. His sweat mixed with the water in the air, and he tasted the asphalt and the hemlocks and maple leaves on his tongue. He had to piss, but he didn't stop on the causeway because someone pushing a stroller, or bird-watching, might show up just when he released. He stood on the pedals and let go. Damp air and sweat washed away warm urine.

Fog mixed with low clouds cut a patchwork through the trees on the distant shoreline. White pine forests disappeared through the opaque glaze and then popped up again, seemingly from nowhere, like dark green ghosts playing tag among fluffed gray pillows.

He stood on his pedals and raised his arms in victory, screaming to let it all out: the breath, the air, his life's uncertainty. He screamed until his throat spasmed with coughs. He sat back down on the stiff racing saddle and swallowed hard. He pedaled a rhythmic cadence that pulled the blood from his toes and fingers, back to his heart, and around the loop of his body. Over and over, until the blood went through the door with his breath, and the difference between wrong and right evaporated beneath the hiss of Baby's wheels.

Pedal, pedal, pedal, and breathe.

Peekamoose Gorge cut through High Point Mountain at the Ashokan Reservoir's west end. He climbed the gorge's east side, ascending fifteen hundred feet in fewer than two miles. He wound his way up through the twists and turns of County Route 42 that curled along the Kanape Brook's banks. At the top, he unclipped one riding shoe from the pedal and took in the view. A break in the clouds revealed most of the reservoir below: a gigantic puddle with soft blue edges. Triangular treetops spiked through the mist as if a child had drawn them with a dull crayon.

He pulled the water bottle from its bracket and took a long drink, rinsed his mouth, and spit. He sensed the mind weeds, returned the bottle to the bracket, clipped his free shoe back into the pedal, and pointed Baby downhill in the direction from which he had come.

The fifteen-hundred-foot vertical allowed plenty of opportunity for John to break previous personal speed records, or at least push the envelope, even with wet roads. He pedaled hard until he reached forty-five miles per hour, then tucked in behind the handlebars and let gravity do the work. Goose bumps bubbled over his skin as fog and sweat evaporated into the wind.

Speed: fifty-five miles per hour.

Heart rate: ninety-one.

Oxygen roared through his veins and made him giddy, like a kid running down the stairs to look under the Christmas tree, throwing caution to the wind, unconcerned about slipping on the carpet. And what if he did fall? Get back up and open your presents. Nobody wants a crybaby at Christmastime.

This ride was a gift. Tears streamed down his cheeks as the wind beat into his eyelashes. He thanked God and pedaled harder.

He kept his hands on the brake levers, and eased Baby into a sharp curve. He heard his cycling coach somewhere in the fog. *Lean with it, don't turn the wheel. Lean with it, and the bike will find the groove in the road, the perfect arc to cut the distance from point A to point B.*

Red taillights blinked up ahead like an angry frog that had been discovered hiding beneath the weeds. *Blink. Blink. Blink.*

There was little time to react. Only a hundred feet of wet road between him and the angry frog's eyes, and he wasn't going to stop in time. He could lay Baby down and slide into the car, or increase speed and pedal around into possible oncoming traffic.

These decisions weren't made by executive teams plotting the direction to take the company over the next few months. They were made by the subconscious, and John was out of the decision-making loop. He squeezed tight on Baby's handlebars, guided her around the angry lights to the car's left side and into oncoming traffic. The lane was clear as far ahead as he could see through the fog. He might pull this one off with no scars or broken bones.

A family of deer—two does and three yearlings—that had all but lost their spots to shabby coats munched on shag bark hickory nuts with their heads down, oblivious to the car that had stopped to observe them. Nor did they notice the bike and rider speeding toward them in near silence.

Time stopped, but not like the time with the turkeys. On this ride, the time stopped for both John and the deer. He smashed into the closest yearling and it bleated a nasal cry as its legs went out from under it. Baby stayed with the yearling, but he continued airborne at full speed into the largest doe. He grabbed her neck, and they lurched over the wet asphalt road as one body, crashing into the rock-and stick-filled ditch.

The doe kicked at the air, got her feet back under her, then jumped up and trotted on shaky limbs to the herd already hiding in the woods. The yearling that had been in the wrong place at the wrong time lay on the wet road and continued to bleat and kick her two good rear legs in an attempt to run. Both front legs were twisted underneath her body.

"Are you hurt? Hey. Are you okay?"

The voice came from the clouds above. *Chocker? God?* A baby cried after the voice.

"Can you hear me?"

Blood thundered in his ears. He opened one eye.

God wore a Land's End parka and a plaid wool shirt. GOING GREEN and RIVERKEEPER patches decorated the pockets. His thick glasses enlarged his eyes so that he looked more alien than even God should appear. *God is a frog?* He had on well-worn brown corduroys and Merrell hiking boots. An angel stood next to him in a matching outfit.

The baby cried again, weaker this time.

"Can you hear me?" God said.

"What?"

"Are you hurt, mister?" The angel looked worried.

John's rattled brain came back from wherever it had run for safety. He remembered the taillights blinking red, flying through the air, and sliding with the doe into the ditch.

Heart rate: one hundred twenty.

He jumped to his feet and took a defensive stance, his weight on his shaky back leg.

"Whoa, fellah." It was only a man. "We want to help." The man stumbled backward with his hands in the air.

John sensed no threat and dropped his guard. "Why'd you park in the road?" he said.

"We were looking at the deer," the man said. "We're sorry. We had the emergency lights on."

"It's a goddamn highway," John snapped. "You don't stop in the middle of the road to sightsee." He wiggled his toes and fingers, and rolled his neck over his shoulders. Nothing broken.

The fiftysomething naturalist puffed his chest and said, "It's the Catskill Park. We didn't think there would be a lot of traffic in a park."

"Park? You asshole. 'Park' is a relative term. People live here. It's not a park." Almost imperceptibly he moved within inches of the man's face. "Go back to Central Park if you want to stop your car in the middle of the road. Stay the hell out of my town."

"Come on, Walter," said the woman. She pulled on the guy's arm. "Let's leave the man alone."

He looked over at the yearling. It hadn't been a baby that cried, but a bleating deer. It kicked the air with its two good legs and rocked in an attempt to get up. John wiped the mud and stones from his body and walked to the injured animal.

"But honey," said Walter. "The man is hurt. He's bleeding."

John looked down at his legs and arms and saw ragged road rash where the asphalt and sand had peeled skin layers from his right thigh, forearm, and elbow. There was a dull pain in his right shoulder. He had landed on it when he fell with the deer in the ditch. He moved it in the socket to check for damage.

The frightened woman looked back at Walter and whispered, "He doesn't need any help and he looks dangerous."

"I'm not going to leave a poor little deer in the middle of the road." Walter puffed up again and said, "We have to take him to a vet."

The woman shook her head and started for the car.

John leaned over the yearling. Both front legs were broken above and below the knee joint, and part of the left leg bone had punctured the skin. It stuck out like a wet ivory twig. The yearling's pupils were dilated and its breath was short. Blood bubbled from its nose and over its tongue. It was in shock and would not survive.

He had seen deer hit by cars before, and they never survived. They were like horses. High-strung animals had, at best, a few hours to live once their legs were broken and they were in shock. They literally scared themselves to death. A wild animal can't live tied down.

His father told him that injured deer were the reason nature invented wolves and coyotes: to shorten the time the animal had to suffer.

Walter shook his head at the deer. "We'll take him to a veterinarian," he said. "He'll be all right."

"It's a doe," said John. "And a vet will put her down. Get out of here. I'll take care of it."

"But you only have a bike. How are you . . ."

John's cold stare stopped the man in midsentence. He held his hands by his side, chin up, muscles visibly flexed. Blood trickled through the tiny holes in his scraped skin and down his leg, soaking into his white socks. A clear liquid oozed from the stitches beneath his riding shorts. He looked like a deranged cycling hermit deerslayer.

"Let's go, Walt. Let's just go." The woman grabbed her husband's arm and tugged.

Walter shook his head in protest as his wife hurried him to the car. He looked back at John as if he wanted to say something, then thought better of it.

John grabbed the deer by the back legs and pulled it into the ditch. It stopped bleating. Its heart beat at a rapid rate through the hairs on its neck. Round pellets of feces rolled from its rectum, and its legs twitched.

The car pulled around John and the deer and drove slowly down the hill. The woman craned her neck to look through the rear window as they made the next turn. She grabbed her cold Starbucks mocha frappuccino from the insulated bottle holder and shook her head.

He brought the rock down hard, and the air in the small deer's lungs whispered a final whoosh of relief.

John picked up Baby and gave her a once-over, straightened the handlebars, and checked the true and round of the tires. *A few scratches on the handlebars.* Otherwise, just like him, ginger peachy.

Bicycle and rider limped home the remaining twenty miles. The adrenaline rush left him exhausted, and lactic acid buildup made his legs ache with every turn of the pedals. He played a scenario over and over in his mind where the two idiots in the car replaced the deer, but stopped when his own sense of well-being slipped away.

He saw Maggie's car in the driveway as he pulled in with Baby and hopped off. He'd check Baby out more thoroughly later and touch up the paint job. What he needed now was a hot bath and a whiskey injection.

A heady meatball and garlic aroma greeted him as he stepped into the kitchen.

"Hey, babe," he said.

Maggie stirred something on the stove, her back to him. She turned around and dropped the spoon. Spaghetti sauce splattered against the white linoleum floor.

"Oh my God. What happened?"

He offered the standard male-stupidity grin and said, "I fell."

"You're bleeding. Look at you." Maggie shook her head.

He looked down at his blood-covered leg and arm. The wind had spread the blood over his now-crimson sock. Maggie went to him but stopped short, as if she might hurt him.

"It looks worse than it is," he said. "I peeled off some skin. No broken bones. I'm going to take a shower, or a bath. I don't know."

"Let me look at you." She ran her fingertips lightly over his face.

He stood still while Maggie knelt down and surveyed his wounds. She jumped up quickly, told him to stay, and brought a wet washcloth from the sink. She rolled it slowly over his thigh and rubbed off tiny pebbles stuck in his flesh. She repeated the treatment on his forearm and elbow.

"You should see the other guy," said John.

"What other guy?" She looked up at him. "Did you get in a car accident or something?"

"A deer," he said. "A bunch of deer ran in front of me around a blind curve, and the road was too wet. I couldn't stop in time."

"What happened to the deer?" she asked. Her eyes went to the kitchen window and looked out at the road as if she expected to see a deer there.

"They're fine. They ran away." No sense in making matters worse. Maggie was a real crier when it came to hurting animals, except snakes and spiders, of course. She was selective with her sympathies. However, deer were definitely on the "do not crush in head with rock" list.

Maggie stood up and started to cry.

"What's wrong, sweetheart?" He put his hand on her shoulder. "Maggie?"

She shook her head and pounded her fist once against his chest. "Don't you know you can't keep playing Daredevil with your life on that bike? What about me? How can I be with a man who won't put his family ahead of his own childish needs to ride a bicycle and tempt fate every time he rides?" She pounded one more time and then turned her back to him.

Family?

Ordinarily, if anyone, even someone he loved and would consider marrying, ever told him riding bicycle was childish, he would end the relationship. If it were a man, it might get violent. John wasn't giving up his rides for anyone, not for love or country. There was more to this outburst than the accident. Women like to simmer, feint with a jab, then hit you out of the blue with a hook from the book when you least expected it. It's something their mothers taught them when they were very young. He didn't go there.

"I love you," he said. He walked past her and went upstairs to take a hot bath.

He poured hydrogen peroxide and isopropyl alcohol over his scrapes, and sat down in the bathtub to soak. More pieces of sand and road pebbles loosened in the hot water, and he rubbed them off with his fingertips. The water turned dirty brown. He stood up and patted his wounds with a dry towel, applied antibacterial cream, and taped some gauze to his shredded flesh. He left his elbow exposed to the air, but he didn't want his bloody leg staining his clothes or Henry's furniture.

He pushed against the sewn-up, self-inflicted wound earned from his encounter with Yoda. It was swollen and red around the edges. He pushed a little harder, and a small drop of puss oozed from beneath one of the remaining sutures. It was time to get back on the antibiotics. He put on loose-fitting sweat pants and a T shirt, and went downstairs to test the ambient room temperature and see if Maggie's mood had simmered.

Maggie brought him linguini, cooked al dente as he liked it. She ladled a serving of red sauce over two large meatballs on his plate.

"This smells really good," he said. "Just what I needed."

"What you need is therapy," she said.

He didn't respond. Maggie wouldn't make eye contact. *Not good.*

He grated some Romano cheese over his plate and took a mouthful of linguini. Maggie had purposely burned the outside of the meatballs a little to give them a crunchy, smoky taste. The Italian women on her mother's side hadn't let their little girl grow up and leave the house without knowing how to cook. Every meal had a special spiciness. Even something as otherwise mundane as linguini with meatballs was a masterpiece in Margaret Mary Castalia's capable hands. Maggie held a PhD in garlic, sage, and oregano.

She picked at a meatball with her fork and drank some wine. They ate like this for a few minutes, and then he put his fork down and looked at her. She wouldn't look up from her plate, so he continued to stare. After a minute or two, he couldn't take it anymore.

"What's wrong?"

"What?" She looked up, her eyes wet.

"What is wrong? I'm sorry I got in an accident. I must have taken at least twenty good falls since I started riding." He turned his palms over and raised his eyebrows. "I can ride, Maggie. When you ride like I do, you fall. It's part of the game. But when was the last time you heard of anyone dying on a bike?"

"People die, John."

"Yeah, when some kid jumps out into traffic on a four-wheeler or something. You don't die because you take a skid and land in a ditch. Jesus Christ, I'm a professional."

Maggie glared at him. He was sure her expression had nothing to do with him using the Lord's name in vain. She went to the kitchen counter, grabbed a newspaper, and slammed it down on the table. The corner landed on his plate and soaked up some red sauce. It reminded him of his blood-covered sock.

The headline read: MAN KILLED IN FREAK ACCIDENT AT FDR PARK.

The subtitle said that the police had persons of interest and that the death might be a homicide. He scanned the article for any mention of a cyclist or the Russian. Nothing.

The article described how a Muslim picnic had turned terribly bad when one of the picnickers had gotten his head crushed by a remote-control helicopter. It was assumed to be an accident, as some hobbyists flew remote-control helicopters nearby, but the police considered it a possible homicide because the victim was Muslim and might be tied to terrorism.

Nice to see profiling hasn't gone out of fashion, he thought. *Anything to sell papers*. There was no way a reporter had specifics about Amjad Ali Khan from the Westchester County police department, because they were clueless as to his terrorist activities. No mention of the FBI. The article closed with a statement about an ongoing investigation.

He looked up from the paper.

"Well?" Maggie said.

"You've got to give me a little more here if you want me to figure out what's bugging you."

"I looked all over this house for your helicopter," she said. "And guess what?"

"What?"

"It isn't here. It's not here, John." She poured on the tears, huffing and hiding her eyes in her hands. He let her cry and catch her breath.

"I still don't get it, Maggie." *Time for the little white lies that keep a relationship together, not to mention the national security of the United States.*

"Tell me . . ."

"Yes?"

"Are you still in the military?"

"What?"

"Are you still in the military? Are you working undercover, or whatever you guys call it?"

He shook his head.

"John, I need to know. Because I can't be with you if you're a killer. I can't."

"And you came up with this theory based on what?" He tried to act annoyed, but was proud of the way her mind worked. He made a mental note not to cheat on her, unless it was in his plans to get caught.

"I looked all over this house for your helicopter," she said. "That man was killed by a helicopter. John, I know you learned a lot in the special forces, and I know you can fly those things." Maggie hesitated, and then said, "So?"

"So you looked everywhere?"

"Yes."

"Everywhere?"

"Yes." The determination in her voice weakened.

He stood up, grabbed her arm, and yanked her from the table. Not in a painful way, but in a way that let her know who was the masculine one of the two linguini lovers.

He pulled her into the living room and turned on the lights.

"Did you look in this room?"

"Yes." Her bluster was gone.

He walked over to the couch and pulled it from the wall. "Did you look here?"

"No," she said. "Why would you—"

"Because, Inspector Clouseau, I needed a place to plug it in, and every outlet in the kitchen is filled by the microwave, toaster oven, mixer, radio, the little television you like to watch when you're cooking, and my cell phone charger . . ." He put his finger in the air as if he had an "ah-ha!" moment. "Oh, and your phone charger, too."

He picked up the little chopper, spun the rotors in his hand, and gave her an Alfred E. Newman grin. "Do I still look like the dreaded picnic killer?"

She ran to him, wrapped her arms around his neck, and nuzzled her forehead into his chest.

"I was alone here," she said. "And you were gone, like you always disappear on these rides for hours." She looked into his eyes. "And then you go camping sometimes without me, and you were in the military, and I know you were there for the right reasons, and I know you were special ops, but then I thought you weren't out of that life, and how would we ever get married, and have children, and then I—"

"Whoa, Maggie, hold on." He brushed a tear-soaked ribbon of hair from her face with the back of his hand, and held her neck softly, caressing the smooth skin behind her ear. "I love you. I'm right here."

"I know, I know, I'm so stupid." Maggie shook her head and squeezed him tighter. "But it seemed so real when I had no one to talk to and you were gone again on the bike, and then when you came home all hurt and bleeding, it was like some kind of . . . I don't know, battle you were in."

He pulled her close and made a soft shushing sound as he rocked her back and forth.

"I will always be riding, honey," he whispered into her ear. "You do know that, don't you?"

"Yes, I know."

"Even when we're retired and living in Florida and all the other old farts are playing shuffleboard, I will be on the bike."

"I know, John," she said with a sniffle. "Do you think we'll be together that long?" Maggie's eyes pleaded for the right answer.

"Longer," he said, and kissed her soft lips. He led her upstairs by the hand.

Maggie dominated him from above, her hands pinned on his shoulders. She needed to know she had some power over him. Then, before it was over, he rolled her onto her back and plunged into her with relentless fury, until she could only respond with short gasps.

He made love to her and burned the present bonfire into oblivion, and then collapsed and left no trace. Maggie curled around him like a helpless child. The fight had left her limbs. In sex, as in combat, you vanquish your partner. At the pyre of their lovemaking, only ashes remained.

Coyotes wailed like tight wires plucked in the wind, and then faded away as if they were temporary spirits sent to remind him of the other side. A few moths beat their wings against the screens, attracted by the light and fleeing from the inevitable winter. Henry Clay Hall thought about winter and how many more he had, and the quiet it would bring the Catskill Mountains in just a few more months. He thought about Christmas stories, especially the one about how nothing was stirring, not even a mouse. It made him laugh that the only thing stirring inside this trailer, besides his aging bones, would be those mice, and his fat cat, when snow blanketed the hemlocks.

Henry was not a heavy sleeper. When he did sleep, it was always irregular and seldom in the early morning. He found that after midnight was the best time to write. He liked the rolling peeps of the frogs in the background, and the soft silence when no cars rumbled on the road. The smell of pine trees was stronger at night as the cooler air brought nature's fragrance through his window screens. He sipped his whiskey, tapped at the Smith Corona Classic 12's worn white keys, and thought about Abe Lincoln.

He looked up for a moment and saw that all the lights were out next door at John's. Maggie's car was parked in the driveway. *Maybe that jarhead is growing a brain*, he thought. Henry felt a warm glow inside that wasn't from the whiskey. He liked to think he had a little to do with her being there. Maybe John didn't want to end up stuck in a trailer, alone with no one but a cat and a dead president. He smiled to himself and took another sip.

Henry had admired the view of his farmhouse across the road thousands of times. He knew every blade of grass, peeled paint strip, and uncut shrub on the property. He knew when the postman had come, when the leaves needed to be raked, and when the first daffodils were ready to pop their heads in spring. Anything out of place caught his eye, and what he just thought he saw was definitely out of place.

A man-sized silhouette had pulled itself up onto the porch roof. *Goddamn perverts*, he thought. *Some kids trying to get a look in the window at John and Maggie*. He got up as quickly as his old frame would allow, grabbed his .357 S&W Magnum from the top of the refrigerator, and hobbled to the door.

He tottered on three legs across the driveway as fast as he could with the .357 at his side, and tried not to huff and puff and give his position away. Whoever it was must have heard him coming anyway, because he saw the guy slide down off the porch roof like a dark shadow when he was fifty feet away.

"Hey! You!" Henry shook the gun at the man. "Stop right there, or I'll blast your pervert ass!"

The man dropped to the ground and began a rapid crawl along the edge of the house as Henry raised his weapon.

"Stop right there!" Henry fired one booming shot into the air as the shadow dissolved into the black woods.

The lights upstairs came on and John was at the front door in seconds. He was leaning a little to one side and had a throwing knife in his hand.

"What the hell, Henry? What are you shooting at?"

"Some pervert was walking around your property." Henry's voice was irritated and disappointed at the same time. "I just wanted to scare him. I wasn't going to shoot him."

John looked around but saw no one. His hand relaxed on the knife's spine. He gave Henry a look of disbelief.

"I'm telling you, John," said Henry. "I was right over there, tapping at the keys, and saw someone jump up on your porch roof. When he heard me coming he slid back down . . ."

"Slid?"

"Like a cat-burglar. The guy was either a real pervert, or he was going to rob you. I didn't want to take any chances." Henry shook the heavy pistol at his side. "I didn't mean to scare you, but I sure as hell didn't want him to get away. I can't believe he ran after hearing the gunshot. Some balls."

John walked off the porch and shook his neighbor's hand. "Having a gun-nut insomniac next door has its advantages.

Thank you, man." He gave Henry a hug, and the old soldier stiffened uncomfortably. "Relax," said John. "I'm not going to kiss you."

"I wouldn't put it past you," Henry said with a wry smile.

"You want to come in?"

"No, no. I've disturbed the two of you too much as it is." He motioned to the upstairs rooms with his head and grinned. When John smiled, Henry said, "I'll get back to my book."

"Next time, use a rifle," said John. "You can just shoot him from your window. I hear you rednecks get all your game that way."

Henry waved his cane in the air and walked across the road to his trailer.

John turned to walk up the porch when he noticed something pinned to the screen door frame. He unpinned it and walked out into the yard a few steps where the light from his bedroom shone down on the small rectangle. It was a photocopy of an image he knew all too well: his own. It was the photograph that Yoda had taken by the chlorine tanks. John saw himself crouched in a firing position. It was a perfect frontal shot of his face and, contrary to Chocker's assessment of Yoda's photography skills, easily identifiable.

He hid the paper under a cushion in the living room for later retrieval, and went upstairs.

"What was that all about?" said Maggie.

John laughed awkwardly and shook his head. "Henry was over there writing about Abe Lincoln's assassination, and he was three sheets to the wind. He thought he saw something—probably a coyote or maybe a bear, who knows."

Maggie laughed as John took her into his arms. "Did you help him back across the road?"

"He was all right. I watched him until he went inside. He'll be fine."

"That gun scared me, John. My God, it was loud."

She snuggled under his arm and turned out the bedside lamp. When John spoke, his voice was soft, and it comforted her.

"I was thinking," he said.

"Yes, hon?"

"Maybe you should think about moving in here, for a while anyway."

"What do you mean?" she whispered.

"I mean, move in. We should practice this marriage thing for a little while. Practice like you play, you know." He squeezed her tighter.

"It's not a football game, John. I play for keeps."

"I know you do, Maggie. I know you do."

He kissed her neck, and he knew she was smiling.

"Yes," said John. "It's me. Do you want to run a voice analysis?"

There was a moment of silence on the other end before Chocker said, "What is it?"

"He's here, and he's stalking me."

"Who?"

"Don't play stupid with me, Pete. You know who. He tried to break into my house last night."

"How do you know?"

"Because my neighbor saw him last night and took a shot at him."

"Good neighbor," said Chocker. "Positive ID?"

"Positive enough," he said. "And I think he might have broken into Maggie's house. Her locket showed up in my barn. I'm telling you, he's right here in my neighborhood."

"I'm going to put you on hold for a second. Don't hang up."

What the hell was this? Chocker was putting him on hold? Was the CIA spook triangulating the location? Was he sending a hit team that would cut the cord of the only man who could tie C. Peter Chocker to illegal murders in the US? John scanned the lawn and woods outside his house for Yoda. It seemed there were shadows everywhere that hadn't been there before.

The pain in his leg was becoming unbearable as the infection grew. John had taken a double dose of antibiotics last night and had hoped for the best. It seemed like the pus that oozed out this morning was brown instead of green, and that meant it was decayed. If the wound was infected deep inside the approximation sutures, he would have to go to a hospital and get it fixed by a real doctor. What kind of questions would that bring up? *Oh yeah, Doc, I fell on my knife and decided to sew it up at home. Doesn't everyone have catgut in their medicine cabinet?*

After Maggie had left for school, he chewed an OxyContin and drank a pot of coffee. He didn't want to, but he couldn't think straight anymore with the pain. Maybe Chocker had a doctor he could see who wouldn't ask any questions.

John went to the windows upstairs and checked the grounds below, and then the trees. He knew that monkey could climb. *How had he found me? Of course, the photo. The photo that was supposed to be grainy.* He went downstairs and pulled it from the cushion. Last night seemed like a dream now: Henry, the gunfire, asking Maggie to stay. He hadn't slept a wink since placing the photograph of himself under the cushion. And he had asked Maggie to move in. What the hell was he thinking? Make a smaller target for Yoda? He'd pick her off more easily if she were alone. The more time they spent together, the safer it was for Maggie.

Where the hell was—?

"Can you get her to stay with you?" said Chocker.

"I already have," John replied.

"Good," said Chocker. "Stay put until you get a call from the FBI."

"You're going to tell the FBI?"

"No. But they've narrowed down the list, and you're on it."

"What?" His voice jumped an octave as he scanned the woods, and then Henry's trailer.

"Agent Gilchrist has your name on a list of bike-riding veterans. A charity. Want to tell me about it?"

He pressed on the wound. More brown ooze was coming through the gauze. "I signed up to take a charity ride," he said. "It's for wives and children of soldiers who died in battle. But I didn't ride."

"Noble act. But you collected money and signed up?"

"I faked some names on the roster and sent in a hundred-dollar money order."

"Gilchrist got the bright idea a cyclist with military skills is behind Brooklyn and FDR, and you went to the top of his list when you didn't show."

"Great."

"No good deed goes unpunished, son. He's pulling in everyone who signed up for the charity ride and wants to interview them. You can handle it. Play the irritated veteran who wants no part of Uncle Sam's war."

"That won't be hard."

Chocker didn't respond right away. John heard another phone ring in the background.

"Are you with me, John?"

"You just find out where Yoda is hiding, Pete. You find him, and let me loose on him. I'll end this now."

"You'll be the first to know. In the meantime, stay low and keep an eye on Maggie. I'm trying to get someone to shadow her now, but it's going to take a while."

"How long?"

"I don't know. Maybe until tonight. I don't have people running around the woods up there."

Chocker sounded irritated. John didn't want to piss off the only man who could assign close personal protection to Maggie, so he kept his thoughts to himself.

"Do your best, Pete. Thanks."

"Stay on point, John. And keep this phone with you at all times."

After Chocker hung up, John realized how truly vacant this old farmhouse had become. He took an inventory of his weaponry and prepared for battle.

Yoda pulled out the lineman's pliers and cut the cable and phone lines. He could not afford interruptions tonight. No phone calls to wake his target.

The night was cloudless, and a toenail moon illuminated the yard better than it had on his first visit. A slight wind gave him background noise. He liked the wind. The wind blew and the peepers stopped; the wind stopped and the peepers sang.

He checked to make sure John's car wasn't in the driveway. It wasn't back at the house when he had checked earlier.

Yoda brought tools with him this time: fifty feet of white, braided cotton cord typically used for clothesline; plastic tubing; and some duct tape. In the backpack were several feet of intravenous tubing with an adjustable flow valve, and a sixteen-gauge needle used in taking blood samples.

Access to the house was much easier than before. Yoda had the kinesthetic muscle memory of a rat in a maze. Once he walked a room's dimensions, he could nearly do it again blindfolded. He stood in the spare bedroom upstairs, dressed in his smooth black skin. He glided over carpet with no more sound than a snake sliding over a glass floor. His only accessories were a black backpack strapped to his shoulders and the Fuji Instax camera.

Yoda's toe bumped against a large duffel bag. It contained clothes and overnight sundries. He quietly went through the belongings. *Was she going somewhere?*

He stared at the large glass fishbowl penny jar in the spare bedroom. He ran his fingertips against the painted sheetrock walls, checked his reflection in the bathroom mirror, and entered Maggie's room. She slept deeply, with the soft orange alarm clock glow throwing shadows on her beautiful features. The heart locket was back in place on the nightstand, draped over a wristwatch, just as it had been the first time he had caressed her while she slept.

Yoda moved silently about the bed as he tied the rope in a nine-coiled hangman's noose. Tradition called for thirteen, but Yoda was not one to stand on ceremony. He laid the noose on the floor beside the bed, leaned down, and inhaled her breath, careful not to exhale on Maggie's soft skin.

He peeled the duct tape slowly and carefully, with no noise, like a Band-Aid from a healed wound. He chewed it free from the roll and stuck one corner to the headboard.

Suddenly, Maggie awoke and rolled to the side of the bed nearest the bathroom. Yoda slid beneath the bed and listened to her pee. He waited another thirty minutes until he heard her sleeping again.

When he was almost ready, he pulled the chair close to her bed and set the duct tape roll on the nightstand. He leaned closer and kissed her eyelid.

Maggie stirred. He kissed the other eyelid and she blinked, and rubbed her hand against her nose as if a small insect had tickled her. Just as she was about to settle back into a deep sleep, Yoda slapped her face hard, and the room filled with the fleeting report of a tiny firecracker.

Maggie bolted upright and stared straight ahead. Yoda thrust the large piece of duct tape over her mouth, dropped the noose over her head and around her neck, and pulled it tight. She kicked her legs, but the blankets around her feet bundled them in knots. She grabbed her throat, eyes wide open, and stared at the man that held the noose tightly around her neck. Her eyes registered a moment of recognition, then panic. She reached out to scratch his eyes, but his arms were too long and her fingernails slid over slippery spandex. Yoda tightened the noose more and her eyes bulged. Her screams were muted behind the duct tape. She clawed at her neck a few more moments. Her struggle was over in less than a minute.

A phone call from the office of Kieran Gilchrist, special agent in charge of counterterrorism and counterintelligence, brought John to White Plains for the third time this month. The first time was as Yossi Mandelbrot, Hasidic Jew and unlikely party planner for a Muslim picnic during the holy month of Ramadan. The second was to eliminate Amjad Ali Kahn and the money supply to terrorist cells overseas. This time, he was Major John Rexford, United States Marine Corps, retired, disabled. In some ways, being himself was a more difficult disguise. On the bright side, the infection in his thigh gave him a convincing limp.

He decided to go country, and wore a Toby Keith T-shirt and a NASCAR ball cap. Good interrogators were trained not to prejudge their interviewees. But they all did anyway, and either

Gilchrist already suspected him, or had already dismissed him, and was going through the motions, hoping something would shine a light on his investigations into the deaths of Abdul Bari and Amjad Ali Khan.

John pulled into the nondescript parking lot where the FBI was located. There were no signs indicating they had an office in the building.

He had a habit of going four or five days without a shave, in case the odd camera picked him up during an assignment. He had shaved today in case an unknown surveillance camera had picked him up on the Bari mission. Big Brother could pop up when you least expect him. There were no surveillance cameras at FDR Park, so no worries there.

The FBI had managed to find the most austere building in White Plains for its substation. The architecture was late-century ugly, with an emphasis on square. The outline was square, the windows were square, even the shrubs were trimmed in little green boxes around the recessed entryway. It had a flat roof, horizontal accent, mostly glass and steel construction.

If their interview skills were as bland, this would be a cakewalk.

The interior door opened automatically. A chrome-framed arrow on the wall directed all visitors to the left. The security guard stood behind a small conveyor belt and a metal detector: six four, short-cropped hair, with dark brown, piercing eyes. His jawline was carved from a cinder block. No rent-a-cop. The bona fide FBI agent had a slight bulge on the left side of his dark blue suit in case one might think otherwise.

"May I help you, sir?" said the agent.

John nodded. "I'm here to see Kieran Gilchrist."

The agent pointed to the roster and handed him a pen.

"Sign here, please."

John signed in and placed the pen back on the roster. The agent asked for identification. He handed over his driver's license and military ID. He carried the military ID around in case it might help him get out of a speeding ticket. A lot of police officers were ex-military and would cut you some slack. He waited for the agent to mention he had been in the military. The agent handed him back the identification and looked back at the signature, with no mention of military service.

"Are you carrying any weapons today, Mr. Rexford?"

"No." This guy wasn't in the mood for small talk.

"Place your change in the basket. Your keys, belt, and anything that may contain any metal."

John complied.

"Is that everything?"

He nodded.

"Please proceed through the archway."

He walked through the metal detector and met the agent on the other side.

"Please gather your things, sir. Proceed to the eighth floor, and check in with the receptionist."

He thanked the guard and walked to the bank of elevators around the corner. A rectangular glass-framed office directory was screwed to the wall. A few letters had fallen and rested at the inside bottom of the frame. The directory showed the FBI on the eighth floor, mixed in with some doctors and small businesses. *Were they all fronts?* John had checked the FBI website before driving down, and learned that their headquarters in New York was at 26 Federal Plaza. The FBI homepage didn't list anything in White Plains. His peripheral vision picked up security cameras at every hallway corner, and another as he stepped into the elevator and pushed the button for the eighth floor.

He started to feel this might not be the cakewalk he had imagined. His stomach fluttered when the car stopped and the door opened. Time to put on the game face. Time to act the part of the confused ex-marine who didn't understand what this was all about but would be happy to help the FBI. If it got sticky, he would invoke his right to an attorney. Citizens had more rights than marines. If it got real hairy, he'd take a hostage, call a press meeting outside the building, and wait for someone from Chocker's team to extract him. Either way, the FBI wouldn't get a word from him.

He stepped into a nondescript hallway and noticed a large ficus plant so shiny it appeared to be waxed. Etched glass windows rested in wooden frame doors to his right. The interior was spartan, with a sense that everything was new.

A receptionist sat at the black granite desk. She was talking into her wireless headset when he walked up to her.

"John Rexford," he said.

She raised her index finger, then said, "Have a nice day" into the mouthpiece. She turned to John. "How can I help you?" she said.

"I'm here to see agent Gilchrist. John Rexford."

"Please sign in and I'll see if he's available, Mr. Rexford."

He filled out the second sign-in sheet and set the pen down. He briefly considered keeping it as a weapon of convenience, but the receptionist's persona indicated she counted paperclips and defended her territory with zeal.

She spoke on the phone to someone, and told John that Agent Gilchrist would see him. He thanked her and followed her directions down the hall to the second door on the left. He knocked, opened it, and walked in, scanning for exits as he entered. One way in and one way out. A small window with frosted glass and shiny, thick aluminum blinds gave the room a cozy, solitary confinement theme. At eight stories up, the window would do him little good.

Kieran Gilchrist rose from his leather chair and walked around the desk with his hand extended. John shook it and introduced himself.

"Did you have any trouble finding the place?" Gilchrist was cordial.

"No."

It would be best to let Gilchrist steer the conversation. If he followed protocol for establishing trust, Gilchrist would ask him some inane question about his occupation, musical preferences, family, and the like. Any question asked, Gilchrist would already have the answer from John's military file and preinterview background checks. He would know in the first few minutes if the FBI agent was going to take the chummy approach or the authoritative angle.

Gilchrist pulled a yellow legal pad from the desk drawer and placed it in front of him.

"Actually, this place isn't on your website," John added, in a friendly, aw-shucks tone.

"We ran out of space downtown and had to set up some temporary offices here." Gilchrist had looked away when he said it. John picked up on the tell: defensive, unsure of himself.

Sure you did, he thought, but knew better. The FBI, along with many large corporations, had moved their most important people a few miles outside Manhattan for security reasons after 9/11. They would be ready the next time New York City took a hit, with key players working from the outside in.

John had been taught effective interrogation techniques from the CIA to question prisoners in Afghanistan. He'd learned to interrogate members of his own staff to see if they were cracking or treasonous, while he made idle conversation.

Body language was the key. Words lie, but the body usually cannot, except in the case of a specially trained professional. Chocker could probably make his retinas lie to a laser scanner.

"Please, sit down." Gilchrist motioned to the leather chair that had recently been filled by Patrick Corcoran, alias C. Peter Chocker. "I hope this meeting isn't too much of an inconvenience. I'm not keeping you away from family or any pressing issues?"

"No," said John. The chummy approach it is.

Gilchrist looked down at the yellow pad and opened a manila folder with REXFORD typed on the tab label. He compared some scribbles on the paper with preprinted documentation in the folder. The fat around Gilchrist's jowls sagged, and his eyes looked like two piss holes in the snow. He had the look of an insomniac on an unsuccessful weight loss program.

"Do you have family in the area, John?"

"No." Chummy.

Gilchrist chuckled at the one-word responses. "Could you be a little more specific?"

"In what way?" said John.

"I mean your family. Where are they? Are you married?"

Gilchrist asked these questions to check facial responses, though he already knew the answers. A seasoned interrogator remembered these facial expressions for later comparison against more important questions regarding the purpose of the interrogation, and ultimately determined whether the interviewee had been truthful.

"As you probably noticed, Agent Gilchrist, I'm not wearing a ring." He raised his hand. "Though I understand a lot of men don't nowadays. But I'm not married."

"Any family?"

"Illegitimate kids, you mean?"

Gilchrist laughed, looked down at the pad, and back up at John, intimidated, ashamed of his question.

It was time to back off on the aggression for a moment, give back the upper hand. "I don't have any kids," said John. "Thank you for asking, Agent Gilchrist." He quickly added, "I do have a mother who lives in Tampa. My father passed away from cancer a few years back when I was stationed in Afghanistan."

"Were you able to return to the States for the funeral?" A concerned look crossed Gilchrist's face.

"No, sir." *But you know that, don't you?* "I was too far in-country at the time. They got word to me, but I couldn't stop what I was doing."

"Which was?" Gilchrist wrote something down on his pad, then looked back at John.

"Fighting the war, sir."

"Yes, I see." Gilchrist wasn't taking the bait of subservience. He looked uncomfortable, sweaty. John had to drop his attitude another notch and loosen up his interrogator.

"You see, Agent Gilchrist . . ." He pulled his chair a little closer to the desk. The body language would show he was reaching out. "My sister lives in Florida, too, and she was there for my mom. You know, to help her with the arrangements, and there was no way I was going to make it back in time. It happened so fast. One day he was in chemo—they said he had six months to live—and the next, he was gone. Just like that." He snapped his fingers. "We had a ceremonial gravesite service when I returned a few months later."

"Cancer is a hell of a thing, John. I had some close friends go that way."

John nodded. *Sure, I'll bet you took civil servant bereavement time off, with pay*. Everyone had a close friend, it seemed. It was different when it was your father or other blood relative.

It was a demon you couldn't raise your hand against, an enemy that didn't fight fair.

"I have some questions for you, John."

Gilchrist's segue had the soothing effect of a lumpy mattress, but he let the poor technique slide. The agent wanted to interrupt the flow to catch him off guard. The chumminess left the room. It was interrogation time.

"Shoot." John smiled and tipped the brim of his baseball cap up a little: the eager redneck.

"Did you see combat in Afghanistan?"

"I was a marine. We don't do a lot of administrative work in the mountains."

Gilchrist nodded and wrote something down. It was probably nothing, a red herring. "And you were special forces?"

"Yes, sir."

"How did you feel about the Afghani people?"

"The same way I do now: some are good, some are the enemy. I don't like the Taliban, if that's what you mean."

"Yeah, that's what I mean." Gilchrist lowered his voice. "Do you hate them?"

"I have no feelings of hate or love for the Taliban. They're the enemy. You must have felt the same way."

"What do you mean?"

"When you were in combat."

Gilchrist looked down and to his right, and shook his head. "I haven't had the honor of military service. Uncle Sam has me stationed here."

"Never stationed overseas with the agency?"

"Let's get back to the topic at hand." Gilchrist seemed irritated that the focus had turned so quickly to him.

Score one for the marines.

"What is the topic?"

"You're the topic, John. We have some problems right here in New York, and it's causing quite a stir in the Muslim community." Gilchrist waited for a response, and when he didn't get one, added, "What do you think about that?"

"I don't know what to think," said John. "I don't know what the problem is, and I don't really care about the Muslim community."

Gilchrist furrowed his brow.

Oops, hit a nerve.

"Well, some of us have to." Gilchrist leaned back in his chair and looked down his nose. "What have you been doing since you retired?"

"I didn't retire, sir. I'm a disabled veteran. I took an IED while on patrol in Taloqan. I wasn't allowed to return to duty."

"How long did you serve?"

"Almost eight years."

Gilchrist lurched forward in his swivel chair. The dark circles under his eyes were puffy, his lips cracked and pale. *This guy needs his beauty sleep,* thought John, *and nailing me would be the next best thing to a vial of Ambien.*

"I hate like hell to have to interview American heroes, John, but I've got a murder on my hands and I need to get to the bottom of it."

"Whoa-up." John raised his palms. "I don't know what you got for problems, but any killing I did was over there. If this is about some criminal matter, then I think I need to get a lawyer."

Gilchrist leaned back and wrote something on his pad.

"There won't be any need for a lawyer. Tell me what you do now that you're disabled. What is your profession, please?" Gilchrist raised his pen like he was pulling a threaded needle, and then set it down on the paper to write.

"I'm into metal."

"Please be more explicit." Gilchrist scribbled as he spoke.

"I make and repair wrought iron, mostly. I do some welding. I have a shop at the place I rent." He put on a scared look when Gilchrist raised his eyes from the pad. He wanted to appear afraid of losing something, his pension check perhaps.

"Nothing else?"

"What do you mean?"

"No other side jobs?"

"No."

"Are you currently employed by the US government in any way, or any of its agencies, either foreign or domestic in nature?"

Gilchrist dropped that bomb with the subtlety of a daisy cutter on a Tora Bora mountaintop. John waited for the concussion wave to pass and his internal organs to readjust. A short answer would defuse the tension.

"No."

Gilchrist looked at him for a moment, as if waiting for more, and then said, "I hear you're a cycling enthusiast."

"Where did you hear that?"

Gilchrist ignored the question. "Do you log a lot of miles?"

"A few."

"Any in the New York City, Westchester area?"

"I come down here once in a while." John paused, and then said, "There are a few good rides. But not many. Too much traffic."

"It says in your file that you're an expert in small arms, hand-to-hand combat, and pretty good with a knife."

John remained silent and waited for a question.

When John didn't respond, Gilchrist asked one. "Would you be surprised to know the person I'm looking for has those qualities, and rides a bike?"

"What person are you looking for?"

"Would you be surprised?"

"I think there are a lot of people who ride bikes that are fairly athletic in other ways," said John. "Some of the guys I ride with are ex-military. So, no, I wouldn't be surprised if you were looking for people with those skills. But why someone with *all* those skills? I wish you'd tell me what the case is. Maybe I can help narrow things down for you."

There was a light knock on the door. Another agent entered and whispered something in Gilchrist's ear. Gilchrist excused himself, and he and the agent left the room. John was familiar with the ruse. They would make him stew for a while, and then come back in and check his pulse. He was supposed to think they had some great new damning evidence. They didn't have a thing. The only thing linking him to Abdul Bari was the dirk, and it was a melted-down, amorphous blob in Henry's barn.

Ten minutes later, Gilchrist came back alone, scribbled something on his notepad, and rearranged his desk. He took another long look at John's folder.

"You say you have no other means of income other than your blacksmithing?"

"No. I didn't say that."

"What exactly did you say?"

"I'm into metal."

"Heavy metal?"

"I said I was a blacksmith. You didn't ask about other income. But I'm sure you know that, as a disabled veteran, I get a small pension and health benefits."

"Why do you think I brought you in here, Major Rexford?"

Major is it? John shrugged. "You're the FBI. I can only guess that someone is killing someone and you think the person who did it is military, or something like military." It was time for him to send up a red herring of his own. "And, if I could guess, I'll bet you think this guy's covering up some drug-smuggling operation, and using his paramilitary training for no good. My guess is some Afghanis are probably bringing heroin or other contraband into the country, and you're close to getting them, but need to get a handle on where their muscle is stateside."

Gilchrist leaned back and put his hands behind his head: cocky, uninterested. "And why would you think that?"

"It's no secret that ever since Blackwater and the CIA have been working together, the amount of heroin coming into this country has doubled, and the production over there has tripled. There's no way they can get it into the country without some help from people inside the States, and those mercenary, soldier-of-fortune types don't trust anyone but their own kind."

Gilchrist mulled this over for a moment. "And you're not one of those soldier-of-fortune types, are you, John?"

He glared into Gilchrist's eyes. "I was a paid soldier for my country. But murder is out of the question. I'd rather put that life behind me. I've got a good woman, and I think it's time to make a life for myself. God knows the military put it on hold long enough." He grabbed the bill of his baseball cap with his thumb and forefinger and shook it once for emphasis.

His own words remained in his head. It sounded so real when he heard it out loud. It was always easier to lie when the truth was sprinkled in. But the truth was that he would trade one more minute in Maggie's arms for a lifetime with assholes like Gilchrist, and every minute here kept him away from her.

"Where do you get your intelligence from?" said Gilchrist.

"My mother, I guess."

"Your information on heroin, the CIA, and Blackwater."

"Same place everyone else does: *Time* magazine and the net."

"And you have no connections to your past military life?"

"The closest I get to the guys I knew in the corps is an annual bike ride to help disabled vets. I bring awareness to the cause. Other than that, I'd like to leave the whole mess behind me. I was proud to serve, but I'm done." John dropped his head for a second and added, "I'm not actually combat-ready anymore, with the knee injury."

Gilchrist knew about the ride, but he wanted to see if his subject would add anything substantially different.

"So what now?"

John raised his eyebrows. "I don't follow."

"You said you're done. What's an ex-marine to do with all the skills he can no longer use?"

"The military taught me more than war, Agent Gilchrist. They taught me to have confidence in myself and to work hard, and let God take care of the rest. I'll make it."

"I know this isn't your first interview." Gilchrist frowned. "On either side of the desk. I know they trained you well over there. But it doesn't mean you're guilty of anything either. All right, then." Gilchrist tore a piece of paper from the legal pad and placed it inside the folder. "If you don't have anything else to say, this interview is over. I appreciate you coming in."

John wanted to leave on a helpful note. Nothing to kiss ass, but enough to show he was eager to help in any little way.

"The paper says you've got an illegal Russian in custody for what happened at FDR," said John. "His being here is proof enough he's doing something wrong—at the very least, evading his country's police or our ICE. But these rivers of illegal immigrants run deep, and it's always something more than it appears. Seems like an undocumented male in custody could be your best lead."

"I appreciate that, John. Thank you for coming in."

"You're welcome. Good luck, Agent Gilchrist." He shook Gilchrist's hand. The grip was strong, but the skin was soft. His nails looked pasted on, white and ragged at the end of his kosher-pickle fingers. John limped ever so slightly to the door.

Gilchrist mulled the interview over in his mind. John Rexford had maintained eye contact most of the time. He hadn't looked away or down at any questions, indicating he probably wasn't lying. The problem with an interview is if you don't ask the right question, the suspect doesn't have to lie and expose his tell.

Rexford wasn't nervous about the subjects of his family or career, but had shown a little agitation when questioned about blacksmithing. Why would that be? Did he think he would lose his job if he was investigated? Maybe he wasn't paying taxes on cash jobs. But Gilchrist wasn't the IRS, and everyone got nervous when those assholes entered the picture anyway.

Did working with metal somehow implicate him?

John hadn't answered the questions too quickly. When a subject was telling the truth, he needed time to remember the details. John had taken the appropriate amount of time. Gilchrist detected no inconsistencies in his speech pattern. The subject appeared reasonably happy he was out of the Marine Corps, if not a little confused about where his future was going; and he was probably in love, and wanted to have kids. Normal enough. The guy wasn't a good prospect for Corcoran, given the liability of romantic ties. But most subjects don't lie; they just don't tell everything.

Patrick Corcoran aside, Gilchrist would have felt a lot better about the interview. But Corcoran was on a long leash at the CIA, and no one, not even the president, questioned his motives or pulled him on the carpet and grilled him as to what laws he broke.

Gilchrist was no further along in the investigation than he was a half hour ago when John Rexford had arrived. He pulled the plastic knife Corcoran had given him from his top drawer. He slid it back and forth across his palm. It was embarrassing to remember how the spook had gotten it through security. The slimly little weasel loved to embarrass his agency.

Gilchrist looked at the folders stacked on his desk. Which one of these boys would be most likely to work with Corcoran? Maybe none of them. But which one was most likely? They all had similar backgrounds, and were all ostensibly out of the military loop.

Maybe a better question was, what did they all have in common?

He scanned the alphabetical roster of men who had signed up for the ride, and wrote each man's disability next to his name. He pointed the plastic knife at their first names, and scrolled down the list: shoulder injury, prosthetic leg, herniated disk, prosthetic feet, knee replacement, knee injury, joints repaired with titanium screws, metal screws, titanium screws . . .

He pushed the button on his phone for the security desk.

"Yes, sir."

"I want all the tapes from every interview performed on the bikers. Give me everything you've got."

"Yes, sir. And the ones you haven't done yet?"

"As soon as you get them, put them on a disk, and get them up to me. I especially want to know if any of them set off the metal detectors."

Gilchrist hung up the phone and watched the blood trickle down his palm and drip onto the roster. *Corcoran has sharp tools. Sharp goddamn tools.*

The rusted-out Honda Civic looked like it was on its last legs, but the Japanese made a great motor, and Yoda was confident by the steady hum of the four cylinders that the car would not let him down. The odometer displayed 255,110 miles. He checked the gas gauge. If it was correct, he had nearly a full tank and would make Yonkers in time. But first he had one more stop to make.

He put on a pair of orange-tinted sunglasses and a baseball cap and pulled into Henry's driveway. The mailbox said HALL in capital letters. Yoda knocked politely on the door and stood a foot away from the bottom tread with a map in his hands. The door opened inward, and Henry looked down at the visitor who had interrupted his writing.

"I don't need any," said Henry.

"I am so sorry to have disturbed your day," said Yoda. "But it appears I can't find Rockcastle Road."

"Never heard of it."

"Yes. I think I am close to it, but I can't find the turn. Would you mind?" Yoda held the crumpled map in front of him and pointed to a spot he had circled earlier.

Henry reached for the map.

"Their ain't no Rockcastle Road in this—"

Yoda slid under the map, placed his left hand on Henry's knee, and pulled the old man's heel upward with his right. Henry hit the floor with a thud and tried to roll over on his stomach to get up. Before he could, Yoda had shut the door and was inside wrapping Henry's legs in duct tape. He pulled Henry's hands behind him and bound his wrists together. To render his victim further immobile and helpless, Yoda used a twisted strand of the tape to connect Henry's wrists and ankles.

"Why the hell are you hogtying me?" said Henry.

"Shut up old man, or I'll add your neck in the loop. How long do you think you'll be able to arch your back before you strangle?"

Henry began to cough and his glasses slid from his face.

"I won't have to gag you if you keep your mouth shut and listen."

"Okay," said Henry. "What do—"

Yoda slapped him on the back of the head. "I said, shut up and listen."

Henry closed his eyes and rolled to one side. He couldn't see the man's face from this angle. What had he looked like? Was he oriental or just one of those young Mexican kids that were always driving around in those little cars? How would he describe the man to the police? Would he even live that long?

"When your neighbor comes home," said Yoda, "I want you to call him and tell him to come over."

"He'll never fall for that," said Henry.

Yoda slapped him on the back of the head again.

"Shut up. He'll fall for it because you will make it believable. If you do not make it believable, you will both die. Do you understand?"

Henry nodded. "What will I say to him?"

"Tell him you've fallen and you can't get up." Yoda smiled to himself.

"And then what?"

Yoda slapped him harder this time. "You don't listen well, old man. You tell him you need help and that's it. He will come like the hero to help his old friend."

"Screw you."

"You almost did last night when you shot your pistol in the air. You should have aimed better, and you wouldn't be in this predicament."

"So you're the pervert, huh?"

"Most importantly, I am the man who decides if you live or die today. Do we understand each other?"

Henry nodded.

Yoda stood quickly and went to the window facing the road. A black four-door sedan had pulled into John Rexford's driveway. Yoda slinked on all fours back to Henry, duct-taped the man's mouth, and forward rolled to the window. He stood to the left of the blinds and watched as two men exited the car. One of them turned toward the trailer, and Yoda slinked back another inch out of view.

Yoda was confident they hadn't followed him here. They were not regular police, probably federal agents of some kind coming after Rexford. He was sure that the photo had evoked this response. If Rexford came home now, Yoda would be trapped and unable to deliver the message he so desperately desired to give the soldier who had prevented his mission from being a complete success. He needed to get rid of the agents. Rexford would have to pay for Yoda's loss of commission and reputation.

Yoda leaned down to Henry and made a shushing sound behind his ear. There was a worn Air Cavalry cap on a nail by the door. Yoda put it on, adjusted the fit, and found a pair of work gloves in a kitchen drawer. He gave the federal agents fifteen minutes to search the house for clues before leaving Henry bound and gagged in the trailer.

Yoda knocked on the door to John Rexford's home.

When Agent Lewis heard the knock, he came out of the living room and opened the door.

"Hello? Can I help you?"

"That all depends," Yoda replied in an anglicized Chinese accent. "Are you here about the lottery?"

The second FBI agent, Jeff Huntley, was upstairs relieving himself when he heard the voices. Huntley carefully lowered the toilet seat. He didn't flush and walked softly to the head of the stairs.

"What is your name, sir?"

"I am Jimmy Wong. I run this place." Yoda pointed a gloved thumb at his chest. "Who are you?"

Agent Lewis rubbed the bald spot on the top of his head, and then scratched at an imaginary itch near the back of his neck. He pulled his suit coat to the side and displayed the FBI credentials hooked on his belt.

"Ah, G-man of the FBI," said Yoda. "Do you have a warrant?"

"I'm Special Agent Stephen Lewis with the FBI." Lewis held up the badge case and flipped it open. "And the man behind me is Special Agent Jeff Huntley."

"It's okay to be here if you have a warrant," said Yoda. "Otherwise, Mr. Hall will be very upset."

"We have a warrant," said Agent Lewis. "But it's for John Rexford's residence. Who is Mr. Hall? Better yet, who are *you*, sir?"

Yoda put his thumb on his chest again. "I am Mr. Hall's caretaker. He has three properties, and I take care of them all. He would not like you nosing around without a warrant."

Agent Lewis wasn't used to being on the defensive end of an interrogation, so he didn't have a ready response. He and Huntley had orders to get to John Rexford's house and execute the warrant. If evidence found led to an arrest, they were to take Rexford down, with force if necessary. If Rexford wasn't there, they were to search for clues to his whereabouts and activities over the last few months: websites, letters, personal effects, alcohol, and drug use. Maybe Jimmy Wong could provide some clues about Rexford.

"Would you mind coming in, Mr. Wong?" Lewis motioned with his hand. "You can see that we will follow the warrant to the letter."

Yoda stepped into the kitchen and gave a quick bow to both agents.

"Please sit down." Lewis motioned to the kitchen table. "Were you in the Air Cavalry?"

Yoda gave an aw-shucks grin, pointed at the hat, and shook his head. "Mr. Hall gave this to me. I'm no soldier."

"Where is Mr. Hall?"

"He stays in the trailer next door. He doesn't need a big house. But he is flat on his back now from an injury. That's why I came over." Yoda sat down and put his work gloves on the kitchen table.

"So Mr. Rexford doesn't own this house," said Lewis, and took a seat at the table opposite Yoda.

Huntley stayed on his feet with a cautious eye on Yoda.

"Mr. Rexford is Mr. Hall's tenant."

"Do you know Mr. Rexford?"

"Oh yes," said Yoda. "Both men are big war heroes: Mr. Hall in the army, and Mr. Rexford in Afghanistan."

"We may need to talk to Mr. Hall later," said Huntley.

Yoda saw the pictures on the wall of John Rexford in a Rutgers football uniform. "Today is a bad day because he sleeps when his back is so bad," said Yoda. "The medication makes him very drowsy. War injury, you know."

"I'm sorry to hear that," said Lewis. "John Rexford is part of an FBI investigation, and we have a warrant to search these premises. It's all legal, Mr. Wong."

Huntley pulled the warrant from his pocket and handed it to Yoda.

"How long will you be here?"Yoda looked over the warrant as if reading the words, nodding with each sentence.

"Not long," said Lewis. "Huntley?"

"I've already got the hard drive and checked most of the upstairs rooms. I'll give it a second glance and we can roll." Huntley turned his gaze to Yoda. "Maybe another fifteen minutes. Where is Mr. Rexford now?"

Yoda shrugged. "He goes out a lot during the day. He has a girlfriend who teaches. He left this morning, and I haven't seen him since."

Lewis knew this to be true because Rexford had already met with his boss in White Plains.

"Go finish up, Jeff," said Lewis. "I'll stay here and talk with Mr. Wong."

"Are you sure, Stephen? I can wait."

Agent Lewis looked at the thin man across the table. He was a little obnoxious but didn't present an immediate threat. "Finish up, and we'll get out of here."

Yoda watched Huntley leave the room, and then he smiled back at Agent Lewis.

"We're in the middle of a homicide and a possible terrorist investigation, Mr. Wong, hence the warrant."

Yoda gave a concerned look and let his mouth drop open. "I see."

"And anything you can do to help would be greatly appreciated. By the way, do you have any identification?"

"Not on me. I keep it at the house."

"The trailer next door?"

"No. I rent a small room in Mr. Hall's other house in Kingston."

"So you don't live next door."

Yoda waved his palm and smiled. "Oh, no. Mr. Hall is a very private person. He doesn't like people under his feet. I just drop off supplies sometimes, and get him odds and ends."

"Are you a citizen, Mr. Wong?"

Yoda beamed. "I am. Three years now. America is the best place in the world. Where I live now, a whole family would live in China."

Agent Lewis gave a pleasant smile, as if he had just received a personal compliment. "Has Mr. Rexford ever told you about his job or personal life?"

"I see him sometimes, maybe once a week. We talk about stuff. He was hero, you know. All-American."

"All-American?"

"A football hero. He almost played for the Detroit Lions, but then went to the marines."

Lewis wasn't sure if Mr. Wong understood the difference between the two teams. The guy seemed to be a little confused, but willing to help.

Yoda scanned the room for more clues about John Rexford.

"Does he ever mention his past?"

"He rode a bicycle in school."

Lewis tilted his head. "What?"

"Did I say something wrong?"

"What do you mean in school?"

Yoda lifted his head and opened his mouth with a wide smile. "Ah. I see. I think I mixed up the phrase. He rode his bicycle *to* school."

"I'm still not sure what you mean."

Yoda jumped up and pointed to the photograph of John in the Tour de Champlain. "You see. He rides his bicycle all the time."

Lewis figured something had been lost in the translation. He heard Huntley coming down the stairs.

"I found this," said Huntley. He held a small remote-control helicopter in his hand. "What do you think?"

Lewis shrugged. "I don't know. Bag it and let's get out of here." Lewis stood up and reached his hand out to shake Yoda's. Yoda grabbed Lewis's big hand with both of his, shook it with three jerky motions, and then bowed his head slightly as if the FBI agent were a dignitary.

"How can we reach you if we need to?" asked Huntley as he shook Yoda's hand.

"Do you have a pen?" said Yoda.

Huntley took out a small notepad and a pen and handed them to Yoda. Yoda scribbled on the notepad and said, "That is my cell phone number. You can call me anytime."

"We'll be going now, Mr. Wong," said Lewis. "Thank you for your cooperation, and I apologize for giving you a start there."

"Start what?" said Yoda.

"Nothing." Lewis smiled and walked out the door, with Huntley a few steps behind.

"I'll close up in a few minutes," said Yoda. "It was nice to meet you gentlemen."

They turned and gave him a polite wave as they got in their car.

"Good-bye, Agent Lewis. See you later, Agent Stuntley."

Huntley turned, shook his head, and got in the car.

Yoda waited until they were out of sight and ran back to the trailer. Henry was still on the floor and appeared to be having a little trouble breathing through his nose. Yoda ripped the duct tape from his lips and took a good chunk of beard with it.

"I have to go now," Yoda said. "The FBI took too much of my time."

"FBI?" Henry grunted.

"It appears your John Rexford is a wanted man. You should be careful whom you associate with."

"Screw you."

Yoda put a fresh duct tape gag over Henry's mouth and stood up. Henry tried to roll over and get a look at his captor, but his belly got in the way.

Henry heard the trailer door close, but the car didn't start up right away. A minute later he heard the car back out of his driveway and sputter as Yoda shifted gears.

John took the back roads home. The route was a little longer, but it would be easier for him to spot a tail if Gilchrist, Chocker, or Yoda were after him. It seemed there wasn't anyone left to trust but Maggie and Henry. This route brought him past Maggie's house, and she should be home from work by now. They had agreed that he would help her get her things and move in. Her car wasn't in the driveway, but she could have parked it in the garage.

The door wasn't locked, so he opened it and walked inside.

"Special delivery!" he announced.

No response.

"Maggie? Hey! Anyone home?"

Maggie didn't always lock her door, but after Henry's gun blast the other night, she probably would have. There were a few dirty plates in the sink. They had breadcrumbs and butter on them. But they were dried out, as if they were from the day before. Maggie often left the dishes in the sink until morning, but she always washed them before she left for work. So these dishes were from yesterday, or else she had left in a hurry. But why?

He heard a beeping sound coming from somewhere in the house. He listened for clues and wished he hadn't come in shouting like that. He ran a checklist in his mind: dryer, washing machine, television, radio—no noise from any of those machines. It was muffled, like a cricket under a blanket. He grabbed a boning knife from the rack on the kitchen counter and proceeded in the direction of the beep.

The carpet was soft beneath his feet, and he made no noise as he ascended the stairs. The pain in his thigh muscle reminded him of Yoda with every step. The beeping sound grew louder at the top of the stairs. He looked to his left, into the spare room. No one was there, but it looked off. Something was missing, but he couldn't get a handle on what it was. He turned back into the hall and opened the door to Maggie's bedroom.

The bed was unmade—not good. Another one of her habits broken. He gripped the boning knife tighter and knelt down to look under the bed. A few dust bunnies stared back at him. He would remember to chide her about her cleaning regime later. He smiled to himself as he imagined her look of surprise that he had been under her bed.

The closets were empty. He pulled the blankets off the floor by the nightstand and already knew what he'd find. The alarm clock was flashing a warning in bright orange. He pushed the ALARM/OFF button and placed it back on the nightstand.

Had she been in such a hurry that she forgot the alarm? The bed was a mess, but there was no indication of a struggle. He noticed her overnight bag by the door. Inside were all the usual items she brought when she stayed over at his house: makeup, pajamas, personal hygiene effects, small hair dryer, and various undergarments. Why was this on the floor? Was she planning on coming back here to pack, and then move in with him? She wouldn't just pack a small night bag. Had it been left from the night before? More likely that was the case, but then, why hadn't she packed to stay with him? Had Maggie changed her mind?

John hurried to the school to see if she was there. Maybe there was a pep rally, football game, or something else she was always talking about, but that went in one ear and out the other. Why hadn't he paid attention to those notices they always sent with the Onteora High School calendar?

He tried not to run in the front entrance. He could feel the soft, ooze-covered gauze loosen from his thigh with each flex of his quadriceps. He was actually limping now, not just for effect. The administration office seemed far away at the other end of the hall. The fluorescent lights threw shadows on the green walls. Posters about upcoming events were everywhere: booster club, French club, cheerleader practice, schedules for fall sports. He wasn't familiar with any of it. This was her world, and he hadn't taken the time to learn a goddamn thing about it.

"Is Maggie Castalia still here?" he said.

"Who's asking?" The middle-aged woman with black dyed hair looked up at him. She pulled one hand down on the frame of her glasses as if it gave her authority.

"John Rexford. I'm her . . ." He stumbled with the words. What was he? The guy who didn't give a crap about her teaching career? Just a self-absorbed bastard playing soldier? "I'm her future fiancé," he said, "but let's keep that between us for now."

"Of course." The woman beamed a smile and gawked over the frame of her glasses. "Maggie talks about you often. You're the Iron Man."

"The what?"

"Oh, I'm sorry," she said, and put her fingertips to her lips. "That was rude. We have a nickname for you: Maggie's Iron Man. That's how she met you, right?"

He tried to not act in a hurry and gave her a humble smile. "I guess you're right. No offense taken. Is she around?"

"Maggie didn't report to work today. We assumed it was a family emergency. She's always very good about calling in if she can't make it." The woman raised a finger and turned her gaze to the calendar on her desk. "But you know her. She always makes it. That girl hasn't called in sick since she started here. Let me see if she had a vacation day coming I wasn't aware of . . ."

"No problem," said John, suppressing his anxiety. "I'll just meet up with her at the house. She said something about shopping, or something. We must have got our wires crossed. Have a nice day, and thank you."

The woman waved and said, "Okay, Iron Man."

His heart sunk even further when Maggie's car was not in the driveway and he saw the envelope posted on the door frame. It was either from Maggie, explaining her change of mind about moving in, or it was from Yoda. Both scenarios were more than he wanted to face right now. He tore it open and a small credit card-sized photo fell onto the porch. He picked it up and felt his stomach drop as the world spun out of control. Now he knew what had been missing from the spare bedroom.

His house had been delicately searched, not tossed as if burglarized by careless rookies. Everything was in place except that which the FBI had taken. As he looked around, it was obvious a professional had turned the rooms over looking for something specific. It had been a neat and orderly invasion of his privacy. Dust outlined the area where his laptop had been. There was duct tape behind the headboard, but the dagger was missing. The cradle for his personal cell phone was in the kitchen, but the phone was gone. The same for the helicopter he kept upstairs in the spare room. It was as if the Grinch had come to Whoville, taken all the toys, and left an FBI warrant instead of stocking stuffers.

The judge had neglected to list the barn in the warrant, and John was sure the FBI would stick to protocol. This meant his bikes and other weapons were still intact. Thank God he had kept his go-bag and medicine with him in the car. John popped a couple more antibiotics and half an Oxy to keep the pain in his leg from distracting him.

He took a quick shower and disinfected his wound as much as possible. It was still swollen and red, but he convinced himself the medicine had started to take effect and the wound would heal without professional help. He wrapped it in several layers of tight gauze and then white surgical tape. There was no time for doctors—only time for Maggie. And without Maggie, there was no time for anything.

The small photograph in his hand looked like a comic book panel. The colors were too bright and the image was exaggerated. Had he been Iron Man, he would have slid inside the comic world and saved the girl. Yoda had failed to cover her beautiful, dark brown eyes when he had taken the picture, and Maggie was staring into the camera. John knew this was on purpose, just another part of the torture designed specifically for him. If he was Jonas from *The Unit*, as Chocker had once told him, Maggie would be trained to give a signal, and he would know where she was. But this wasn't television, and Maggie was trained to teach small children how to survive the school world, not Yoda's world.

Maggie was dressed in a long skirt, sneakers, and a ragged sweater she kept saying she was going to throw out. Her left arm was tied tightly to her torso with a thin rope as she sat in an old wooden chair. The wooden chair was tied to an old furnace so she couldn't rock in place and break free. Her feet were also bound tightly by the rope. Her right arm was immobilized against the chair with duct tape. There was a silver needle in the crook of her elbow. A three-foot piece of IV tube ran from the needle to a large fishbowl on the floor. Maggie's blood covered the bottom of the bowl. Not a lot, not yet, but enough to get the point across. On the floor next to the fishbowl was a prescription bottle. Had he drugged her? Was it a blood thinner?

There was an electric alarm clock on top of the rusted furnace next to her head. The time shown in goblin green: 12:07. The small P.M. dot on the bottom was lit.

The back of the photograph had four words hand printed in black ink: HALF PINT PER HOUR.

Yoda had set the valve on the needle to bleed Maggie out at a half pint per hour.

There were ten pints of blood in the average adult, but you could only lose about four pints and still survive. John had already done the calculations. Maggie had eight hours to live.

He paced every room in the house, over and over, trying to think of a way to find her. He held the photograph in his hands, pressed it against his heart, and reexamined it for something he might have missed. Tears streamed down his face, his expression contorted in pain and fury. There was nothing he could do. The room she was in was dark, like a basement, but Yoda had been careful not to leave any objects in the picture that might give him clues.

He took Chocker's phone from his pocket and was about to dial when it rang in his hand and he almost dropped it.

"He's got Maggie," John said into the phone.

"How?" said Chocker.

"I don't know. He left me one of his little calling cards with a picture of her."

"Is she all right?"

"No, Pete, she's not." John's voice turned morbid. "She's got an IV in her arm, and she's bleeding out. She's got less than eight hours to live."

"I've got a lead on Yoda," said Chocker.

For a brief moment, John's heart lightened. It was as if he had won a small battle in the war he would inevitably lose. "What is it?"

"A single male purchased a one-way ticket to France. The credit card he used was pinged later as buying another ticket from France to Algiers, and then Yemen. It wasn't Yoda who bought the ticket. He had some flunky do it, but it's got to be him. The credit card belonged to a guy who was found dead in Yonkers. The guy who bought the ticket worships at a mosque where I already have people stationed."

"I want him, Pete. He's the only person who knows where Maggie is."

"Then I need you to get down to the Al-Farooq Masjid mosque on McLean Avenue now. Perform surveillance of the area on your bike, and then wait until the mosque lets out all the hajjis at three o'clock. We don't know how he'll be dressed, but most likely he'll blend in with them in their prayer garb. But you know him, Johnny. You'll be able to find him."

John looked at the wall clock. When had he gotten home? Was that the real time? He needed to leave.

"I'm out."

"Wait. You can't take your car. The feebs have made you. They're probably on their way there."

"They've already been here." John stood up near the sink, got dizzy, and slid back down the wall. "They went through the whole house."

"Did they get anything?"

"Nothing incriminating." John flashed on the space where his computer had been. What else was missing that he hadn't noticed? "I don't think so, anyway. How the hell did they justify a warrant?"

"Gilchrist figured out you might be working with us."

"How could you let that happen?"

"He has no evidence. It's all circumstantial. He can't place you anywhere, but he knows a bike was used at the bus stop, and he tied you into biking through the VA records and your charitable ride. Also, you didn't set off the metal detector when he interviewed you."

John knew that would come back to haunt him. The things he didn't think of. *It's always the case.*

"And you know this how?" said John.

"Now you sound like Yoda." A few seconds of silence followed. "Sorry. You know how. I can neither confirm nor deny."

Chocker didn't give up his sources.

"What's the next move?"

"Get another vehicle. Get your bike close to Yoda, and point him out. Bring this phone and call me if you need to. Otherwise, complete radio silence until you hear from our guy. I don't think Gilchrist can triangulate this sat phone. It's encrypted anyway, but he might zero in on your location with it. Take the battery out until you get to Yonkers. It will buy you some time if they already traced it to your house. And if you have your own cell phone, don't bring it. You're made."

Chocker waited for a response. His man didn't sound 100 percent on board.

"John?"

"Yeah?"

"Now's your chance. Go down there and get this animal. As soon as you see him, point him out to the team. I've got three guys on the inside and a few on the roof. Walk toward him. When you get close enough, bump him and get the hell out of there. We'll take over. I want you gone before the FBI shows up. Understood?"

He understood that there was no way out. Evading the FBI would be impossible. They were so hot for him they'd probably shoot him in the street. If they tried, he'd be sure to take out Yoda first, and let the chips fall where they may. That psycho wasn't giving up Maggie's location to the FBI, regardless.

"The bright side is you get to meet an old friend of ours," said Chocker.

"Who would that be?"

"He used to ride a Honda scooter if that helps."

Canaan. Small world. It made sense. Chocker would have a man who could pass as a bona fide Muslim living in the community.

"Always good to see an old friend," said John. Knowing Canaan was on the team calmed his nerves a notch. It was nice to have a tiger on the loose when you were surrounded by a zoo full of unfriendlies.

"He's going to ask you something about the Tour de France, and you will respond with 'Lance should have stayed postal.' Got it?"

"Yep."

"You can't kill him, John."

"Not until I find out where Maggie is."

"Not even then. This operation will be run by my people in the mosque. Their cover is paramount."

"Fuck you, Chocker! I'm going down there to capture, interrogate, and then kill the scumbag. Any of your people get in the way, I won't be responsible."

"You *are* my people, John."

"Not anymore. You said you had my back. You were supposed to save my ass when the desert burned. Well, the flames are all around me, and I don't see you anywhere. You're just another powerless bureaucrat with your thumb up your ass, giving orders and watching other people die."

"Don't mess up this mission, John." Chocker's voice was calm, steady. "Yoda's the only man alive that can save Maggie."

"The only man alive that can save Maggie is about to hang up the phone on you, Pete."

He had trouble completing his internal dialogue with his head draped in an anesthetic pillowcase. His throbbing thigh wound reminded him he was alive, but it was only a distraction. It didn't hurt. It pulsed without pain. If the hillbilly heroin wasn't still in his system, a four-inch-long infected gash through his hamstring muscle wouldn't feel like a distraction. It would be more akin to a small, razor-toothed rodent gnawing his leg from the inside out.

He couldn't shake the moment's dream-like quality. The phone call with Chocker may have happened hours ago—or had he imagined it?—but he had just hung up the phone. The world was filtered, and he couldn't wipe the fog off the lens. It was the OxyContin, coupled with fatigue. He hadn't taken one in a while, but its strong narcotic stayed in the system for at least twelve hours. Proper surveillance of a world-class assassin was difficult enough when your mind was clean. What were his chances of defeating Yoda with an infected wound, while under the influence?

He limped to the car and located his go-bag and portable pharmacy. He needed something to counter the Oxy. He needed to boost his metabolism a few notches, and Uncle Sam had provided the prescription.

Crank increased the release of the neurotransmitter dopamine, which stimulated brain cells, enhancing mood and energy. At low doses, its effects were increased wakefulness, increased physical activity, increased heart rate and blood pressure, and mild euphoria—all beneficial effects to a warrior, but you had to moderate your intake. High-dose chronic use caused irritation, paranoia, and aggressive and violent behavior.

Desoxyn was the pharmaceutical grade of crank Uncle Sam provided for its elite personnel. In Afghanistan, John had seen a few guys who refused to come in from the hills. They had learned to hoard their Desoxyn rations, and then go on a binge that kept them fully tweaked for a week or more while they were hunting, tracking, killing, or hiding in a cave until someone came in they could kill. It wasn't good, normal, or soldier-like. These boys had slipped through the psychological testing and shouldn't have been in the field with weapons.

The bingers returned to base sallow likenesses of the warriors who had left only days before. Their commanders knew what was going on, but they considered it a morale buster to pull someone in who was getting the job done—and those boys got the job done. That is, until they crashed. Some turned into animals while under the drug's influence and sleep deprivation, forsaking their moral compass. When they came down, reality was sometimes too much to bear. The lucky ones went through convulsions and swore off the drug. The unlucky ones were relieved of duty and sent stateside, where they either got help or ended up rotting away in a trailer park, looking for their next fix and remembering their brief glory days.

John had known a ranger who was so despondent that he volunteered for a night jump and ate dirt from four thousand feet. When they inspected his flattened body, they found he hadn't pulled his main chute or auxiliary cord. It was suicide by plane.

John weighed the pros and cons, then popped a ten-milligram Desoxyn into his mouth and chewed the bitter pill. A quad-macchiato wouldn't cut it today. Uncle Sam's crank went down with trepidation. He thought of tweaked-out soldiers curled up in a rocky ditch, waiting for the tremors and paranoia to wear off.

He pressed his fingertips against his red, swollen wound, still puffy around the edges. He rubbed some antibiotic gel over the wound's edge, pulled on ankle-length cycling pants—careful as he slid them over his thigh—and slid another Desoxyn into the pocket. Experience dictated that he would need two doses to get through the day. If he took them both, they would overload his system. If he timed the doses right, he would peak at McLean Avenue in Yonkers.

His psychological dial was set on kill. Tracking and pointing fingers wasn't going to satisfy John's instinct for revenge. Yoda had tried to kill him and was well on his way to draining the lifeblood from Maggie. John's gut told him he would do more than spot Yoda for Chocker. His warrior id wasn't going to let social mores override its drive for amoral and egocentric pleasure. Once he found out where Yoda had stashed Maggie, nothing but a confirmed kill would satisfy him.

He stuffed the pharmaceutical go-bag under the seat and went back upstairs. He placed the old wound dressing and bloody towels in a plastic shopping bag, and then threw them in the trash outside. He stuffed his helmet, windbreaker, balaclava, long-fingered riding gloves, and sunglasses inside. He locked the door and walked across the street to Henry's trailer. His wireless earphone and transmitter were already in the go bag.

John pounded on the door as obnoxiously as he could, but Henry didn't answer. He double-checked that the truck was in the driveway. Of course it was; he had walked past it seconds ago. Hadn't he? He checked again, and then pounded on the door so hard the hinges rattled. Something had fallen over inside.

"Henry?" He waited a moment and listened for the sound again. There it was. Someone was in there. Screw the old bastard; the door was coming down.

John shouldered the flimsy trailer door. The lock pulled away from the frame, and the hollow door smashed against the wall.

"What the hell?" said John.

Henry was hogtied on the floor, his head in a puddle of drool. John knelt down and checked his pulse. He got a kitchen knife and cut the duct tape from Henry's ankles and wrist, then pulled the strip from his mouth. A slow groan came from his friend's throat. He helped Henry into a sitting position and leaned him against the wall.

"You gonna make it, old man?" John slid Henry's glasses over his ears and let them fall gently on the bridge of his nose.

"Yeah. I guess."

"Who did this?"

"Some little foreign pervert," said Henry. "You know him?"

"I don't know. Was he Chinese?"

"Could have been."

"Did he take a picture of you?"

"What?" Henry's eyes opened fully. "No. What do you mean?"

"Nothing. It was probably a little Asian punk I've been having some trouble with."

"Are you going to tell me what this is all about? Or do I have to beat it out of you."

John smiled. "I'm in some trouble, friend. I need to borrow your truck."

Henry coughed and wiped some spittle from his beard. "I'll say you are. The FBI searched your house this afternoon, and that little prick who tied me up was in on it. He went over there and chatted with them, I think. Can't be sure. I was indisposed."

"I know. I saw the warrant on the table when I came home."

"Why don't you grab that bottle of rotgut from my desk, and we can talk about it?"

John retrieved the whiskey, took off the cap, and gave Henry the half-empty bottle. Henry took a three-gulp pull and sat it on the floor next to him.

"I can't join you now," John said. "I've got to get out of here. There's a bad guy buffet and I'm on the menu."

"Why don't you stay here, John?" Henry put his hand on John's shoulder. "Let's talk this out first. Another point of view will give you some perspective on the situation. It may not be as bad as you think. You look a little strung out, and I know it ain't from coffee."

The old bastard must have noticed his pupils, or his shaking hands. The Desoxyn's effects would already be apparent to a trained observer, and Henry Hall must have seen a lot of strung-out soldiers in his long military career.

"The time for talking is long past. They've got Maggie, Henry. Someone has her stashed in a hole somewhere, and if I don't get to her within the next several hours, she'll be dead."

"Jesus H., son." Henry bowed his head and rolled it from side to side. "What in God's name have you gotten yourself into? I knew you were up to something, but I never figured you to go in with no drug gang."

"It's not that, Henry. You know me better than that." John rolled his biking shorts down over his thigh, exposing the brown and bloodied gauze. "I'm taking something now for the pain. I've got a gash in one side and out the other, and I don't really care what you think about my drug abuse." He rolled his shorts back up. "Now I need to get going, and fast, and I can't use my car. So are you going to let me borrow the truck, or am I just going to take it?"

"Keys are in it. The Asian guy said the FBI has you on a wanted list. That true?"

John stood up. "If it wasn't then, it will be in the next couple of hours."

"You're going to go down there and murder that guy? John, they'll fry you for that. Let someone else handle it."

John wanted to explain, but he just said, "Are you going to be all right?"

Henry nodded. "Just throw my cane over here, and get me the phone on the table. I'll try to get up. If I can't, I'll dial 911."

John dropped the cane and phone next to the bottle. He secretly wished there was a 911 number that could help him find Yoda. Chocker's emergency services were the only ones available at the present time.

"There's gas in it, isn't there?" said John.

Henry flipped him the bird and took another three-gulp pull.

YONKERS

He took his mountain bike from the Subaru and lowered it into the F-150's bed, and then covered it with a tarp and weighted it down with some cinderblocks. After a mental checklist confirmed he had everything he needed, including the satellite phone in case things went south, he pulled away from his house and hit the horn once for Henry.

He saw parents and their kids in costumes as he passed cars on the highway. Presidents and dictators were popular disguises this year. Ronald Reagan drove by in an SUV, and Fidel Castro blew by him in a Honda Civic. Halloween was still weeks away, but a lot of people had made an early holiday of it. With the economy in a tailspin, Wall Street still up against the ropes, and the housing market knocked out and staying down for the count, people looked for any reason they could to celebrate.

The whole country wanted to put their heads in the sand. To add insult to injury, the current president traversed the globe and bowed to every third-world tyrant with whom he could get an audience. A general malaise permeated the air, and it was no wonder people wanted to dress up and be someone else.

John had missed morning rush hour traffic, so the Tappan Zee wasn't backed up its usual three to four miles into Westchester County. He rolled down his window and inhaled the fresh fall air deep into his lungs. He looked over the guide rails and up the gray Hudson River, where a few small sailboats battled a stiff October wind. The pain in his leg had subsided, but his head started to ache, and sweat beads formed on his brow.

Resting heart rate: one hundred.

Not good.

The downside to less traffic was that he would stick out like a sore thumb in the old pickup truck. Expensive luxury cars, SUVs, and late-model commuter compacts owned the roads fifty miles north of New York City. Most people wouldn't be caught dead in a fifteen-year-old, two-wheel-drive pickup with a bumper sticker that read, You Drank the Kool-Aid, Now Get Out Your Checkbook. Henry's Ford smelled like a cheap cigar smoldering in a wet sock. Candy wrappers and snack-cake cellophane littered the floor. The old bastard wasn't winning any points with his doctor on this diet.

A multi-themed gauntlet of bars, delis, and copy shops decorated McLean Avenue. The storefronts had been taken over by Asians who worked nonstop to eke out a life for themselves in the land of milk and honey. John drove until he found an outdoor parking lot a few blocks from the Al-Farooq Masjid mosque. He parked between two gargantuan SUVs, locked the truck, and took his mountain bike from the bed.

Compared to Baby, the Cannondale RZ One Twenty was a Clydesdale. The One Twenty was an ultra-endurance bike, with an adjustable suspension, invincible rear-wheel tracking, and relatively light weight for a mountain bike. It had a thirty-six-hole rim to absorb boulders in the mountains, and for jumping over curbs and trash cans in urban terrain. The RZ also sported an all-aluminum frame with minimal welds, and a monster front shock so the frame resisted cracking if you happened to nosedive into a tree or hit an open manhole cover.

John had left it stock white with blue trim because it looked more like something the average Joe might ride. Messengers liked to paint their bikes black or brown and scratch them up on purpose to discourage theft. A messenger was also a good cover for someone trying to get into places in the city where he didn't belong. Yoda might key in on a messenger, but he would likely dismiss some yuppie tooling around town on a new, clean, and unblemished bike.

He made sure that the helmet strap covered the earpiece phone. The phone was an expensive German make Chocker had provided him via FedEx after their first meeting. It consisted of a combined microphone and earpiece with a small, wireless transceiver that clipped to his waistband under a lightweight windproof cycling jacket. A belt was strapped around his torso, with two sheaths designed for easy release of the daggers he had chosen for Yoda. The daggers were handmade and perfectly balanced for throwing, with extra-wide hilts to protect his hands during thrusts. He would ram the nine-inch blades in one side of the skinny little freak and out the other, after he extracted Maggie's whereabouts.

The early fall air was a brisk fifty-five degrees with a ten-mile-an-hour wind. He put on the balaclava. It was black and decorated with the well-known smiley face yellow icons. He would leave it over his mouth and nose for now, but pull it down under his chin when he got close to the mosque. Even with the happy faces splattered all over it, the balaclava looked a little ominous. But with it down around his neck, it gave the impression of a rich guy's attempt at being trendy.

The satellite phone was in his jacket pocket, charged and on. He pushed the power button for the earphone's remote transceiver and gave it a moment to fire up. It was preset to listen in, so he adjusted the toggle to speak and hear, and then pedaled toward the Al-Farooq Masjid mosque at an unhurried pace.

A few minutes later, a static bleep came into his right ear, followed by a familiar voice. The reception was clear, as if a little man were inside his head.

"The *maillot jaune* looks like a rag without Lance."

"Lance should have stayed postal."

"What's your twenty, old friend?" asked Canaan.

"Three minutes."

"It's good to hear your voice. Nice to have you home again."

Short-range transmitters could get picked up by local listening devices, so they weren't going to get into any details. They didn't need some mullah's kid listening to the Yankee game to figure out they were up to no good, at least by mullah standards.

"It's lonely in here," said Canaan.

John understood. Canaan was working alone and inside the mosque. They hadn't had time to devise a code, so they had to wing it.

"Has the parade started?"

"Not yet. The band is still seated," said Canaan.

"Any sight of the mayor?"

"The mayor may not show for this fete. Would you know him if you saw him?"

"Like my own flesh and blood." John flashed on Yoda's blood mixing with his own during their struggle. "He's got my wife-to-be, Major." John's words rang cold in his own ears, and it bothered him that the first time he'd called Maggie his wife might be the last.

"Say again."

"He took my woman. I need him one-on-one."

There was an uncomfortable moment when Canaan didn't respond. Would he help? Or was he too loyal to Chocker?

"Come on down, then. Get a good seat."

He circled around a few blocks to shake off the butterflies and check for Chocker's spotters and the FBI. The perimeter was clean. If any observers were in the neighborhood, friendly or not, they hid in cracks and crevices like insects. John didn't see them—and locating and exterminating pests was his specialty.

In ten minutes the mosque would let its worshippers out the main doors and onto McLean Avenue. Gophers sent to take out Yoda, or capture him, would pop their noses in the air for a whiff. He rolled the balaclava under his chin, but kept his sunglasses and helmet on. He wore Oakley M Frame Sweeps with light gray polarized lenses. They had excellent optics and were dark enough to cut glare, but not so dark it looked like he was trying to conceal his eyes.

He stopped at the street corner diagonally from the mosque and leaned the bike against a parking meter in front of a boutique coffee shop. It was a small operation that appealed to the Starbucks crowd, without the guilt of contributing to a multinational corporation.

John wrapped a plastic-coated steel cable around the Cannondale's frame and a parking meter. He pushed the padlock's shackle into the case, but stopped before the locking mechanism clicked. There was no time to play with the combination during a hasty exit. He made a fuss about locking it, in case anyone had the bright idea to steal his escape vehicle. Satisfied that the bike would appear to the casual bystander as securely locked, he took off his helmet and walked toward the coffee shop. He left his glasses on.

Police walked with power, arms away from their waists because of overloaded utility belts, and a slight back-and-forth sway in their shoulders that projected authority. Undercover police kept their hands to their sides, but still had command presence and maintain eye contact with those around them. They focused on what could hurt or kill them. In general, a cop wouldn't approach a person unless he had to. They preferred that the subject approach them. The person moving in was the most vulnerable. He was too focused, whether he was a criminal or a citizen in need of directions.

Beat cops, undercover cops, and assassins seldom touched their faces. It revealed insecurity or possible deception. Under the assumption that Yoda was nearby, maybe even in the coffee shop, John maintained a nonaggressive posture: his hands held loosely at his sides, a slight bend at his waist. He rubbed his hair vigorously and scratched his scalp with his fingers. It made him appear to be another guy on the street with his bike who would have been just as comfortable at home on his couch. It was a casual move, and it put people around him at ease. He scratched his balls for good measure and pulled his shorts away from his crotch in the universal adjustment maneuver.

He kept his chin down and studied some scratches on his helmet as he walked into the coffeehouse. He continued to roll the helmet over in his hands as his eyes inconspicuously scanned the room. A couple sat to his right near the window, drinking lattes and reading *Chronogram*. A few young Goths sat at a far table, in deep conversation that relied heavily on Yonkers sign language, with much hand-waving, their mouths staying open after they spoke. No one had his back to the wall, looking out.

A spike-haired barista sat on a bar stool behind the counter, with one fingertip in his mouth as he waited for customers. It didn't appear the coffee shop clientele represented any of the factions involved in today's stakeout. You could never be 100 percent sure, but his internal radar was on low as he walked up to Spike Hair.

He craved sugar but didn't need any more speed in his bloodstream. A low-level drug like caffeine would screw up the cocktail. He ordered a layered caramel mocha decaf macchiato doppio grande just to mess with Spike Hair. The barista whipped it up like a pro, and took his fingertip from his mouth long enough to make change.

John threw a buck in the plastic tip cup and sat down one table from the window with a street view, his back against the wall. The first delicious sip burned his lip a little. The macchiato tasted like a cup full of warm cake to a homeless man.

He had a clean view of the front door and the bathroom in the rear. He saw his bike's front tire on the street to his left. He instinctively kept an eye on what was his, especially in a battle zone with such a diverse criminal population as Yonkers.

He watched several earthlings enter a street-level pizzeria in a brick trapezoid building two doors down from the mosque. Telephone wires draped from the roof and disappeared overhead on his side of McLean Avenue. The first store on the next block displayed a purple sign with the name of a boutique, something having to do with hair. The paint had peeled away from the first part.

Small trees had been planted in holes in the sidewalk to beautify McLean Avenue—part of Yonkers's dying dream to revitalize the downtown district. They were out of place, as even the lamest architect should have known—trees don't grow in concrete. A Mexican hottie in a Subaru waited in front of the boutique with the motor running. She could be an actor in this play, but she looked too young. *Definitively not Chocker's people. Perhaps a new FBI recruit.* An out-of-place, fluffy pampas grass plant covered most of the boutique's window. Not a good hiding spot. If you sat there long enough, someone might cut your hair.

The white-bread Yonkers John had known as a kid was gone. Now the city made you pay a tax if you sold your house and left the town. It was supposed to discourage white flight, but it had only succeeded in raising home prices the amount of the tax, and discouraged working people from moving in. Social engineering at its finest.

He picked up a local real estate magazine and thumbed through the pages to keep his hands busy. The crank made him jumpy, and he didn't like this sitting and waiting game.

"Anything?" It was the little guy in his head.

He picked up his coffee, took a drink, and feigned licking his lips. "Nope."

"The parade starts soon," Canaan said.

"Roger that."

His eyes followed the telephone wires back to the roof. Something had distracted him. A reflection? Movement? Was something or someone on the roof? It might be a pigeon behind the façade, or one of Chocker's people with a scope. He didn't assume only he and Canaan were on the line. Chocker's spotters and snipers would be in the area, and they would have been told to maintain radio silence as they listened in on his conversation. What the hell else could they do anyway? Shoot a man in broad daylight on a Yonkers street in front of a mosque? Doubtful. Maybe they were there to protect him. Or maybe the Desoxyn had worn off and he was getting loopy. Had Chocker hung him out to dry?

John felt for the other pill in his pocket, palmed it, put it in his mouth with a phony cough, chewed it, and washed it down with the extra-sugary macchiato. Psychologically, his heart rate increased. He willed it back to a resting pulse and waited.

He started to second-guess his choice of the bike as cover. No one else had ridden by in the few minutes he had been there. It was too cold for all but die-hard enthusiasts. But he didn't have any other options for a good disguise, and if all hell broke loose, getting out in a car would be difficult. He would have to make the best of it.

The clock on the wall behind Spike Hair showed it was the top of the hour. The parade would indeed begin soon, and still he hadn't seen anyone who remotely resembled Yoda. No one had entered or exited the mosque during his coffee break.

What should he look for? Would Yoda slip into formal Muslim prayer garb, or would he try to look like a nonbeliever strolling through, and then disappear in the crowd? Would he even show? Was this entire operation flawed? Was Yoda already having breakfast on an inbound flight to Yemen's capitol of Sana'a?

He snapped to mental attention when the Al-Farooq Masjid mosque's large wooden doors opened, but he willed his body to stay calm despite the Desoxyn in his veins.

The worshippers were dressed for prayer: the men wore hats and black coats, most of them bearded, and the women wore burkas with their heads covered. This wouldn't be easy. He knew Yoda's general build and height. This fact removed most women from the equation, so he thought he should focus on the men. However, the sly yogi might slouch and throw some padding under a burka.

"Still there?" said the voice in his ear.

"Yep." John's lips barely moved.

"Anything?"

"Nope. They all look alike." More silence as he watched the crowd enter the street. "How many more?"

"The last ones are going through the door," said Canaan. "I'm bringing up the rear. I'll remain inside for the present."

He understood. If Yoda got spooked, he might run back inside, or he might still be in there without Canaan's knowledge.

His heart fluttered, and the valves pumped harder. The tiny phone pressed against his eardrum reverberated the pulse of his heart's rhythm. His skin tightened against his muscles. The crank interfered with other more instinctive messages his body normally sent him in stressful situations. Was the hair on his neck up? Or was he tweaking?

How long his knee had been involuntarily shaking under the small table was anyone's guess. He pressed it against the floor, and a sharp pain ran from the wound up through his pelvis. He needed another OxyContin, but purposely didn't bring one for fear it would take away the edge.

The mullah shook the hands of the Muslim worshipers as they exited through the big wooden doors and walked into the street. There were too many of them. John couldn't pick out a single face or gait. The coffeehouse suddenly became too small. No good. He had to get into the street, get closer and hope his disguise held. He had to move.

He stood next to his bike and sipped the macchiato prop. He threw the paper cup in a metal wastebasket chained to a telephone pole. *They even steal wastebaskets in Yonkers?*

His skin seemed to stretch even tighter, and his internal radar told him something wasn't kosher. Where was his bike? There it was, right beside him. Someone was behind him. *Calm down, of course someone is behind you.* There are 750,000 people in Yonkers, not counting the unregistered Central Americans.

Desoxyn aside, he trusted his gut. He unzipped his windbreaker enough so he could slide his hand inside and get to a dagger if necessary. He turned and stepped back with his right foot. The person behind him didn't expect it. Their clothing rubbed, and he caught a glimpse of a bearded Muslim with the blackest eyes, like marbles, with no pupils. The man looked at him with distain and said, "Bebakhshid." *Excuse me.* John recognized the accent: Iranian, not Afghani.

Dark Eyes walked across the street and into the crowd. *Where had he come from?*

John turned toward the deli next to the coffeehouse. From the angle they had bumped, Dark Eyes likely came from the deli. He looked back across the street, but Dark Eyes was gone. A Yankees cap appeared in his peripheral vision. He didn't turn his head. Its owner was headed his way, and he didn't want to seem interested in every passing citizen. He was, after all, just a cyclist dropping in for a coffee.

Yankee Cap was thin, about six one, with Asian features and a beard. John couldn't get an angle on his face to see if it was Yoda, but so far he fit the bill. Dark Eyes and Yankee Cap must have been in the deli together, having a snack or reading the paper while they waited for the mosque to empty so they could melt into the crowd. Only a sheetrock wall had separated them while John sipped his coffee.

Yankee Cap walked several yards to the corner and hailed a cab. John got a good look when the man ducked into the rear passenger-side door. Yankee Cap grimaced in pain as he slid into the seat and closed the door.

"I got him," said John. He unwound the steel bike cable and dropped it in the gutter.

"Say again."

"I got him. He's in a cab across the street. Get out here now. Go, go, go!"

But nothing happened. No shooters, no agents ran from surrounding buildings.

"Calm down," Canaan whispered. "I'm at the door." Canaan nodded at the cab, and John nodded back.

The cab pulled away from the curb.

"Get someone on this guy. We're going to lose him."

Blue smoke puffed from the cab's exhaust pipe as the driver accelerated away from the curb. John pulled the smiley face balaclava over his nose and mouth, pushed his sunglasses tight against his forehead, jumped on his bike, locked his feet into the clips, and sprinted toward Yoda. The light had been red for a long time. Then the stale red turned yellow, then green in an instant. The streetlight changed quickly, but the world around it slowed down. He had the sensation of gasoline being poured on his wound. He stood in the saddle for more power. Thread by thread, his stitches tore through their holes.

Canaan ran from the door and across McLean Avenue. John pedaled harder to catch up with the cab. He wouldn't make it. He was too slow. *Everything. So. Slow.*

Two pedestrians jumped out of his way. Another one wasn't so lucky and took a handlebar to the elbow. John lost his balance for a second but kept on pedaling. The man went down hard on the concrete and yelled profanities as he wiped the spilled coffee and sandwich from his jacket and pants.

The cabbie picked up speed at the middle of the intersection. John pulled up on the handlebars with all his strength and hopped off the curb and into the street. He would block the cab and wait for Canaan, or Chocker, or the FBI, or the police, or the cavalry. Somebody better show up, or Yoda would disappear into the woodwork like a cockroach.

He flew off the curb, with his front tire in the air, and banked toward the cab. The cabbie saw him coming and tried to wave him off. The rider in the backseat looked over his glasses and smirked.

Yoda.

Why in the hell was he smiling?

John got one last look at the Yankee trademark before McLean Avenue engulfed him.

Blood oozed purple through the yellow smiley faces on the balaclava. Canaan checked for vitals and then patted John down. Four FBI agents jumped out of the SUV that had slammed into John Rexford's airborne body and bicycle. They drew their guns and yelled for Canaan to back away. Canaan glared at them, ready to strike. They leveled their pistols at his center mass from six feet away.

"My son! My son!" Canaan wailed in Pashto. "They have killed my son."

"Step away, sir. Step away from him now." The largest FBI agent kept the muzzle of his Glock 22 pointed at Canaan's head, his finger on the trigger.

"Help me, my brothers. Help me. The FBI has killed my son!"

Dozens of Muslim men ran from the street outside the mosque to the accident scene. Canaan continued to scream about how the FBI had killed his son, wailing and crying as he rocked over the body, cradling John, protecting him. He felt the dagger and satellite phone beneath John's riding jacket. He wrapped his arms around John's head and shoulders and checked for a pulse. Nothing.

"Stand back." The lead FBI agent and his three partners trained their Glocks on the crowd and aimed over their heads. "Stand back. FBI!"

An old man in the crowd knelt down beside Canaan, oblivious to the FBI's commands. Several more worshippers broke ranks and encircled Canaan. The FBI continued to shout, but the dam had broken, and every man in the crowd rushed the scene. The Muslim worshippers formed a wall of human flesh around Canaan, with their backs to the FBI as they circled their fallen brethren.

Canaan continued to wail as he searched John's body. He removed the microphone from John's ear and the transceiver from his waist, and hid them and the daggers beneath his own robe. He grabbed his satellite phone, scrolled to the menu, and dialed the only number there.

"Cock."

"Tails and ginger ale," said Canaan.

"What the hell?"

"He's down. Lance is down."

"And the bird?"

"The bird has flown," said Canaan.

"And Lance?"

"Unknown. Taking him to the doctor."

"We'll be ready."

"Out."

The phone went dead.

The male worshippers had successfully pushed the FBI back ten men deep from Canaan.

"Help me." Canaan motioned to the four men closest to him to reach under John's body and lift. They formed a human stretcher and, in a crouch, moved John's body through the crowd toward the open doors of the Al-Farooq Masjid mosque. The men, women, and children of the mosque sealed off the entrance from the FBI with their bodies.

The FBI held their positions at the crowd's edge, communicating into visible earpieces, guns at their sides. The US attorney general wouldn't back them for any collateral damage they created while attempting to apprehend a possible suspect. In fact, since the man wore a balaclava, sunglasses, and helmet, the agents wouldn't be able to testify in court that the man they had killed was in fact the person targeted for apprehension. They would have a tough time explaining why they ran over an unarmed citizen on a bicycle. The stakeout thus far could be summed up in one acronym: FUBAR.

Two of the men holding John were from Chocker's team, planted in the mosque three months before Canaan had arrived from Afghanistan. Given his rank within the CIA and his proficiency in all things Muslim, Canaan was de facto commander of the surreptitious team that had infiltrated the Al-Farooq Masjid mosque, a place of worship frequented by men known to raise money for terrorists overseas. Canaan waved off the two people who weren't team members, and ordered them to lock the large wooden doors to the mosque.

Canaan and his soldiers hustled to a back room where the mullah held private meetings. They hurried John's body down two flights of stairs and into the boiler room. Wooden pallets were stacked against a wall in the back of the room behind an archaic oil-burning boiler. Canaan pushed the pallets aside, exposing a steel door five feet high. He picked up a sledgehammer hidden behind the pallets and smashed it against a steel padlock that secured a hasp to the wall. The padlock shattered into several pieces, and the door swung inward.

Canaan waved his men through the door into a small room with a ten-foot ceiling. His reconnaissance of the building's layout had shown him that, during Prohibition, the mosque's basement had been a speakeasy, and the Irish mob used this back hallway for hooch deliveries and quick escapes during raids.

Canaan pointed to a smaller steel door on the back wall. "Set him down," he said. "Go outside and confirm that the van is there. It will have yellow lettering and keys in the visor. Then get your asses back here, and let's get our soldier the fuck out of here."

Canaan placed his hand on John's throat. His own thumb and forefinger pulse was too strong to discern if John had a pulse of his own. Canaan lifted the soldier's eyelids to check for a reaction. The pupils were dilated and the corneas were bloodshot. All bad signs. Still, an accurate diagnosis couldn't be made in the poorly lit anteroom.

Canaan watched the two men until they disappeared into the blackness. He heard a door open at the narrow channel's far end, saw some light enter the passage, and heard the door shut again.

Canaan wondered if he should go back and inject himself into the angry mob in a show of solidarity. Or should he ride with John to the doctor? As with most mission elements, preparation allowed for improvisation. It sounded easy until you tried it for real, with your heart pounding, an angry mob outside, and the FBI on the street, armed to the teeth.

As if this wasn't enough, the only man who could identify Yoda might be dead. Was Yoda watching the whole thing from an apartment across the street? A mistake on Canaan's part would blow a cover that had taken years to cultivate. Should he leave the mosque without a word? Would his fellow worshippers think he was undercover Al Qaeda and laud his disappearance? They might even think he was a hero. But how would he explain his newfound son? There were too many questions. He had survived this long by making quick decisions. In a SNAFU like this, the only real option was to make a decision, go with it, and survive to adapt your plan later.

First he would close the door that led to the boiler room. Then he would step into the bootleggers' escape tunnel, carrying John, and lock the inner door from the other side. The Prohibition-era rumrunners had the foresight to install a steel bar and a deadbolt that would hold during their escape, even against a police battering ram. Simple but effective 1930s technology.

He turned to close the outer door to the boiler room, and heard the soft swish of nylon clothing behind him.

"So, Major Dan Canaan. We missed you in Turkmenistan."

"It speaks," hissed Canaan.

"But I didn't miss you partner," said Yoda. Yoda's broken English reminded Canaan of old black-and-white Charlie Chan movies, but not so funny. "I folded him up in nice package. CIA must have save money on the casket."

The "partner" had been an expert hand-to-hand combat soldier under Chocker's command. Tim Horton had been an aikido and Thai boxing master—an unorthodox but deadly combination. Horton had agreed to fight Yoda in order to maintain his cover. He ended up with his back broken, his ribcage split for open-heart surgery, and his sacroiliac separated from his pelvis. It all happened in one quick move delivered by the deadly yogi.

Canaan quickly weighed his options. *Pick up John, run through the door, and bolt it shut. Take care of John today, and pick another day to die.* He had been given direct orders from Chocker not to engage this freak of nature. Option two was to stay here and kill the skinny little prick once and for all, and maybe die now. Canaan almost reached for the gun in his ankle holster, but he wanted to inflict more pain on this bastard than a bullet would allow.

"Deer should not toy with tiger," said Canaan.

"Ah," said Yoda. "You are Confucius."

"Charlie Chan, fuckhead."

There weren't many people in this world Canaan couldn't kill in a few seconds of hand-to-hand combat. Every bone and muscle fiber in his body had been shaped by the rigorous and painful practice of body hardening known as iron shirt. His body had been hammered repeatedly over several years—first with soft, dried bamboo shoots, and later with kendo sticks that formed tiny rips and cracks in his muscle tissue and fascia. The injuries healed so many times that they became dense beyond nature's intent, and were weapons in themselves.

Canaan bowed, careful to keep his head up and his eyes on Yoda. Yoda slid his Yankee cap, jacket, and sneakers off, and walked toward Canaan as if taking a stroll in the park.

Canaan placed his left toe on the ground in front of him. He raised both hands in a classic cat stance: strong, sharp fingers spread like tiger claws. Yoda ignored the stance and continued his leisurely pace. One step, two, three, and Canaan struck. He dropped his toe, shifted his weight to his left leg, and thrust his right foot in a short kick that caught Yoda in the tibia. Yoda walked through the kick, though the pain must have been excruciating. Canaan brought his right leg back to the ground as fast as he had lashed out, pushed off his right foot, and jabbed at Yoda's neck with a sharp left hand, claws extended. Yoda countered by dropping his chin into his chest, guarding his soft neck tissue. The blow missed Yoda's tender throat muscles by a split second, but the sharp claws took off the left side of his nose. Canaan saw Yoda's exposed and bloody sinus membranes.

Canaan lashed out with another kick, slightly off-balance this time, not expecting Yoda to walk into his jab. Opponents never walked toward you—ran, maybe, or walked, then feinted—but they never simply strolled into your attack. The top of Canaan's foot nailed Yoda squarely in the crotch. Yoda winced, ducked under Canaan's arm, and was behind him in a torso lock before Canaan could spin away and grab his fingers to prevent the hold.

It was time to panic.

Canaan had seen Chocker's video of Yoda in action and realized he was about to experience it in real time. He had mentally practiced a defense for several years. He theorized that if he could stand up straight and not go down, even Yoda's legs weren't flexible enough to get double grapevines in twice around his ankles. He needed to stay erect and keep his legs extended until an offensive opportunity presented itself.

Canaan didn't expect the full nelson that already had his scapulas pressed in a V formation, forcing them into his spine with his hands over his head. It was a simple wrestling move designed to snap your neck at the sixth and seventh cervical bones if applied with enough pressure. Canaan gasped for air, and his lungs spasmed violently as the predator's slender ankles wrapped around his own. Option number one looked better now.

Canaan expanded his lungs. Yoda waited for the contraction before he completed his deadly maneuver. When he could hold his breath no longer, Canaan pushed all the air from his lungs in one rapid exhale, leaving the slightest space between his right armpit and Yoda's bicep, and yanked his arm down in an attempt to free one side and leave him in a half nelson. Yoda felt it coming and ratcheted the full nelson even tighter so that Canaan's vertebrae began to separate.

With his windpipe nearly closed, the room sparkled with tiny stars in Canaan's peripheral vision. Yoda's lips pressed against the bend in Canaan's neck, and he whispered, "I hear angels call your name, Major. Do you hear them?"

Canaan shivered from Yoda's warm breath on his skin as he faded. He felt his legs tingle, and then ache, as electric shocks jolted his nerve endings. He felt his bowels begin to relax, and all the warmth of his body pooled in his groin. His head began to cool, and his penis grew hard. Someone rubbed his ankle. Someone cared enough about him to rub his aching body before he died.

Bang! Bang! Bang!

Did Canaan dream it? Was he dreaming? Was he already gone, and the angels were firing off his salute?

Yoda released the full nelson and slid down Canaan's spine, his arms draped over Canaan's ankles and his head wedged between Canaan's knees. Canaan looked down and then collapsed backward on top of the yogi assassin. He rolled to his side and saw John Rexford's face next to him, his own pistol in John's hand . . . and then Major Daniel Canaan passed out.

The corners of John's mouth twitched for a second, and then he went limp with the gun in his hand.

"Major!"

Someone pushed against his shoulder.

"Major! Get up! Are you okay?"

Canaan's eyes opened. He saw one of the soldiers he had sent to check on the van. He coughed and rolled to his side. He saw the bullet holes in the back of the assassin's spandex shirt. They seemed too small, shaped like tiny tears. *This was all it took to bring down the devil? Bullets?*

Canaan got up slowly and motioned for his man to take John into the tunnel. He tried to talk, but his throat was still frozen from the full nelson. He swung the steel door shut and lowered the metal bar on the other side, then fell to the ground inside the dark tunnel, spent and in pain.

The full nelson had drained all strength from his shoulders, and his hips had been stretched to the breaking point. He took a few breaths to clear his mind, and flexed his legs to regain muscle control. When he was ready, Canaan half-ran to the end of the escape passage. He jumped in the van's side door.

"Let's roll, boys. The FBI is pee-issed!"

He sat on the carpeted floor of the van and giggled like a little kid. He composed himself and then crawled over to John, wincing with every breath.

"You all right, Lance?" he said.

The driver looked over his shoulder and back at the road. "He hasn't said a word, sir."

Canaan felt John's faint pulse and checked his pupils again. They were still dilated, and his breath was shallow.

"Take the GWB—the lower bridge. It'll take us out at the Fort Lee exit, and we can get this soldier some help."

"George Washington Bridge, lower level. Be there in fifteen minutes. Who's this guy, sir?"

"NTK, soldier."

"And I don't need to know, sir. Sorry I asked."

NEW JERSEY

Dr. Sarah Wahler spent four days a week, sixteen hours a day, at Manhattan's hospital for special surgery, where her delicate and precise hands performed orthopedic miracles on adult and pediatric cervical, thoracic, and lumbar spine injuries and deformities. She specialized in trauma-induced spinal stenosis, a narrowing of the space between the vertebral discs, most common among the elderly as a symptom of the aging process. It was also one of the most debilitating injuries a soldier could endure when thrown into the air after his vehicle ran over a landmine or improvised explosive device, or when the percussion from a bomb sent him flying and he landed on his head or tailbone.

After completing medical school at Tel Aviv Sourasky Medical Center, where she studied internal medicine, Sarah transferred to Assuta Medical Center in the same city and obtained certification as an orthopedic surgeon. She learned to operate on any bone in the human skeleton. There was no patient shortage, with Hamas and Hezbollah lobbing shells and placing mines along the patrolled Lebanon/Israel border and Gaza Strip for the last thirty years. Her residency in Tel Aviv had put her in the geographic center of the country, and brave soldiers who didn't die on the field were brought to her to repair them as best she could.

She had been introduced to C. Peter Chocker at Assuta. Chocker's team had fought alongside Israel's Shin Bet, their FBI equivalent for internal national security. With help from International Fiber Resources, she obtained a visa for the United States and a position as assistant chief of orthopedic surgery at HSS in Manhattan. Each summer, to assuage the guilt for leaving her homeland, Dr. Wahler returned to Assuta Medical Center and performed *au gratis* surgery for anyone who couldn't afford the needed procedures.

Her payoff to the CIA was that they could call upon her special talents 24-7 and she would be available. A special trauma unit and operating room had been leased for her use at a facility in Fort Lee, New Jersey, courtesy of C. Peter Chocker and his humanitarian organization.

Sarah had already prepared the operating room for whatever emergency Chocker was about to dump in her capable hands. They provided her with state-of-the-art equipment and an on-call anesthesiologist. He helped her prep the room and sterilize her surgical instruments while they waited for the patient.

Canaan pressed the buzzer, and a moment later the electronic latch clicked. He pushed the door open, and his two men carried John to the operating room and placed him on the table. He ordered them to park in a nearby underground lot until summoned. Someone in Yonkers might have seen the white van pull away from the mosque, and he didn't need an overzealous Barney Fife snaring his men in a routine traffic stop.

"What happened?" said Sarah.

"He was hit by a car, an SUV." Canaan pulled out a knife. Sarah didn't move. He cut off John's shirt and cycling pants, and then took off his shoes and socks. He found the photograph of Maggie in John's jacket and quickly stuffed it in his pocket.

"Who butchered the stitches?" Sarah pressed lightly on the open wound with her fingertips. Trickles of creamy, opaque pus beaded to the surface.

Canaan wondered about the deep gash on John's thigh, but explanations would have to wait. "I have no idea."

Sarah checked for a pulse.

"There's no pulse. How long as he been like this?" She was already walking toward the wall-mounted automated external defibrillator.

"He had a pulse on the way over." Canaan's eyes met Sarah's. "I checked him two minutes ago and it was there, but faint."

"So maybe two minutes, three without a heartbeat. That lowers his chances to 60 percent, with no damage to the heart or brain." She placed the self-adhesive electrode pads on John's upper right and lower left chest. A red light on the AED flashed. "He's in ventricular fibrillation. The good news is he's not dead, yet."

"Cheer up, Doc. He's a marine."

"Why didn't you perform CPR on the way over?"

"I'm telling you, Doc. He was breathing and had a faint pulse until we came through the door."

"Let's save this soldier." It was a phrase Doctor Wahler had used more than once in Tel Aviv. She checked to see if the electrode cables were properly fastened to the AED and waited for the green light. A digital voice from the AED indicated that a shock was needed. Sarah yelled "Clear!" and pushed the SHOCK button. She immediately began CPR for two minutes and checked for a pulse. The AED voice came on again, prompting another shock. She yelled "Clear!" and pushed the SHOCK button, followed by another CPR cycle.

This time the AED indicated a shock wasn't needed. She grabbed a stethoscope and listened to John's chest.

Sarah let out a breath. "He's back. Let's see what there is to see."

Canaan smiled and took a breath. He took the photograph from his pocket and stared at the horrifying image. He was no stranger to death, but he had never gotten used to the torturing of innocents.

John bolted up from the table into a sitting position and caught them both off guard. Sarah jumped back. Canaan placed a hand on his shoulder. John grabbed the photograph from Canaan and fell back down. Canaan tried to take it from John's hand as his wide eyes burned into the image.

"Take it easy, soldier," said Canaan. "I'm right here." He tried to ease the photograph from John's fading grip.

John's eyes closed and he began to mumble softly. "The Iron Fireman . . ." His voice trailed off. Canaan leaned closer to his lips. John grabbed hold of Canaan's wrist and squeezed with his last ounce of energy. "It's the Iron Fireman. Go to the old school."

Canaan took the photograph and stepped back as John's hand fell off the side of the table.

"Please sit down, sir." Sarah motioned to a chair against the wall.

"I have triage experience if I can be of any help, Doctor."

Sarah nodded dismissively, removed the electrodes, and began her examination. Her small hands moved quickly over the joints in John's legs and arms, feeling for protrusions and swelling. She reached gently behind his neck and ran her thumb and forefinger along each of the cervical vertebrae. Next, she massaged his scalp for bumps and contusions. When she was finished, she went to his feet and started the process again. She felt each toe, the bones in his feet, then worked her way up the legs to his hips and chest area, and completed her exam with the cervical spine.

Sarah picked up some loose papers from a stainless steel table against the wall. It was John's medical history. Chocker had faxed it over before they arrived.

"How well do you know this man?" she asked Canaan.

"I serve with him."

"His record shows several injuries, lots of combat action, otherwise good health." She shook her head. "How ridiculous is it that military leaders take young men, build them up to the peak of physical and mental performance, and then send them places where the enemy can tear it all down. Such a waste."

"How is he?"

"Nothing big is broken. I want to perform some tests, but it says in his file that he's had knee surgery and there's a layer of Teflon near the meniscus, so I'm limited in scope as to what I can do. In other words, no MRI."

"Isn't Teflon a plastic, Doc?"

"Yes. But some companies weave a thin layer of titanium into the mesh for durability. I have no way of knowing what's in him without knowing the manufacturer."

How far could he go with Dr. Sarah Wahler? Chocker had cleared her and that should be enough, but only to a point.

"What's the downside?"

"If we don't perform an MRI, a lot of unseen damage could be missed." She tilted her head to the side. "On the other hand, if we do, and there's titanium in his knee, the magnet will pull the metal through his skin like it was made of paper."

"I need more options, Doc." Canaan looked into her eyes with a cold stare.

"The only other option is for me to go in and find out what type of mesh is holding his knee together."

There was no time for exploratory surgery, and it was unnecessary anyway.

"Give him the MRI, Doc."

"What? We can't do that."

Canaan took the medical report from her hand, folded it in half, and stuffed it in his pocket. He walked over to the fax machine and cleared out the incoming calls memory, then unplugged it. "There's no metal in his knee."

She almost asked him why, but then realized it was pointless. "Nothing is ever what it seems with you guys, is it?"

"Sometimes excess reality can be a painful thing."

She motioned the anesthesiologist to the examination table. "Let's get him an MRI and a CAT scan."

"Both machines are warmed up and ready, Doctor."

"Wheel him in."

Canaan tried to follow, but Sarah ordered him to sit with a wave of her palm.

"I need to be with him, Doctor."

"You can watch from behind the glass. I have security clearance, soldier. He's not giving up any state secrets in this condition."

"With all due respect, you don't have this level of clearance. And this man won't leave my sight for even one second."

She stared at Canaan's uncompromising gaze as if cataloging his expression. "Or what?"

"Or I take him out of here." He appealed to her Hippocratic Oath. Dr. Sarah Wahler wouldn't let Chocker's man die on a table over a turf war.

"Very well." Disgusted, Sarah shook her head. "Walk him into the MRI, but you can't be in there when we turn on the machine. It's a very strong magnet and I don't need two victims."

He smiled. "Are you insinuating I might have metal plates in my head?"

She almost smiled, but shook her head again. Canaan followed John and the anesthesiologist into the MRI room. He went into the observation room and sat behind Sarah.

Sarah instructed the anesthesiologist to give John a dose of thiopental to induce a temporary barbiturate coma. She explained to Canaan that if John woke up inside the MRI tube and began to thrash around, he could do serious damage to himself. Canaan checked the label on the thiopental bottle and nodded. Sarah explained the drug would also reduce any intracranial pressure if John had suffered a severe concussion. Better to release the pressure in case of traumatic brain injury and not wait for the MRI and CAT scan results.

"Not your first experience, hey, Doc?"

"Hardly."

Forty-five minutes later she instructed the anesthesiologist to bring John out. They all went to another room where a CAT scan was performed on John's breathing but motionless body.

Another half hour and the procedure was finished. Sarah instructed the other doctor to put John back in the operating room and hook him up to an electrocardiogram to monitor his heart, an EEG to monitor his brain waves, and to check his blood pressure every five minutes.

"What's the prognosis, Doctor?"

"The axial and coronal images are negative for abnormal structures, aside from a slight concussion. No haemangioma." She saw she had lost Canaan with the phrase, and added, "No internal vessel hemorrhaging, no clots, no tumors." Canaan nodded that he understood. "He's stable. Other than a few scrapes and bruises and that gash in his thigh from an earlier injury, he's uninjured."

"Then why was he unconscious?"

"Was he able to talk after the accident?"

"No. He didn't say a word."

"It's a Grade 3 concussion. His body went into total shock from the trauma. From what you explained, the SUV must have hit him broadside. Imagine all the electricity in your body getting rerouted instantaneously. His circuitry shut down. The mild concussion kept him under for a while, but his brain slowed everything down while it tried to figure out what was wrong with him."

"Thank you, Doctor. He's very important to us."

"Everyone's important, soldier."

"Some are more important than others."

"Unfortunately. I'm going to take him out of the coma."

"No, Doc."

"Pardon me?"

"I have to make a call and check in. Let him rest."

"Rest?" Her expression turned angry. "I don't understand."

"I'm not asking you to. Just leave him. I have to update my superiors as to his condition."

"You make your call," she said, her face inches from Canaan's. "You've got five minutes, and I'm waking him up."

"Sit down, Doc, please. I'll be right back."

She sat down, flabbergasted at how easily she had lost control of her operating room.

"Cock." Chocker answered after one ring.

"Tails and ginger ale." Canaan looked at the photograph of the doomed woman.

"What's the status, Major?"

"He's in a barb coma. He'll live. No serious injuries, but he must have been in one hell of a knife fight."

"Anything else?"

"I've got a small photograph of the woman I think is his wife. She's tied to a chair and has an IV drip in her arm. But it's not for medication. It's draining her blood into a bowl."

"Did he say anything?"

"Yeah, he did. He woke up for a moment and said something about the Iron Fireman and the old school."

"He said school?"

"*The* old school. Mean anything to you?"

"The woman is a teacher. I'll look into it and get someone there ASAP."

"Next step?"

Chocker gave Canaan explicit instructions on the condition John Rexford would be in when he left Dr. Sarah Wahler's care.

Canaan paced the room like a caged animal. "He saved my ass in Afghanistan. We can't replace him, you know."

"I know. It's the only way, Major."

"The only way sucks, sir."

"I know."

Canaan hung up and jammed the phone into his pocket. He looked at the photograph again and noticed a small, circular insignia on the furnace next to the woman's head. Much of it was rusted, but still had a little red paint in the middle. Inside the circle was a tiny tin man holding a shovel. Canaan narrowed his eyes and could just make out one of the words beneath the logo: IRON.

He returned to the operating room to tell Dr. Wahler what must be done.

Agents Jeff Huntley and Stephen Lewis were molar deep into the sweetness of the Pine View Bakery's homemade, sugar-glazed apple-cheese Danish when the call came to go to the mothballed school on Randolph Street. Lewis left a twenty on the table, slurped once more on the strong black coffee, ignored the splatter on his tie, and rushed out the door.

"She's got to be in there," said Lewis. He switched on the flashing grill-and-dash strobe lights, activated the siren, and raced the turbocharged Ford Taurus to seventy miles per hour in a forty-five zone.

"This is Rexford's woman?" Huntley said. He checked his pistol and clip while trying not to look at the road. He didn't like to speed unless he was behind the wheel.

"Gilchrest thinks so," said Lewis.

"Anonymous tip?"

"It could be Rexford himself who called it in," said Lewis. "He may be so fucked up that he tried to kill her and then had second thoughts."

"Why?"

"Eliminate anyone who knows him. He's in the wind, and maybe, just maybe, he doesn't want a murder rap to contend with."

"Or maybe he loves her. Maybe he . . . Watch out!"

The red-and-black Woodstock Fire and Rescue truck pulled out from a side road off Route 28 into the direct path of the Taurus. Lewis pumped the brakes, gave up on the antiskid technology, and slammed them hard. All four tires grabbed the asphalt with the wail of big dog.

They followed the fire truck for seven miles before it turned off, unable to pass the behemoth due to oncoming traffic.

"Looks like they're going our way," said Huntley as they turned on the same road as the fire truck. Three police cruisers followed close on their rear bumper.

"You think Gilchrist called the locals?" said Lewis.

"I think he called everyone in the county, and it's a race to see who gets here first. If this woman is in trouble, she could be shot, unconscious—anything."

The car had barely stopped when Huntley jumped out the passenger side. Both agents ran to the front door, where two police officers were taking turns trying to breach the steel doors with a battering ram.

"Anyone bring a key?" said Lewis, trying not to sound too much like a smart-ass.

The two cops ignored him. A third sidled up and said, "This place has been closed for over a year. No one seems to know where the keys are. We got someone going over to the high school now to see what he can find."

"It might be too late by then," said Lewis. "Let's take out a window."

At that moment the doors broke inward and a whoosh of stale air escaped.

Lewis turned to see an EMT ambulance race down the narrow asphalt service road along the south side of the building.

"Where's he going?"

The cop shrugged and said, "Back door?"

The scanner had crackled, and the dispatcher said something about a hostage situation or possible homicide at the old school. Tom Foster was off duty as a janitor for Onteora school district, but on call as a volunteer EMT. When he pulled into the school parking lot and saw flashing lights, he was a little relieved that the cavalry was there. But when he saw the two cops trying to batter in the door, he knew there was a better way. Foster had cleaned every square foot of flooring in the building for ten years, and had continued to run monthly maintenance checks on the plumbing and electricity. He had a key that would open the back door to the basement.

He backed the ambulance up to the basement stairwell, and he and his partner ran to the door with a minimum of breakout gear. In less than a second, he'd located the proper key on his chain and opened the door.

Both men walked briskly through the dark hallway of the basement and scanned the rooms on either side with their flashlights.

Foster heard yelling from the floor above and voices shouting "Margaret Castalia."

He only knew one Margaret Castalia in this town, and it had to be Maggie. His mind went back to their last date, over a year and a half ago. They had broken off their relationship when she started dating the blacksmith.

"Maggie!" He heard his own voice echo back off the damp cement walls. "Maggie!"

His partner gave him a look and said, "You know, Tom, there could be somebody with a gun down here."

Foster replied by pulling up his pant leg and exposing a small-caliber pistol strapped to his ankle.

The voices above were closer now, and Foster heard footsteps running down the stairwell. Someone yelled, "Boiler room!" It was all he needed to pick up the pace and race to the end of the hall, where the old Iron Fireman burner was located. Foster knew the touchy old firebox too well, having busted his knuckles more than once cleaning the filters. It still worked, but it was set on a slow burn—just enough to keep the pipes from freezing in the winter. He pushed open the door, heard sand and grit scrape beneath the metal sweep, and felt a warm rush of air against his face. The smell of oil and urine filled his nostrils. His eyes followed mouse scat across the floor to where the numbers on an alarm clock glowed green: 6:07.

They froze at the threshold, afraid to break the plane that would commit them to the room.

"We better wait for the cops," said his partner.

He gasped, and then whispered, "Holy shit."

A scarecrow was slumped forward and strapped down in a wooden chair. Its head folded onto its chest, as if all the straw had left its neck. Strands of black, sweat-drenched hair covered its face and stuck to its chest like warm tar. It wore a ragged sweater and a long skirt, both drenched in sweat and stuck to its body. Foster followed the line of the scarecrow's legs to its dirty sneakers. Its swollen and bleeding ankles were tied to the chair legs. The struggle for freedom had torn all the skin from its shins, and one ankle was rolled over against the floor. Thin ropes were tied tight against its arms: one piece held fast to its torso, the other held its arm strapped to the chair.

He followed the duct tape to the crook of the elbow, where an IV tube ran from its veins to a large glass fishbowl on the floor.

It has to be a prank, thought Foster. *Kids playing with the cops, or something left over from a dare, or a Halloween party*. But scarecrows don't bleed, and the fishbowl was about one-third filled with blood. *Or was it a game, not blood? Just some soda, or frosting, or something? Anything but blood.* And there was an electric alarm clock on the rusted furnace. *Why?*

"Freeze!"

Foster lowered his flashlight and turned toward the voice.

"Get away from the body! This is a police investigation." Lewis lowered his automatic about a foot to show that he had no intention of shooting, but kept the weapon pointed in Foster's direction. Someone flipped the wall switch, and a florescent bulb began to warm the room with expanding light.

"It's Maggie." Foster looked at Lewis and then back at the clock. "She's dying. We've got to do something."

"She may be dead, sir," said Lewis. "We have to proceed with caution. Now back over to the wall, and let us do our job."

Foster gave Lewis a blank stare and said, "Your job?"

"This woman is in danger, but so are the rest of us if she's booby trapped. We have to get the bomb squad in here before we touch her." Lewis cocked his head and gave Foster a soft but determined gaze. "Please step away."

Foster turned his back to Lewis and walked over to the oil burner. Lewis and Huntley raised their weapons and shouted for him to stop. Foster placed his fingers gently alongside Maggie's neck.

"There's no pulse," he said. "We've got to get her off the chair and to a hospital."

"Stay right the fuck where you are, sir! This is no time for heroics. That clock may be a bomb." Lewis raised his weapon toward Foster's chest.

Foster looked at the alarm clock, back at the guns pointed at his critical mass, and then to the woman he still loved. He didn't see any wires connected to the alarm clock. There were no explosives nearby—nothing to indicate it was anything more than an alarm clock. Still, he was no expert. What if they were right?

He stretched his arm toward the green glow of numbers.

Lewis screamed, "Hit the dirt! Everyone out!"

Foster's hand trembled as he reached for the clock. He turned his face away and grimaced, as if it would protect him from an explosion.

He grabbed the clock, stared at the time, and waited for the big boom.

Nothing happened.

Foster pulled a jackknife from his pocket, cut the IV, removed the needle from her arm, and cut the duct tape that held her in place. He cradled Maggie's limp body as it rolled to the floor. He pulled strands of wet hair away from her face and gently lifted an eyelid to check her pupils. He felt resistance as Maggie's eye muscles twitched beneath his shaking fingers.

"She's alive!" Foster turned to the door. "Get a stretcher in here. She's alive!"

Lewis and Huntley stepped inside the room. Lewis turned back to the hallway and shouted for a stretcher and more EMTs. Within seconds, another crew of paramedics was in the room, checking Maggie's vitals.

"Is she alive?" Lewis asked.

One of the paramedics shook his head. "No pulse, no response. We can immobilize her and get an IV in her arm for fluids. That's about it, until we get to the hospital."

Lewis looked at the oil stains on the ground, the limp body, the blood in the fishbowl, then back at the paramedic. "You're in charge of the body," he said. "Don't touch anything else. Get her out of here as fast as you can. You are not to speak to anyone. This is an FBI investigation. Do you understand?"

The paramedic nodded and motioned for his team to roll Maggie onto the fiberglass stretcher. Foster walked over to help.

Lewis motioned for Huntley to follow the paramedics. He caught the eye of one of the Woodstock police officers, and then pointed to Foster and said, "Would someone please arrest this asshole?"

THE EQUUS

The village of Tarrytown, New York, rested on the Hudson River's east bank, about a half hour north of midtown Manhattan. It was famous for several reasons, not the least of which was that it was where Revolutionary War spy Major John Andre had been captured, interrogated, and searched by armed militiamen. Inside his boot they found diagrams of West Point drawn in Benedict Arnold's hand, showing the British how the fort could be taken. Arnold escaped to the British side, and Andre was later hanged across the Hudson in the town of Tappan, in October 1780.

North of Tarrytown was Sleepy Hollow, where Washington Irving drew inspiration for *The Legend of Sleepy Hollow*, a novel that gave birth to one of the world's most frightening specters, the Headless Horseman. Irving was buried there, in the Sleepy Hollow Cemetery.

Tarrytown and surrounding villages had thrived for over two hundred years due to their place in history, location on the

Hudson River, and access to trains and major roadways. When General Motors decided to close a major manufacturing plant in the 1990s, the town took a nosedive and had to allow for lower-income residents. The blueblood core still remained, but Tarrytown was under siege by exorbitant taxes and the multicultural influx spreading across their borders from low-rent districts such as Elmsford and the train-depot towns of Ossining and Dobbs Ferry. Many idle rich stole away under night's darkness, in much the same way British spies slunk to points south and west to escape capture over two hundred years ago.

For those who remained because they were attached to the area, or had trouble selling their million-dollar-plus properties, there were places such as the Equus to encourage the illusion that they weren't part of a dying community. Equus offered a five-star diner's dream inside a stone-walled castle on the Hudson, built in the early 1900s by the son of a Civil War general. It had been recently renovated into a modern hotel on the inside—the outside was a designated historical landmark—with luxury suites, fitness centers, a heated pool, and tennis courts.

John couldn't think of an appropriate place to take Maggie for this special occasion, so he fell back on the HudsonVhappenings.org website and found Equus. Maggie needed something special to take her mind off the past month. He had convinced her he wasn't a killer—a white lie when you considered the stakes. He was just a man who was doing a job, albeit a secret one, for the military. The CIA had refused to give him the necessary change of status to divulge to her that he had worked with them. She accepted that he was only part of a domestic, peripheral support team collecting intel for the military, and that he hadn't been actively involved in combat, but things had gone wrong on this one mission—very wrong.

After the FBI had crushed him on the streets of Yonkers, John needed several weeks of at-home rehabilitation. The scars on his legs and bruises on his ribcage couldn't be explained away by another bike accident. He had told Maggie he was collecting intel on bad guys and that the car accident was unrelated. He wasn't sure whether she believed him, or just wanted to believe him, so they could get past this painful gorge dividing their trust. He stressed that he was officially out of the loop, and free to go on with his life. In other words, his obligation to his country was fulfilled, and she was the only obligation left in his life.

It wasn't a total lie. When they met again, John would press Chocker for complete absolution, a clean cut, even if it meant giving up the bogus pension the CIA had finagled through his fictitious knee injury. John would prefer to keep the money coming in, but if Chocker pressed him on the issue, then he would take the pay cut. Worst case scenario: he would become a liability to the agency, and they might even want him reassigned—a nice way of saying "dead." The absence of IFR's senior account executive during John's rehabilitation was not a good sign.

This would have been a hell of a lot easier had Yoda not involved Maggie. She was seeing a therapist now to get over the feeling of powerlessness, and John was patient and smart enough to let her express herself. No macho man-of-the-house stuff. Maggie was given full reign in all their decisions. It was nice to nurture her for a change; God knows she had been there for him.

The valet hid his displeasure at John's dirty Subaru and took the five-dollar tip. Another employee dressed in a tuxedo escorted them to their reserved window seats overlooking the Hudson River.

"John, this is so beautiful. How did you find this place?" Maggie wore a silk black-and-rose-colored Bianca Nero cocktail dress, with sheer shoulder straps and a low V-cut that accentuated her assets nicely. John had splurged on a private shopper at Nordstrom. Tonight would be like no other Maggie had ever known. Her long black hair was pulled up in a French twist, and sparkling one-carat etched diamond hoop earrings accented her slender neck. The earrings cost over a thousand dollars, but John had managed to win the closeout bid on eBay and picked them up for five hundred. They were new, so he didn't feel too much the heel for trying to win her appreciation on the cheap. What she didn't know wouldn't hurt her.

"Believe it or not," he said, "Henry told me about it when I told him I wanted to take you someplace special. It turns out the original owner was a Civil War hero."

"I'll thank him for upgrading your taste when I see him again." She unconsciously ran her middle finger over one of the earrings. "How is he, by the way? Did his knee heal?"

"Nothing whiskey won't cure, he says."

They both laughed. Maggie was under the impression that Henry had fallen on his steps one morning when he slipped on a black ice patch.

Henry was cool with the story. His run-in with the Yoda was a bit of an ego smasher, and he didn't think anyone other than John needed to know the details. John had apologized repeatedly for what had happened, and had assured Henry that his clandestine days were numbered. He had concurrent lies running with the two closest people in his life, and he didn't feel right about either one. Lately, he felt as far from mushin as he could be.

John had ordered a 2006 Laetitia Pinot Noir, La Montee, from the wine cellar, and he and Maggie were halfway through the bottle.

"Drink up" he said. "There's no designated driver tonight."

"What do you mean?"

"I reserved a room for us in the tower suite tonight—fireplace, four-post bed, marble bathrooms—you know, the usual." He reached over and held both her hands. "When we wake up tomorrow, we should have a sunny view of the Hudson River, and maybe even the Manhattan skyline."

Maggie put her hand to her breast, smiled, and rolled her eyes. She raised her glass and said, "A toast."

"To what?"

"To us. And to the fact that you clean up real nice, Mr. Rexford." She clinked her glass to his and took a sip. "And to the FBI for killing the bastard."

Maggie had brought up Yoda several times in the last few days, and each time her pleasure at his death was more gleeful than the last. He believed that if Yoda were standing right there, his lovely Italian bride-to-be would not hesitate to kill him. It was a bad sign. The doctor had warned him that Maggie might become more aggressive as she digested the memory of her captivity. Maggie was not violent by nature, and the more of this trait she expressed, the less of her core personality remained. John tried not to show emotion, but his expression gave him away.

"What's the problem?"

"Nothing," he said. "I just don't know how much we should talk about him. I mean, it's a bad memory, and I know you've got to get it out, but maybe not tonight. Okay?"

Her visage changed from friendly date to a possessed puppet under another's control. "He is dead, isn't he, John?"

"Maggie, we talked about this . . ."

"You need to answer the question, John. I don't want your platitudes and military jargon." She stared straight into his eyes with hate, but he knew he was just the target, not the source.

"The FBI put three slugs in his back at point-blank range. That much I can confirm, from a man I trust very much."

"That doesn't mean he's dead, John." Maggie's words left her mouth with a hiss. "You didn't see him."

"I didn't have to see him, Maggie." John had left out the part about who shot Yoda when he explained the story to Maggie. He gulped his wine and put the glass back down a little too forcefully. It startled her, and he regretted the move immediately. "You saw the news reports. 'Suspected terrorist shot at Yonkers mosque.' Who are you going to believe?"

"Shot doesn't mean dead."

"Sweetheart, we've been over this before, and I don't mind. But have a little faith."

"In you?"

"That's not fair."

Tears rolled down her soft cheeks. He reached across the table and touched her wrist tenderly.

He was starting to think this was a bad idea. Maybe it was a little too soon for her to spend the night away from home. After all, it had only been a few weeks since she had been rescued from the boiler room of the old school, with three pints of her blood in a glass fishbowl. On the other hand, getting her the hell out of the woods would let her see that the world still existed. Maggie needed to learn that you locked your doors to keep the bad guys out, not to lock yourself in.

She tried to sip her wine between sniffles, but it wouldn't go down. "I just need to know. I hate not knowing."

"Sweetheart, I can't deliver the corpse. I'm sorry."

"Then who can?" She looked up at him as if delivering Yoda's dead and bullet-riddled body was a perfectly normal request.

When he couldn't provide a good answer, he fell back on what came from his heart. "I love you, Maggie. I will always love you, and stay with you, and be by your side. I am your man and your protector, and we will get through this because nothing—nothing in this world—matters more than that."

She nodded and wiped away the last of her tears. "I know, I know. Will we really get through this?"

"We have to," he said. "I can't afford to keep taking you to places like this."

Maggie snorted a muffled laugh, and the ice that covered her lovely face melted with her smile.

"You don't except me to wear this monkey suit too often, do you?"

"Once a year will do it." She gave a half-hearted smirk. "I think any more for a redneck like you would be cruel and unusual punishment." She squeezed his hand and said, "Now let's get drunk and eat this expensive food."

They clinked their glasses and drank. He poured more aromatic Pinot Noir.

It was like watching a split-screen movie, the way Maggie changed like that. He was never sure which show would dominate the picture. It wasn't normal for anyone to flash from murder to party mode so easily. At first glance, she seemed so much the old Maggie, but he knew better. The scars that Yoda had left were all internal, except for one tiny pinhole reminder in the crook of her elbow that might as well have been an open floodgate. So much more than blood had flowed from that small puncture wound.

The waiter placed their appetizers on the table and removed the empty bottle. John asked Maggie to order another wine. She chose a Sonoma County Vérité Winery La Muse. He had asked the sommelier for a wine list with no prices, so Maggie didn't know that she had blown 150 dollars.

She ordered the apple and celeriac soup for an appetizer, and he had the roasted king oyster mushrooms in garlic broth.

They enjoyed their delicacies in silence and exchanged knowing smiles. When they weren't looking into each other's eyes, they turned to the window and enjoyed the view of Westchester County below.

"John?"

He looked up from his plate, keen to any miniscule change in her voice. Maggie had that sound in her voice women get before they say something they know a man doesn't want to hear.

"Did you mean what you said about 'longer'?"

"Huh?"

"A while ago I asked you if you thought we would be together long enough so we could watch the other old farts play shuffleboard in Florida, and you said, 'Longer.'" She ran her finger around the top of her wine glass. "Did you mean it?"

"Am I supposed to feel trapped?"

"No. But you could answer the question without asking a question." She looked down at the table, disappointment on her brow.

"Maggie." He held up his glass. She raised hers. "I cannot imagine a future where you and I aren't joined at the hip." He paused and they toasted. "I don't think that came out real good. Did it?"

"It was fine." Her eyes welled up, and the sparkle of her tears was vastly more beautiful to him than the glint of the diamond hoop earrings.

Maggie's entrée was a sumptuous portion of sea scallops and foie gras, and he had rack of lamb dusted with cumin seed. He ordered a side dish of smoked wild salmon in jalapeño vinaigrette, which they shared between bites of entrée.

The waiter brought over a highly polished sterling silver champagne bucket half filled with ice. A blanketed champagne bottle rested on his arm. He pulled the cloth away ceremoniously and exposed the name KRUG.

"I'm sorry," said John. "We didn't order champagne."

"Of course, Mr. Rexford. Compliments of the two men to your right."

John's radar spiked. He prepared to push the table up to protect Maggie, and quickly scanned the room for weapons of opportunity. He turned slowly and saw C. Peter Chocker's smiling face, his hand holding a champagne flute lifted in their direction. A thin man sat next to Chocker, and there was a cane leaning next to his chair. He sported a well-groomed handlebar moustache and wore round spectacles. A brown bowler derby rested on the chair seat next to him. He wore a beige three-piece suit, a brown shirt with white stripes, and a beige-and-brown bow tie. John recognized the eyes but would need a closer look.

"Thank you." He dismissed the waiter. "I'll take care of this, Maggie. Don't worry. I think I know what they want."

"John? Is this someone from . . . you know . . ." Her smile was replaced by a straight-lipped, fearful expression. She started to play with her earrings again.

He shook his head. "I don't know the guy with the moustache, but I know the other one." He kissed her forehead. "I'll be back before it has time to cool. Eat up."

"Johnny. How the hell are you, son?" Chocker stood up and gave him a two-handed pump. "Let me introduce you to Mr. Wiggles."

John shook the Englishman's scarred hands and looked into the shiny and lethal eyes of Major Daniel Canaan, most recently stationed at the Al-Farooq Masjid mosque in Yonkers.

"I'm glad to see you, John." Chocker moved a champagne flute toward him. "It's nice we can all be together. The first time is always the most memorable."

"It's not the right time, Pete." He looked across the table. "What's with the outfit, Mr. Wiggles?"

"My name is Bond, James Bond." Canaan had a lame English accent.

"Bond doesn't have a handlebar moustache."

"Right-O, chap. But other than that, it's pretty MI6, don't you think? You know, 'Q' and Moneypenny and all that."

"Why the getup?"

"Well, John," said Chocker. "We are spies, after all." He laughed and took a drink. "Nice to see you upgraded your suit collection." He slapped John on the shoulder a little too hard, and Canaan's eyes darted from John to Chocker and back.

"And you're what? A captain of industry?"

"None other." Chocker placed what looked to be a cell phone on the white tablecloth and kept talking while the machine scanned for electronic devices.

"What happened to the other one?" John pointed at the device.

"Obsolete, John," said Chocker. "The champagne is Krug, Clos du Mesnil 1995. Only twelve thousand bottles produced, and the Saudis picked up almost all of it. I know the wine steward here. Told him we were coming, and he managed to grab a few bottles that were floating around." Chocker poured John a fluteful and raised his glass. "Here's to us. The thin line of sanity."

John shifted uncomfortably in his chair and drank half the glass. He didn't like his back facing the entrance. Chocker and Canaan had their backs to the wall.

"Nine hundred dollars a bottle, Johnny. You just swallowed fifty bucks. Like it?"

"I like it." John took another sip. "But it's missing something."

"What's that?"

"Whiskey."

"You're a clown, my friend."

"I was thinking . . ."

"Yeah?"

"If the bad guys wanted to strike a serious blow to democracy, with the three of us here, this would be an opportune time."

Canaan looked at Chocker and gave a knowing smile. "We seldom get together, John. And when we do, the perimeter is well-fortified, as well as the inside of these castle walls. No bad guys can make it over the moat." Canaan slugged his Krug and poured another.

"Yeah," Chocker added in a western accent. "We got the place surrounded, sheriff."

"What about Gilchrist's people?"

Chocker shook his head. "They didn't follow us. And no one followed you." Chocker paused for effect, and then added, "Besides, we're leaving in a linen truck."

He surveyed the room. If these waiters were on Chocker's payroll, they did a good job hiding it. Chocker waved to Maggie and smiled. She waved back and raised her glass, ever the gracious date.

"What about the FBI?" said John.

"I already answered that question," said Chocker. "You all right?"

"I mean follow-up investigations. They basically told me not to leave town."

"I don't think they'll bother you much more. They might bring you in for questioning one more time. No one got a look at you in Yonkers, thanks to Mr. Wiggles over here."

Canaan raised his glass again and drank. "Another fifty bucks down the hatch. I'll have to cash in some frequent assassin miles."

"I thought you Muslims didn't drink."

"But today I'm British, and we're all sots." Canaan poured himself more champagne. "When in Rome . . ."

"I haven't had a chance to thank you. So, thanks." John reached over to Canaan, and they shook hands.

"Just returning the bloody favor, old chap," said Canaan. "I'd still be in a hill country ditch if not for you. And I hate to admit it, but the freak had me dead to rights. I was going down, John, without you, I was a dead man."

"Back to the feebs, John," said Chocker. "That chainker Gilchrist might bring you in because you failed to set off his metal detectors. A slight oversight on your part, don't you think?"

"What was I supposed to do, shove a paperclip up my ass?"

Chocker laughed. "Not to worry, Johnny-boy. Mr. Wiggles here had the surgeon who patched you up leave a little surprise for the FBI."

"Surprise?"

"There's a small sliver of sterile titanium nickel alloy behind your medial meniscus. If they call you in, you'll light up the metal detector like a menorah. The downside is that you can't go through any airports without using a special passport."

Why would Chocker go to these lengths to protect him from the FBI, only to kick him out? And if he was staying in, why not get him the hell out of here and start a new life away from the Catskills? It had been done before. Why put the damn metal in his leg? He wasn't sure he wanted titanium nickel alloy behind his knee, even if it was sterile.

"You looked concerned, son. Don't worry. The doctor put it in a place where it will have no effect on your range of motion. You can still ride in the Tour de France if you want." Chocker winked and topped off John's champagne.

"And what do I tell the Feds?"

"Tell them the same thing you did the last time: you don't know what the hell is going on."

"Okay. Now what?"

Chocker gave Canaan a serious look.

"You saved the free world, John." Chocker raised his glass and took a drink. "You're a success. Be proud. We're proud of you. You can stop chasing ghosts. But you can't come back."

"And what if I want to?"

"Did you see the movie *Highlander*?"

"Yeah?"

"There can be only one." Canaan leaned closer, his cabled forearms pressed on the white tablecloth. "With Yoda in the dirt, the hajjis don't have a clue who you are, but the FBI's going to sniff around your personal life for a few years. As is often the case, your biggest problem is getting nailed by your own side. You have to make a clean break, partner."

"Anyway," Chocker said, "your cover's blown."

"You mean Gilchrist? Mr. Wiggles here said they didn't have a thing on me."

"I'm not worried about the feebs," said Chocker. "I could always fix you up with a little plastic surgery, and then bury you so deep you won't even remember who you are, let alone the FBI." Chocker looked over at Maggie, then back at John. "You're blown, son. You've got a liability."

John's emotions coiled around his heart with fury and elation. He had wanted out, but he wanted to make that decision on his own. He didn't like being put to pasture like some injured rodeo bull.

"And if I get rid of my liability?"

"You're no two-timer, John. You can't love me and Maggie at the same time. Besides, when you propose to her, I want you to have a clear conscience." He slapped John on the shoulder again, softer this time.

"Do you have me under surveillance, Pete?"

"I never give mission-specific information to outsiders." Chocker smiled. "But in your case, what the hell?" Chocker clasped his fingers together.

John looked at Chocker's scars and swollen knuckles, then at Canaan's paws. John knew these two men had shared a lot of life, and a lot of death. If there was a *Pound Your Face Monthly* magazine, Canaan and Chocker could be the hand models.

"So how did you know?" said John.

"I reviewed the surveillance tapes in the mall," said Chocker, "and saw our friend Yossi Mandelbrot." Chocker made annoying little quotes with his fingers and smiled like an idiot when he said "Yossi Mandelbrot." "And it turns out he went into David Yurman jewelers and spent a half hour. I noticed when he came out there was a small bulge in his bag that wasn't there when he went in. So I had another Yossi"—Chocker made the air quotes again—"go in a few days later and ask to see the ring his friend had purchased. His friend was a fat guy in a windbreaker with a beard and yarmulke. The guy remembered Mr. Mandelbrot."

"Nice diamond," said Canaan. "She'll love it. But to get back on point, you do have a liability."

"Why waste a good trip to the mall, right?"

They raised their glasses and toasted each other.

"Anyway, son," said Chocker. "When your bride-to-be comes back from the ladies room, we'll be gone. So we'll say goodbye and let you get back to your current mission. And don't worry about your retirement. You're forever disabled, soldier."

John wasn't sure which upset him more: his new freedom, Chocker's recognition of his victory, or that he would never see these two comrades-in-arms again.